ADVANCE PRAISE
AMONG THE FAIR MAGNOLIAS

"The era of America's Civil War is ripe with dramatic, heart-wrenching stories, and here are four you'll long remember. Four novellas, four stories of strong women challenged by the times, yet overcoming through love and faith."

—ANN TATLOCK, award-winning author

"Four intriguing novellas rich with period detail, dynamic characters, and surprising premises—each filled with romance, spiritual depth, and redemption. This collection set in the nineteenth century took me home to times and places in the Deep South I've visited only in my dreams. An absolute pleasure to read. An absolute *must read*."

—CATHY GOHLKE, BESTSELLING AND CHRISTY AWARD-
WINNING AUTHOR OF *SECRETS SHE KEPT* AND *SAVING AMELIE*

"Four talented authors have penned a charming collection of stories that take place in the Deep South. Passions simmer, romance blossoms, and history comes alive. The settings are so real you can almost smell the sweet scent of magnolias on every page. This all adds up to a winning combination that was truly a delight to read."

—MARGARET BROWNLEY, BESTSELLING AUTHOR OF THE BRIDES
OF LAST CHANCE RANCH AND UNDERCOVER LADIES SERIES

"Grab some sweet tea and find a rocking chair underneath the ceiling fan of a wide front porch. You are in for a treat! *Among the Fair Magnolias* reminded me of *Gone with the Wind* mixed in with *Gunsmoke*. Tamera Alexander, Shelley Gray, Dorothy Love, and Elizabeth Musser each pen exciting, romantic tales of the Old South and the great state of Texas. Set before and after the Civil War, these four stories speak of genteel ladies and gallant gentlemen, with a few charlatans thrown in for good measure. I loved getting caught up in these hugely romantic tales of love in the time of a changing America. And with recipes from each story to add to the charm, this collection is best read . . . under the fair magnolias. I loved it!"

—LENORA WORTH, AUTHOR OF *AN APRIL BRIDE* AND *LAKESIDE HERO*

"*Among the Fair Magnolias* will sweep you into the past, carrying you into the beauty and battles of the Old South. You will love, laugh, and lament as your heart is inspired to face life with courage and live it more fully."

—CINDY WOODSMALL, *NEW YORK TIMES* AND CBA
BESTSELLING AUTHOR OF AMISH FICTION

AMONG THE FAIR MAGNOLIAS

Other Novels by These Authors

TAMERA ALEXANDER
The Belle Meade Plantation Series
To Whisper Her Name
To Win Her Favor

The Belmont Mansion Series
A Lasting Impression
A Beauty So Rare

SHELLEY GRAY
The Chicago World's Fair Mystery Series
Secrets of Sloane House
Deception on Sable Hill
Whispers in the Reading Room (Available November 2015)

DOROTHY LOVE
A Respectable Actress (Available October 2015)
The Bracelet
A Proper Marriage (e-novella)
Carolina Gold

ELIZABETH MUSSER
The Secrets of the Cross Trilogy
Two Crosses
Two Testaments
Two Destinies

The Swan House
The Dwelling Place
Searching for Eternity
Words Unspoken
The Sweetest Thing

Waiting for Peter (novella)

AMONG THE FAIR MAGNOLIAS

FOUR SOUTHERN LOVE STORIES

TAMERA ALEXANDER, SHELLEY
GRAY, DOROTHY LOVE, AND
ELIZABETH MUSSER

THOMAS NELSON
Since 1798

NASHVILLE   MEXICO CITY   RIO DE JANEIRO

Published in Nashville, Tennessee, by Thomas Nelson. Thomas Nelson is a registered trademark of HarperCollins Christian Publishing, Inc.

Elizabeth Musser is represented by MacGregor Literary, Inc.

Interior design by James A. Phinney

Thomas Nelson titles may be purchased in bulk for educational, business, fund-raising, or sales promotional use. For information, please e-mail SpecialMarkets@ThomasNelson.com.

Scripture quotations are taken from The King James Version of the Bible.

Scripture quotations are also taken from the *Holy Bible*, New Living Translation, copyright © 1996, 2004, 2007, 2013 by Tyndale House Foundation. Used by permission of Tyndale House Publishers, Inc., Carol Stream, Illinois 60188. All rights reserved.

Library of Congress Cataloging-in-Publication Data

Among the fair magnolias : four southern love stories / Tamera Alexander, Shelley Gray, Dorothy Love, and Elizabeth Musser.

pages cm

Summary: "Four Southern women are at a turning point in history. and in their own hearts. To Mend a Dream by Tamera Alexander The Civil War cost Savannah Darby everything--her family and her home. When Aidan Bedford, an attorney from Boston, buys the Darby estate, he hires Savannah to redecorate. Can she find a mysterious treasure before her job is finished? An Outlaw's Heart by Shelley Gray When Russell Stark returns to Fort Worth, he's determined to begin a new life. But when he arrives at his mother's homestead, he discovers that she is very ill and the woman he loved is still as beautiful and sweet as he remembered. With time running out, Russell must come to terms with both his future and his past. A Heart So True by Dorothy Love Abigail knows all too well what is expected of her: to marry her distant cousin Charles and take her place in society. But her heart belongs to another. A terrible incident forces Abby to choose between love and duty. Love Beyond Limits by Elizabeth Musser Emily has a secret: She's in love with one of the freedmen on her family's plantation. Meanwhile, another man declares his love for her. Emily realizes some things are not as they seem and secrets must be kept in order to keep those she loves safe"-- Provided by publisher.

ISBN 978-1-4016-9073-1 (paperback)

1. Love stories, American. 2. Women--Southern States--Fiction. 3. Christian fiction, American. I. Alexander, Tamera. II. Gray, Shelley Shepard. III. Love, Dorothy, 1949- IV. Musser, Elizabeth.

PS648.L6A49 2015

813'.08508--dc23

2015003948

Printed in the United States of America

15 16 17 18 19 20 RRD 6 5 4 3 2 1

# CONTENTS

A HEART SO TRUE

Dorothy Love

For My Mother

A NOTE FROM THE AUTHOR

DEAR READERS,

Since childhood, the beach is the place where I have felt most alive and closest to God. There is something about the power and beauty of the ocean, the golden light of a sunrise over water that calms my heart and fuels my creativity. Many of my books were first conceived during an early-morning beach walk. When I was offered the chance to write a novella for this collection, I knew right away it would be set on Pawleys Island, South Carolina, one of my favorite places on earth.

If you have read my novel *Carolina Gold*, this setting will be familiar to you. My fictional character Charlotte Fraser grew up spending her summers in her family's cottage on Pawleys. For *A Heart So True* I couldn't resist returning to a place I love to give you another glimpse of Charlotte at age fifteen, before she became mistress of Fairhaven, her father's rice plantation on the Waccamaw River. And I've included a scene in which you will catch up with Celia Browning of *The Bracelet*, a year after her marriage to her childhood sweetheart, Sutton Mackay.

Now I hope you will enjoy meeting a new heroine, Abby Clayton. In *A Heart So True*, a beach barbecue sets the stage for events that compel Abby to make hard choices that change the course of her future.

Be blessed,
Dorothy

CHAPTER ONE

Pawleys Island, South Carolina
May 1860

HAD WADE BENNETT TRULY FORGIVEN HER?

Skirts tucked up, shoes dangling from one hand, Abigail Clayton stepped over the pungent remains of a horseshoe crab and studied the tumbling surf as if the answer to her question might be written there. A storm had blown ashore after midnight, leaving in its wake piles of broken shells, burrowing whelks, and clumps of rust-colored seaweed. Under the warm spring light the deserted beach took on a particular radiance that illuminated a pair of orange-beaked skimmers searching for sand crabs and a flock of brown pelicans gliding above the breakers.

Despite her worry, Abby released a grateful sigh. How perfect was God's creation, how delightful the rhythm of life on Pawleys Island.

Last week, with the last of the rice fields planted, Papa had closed Mulberry Hall and moved the household—furnishings, livestock, house servants, and all—here. To Osprey Cottage. The twelve-mile journey—nine by water down the Waccamaw River and three by land—had been accomplished by nightfall. The days following passed in a blur of activity. After a thorough cleaning and airing of the cottage, Mama had supervised the unpacking of dishes and lamps, silver and crystal, and set about preparing for the Claytons' annual spring barbecue. On Friday the beach would ring with the sound of dozens of their guests gathering for a three-day visit before leaving for summer homes in Saratoga or Europe.

Abby dropped her shoes onto the sand and stooped to examine a tiny fan-shaped shell. Mama was counting on her to help with the preparations, but all she could think about was Dr. Wade Bennett. Would he attend the party or stay away? Was he still holding on to his anger in the wake of their quarrel?

She heaved another sigh. If only she could take back her hurtful words. If only she could tell him that—

"Miss Abigail!" Rapid footsteps sounded behind her, and Abby turned to see her mother's favorite house servant, Sophronia, hurrying along the beach. Sturdy and compact, Sophronia reminded Abby of the steamers that plied the Lowcountry rivers. All she lacked was a smokestack and a whistle. And despite her small stature, she could move like wildfire through kindling when on a mission from Mama.

Clearly that was the case now. Sophronia hove to a stop in front of Abby, hands on hips, a frown creasing her smooth brown face.

"Where you been? Your mama sent me to fetch you half an hour ago."

"I went down to the boathouse." Abby jumped as the cold surf rushed over her bare toes. "I wanted to be sure my rowboat survived the winter. I must have lost track of time."

"Humph. You know Miss Alicia don't like you taking that boat out by yourself. It sure ain't ladylike, and 'sides that, it ain't safe."

"I've had a boat since I was ten years old. And I don't take it into open water. I stick to the marshes."

"Where the alligators just waitin' to gobble you up for breakfast." Sophronia glanced at Abby's feet. "Better not let Miss Alicia catch you running 'round with no shoes on."

"I know it. Mama can be such a stickler for propriety." Abby plopped down on a patch of dry sand to pull on her stockings and shoes. "Honestly, I don't see why she must stand on formality even here at the beach."

Sophronia's brows went up. "Maybe 'cause your daddy got his sights on running for office, and the governor hisself is on the way here for the barbecue."

Sophronia held out a hand and hauled Abigail to her feet. "Come on home now 'fore your breakfast gets cold as stone."

Abby followed Sophronia up the path to the cottage that had been her summer home for her entire life. Constructed of plain clapboards, it was not quite as large as the summer homes of their neighbors, the Westons, the Frasers, and the Allstons, but it boasted a prime location on the four-mile-long spit of land that was Pawleys. A wraparound porch provided a shady spot to while away a summer afternoon, watching the seabirds and the occasional pod of dolphins. The rear of the house faced the golden marshes and the endless serpentine creeks that fed into the broad, blue Waccamaw River. A sight that never failed to soothe her spirit.

"There you are." Mama stood on the porch, leaning on her walking cane, watching Abby's approach. Her voice was stern, but her brown eyes held a hint of merriment. "I might have known you'd come home damp and sandy. Don't track that dirt into the parlor, please, Abigail. Your father is expecting Governor Gist this afternoon, and Molly has already cleaned it. And for heaven's sake, do something with your hair. It looks like a rat's nest."

"Yes, Mama." Abby ran lightly up the steps and planted a kiss on her mother's cheek. "I'm sorry you had to send out a search party. I didn't intend to be gone for so long."

"You're here now, and no harm done. Your breakfast is waiting in the dining room. Please tidy up and meet me there. We have a million things to do before Saturday."

Ten minutes later Abby was seated in the dining room, a plate of eggs, sausage, and Molly's delicious spoon bread in front of her. Molly bustled in and poured coffee into Abby's paper-thin china cup. She set down a cut-glass pitcher of warm syrup. "Here you are, missy. Molly knows you partial to havin' syrup with spoon bread."

Abby drizzled syrup over the bread and took a bite. "Delicious, Molly. Don't I always say you make the best spoon bread in the Carolinas?"

With a gentle nod Mama dismissed Molly. She opened a leather-bound book and picked up her pencil. "Our dresses have arrived. You must try yours on at once in case it needs any last-minute alterations."

"All right." Abby took another bite of spoon bread, letting the warm sweetness linger on her tongue. She peered at the stack of mail on the table. "More replies for the barbecue?"

"Yes. These came yesterday, but I was too busy to open them." Mama withdrew a sheet of paper from a thick envelope. "The Frasers are coming. Poor Francis. I feel so sorry for him, trying to raise Charlotte all alone. You must remember to make time for her, Abigail. She's much younger than you, but desperately in need of female friendships."

Abby dug into her eggs. Fairhaven, the Frasers' plantation, was their neighbor on the Waccamaw. On her visits home from boarding school, she'd caught occasional glimpses of a small, sturdy girl traipsing after her father in the rice fields, her dark hair flying, her too-large boots sinking into the marshy ground. Abby couldn't help envying the younger girl's relationship with her father. Mr. Fraser seemed to dote on his only child, whereas Abby's own father believed girls were meant to be seen and not heard.

"The Averys are coming up from Georgetown tomorrow," Mama continued. "Theodosia will room with you."

"Oh. I was hoping to see more of Penny Ravensdale. It's been ages since we last spoke."

Mama scribbled in her notebook and spoke without looking up. "You'll see plenty of Penelope. The Ravensdales will be staying here for the weekend. Besides, Theodosia is perfectly lovely. And so ladylike."

"And I'm not?"

"I didn't say that, darling. Only you must try to comport yourself with great care this weekend. For your father's sake." Mama's brown eyes bore into Abby's. "You know how strong his political aspirations are. We owe it to him to do all we can to make a favorable impression on Governor Gist. The governor's opinion will carry a great deal of weight when the state legislature meets to choose his successor." Mama reached across the table and cupped Abby's chin in her hand. "Whatever your opinions, please try not to voice them."

"After all the money Papa has spent filling my head with knowledge, I don't see why now I'm obliged to conceal it, but all right." Abby raised one hand, palm out, as if taking an oath. "I will be the walking definition of 'seen and not heard.'"

Mama tried and failed to suppress a smile. "Thank you. Will you please see that Sophronia makes room in your clothespress for Theodosia's things?"

"Fine. But my room is so small we'll be tripping over each other all weekend."

"I know it. Osprey Cottage will be full to the rafters when everyone gets here. But it's only for a few days. The Averys are sailing for New York a week from Thursday, and after this weekend the

Ravensdales will be staying at the Wards' cottage. Emily and John have already left for the Continent." Mama flipped a page and consulted her list. "Seventy-five people coming, so far."

"Heavens. They'll overrun this poor little island." Abby tried to lighten her tone, but she was desperate for news of one certain invitation Mama hadn't yet mentioned. "Any word from the Bennetts?"

"Nothing so far, but I'm sure Dr. Bennett and his parents will attend, just as they always have. Judge Bennett is not one to miss a chance to go fishing with your father."

Memories of her last evening with Wade Bennett set Abby's insides to churning. Three months apart had made her realize just how deeply she cared for him. How fervently she hoped he felt the same way about her. Last Christmas she'd thought he was ready to propose, but the holidays had come and gone without any declaration on his part. Then in February had come the unsettling quarrel that still brought tears to her eyes if she thought too long about it. What if they could never recapture the mutual delight and perfect harmony they'd once enjoyed? What if she couldn't convince him of her change of heart?

Mama smiled and patted Abby's hand. "You mustn't fret, darling. Whatever your disagreement, it can't be all that serious."

But it was. They had discovered a deep and fundamental difference in what they expected from life. As dearly as she loved him, as ready as she was to admit to her faults and seek a compromise, she had wondered and worried all spring about whether things between them could ever be put to rights.

Mama opened another envelope and drew out a single sheet of ivory vellum covered in small script. "Here's a note from Celia Mackay in Savannah. She says that she and Sutton can't join us this time. She's going to become a mother this autumn."

Abby noted the tears in her mother's eyes. "But that's happy news, isn't it?"

"I'm delighted for Celia and Sutton, but terribly sad that her father won't ever know his grandchild. David Browning was the most devoted father I've ever known. Apart from your own father, of course."

Abby took another bite of spoon bread. She didn't doubt her father's affection, even if he didn't often show it. She loved him too. Respected him. But a part of her feared him. Not so with her mother, who was the very soul of parental tenderness. For all of her life, Mama had been the one to indulge her only daughter's passions, to encourage her in her various pursuits.

Seeing her mother's sadness, Abby felt an overwhelming rush of love. A riding accident at age twelve had left Mama with a severe limp that required the use of a walking cane. But she hadn't allowed her infirmity to sour her disposition, to weaken her faith in a merciful God, or to dampen her enthusiasm for life. Even though Abby was a grown woman now, it was still her greatest joy and pride to win her mother's approval, and her praise meant more than that of anyone else.

On a long breath, Mama set aside Mrs. Mackay's letter and opened the next one. "Ophelia Kittridge is coming. And Charles is attending as well."

Abby's cup banged into the saucer with more force than she intended. Her appetite fled at the recollection of her unpleasant encounter with Charles Kittridge last summer. She hadn't told anybody what happened—not even Penny, who was her closest friend this side of heaven. It had been too upsetting. Even now the memory of it made her feel ashamed. As though the entire disgusting episode had been her fault. She pushed her plate away. "Oh mercy. What an insufferable pest Charles is, and his mother is the worst gossip in the entire Lowcountry. I don't see why—"

"They're your father's cousins."

"Yes, but such distant cousins they hardly count as kin at all."

"Nevertheless, we can't very well exclude them. Your father still has hopes that you and Charles might one day—"

"I know what he wants, but I wouldn't marry Charles Kittridge if he were the last man breathing."

Through the window Abby watched the brown pelicans diving into the surf. She would have to at least greet the odious Charles. She might even be forced to dance with him. But the only guest she was interested in seeing was Dr. Wade Bennett. And so far, he was silent.

————

Standing in the middle of her bedroom, clad in her chemise and petticoats, Abby lifted her arms as Sophronia slid the ocean-blue silk dress over her head. The voluminous skirt settled over her crinoline hoops, rustling as the maid did up the dozen tiny buttons in the back. Abby tugged at the scooped neckline to show off a bit more of her shoulders.

Sophronia frowned and rearranged it to her own satisfaction. "Now. That looks more like the lady you s'posed to be."

"Oh, for goodness' sake." Abby scowled. "This is 1860. And I'm twenty-three, not forty."

"Don't make no difference. Ladylike is ladylike." Sophronia opened a box and drew out a pair of kid pumps. "Try these slippers on your feet. I hope the heel is high enough so's I don't have to take up the hem of that gown. I got plenty more to do 'fore Saturday gets here."

Abby slid her feet into the shoes, not bothering to do up the buttons, and clumped over to the big cheval glass in the corner. She twirled around, the skirt belling about her ankles. This was not the gown she'd wanted. She had hoped for something more sophisticated. But Mama had enlisted the modiste, Mrs. Finley, in her cause, and Abby had finally given in. Now she had to admit her mother was right. The cut of the bodice flattered her small waist. The shimmering blue silk showed off her glossy brown hair and brought out the faint blush in her cheeks.

Even Sophronia, who rarely smiled, beamed when Abby turned to study the back of the gown in the glass. "You sure is a vision, Miss Abigail, and that's the truth. Won't be no empty spaces on your dance card."

Abby kicked off the shoes, which were already beginning to pinch her feet. "We won't have dance cards. Despite the fancy clothes, the dance is informal—though you wouldn't know it, the way Papa is carrying on."

"He wants to be gov'nor real bad, I reckon. Got to impress the muckety-mucks so's they'll vote him in come wintertime." Sophronia retrieved the kid shoes and returned them to the box. "He sure is excited that the governor hisself accepted his invitation."

"He was on pins and needles for an entire week, waiting for Governor Gist to reply." Abby's face clouded. "I've hardly seen anything of Papa all spring."

Turning her back to Sophronia, she motioned for the maid to begin undoing the buttons. "Though these days Papa's no fun at all anyway. It's as if he's forgotten how to talk about anything except politics. Secession this and secession that. It gives me a headache."

Sophronia chuckled. "I don't understand politics neither."

"Oh, I understand it. But since the men are the only ones who can vote and will do as they wish regardless of what the women think, any discussion of it seems entirely pointless." Abby stepped out of the blue gown and reached for her simple green day dress. She slipped it on and adjusted the matching satin sash. "I do miss taking the boat out with Papa."

"The summer just beginnin' though. You and your daddy'll have plenty o' time once this weekend is over." Sophronia carefully folded the dress and returned it to its muslin nest.

Outside, a horse and rig clopped along the beach road. Abby parted the curtain and looked out. A tall, broad-shouldered man with dark curly hair got out and brushed the dust from his gray jacket and trousers. He glanced up at her window as if he expected to find her waiting there.

Abby's breath caught, and her heart expanded with sudden joy. After three long months, Wade Bennett had come home.

CHAPTER TWO

"Quick!" Abby flapped a hand at Sophronia. "Help me with my shoes. I want to catch Dr. Bennett before he—"

"No, ma'am. You ain't gonna go chasin' after no man. Not even Mr. Wade. You just go wait in the parlor like the lady you was raised to be." Sophronia picked up Abby's hairbrush and began dragging it through Abby's tangles. "'Sides, you ain't even done up your hair this mornin'. Looks like the rats done slept in it." Sophronia clucked her tongue and shook her head. "No, ma'am. You ain't ready to receive no gentleman callers."

Abby sighed and submitted to the maid's attention, her ears straining for the sound of Wade Bennett's voice in the downstairs hall. But it was the creaking of wagon wheels and the sound of female laughter that drew her attention back to the window.

"Looks like more guests arrivin' from the ferry." Sophronia reached for Abby's jet hair combs. "I reckon Miss Avery and Miss Ravensdale be glad to see you."

"I suppose."

Sophronia anchored Abby's hair combs and handed her a small round container. "Put some rice powder on your nose. Then go make our comp'ny feel welcome."

Abby dabbed her nose with the powder, then fastened her shoes and made for the door. Sophronia was right of course. As eager as she was to see Dr. Bennett, it was better to wait for him to seek her out. With her luck Papa would be watching, and he seemed always to be looking for some reason why the handsome young doctor was unsuitable company for her.

She ran downstairs to the foyer, where Penny and Theodosia stood surrounded by a mountain of hatboxes, trunks, and portmanteaus. Both girls squealed when they saw Abby, and the three joined in a noisy, awkward embrace.

Theo Avery pulled away, her green eyes dancing. "Guess who was on the ferry with us this morning."

"Dr. Bennett."

"Yes!" Penny sent Abby a triumphant smile. "Didn't I tell you there was nothing to worry about? Didn't I say he'd be the first one off the ferry for this party?"

"You did." Abby grinned. The thing she loved most about Penelope Ravensdale was that Penny always saw the bright side of any situation. No matter how hopeless it seemed, Penny simply assumed the best would happen.

"Well then?" Theo glanced out the foyer window to the group of other guests gathering outside. "Where is he?"

"I saw him arrive, but he must have gone on to his family's cottage."

"Well, he'll be here soon enough," Theo said. "Maybe it's better if you don't see him until the dance. Make a grand entrance in that stunning new gown."

At Abby's questioning look, Theo went on. "Mama and I were at Miss Finley's last month to pick up our own dresses, and we saw her putting the finishing touches on that beautiful blue skirt. She told us it was yours. Honestly, Wade Bennett is going to melt right through the floor when he sees you in it."

Hector, the Claytons' driver, came in with more luggage. Mrs. Avery and Mrs. Ravensdale trailed in his wake. Hector nodded to Abby. "Where you want these things, miss?"

"Theo, you're in with me," Abby said. "I'm not sure which room is Penny's. Mama has a list somewhere."

"Well, no matter." Mrs. Avery turned to Hector. "Just leave it all here for now. We'll sort it out later. Hello, Abigail my dear." The older woman planted a cool kiss on Abby's cheek. "You're looking well."

"You too. Mama says you're leaving for New York next week?"

"Yes. Spending the summer in Saratoga. We always enjoy it so. Don't we, Theodosia?"

"Yes, Mama," Theo said, rolling her eyes and shaking her head no to Abby.

Penny, her blue eyes merry, stifled a laugh. "We're staying right here on the island this season. There is no place on earth better than Pawleys."

Mama entered the parlor, leaning heavily on her ebony cane. "I'm sorry to keep you all waiting. There was an urgent problem in the kitchen, but it's sorted out now. Luncheon will be served shortly, but I imagine you're ready to get settled after your trip."

Mama removed a list from her pocket and swiftly directed everyone to their rooms. As planned, Theo was assigned to Abby's room overlooking the ocean while the Ravensdales were given a larger room facing the marsh and the tidal creeks. Mrs. Avery took a smaller room at the back of the house.

"Abigail, I need your help," Mama said as their guests headed for their quarters. "Augusta Milton has offered to let the Kittridges use her cottage this week. I meant to send Hector for the key, but it slipped my mind. Miss Augusta left it beneath that red flowerpot on the piazza. Would you be a dear and run over and get it for me?"

"Right now?" Abby wanted to catch up with Penny and Theo before they had to sit through a long and tedious meal, during which Papa and the men would talk politics and the ladies would sit smiling politely and mute as death.

"Yes, please. The Kittridges are due on the afternoon ferry, and I don't want Ophelia to have to wait to settle in. Her health hasn't been good this spring, and she will be in need of a nap when they arrive."

On the other hand, Miss Augusta's cottage was just down the beach, nestled in the dunes next to the Frasers' Pelican Cottage— and just steps from the Bennetts' cottage. Perhaps she would see Dr. Bennett after all.

Abby grabbed her old straw hat from the peg beside the door and set off down the beach. Later in the season the air would be humid, thick, and still, but today a cooling breeze lifted her hair and stirred the stands of sea oats dotting the dunes. Down the beach a couple of young boys, their bare arms already reddening in the sun, launched a dinghy into the glittering surf. They waved to her as she crested a dune and started up the short boardwalk to Miss Augusta's cottage.

Abby found the key beneath the red flowerpot and took a moment to savor the view from Miss Augusta's piazza—the undulating sea oats in the powdery-white dunes, the gentle curve of the wide beach reaching out to the sea. She shaded her eyes and looked toward the Bennetts' low-slung cottage, but the dunes obscured her view. A gust of wind sent her hat tumbling across the sand. She lifted the hem of her skirt and chased after it, stopping when someone called her name.

Charles Kittridge bounded across the sand, one arm raised in greeting. He scooped up her hat and jogged over to where she stood.

"Hello, Cousin," he said, proffering her runaway hat. "This is yours, I believe."

Abby jammed her hat onto her head and started for home. "My mother wasn't expecting you until later."

"The *Nina* docked early in Georgetown, and we caught the noon ferry." He swung into step beside her. "What's your hurry?"

"My mother needs me. I don't want to keep her waiting."

"Ah. I'm glad to see you too, Miss Abigail."

She strode on, the spring sunshine warm on her face, the key to Miss Augusta's cottage pressed into her palm.

"Aren't you glad to see me?" Charles asked.

Abby didn't bother turning her head to look at him. "You have some nerve asking me that after what you did last summer."

"You aren't still miffed about that, are you?"

"Miffed?" She stopped walking and regarded him, arms akimbo. "I was never merely *miffed* at you, Charles. I was furious, and I still am. If I'd had my way, you never would have been invited to this barbecue, so I'd be grateful if you'd stay away from me for this entire weekend. Do that, and I might not tell Papa about your disgusting behavior."

He laughed. "I doubt he'd be too upset. After all, he's given me to understand he might look quite favorably upon my asking for your hand."

"Yes, I know he hopes for just such an outcome, chiefly because then our plantations would be joined as well. But I can assure you that I will never consent to marry you. Not in a million years."

His smile vanished. He flushed beneath his tan. "I wouldn't be too sure about that if I were you."

She resumed walking. "Short of kidnapping me, you have no chance."

"Because you've got some silly, girlish notion in your head about that common country doctor, Wade Bennett."

"He is a doctor, but far from common."

"Your father thinks he is."

"My father thinks the same of anyone who is not a planter. It's one of his shortcomings."

"He adores you, Abby, and only wants your happiness."

"If that's true, then I have nothing to worry about. Because what would make me happy is to marry Dr. Bennett."

"Yes, Mother mentioned that you tagged after him last fall, collecting plants and such for some kind of scientific experiment. Personally I can't think of anything more tiresome than tramping through the stinking pluff mud looking for heaven knows what."

"I wouldn't expect you to understand. You think of nothing besides your horses and hunting and going out with your friends."

"What else is a gentleman of means to do with his time? I've plenty of servants to look after my plantations. It's one of the things I love best about being rich. My time is my own. I can't imagine wasting it on some nonsensical experiments that won't ever amount to anything."

"Dr. Percy doesn't agree. That's why he asked Dr. Bennett to work with him in Washington this spring. They're making wonderful progress."

"You sound loyal to your Dr. Bennett now, but from what I heard, it was that very trip to Washington that was the source of your disagreement last winter." Charles shook his head. "You're like most girls I know—unable to make up your mind about anything. But let's be honest, Cousin. You are rich. You've always been rich. You will never be happy married to some poor doctor, irrespective of how he makes your foolish heart flutter."

Abby turned away and swiped at her eyes. The last thing she wanted was for Charles Kittridge to see that he could make her cry.

"Marry him, and you'll find out that being poor is not in the least romantic." Charles jammed his hands into his pockets.

"The Bennetts aren't poor. They own a fine house in Charleston and a cottage here. Judge Bennett is one of the most respected men in the state—even Papa will admit to that. And Dr. Bennett is developing a reputation in Washington. I won't be surprised if he becomes as important as Dr. Benjamin Rush."

Charles let out a long breath. "I'll grant you there is a decent living to be made in medicine if a man takes the right kind of cases. But even the most successful physician can never hope to earn the kind of money that the rice trade affords. If we were to marry and join Mulberry Hall with my place, we'd own more land than anyone in Plantersville besides the Allstons. And maybe the Wards."

She glared at him. "Is that what I represent to you, Charles? An opportunity to get richer than you already are?"

"Not entirely."

"Not entirely?" She shook her head. "You don't give one whit about marriage. You want only an economic merger, completely devoid of any tender feelings."

"That isn't true. I'm very fond of you. You're everything a man could want in a wife—beautiful, well-read, skilled in the ins and outs of running a big house." He paused, his smile returning. "What's wrong with that?"

"What about affection and companionship? What about being able to share your real, true heart with someone?"

"There will be time for all that after we're wed."

"I doubt it. And anyway, I am not interested in finding out. I know what I want."

"And you're willing to defy your father to get it?"

"I don't want to defy him. I hope I won't have to. I want him to see that what is best for me is to marry someone of my choosing. Not his."

They reached her cottage and found a creel full of perch on the porch next to Papa's favorite hat and two fishing poles. In the yard, Amos the stable hand was tending to the horses. Papa had returned from a fishing trip, probably with Governor Gist.

Abby paused, one hand on the banister. "If you'll excuse me, I must speak to my mother."

Charles bowed from the waist. "Of course. Mother and I must forgo your wonderful luncheon so she can rest. But I'll see you at supper this evening."

Abby hurried up the steps. *Not if I see you first.*

CHAPTER THREE

MOLLY AND THE KITCHEN GIRLS HAD LABORED ALL MORNING to prepare a lavish buffet, the remains of which now littered a long table on the piazza overlooking the sea. Papa and the menfolk retreated to the sandy yard to enjoy their cheroots while the ladies claimed rocking chairs on the shaded piazza or sat on the steps leading to the sand.

Abby was wedged between Penny and Theodosia on the top step as they polished off the remains of Molly's strawberry pie. The younger girls were playing tag with the surf, their laughter riding the late spring breeze.

Penny nodded toward one of them. "I'm glad Mr. Fraser brought Charlotte," she said, her blue eyes full of sympathy. "Poor girl."

Abby ate the last crumb of her pie. "So am I. I can't imagine what it would be like to lose my mother."

"Charlotte seems happy today, though," Theo said, watching as the girl stopped to examine a shell. "It looks as if she and Bessie Allston are having a grand time."

"Bessie Allston can cheer up anybody," Penny said. "I remember her at school. Everyone at Madame Togno's loved her from the time she was very young." Penny drank from her perspiring glass and set it down. "Anyway, Bessie is turning fifteen at the end of the month, and this will be her first grown-up dance. Charlotte's too."

Theo twisted around and set her plate on the porch. "Perhaps we ought to call Bessie over here to cheer you up, Abby. You've been moping all morning."

"Because Dr. Bennett has yet to make an appearance," Penny said. "I do admit I am puzzled as to why he got off the ferry and then vanished."

"He's avoiding me," Abby said. "I don't suppose he has forgiven me yet for our quarrel last winter."

Theo frowned. "He doesn't seem like one to nurse a grievance. There must be some other reason he and his parents didn't come to dinner today."

"You don't suppose they have taken ill?" Penny looked stricken. "That would be too awful if Dr. Bennett were sick and missed the dance."

"And missed seeing Abby in that dream of a dress." Theo rose and brushed at the back of her skirt. "Well, I suppose there's only one way to find out."

Abby shot to her feet. "What are you going to do? Please, Theo, don't say anything."

"You want to know, don't you?" Theo frowned. "Don't worry. I'll be discreet."

With a backward glance, Theo ran lightly down the steps and onto the sand. Papa and the governor and several other men acknowledged her with polite bows as she walked past before resuming their political talk, their animated voices carrying on the breeze. Theo stopped to speak to Charlotte and Bessie and knelt with them in the sand to examine a mass of seaweed just washed ashore.

Abby moved aside so the servants could begin clearing the table and let out an exasperated breath. "Why is Theo beachcombing when she's supposed to be talking to those girls?"

"If I know Theodosia Avery, she has a plan up her sleeve." Penny grinned and patted Abby's hand. "Be patient. If anyone can find out about the Bennetts, it's Theo."

Abby saw Theo whisper something to Bessie Allston, who rose from her inspection of the seaweed and ran over to where her father stood talking to Governor Gist. Moments later Bessie rejoined Charlotte and Theo, then gestured toward the causeway. Theo gave Bessie a quick hug and hurried to rejoin Abby and Penny on the piazza.

"Mystery solved," she said with a triumphant smile. "The good doctor passed the Allstons' cottage this morning, at which time he indicated he was off to Georgetown to pick up a parcel he's expecting."

"You see?" Penny gave Abby's arm a playful punch. "Didn't I tell you there was a logical explanation for his—"

"Abigail." Papa appeared on the piazza. "Where's your mother?"

Abby looked around. "She was here a few minutes ago. Perhaps she has already gone up to her room for her nap."

"Governor Gist wants a look at our salt works. If your mother inquires as to my whereabouts—"

"I'll tell her, Papa. When will you be back?"

He indicated clouds building on the horizon. "We won't stay long. Looks like we might get a storm before the afternoon is through."

"All right."

Papa clasped both her hands. "When I get back I want to have a talk with you."

Looking past his shoulder she saw Charles Kittridge watching them. Alarm bells sounded in her head. "What about?"

"A private matter. I'm sure your friends will excuse us for a while."

"Of course, Mr. Clayton." Penny bobbed her head and looped her arm through Theo's. "Any time we get in your way, why, all you have to do is say so."

Papa smiled. "Well, I wouldn't say you're in the way, Miss Ravensdale. It's simply a matter of—"

He broke off as Governor Gist came up the steps. "I hate to rush you, sir, but it does look as if we're in for a rain, and I am quite keen to take a look at that salt operation of yours."

"Of course." Papa bowed to all three girls and left with his guest.

"So." Theo brushed her palms together as if dusting them off. "Mission accomplished. Dr. Wade Bennett ought to be on his way back here even as we speak."

"Well, I'm glad to know he intends to return, but I do hope Bessie Allston won't tell him we were asking after him."

"Bessie is sworn to secrecy. I promised to lend her my diamond dress pin for the dance if she promised not to tell anyone we asked about Prince Charming." Theo suppressed a yawn. "Now, if you will excuse me, I think I need a nap. Sleuthing is exhausting. And I'm full as a tick."

"Me too," Penny said. "I can't remember the last time I ate so much food."

The two started inside. At the open doorway, Penny turned. "Sure you don't want a nap, Abby?"

"I'm sure."

The servants were just clearing away the rest of the dishes. Molly folded the white linen tablecloths and took them inside. Mrs. Ravensdale had settled herself into a rocking chair and was absorbed in her book. The rest of the ladies had gone for a walk on the beach or were napping. Penny frowned. "What will you do all afternoon, all by yourself?"

"I'll think of something."

"Suit yourself." Penny waggled her fingers and followed Theo inside.

Abby waited a few minutes until her guests were settled. Then she took her hat from its peg in the foyer and headed for the causeway. The ferry was due in half an hour. One look at Wade Bennett's face would tell her whether the brief, stilted letters of apology they'd exchanged had truly reconciled their hearts. Only then would she be able to relax and enjoy the rest of the weekend festivities.

She arrived at the landing just as the ferrymen secured the ropes and began letting the passengers disembark. Abby stood aside to let a horse and rig exit the ferry, followed by a parade of couples carrying picnic baskets, businessmen in their serious suits, children carrying kites and satchels. At last she saw Wade talking with one of the ferrymen and her heart lurched. She never would have believed he could get any more appealing. But as she watched him, his head inclined toward the shorter man, she was struck anew not only by his good looks but by his quiet confidence and the kindness he showed to everyone. She blinked against the sting of tears, realizing all over again just how wrong she had been and how deeply she had missed him.

He handed the ferryman a coin, picked up his satchel, and strode off the ferry. Then, spotting Abby, he stopped short. "Miss Clayton. I didn't expect a welcoming committee."

The look in his eyes—a mixture of pleasure and amused surprise—heated her cheeks and made her heart stutter. From their first introduction at a St. Cecilia Society ball six years before, Wade Bennett had always had that effect on her.

She dropped a small curtsy, her eyes never leaving his face. "I saw you when you stopped at my cottage this morning, but you drove away before I had a chance to greet you."

He guided her out of the way of a passing rig. "I wanted to see you, too, but I met your houseguests on the ferry and knew there would be no time to talk."

She wanted simply to stand there, drinking in the sight of him while they caught up on the news of these last lonely months and poured out their hearts to each other. But he offered her his arm and set off, matching his stride to hers as they started down the sandy, sun-dappled road. "I trust that Miss Ravensdale and Miss Avery are well."

"Very well." She glanced up at him. "You're looking quite hale and hearty yourself."

He smiled. "And you are more beautiful than I remembered."

"I'm pleased you think so." She paused, relieved that he didn't seem to be out of sorts with her at all. But perhaps it was too early to judge. "I heard you went to Georgetown this morning to pick up a parcel."

"There are no secrets on Pawleys Island."

"Not many."

"I went to retrieve a manuscript that came from Washington. I didn't expect it until next week, but Mr. Kaminski sent word that the package arrived on the *Nina*, and I was eager to get it."

"What kind of manuscript? Don't tell me you've written a novel."

"Hardly. I think I mentioned my colleague, Dr. Archibald, in my last letter to you."

"The one who's helping you and Dr. Percy with your work on the extract replication?"

"Yes. He's written an article about our work that we hope will be published in the Medical Society journal. I'm to read it and add my own notes before he sends it off to be reviewed. If it's chosen for publication, it could bring more attention to our work and perhaps the funding we need to continue our experiments."

"I see. Your work there isn't finished then."

"When it comes to finding better treatments and better medicines for those who are ill, the work is never done."

Abby shoved her fists into her skirt pockets. Clearly, a life with Wade Bennett meant that she would always share him with everyone else. Would it be enough to come second, behind his work and his commitment to others? Even though she was reconciled to it, she couldn't help feeling that they were back where they started. Back to that cold February morning during Race Week when everything had come undone.

They passed Pelican Cottage. Charlotte Fraser paused in her walk on the dunes to wave and call out a greeting.

"Lovely girl," Wade said, tipping his hat. "My mother was quite distressed when the poor girl's mother died. I think Mother had half a mind to—" He stopped walking and peered into Abby's face. "What's the matter?"

"Nothing."

"Is this about my work?"

"I know how important it is to you. And I do understand the implications of it. If a way can be found to standardize the strength of those plant extracts—goldenseal, for instance—who knows how many illnesses might be prevented."

"But?"

"I was hoping your colleagues might carry the work forward and allow you to return to your practice in Charleston. Your patients must miss you so."

And I miss you. More than anything.

"I have no plans to neglect my patients. Dr. Howard has performed admirably in my absence, but I'll be taking over again in a couple of weeks. There's nothing more to be done in the laboratory until those test crops we planted are harvested and processed. And as much as I wish it were otherwise, I'll be needed when the yellow fever arrives this summer."

"Yes. Mother and I were just discussing it last week. It's too bad there is no cure for such a deadly plague."

"I'm glad you understand." He squeezed her arm. "One day we'll figure it out, just as Dr. Snow discovered the cause of cholera, and the fever will be a thing of the past."

They reached her cottage. Papa's rig sat beneath the piazza, the horse tethered in the shade at the edge of the maritime forest that separated the tidal marshes and the beach. Through the open window of the study she heard her father's voice and that of the governor, and she let out a shaky breath. She had an idea what Papa wanted to talk to her about, and she wanted to delay the conversation as long as possible. Besides, she wasn't through with her conversation with Wade.

"I left Mama and our guests napping. I'm sure there's tea, if you'd like some."

"I would." They mounted the steps just as the first fat raindrops plopped onto the sandy yard. "In any case, I must wait out the rain."

Rather than summon Molly and risk attracting Papa's attention, Abby gathered the tea things herself. She put some shortbread on a plate and motioned Wade into the small room next to the parlor overlooking the sea. For a time it had been her mother's sewing room, but now it was furnished with two upholstered chairs, a small table, and a shelf of tattered books. Filmy curtains stirred in the sea breeze that brought a faint tang of salt and rain.

Abby closed the window, poured tea, and picked up the sugar bowl. "Two lumps, if I remember correctly."

He smiled. "Please."

She added the sugar and passed him the milk pitcher.

"I want to say—" she began at the same instant that he said, "Abigail. I wish to apologize for—"

They set down their cups and laughed, and Abby felt a surge of relief. Perhaps everything would be all right after all.

"I should have been more respectful of your feelings," Wade began. "I was so taken with the prospect of working with Dr. Percy that I didn't stop to consider the importance of social events to a lady. Especially the importance of Race Week."

Abby stirred her tea. "I won't deny that I was deeply disappointed to miss the picnic and the balls. I had so looked forward to them all year. But since we've been apart, I've realized it was selfish of me to set such store by them when you had the chance to do something truly important." She watched rain trickling down the wavy glass like streams of quicksilver. "Perhaps in a way I envied you."

"Oh?"

"Well, think about it. What can a woman of my station do with her life? Apart from marriage and motherhood, I mean. It's all we're trained for. A proper marriage is the pinnacle of achievement for girls like me. We don't get to choose anything in life except a husband and a church."

"I suppose you're right. But things are changing. For instance, the Blackwell sisters have paved the way for women who wish to get medical training." He sipped his tea.

"Papa would never hear of that. But honestly, I'm not medical-school material." She eyed him over the rim of her cup. "I'm ashamed to admit it, but I faint dead away at the sight of blood."

He smiled. "That would be a significant barrier to a medical career."

"But I do want to contribute something. In my own way."

"You already have. Your assistance in collecting the plant speci-mens was invaluable to me."

"My cousin Charles Kittridge doesn't think so."

"Do you care what he thinks?" Wade took a bite of shortbread.

"Not in the slightest."

"Good. Because on the way back from Washington, I was thinking about all the help I'll need once we get the new specimens harvested. We've planted goldenseal, feverfew, and a new plant, a purple coneflower, in several locations that will expose them to various amounts of water and sunlight and various kinds of soil. All of that information will have to be collected and cataloged. And once the chemical components of the plants are extracted, we'll need to record any variations in the makeup of the compounds and their strengths."

Abby set down her cup again, struck by the passion in his voice and by her own growing desire to become a much more vital part of his work. Picnics and horse races and dances, though they were indeed great fun, paled in comparison to curing fevers and saving lives.

"Abigail?" Wade frowned. "Are you all right? I haven't offended you again?"

"Far from it." She was swept along on a powerful wave of emotion that made her want to weep. "While you were away, something happened inside me. I can't explain it exactly, but you will be pleased to know that you will encounter no further resistance from me in your pursuit of medical discoveries."

"And I promise we'll attend Race Week next winter."

"Can you spare the time?"

"I'll make time." He cupped her chin in his hand. "These past months I, too, have had a lot of time to think. It was unreasonable of me to expect you to ignore the social season altogether. Next year we'll take in every race and every picnic, and I'll brush up on my dancing so I don't step on your hem during the St. Cecilia ball."

She laughed because they both knew he was one of the best dancers in all of Charleston. "I'm relieved that our quarrel is truly forgotten. And I would dearly love to assist in your work, in any way I can."

"You may regret having made that offer," he said, his eyes alight with happy excitement. "There will be a mountain of work to do come autumn."

"I won't mind, so long as we're together."

They rose, and he took both her hands in his. "Dearest Abigail. I wonder if you know—"

Her breath caught. If only Wade Bennett would declare himself, Papa would have to listen to her wishes. To take her feelings into account and—

The door crashed open, and Papa came in, his blue eyes blazing. "There you are, Abigail. Have you forgotten that I wish to speak to you?"

Abby took in a deep breath to steady her voice. "Of course I haven't. But you were talking with the governor when we came in. And Dr. Bennett has just arrived from the ferry. We're having tea, waiting out the storm."

"So I see." Papa cleared his throat. "Good afternoon, Doctor. I trust you're well. We haven't seen much of you this spring."

"I've been away, working with Dr. Percy at his medical laboratory in Washington," Wade said easily. "But the work is done for now, and I'm delighted to be home. All of us Bennetts are very much looking forward to the barbecue and the dance."

Papa nodded. "It's always a pleasure to talk with your father. He has a fine legal mind. We need his kind in the legislature."

"I couldn't agree more, sir, but my father has said many times he has no interest in politics."

"Too bad."

The three fell silent. At last Wade said, "The rain has stopped, and I ought to be getting home. It's Mother's birthday, and unless I miss my guess, Father has some kind of surprise planned."

"We'll see you at the barbecue," Abby said. "And for the dance afterward."

"I'm looking forward to it." Wade tucked his satchel under his arm and retrieved his hat from the back of his chair. "No need to see me out. I know the way. Good afternoon, Miss Clayton." He inclined his head toward Papa. "Sir."

When the sound of his footsteps faded, Papa motioned her into her chair. "It's time we talked, Abigail. Sit."

CHAPTER FOUR

Abby sat. "If this is about Charles Kittridge—"

"It is. Please do me the courtesy of hearing me out."

"I have heard you on this subject before, Papa. I know you would have me marry him, but I don't love him."

"I'm well aware that your heart belongs to the young doctor." Papa stared out the rain-streaked window. "I imagine everyone else knows it too. You're wearing your heart on your sleeve, my girl."

"Then why keep bringing up Charles when even you can see my affections lie elsewhere?"

"The making of a marriage is about much more than mutual attraction. You must think of the future. Charles has acquitted himself admirably this year. His investments in the Nevada silver mine and the oil drilling in Pennsylvania have paid off quite well. Added to the profits from the Kittridge rice plantations, they make Charles easily one of the wealthiest men in South Carolina." Papa peered at her over the top of his spectacles. "He will be even wealthier when I give you your dowry. I intend to give you Arrington Place upon your marriage. It isn't as large as Mulberry Hall, but it's well situated, and it has always turned a profit. And when your mother and I have passed on, of course, Mulberry will be yours too."

Abby chewed her bottom lip and watched a group of children emerge from their cottages to play in the puddles the rain had left on the beach. She could think of at least six reasons why the prospect of marriage to Charles made her skin crawl—starting with his reprehensible behavior last summer and including the fact that he cared so little for books—but there was little to be gained by reiterating her feelings. Papa wanted what he wanted, and nothing would dissuade him.

Papa reached for her hand. "So will you think about it?"

"Why the big hurry? Can't we enjoy our guests? Why must you pressure me for an answer now?"

He removed his spectacles and polished them on his sleeve. "Rumor has it that one of the Drayton girls has set her cap for young Kittridge. And she's coming to the barbecue."

"Good. She's welcome to him."

"I want to see you settled, Abigail, in case the worst happens."

"Oh, Papa. I know you're worried about secession, but—"

"The situation is grave, my dear. John Bell of Tennessee is a fine man, but nobody believes he can beat Mr. Lincoln for president this fall. And Lincoln has made it quite clear that there is no room for compromise on the slavery question. If he wins election in November, I have no doubt South Carolina will secede, and that will bring us one step closer to war. I want to know you will be secure, no matter what happens."

She looked up, alarmed. "Are our fortunes at risk?"

"No more so than those of any other rice planter."

"If that's true, then I don't see how marriage to Charles will protect me."

He sighed. "I won't live forever, Abigail. You will need a man to look after your holdings and to deal with the bondsmen. To secure your future and that of your children and their children."

"Any reasonably intelligent man can do that."

"You mean Dr. Bennett."

"Yes. After all, he is far better educated than Charles."

"But Charles has the instincts of a born businessman. He knows when to take a risk and when to cash in. I've no doubt the good doctor knows his way around a stethoscope and a laboratory, but—"

Abby rose and began to pace the small room, her thoughts and her stomach churning. Couldn't Papa see that her heart had a mind of its own? That she was powerless against its pull on her?

"Why do you find Charles so objectionable?" Papa asked, frowning. "He's more than reasonably attractive to the ladies, or so I've been told. He doesn't drink to excess, he's competent on the dance floor, and he has the added advantage of kinship."

"He doesn't care for me," Abby said. "And he—"

"That will come with time. With shared burdens and shared joys. Youthful attraction fades, my dear. It's exciting at the outset, but it is quite an insufficient foundation for marriage. You must trust me about this."

Abby studied her father's face. Despite all he did to vex her, she didn't doubt that he wanted the best for his only child and heir. But he wouldn't understand her concerns about Charles's character, much less her need to do something that mattered in the world, something that would transcend her own time on earth. She sighed. "I do trust you, Papa."

He drew her close and planted a kiss atop her head, the way he had when she was small. "Just give it some serious thought. That's all I ask."

"All right."

The clock on the stairway landing emitted a series of faint chimes.

"Fair enough. Now I must see to my guest. The governor will no doubt want to go poking about the island again this afternoon."

Papa returned to his study. Abby picked up her hat and headed outside to the boathouse. She needed time on the water to calm her heart and clear her head. Once there, she found her paddle and wrestled her small rowboat into the tidal creek. It swayed on the still waters as she settled herself on the seat and pushed off. The creek rose slowly as the tide came in, obscuring the mud flats and sending the birds to higher ground. A squirrel's tail flashed in the limbs of an old oak tree. Above the brown water a cloud of insects rose and fell. Abby felt her anxiety fading away. This island had always been her refuge. The place where she came to think. To dream. She closed her eyes and let the boat drift.

Papa would expect her answer soon, and though she knew what her answer must be, she would have to figure out a way to make him see things her way. Perhaps if Wade declared his intentions toward her, perhaps if he himself spoke to her father and explained what he wanted to accomplish, Papa would see that there were things in life more important than making gobs of money. That she was fit for more than giving teas and paying social calls.

She appreciated Papa's concern for her future and his generosity in giving her Arrington Place. It was one of the finest plantations on the Pee Dee and a close neighbor to Mr. Allston's magnificent Chicora Wood. But perhaps Charles Kittridge had been wise to invest in the Comstock Lode out West and in the Titusville oil-drilling operation. If the day came when there were not enough men to plant and harvest rice, those investments might well save the day.

Tears leaked from her closed eyes. Marrying Charles might be the practical choice, but what about her heart? And could she really trust a man who simply took what he wanted with no regard for her own feelings? His behavior last summer was bad enough. She could imagine how much more demanding he might become once they were wed.

A loud splash near the boat interrupted her reverie. The gray, ridged back of an alligator appeared just yards away. The tobacco-colored water roiled as the gator neared the boat. Abby grabbed her paddle and tried to turn the boat in the narrow creek. But the alligator glided closer, its large teeth showing as it rose and clamped onto the stern. A chunk of the dried-out wood came away, and the boat began taking on water.

Abby screamed and tried to beat the creature back with the paddle, but the alligator came halfway out of the water and tried to slither into the boat. Abby paddled toward the boathouse, now barely visible in the distance, but the boat was sinking fast. Her only option was to abandon it to the angry alligator and take her chances crossing the marsh on foot.

Holding fast to the paddle, she jumped out of the boat and landed ankle deep in pluff mud that sucked at her shoes as she ran, turning left and right in a frantic zigzag motion to slow and confuse the alligator. The water, cold and slimy, rose to her waist. The sharp sawgrass tore at her heavy skirts and scratched her arms and face. One of her shoes came off as she crossed the last few yards to the boathouse, her heart hammering, her sides aching.

She pushed open the boathouse door and collapsed, shaking and gasping for breath, onto the short bench where paddles and extra hats and fishing poles were kept. When her breathing slowed, she removed her sopping stockings and her dress and hung them on a nail to dry. She wrung water from the tattered hem and tried to brush away the mud clinging to the sleeves.

Supper time was still a couple of hours away. Perhaps by then her dress would be dry enough that she could at least wear it into the house. Sophronia would be furious, but she would help with a bath and fresh clothes before Abby was expected for supper. There wouldn't be time to wash and dry her hair though, and her arms and hands were red and covered with angry-looking scratches.

Thankfully Wade Bennett was busy tonight. At least she would be spared the mortification of his seeing her in such a state.

Shivering in her sopping chemise and pantalettes, Abby pressed a hand to her throbbing side and rubbed at the stinging red marks on her hands. What she needed was some of Sophronia's elder-bush salve. Perhaps the marks would fade before tomorrow night. If not, her long gloves would hide the worst of—

"Abby?"

She gasped as the door to the boathouse opened and Charles Kittridge strode inside. She grabbed for her dress and heard the fabric rip as it caught on a nail. "Get out."

He frowned. "I was coming back from the creek when I saw you running across the marsh like the devil himself was after you. What in the world happened?"

"It doesn't matter. I'm fine." She clutched her ruined dress to her chest. "Please go."

He moved closer and folded his arms across his chest. "Not until you tell me what happened."

Through gritted teeth she explained about the boat and the alligator. "It was my fault. I was distracted and let the boat drift too close. She was defending her nest."

"My lord, Abigail. You might have been killed."

He drew her into an embrace so tight she winced. "Let go. You're hurting me."

"Shh. Just let me hold you."

She pushed against his chest, but he held on, his cheek resting against her hair.

"I said let go!"

The boathouse door squeaked. Abby twisted her head away and found herself looking squarely into the startled face of Governor Gist.

CHAPTER FIVE

THEODOSIA ANCHORED A DIAMOND COMB INTO ABBY'S
elaborate cascade of curls and stood back to admire her handiwork.
"There. You look perfect, Abby."

Abby tried to smile, but tears threatened. Since the incident in the
boathouse yesterday, a pall of unease had settled over the cottage like
dust in an abandoned room. Mama moved about in strained silence.
Papa had shut himself into his study and remained there all evening,
so angry with her that he hadn't even emerged for supper.

This afternoon he had appeared at last, stone-faced and silent, to
host the barbecue. Wave after wave of guests had made their way up
the beach road from the ferry landing, eager to sample the dozens of
dishes Molly set out on long tables on the beach. Papa had been too
busy or too angry to pay Abby any notice, and she had been certain
to give him and the governor a wide berth. But Mama had insisted
that Abby stand in the receiving line, and by the time she'd greeted
the merchants, factors, lawyers, and their wives and children, the
barbecue was almost over and she'd had little time to spend with
Wade at all.

She could well imagine what the governor thought of the scene
he'd stumbled upon in the boathouse, but she consoled herself with

the thought that he himself possessed less than a spotless reputation. It was rumored that he had once killed a man in defense of a lady's honor. And according to Ophelia Kittridge, the governor's parents had never been married—at least to each other. He had been expelled from school and twice been involved in duels, though he'd never been punished for it.

With such a checkered past, the governor was hardly in a position to criticize her for the situation he had come upon in the boathouse. But Charles Kittridge was not constrained by his own past deeds. He would do anything to get his way, even if it meant causing a scandal.

"Abigail Clayton, whatever is the matter with you?" Penny Ravensdale, dressed for the ball in a pink confection appliquéd with white rosebuds, collapsed onto Abby's bed like a weary soldier returning from battle. "You haven't heard a word I've said. And it's good news too."

Abby sighed. "I could use some good news."

Theo leaned into Abby's mirror to put the finishing touches to her own hairstyle. "Listen, Abby. Penny and I both know something's wrong. You look as if you've lost your last friend. What happened?"

"My father wants me to marry Charles Kittridge. I'm considering entering a convent."

"That's old news," Theo said. "Mr. Clayton has wanted you to marry Charles since you turned eighteen."

"That's where the good news comes in," Penny said, rising from the bed. "Guess who arrived here this morning. Jane Drayton. And I overheard her mother telling my mother that there's to be an engagement announcement soon. Maybe even this evening."

Abby dropped her powder brush onto the table. "Engagement? You're sure?"

"Sure as Sunday follows Saturday."

Abby jumped up and embraced her two friends. "What a relief! Papa told me one of the Draytons had set her cap for Charles, but I didn't think it was serious. Oh, I do hope it's true."

Through the open window, Abby heard the musicians her father had hired warming up. The first strains of a waltz drifted on the cool ocean breeze.

"We won't find out sitting up here, will we?" Penny adjusted the pink sash on her voluminous skirt and twirled around. "I for one am ready to dance."

"Me too." Theo buttoned her white kid gloves, then planted a kiss on Abby's cheek. "Don't worry. Everything will be all right. I saw your Dr. Bennett arriving just ahead of us." She clapped one hand to her chest. "He's in the parlor. And may I say he looks absolutely divine. You're lucky to have such a handsome and distinguished suitor."

"He isn't a suitor yet, at least not formally," Abby said. "But I hope he will be soon."

"He won't be able to resist when he sees you in that dress," Penny said. "Wait here. Let Theo and me go down first. That way you can make a grand entrance."

Abby watched her two friends descend the stairs. With a final glance in the mirror, she picked up her ivory fan and started down.

Dr. Bennett stepped into the hallway just as she arrived at the bottom of the stairs. "Abby."

He clasped her hand, and she read the affectionate approval in his eyes.

"I'm glad you're here," she said.

"Wouldn't miss a chance to spend an evening with you for the world. And nobody entertains with more style than your father. He tells me the violinist is newly arrived from France and is quite the sensation in town."

"Yes. He told me that too."

Wade frowned. "You seem awfully subdued. Is anything wrong?"

If only she could pour her heart out to him about the awful incident in the boathouse. But this wasn't the time or place. "I'm all right. A bit tired after the receiving line this afternoon."

"It doesn't show," he murmured. "I've never seen you looking more beautiful."

"I'm glad you approve." She squeezed his hand. "I should go find Mother. She so loves this party, but it is tiring for her."

"Can you spare a few moments for me first? I hardly saw you at all this afternoon. I had plans to speak to you earlier, but you were kept so busy I abandoned them."

She smiled up at him, her heart thudding. "What sort of plans?"

"Come into the parlor."

She followed him into the spacious room overlooking the sea. Below them, on the temporary wooden dance floor Papa had erected, guests were already pairing off for the first dance, the men regal in their dark suits and silk cravats, the women in their silk and satin gowns as bright as a flock of exotic birds. Molly and Sophronia wove their way among the guests offering cups of punch in crystal glasses that caught and reflected the waning sunlight.

Wade stood behind Abby at the window and slipped both hands around her waist. "I wanted to ask you something. I suppose I ought to say this quickly before we're interrupted again."

He turned her around so she was facing him. "After our parting last February, I had plenty of time to think about the future, about what I want in a wife. And even before you told me that you wanted to work alongside me, somehow I knew you were the one for me."

She nodded, afraid to speak and break the spell. But she felt exactly the same. True hearts didn't simply meet by chance somewhere; they were meant for each other—waiting for each other all along. How grateful she was that they had both discovered this before it was too late.

Wade made a small sound in his throat. "So what I am asking is whether you will allow me to speak to your father about us. I can't offer you a great fortune or even an aristocratic name. All I have to offer is my abiding affection and my promise to treasure you and to protect you for the rest of my life." He pulled her close, his eyes seeking hers. "You must think carefully about whether this is enough."

"I have thought of nothing else since you went away. You are more than enough for me, Wade Bennett. You always will be."

He glanced around, drew her away from the window, and kissed her with such fervor she nearly lost her breath.

They finally drew apart, and he smiled into her eyes. "Shall we go find your father?"

"Yes. In a little while. Right now I'm so happy I want to keep this secret just for the two of us." She took his hand and drew him out of the parlor, leading him through the doors and down the steps to the dance floor. Wade took her into his arms, and for the next hour they danced every dance, keeping to the shadows, murmuring together.

When the sun went down, turning the sea and sky to shades of apricot and gold, the musicians took a break. Hector lit torches and placed them in buckets of sand. Molly and Sophronia brought out platters of sandwiches and sweets and another round of punch.

"Will you excuse me?" Abby asked Wade. "I ought to check on Mother."

"Of course." He placed a swift kiss on her cheek. "Don't be long."

Abby found her mother seated in her rocking chair on the piazza, deep in conversation with Mrs. Ravensdale.

"Oh, there you are, darling." Mama smiled up at Abby. "I was right about your gown. It becomes you."

Mrs. Ravensdale snapped open her fan and nodded to Abby. "It is lovely, my dear. But something more than that blue silk gown has put the roses in your cheeks."

Abby smiled, wishing she had found her mother alone. She was bursting to share her good news, but now was not the time. Not before Wade had spoken to Papa. And anyway, Mama looked pale tonight, and terribly tired. "Are you all right, Mama?"

"I'm afraid I had a restless night. I hardly slept a wink. Have you seen Charles Kittridge this evening?"

"No. But I haven't looked very hard to find him." The memory of their encounter in the boathouse burned like acid in her veins. But she wouldn't let it spoil the perfect wonder of this night. Because no matter what Papa said, she intended to marry Wade Bennett. Nothing could change that.

"You ought to speak to him right away, Abigail. And your father too."

"I will. Do you need anything before I go? Some more punch? Your shawl? It's bound to cool off quickly now that the sun has set."

"I'm fine, dear. And Mrs. Ravensdale is here to keep me company."

"You go along with the young people," Mrs. Ravensdale said. "Enjoy the dance. I'll sit with your mother awhile longer." She patted Mama's hand. "The two of us have much to discuss this evening."

"All right." Abby bent to kiss her mother's cheek just as the first strains of a waltz floated on the breeze. The musicians had returned. She hurried to find Wade, but he had disappeared. Penny and Theodosia found her standing in the spot where she had last seen him.

"Well?" In the flickering torchlight, Penny's eyes shone. "What happened in the parlor?"

Abby's happy laugh bubbled up from deep inside. "Can you keep a secret?"

Both women nodded. "Do tell," Theo prompted. "Did Dr. Bennett propose?"

"Yes, but you can't say a word to anyone. Not until he has spoken to Papa."

"Oh, aren't you the luckiest thing?" Penny grabbed Abby's hand. "I'm delighted. And slightly jealous. I only wish that someday I—"

"Ladies and gentlemen." Papa's voice rose above the music and the guests' animated chatter. "May I have your attention?"

He motioned to Abby, and she made her way through the crowd, searching for Wade. Perhaps he had spoken to her father already. Finally she spotted Wade standing near one of the torchlights, deep in conversation with the governor and Judge Bennett.

The guests gathered in the yard where Papa and Charles Kittridge waited. To Charles's left stood Jane Drayton in an exquisite pale-lilac satin gown, an expectant smile on her face.

The music stopped, leaving the whisper of the sea as the only sound.

"Friends," Papa said. "You honor us with your presence here tonight. A night that is even more special because we have a betrothal to announce."

Theo and Penny crowded in next to Abby. "See?" Penny whispered. "I told you so. Charles is going to marry Jane Drayton. And you'll be free to wed Dr. Bennett."

Papa placed his hand on Charles's shoulder. "Tonight I have the honor of announcing the engagement of my cousin Charles Kittridge. To my beautiful daughter, Abigail."

———

In the deeply shadowed room, cool hands rested on her cheek and forehead. Voices drifted on the breeze coming through the open window. Her whole body felt heavy, her throat raw and dry.

"What happened?" Abby struggled to open her eyes.

"You fainted dead away is what. Jus' lie still, child." Sophronia dipped a towel into a basin of water and pressed the cooling cloth to Abby's brow.

Abby attempted to sit up. Somehow her blue gown and her corset and crinoline had been removed. She was lying in her bed clad in her chemise and pantalettes. The curtains billowed at the window, letting in a narrow strip of bright sunlight that revealed all of Theodosia's things—her silver hairbrush and mirror, her hatboxes and trunks—were gone. "Sophronia, where is Theo Avery? What time is it?"

"The Averys took out of here last night. And I 'spect it's nigh on to ten o'clock."

"Ten o'clock. In the morning?"

"Sun don't shine in the nighttime." Sophronia fluffed Abby's pillows and opened the curtains. "Once Dr. French gave you that nerve potion, you slept like the dead. Best thing for you, considerin' the circumstances."

The circumstances. Now the entire horror of last evening came roaring back. Papa's stunning announcement, Charles Kittridge's triumphant smile, and her sick disbelief before everything went black. "Dr. French looked after me? Where was Dr. Bennett?"

The maid shrugged. "I wasn't there. It was Mister Clayton hisself that scooped you up and carried you inside. Miss Alicia brought in the doctor. Lucky he was still here. Anyway, your papa told me to fetch him when you woke up."

Hot tears spilled down Abby's face. "I wish I'd never woken up."

"Now you take that back, Miss Abigail. It's bad luck to say such things."

"Oh, Sophronia, the worst thing that can possibly happen to me has already happened."

"You mean 'cause you engaged to Mister Charles? Some girls would give anything to snag such a rich husband."

"Well, I don't care one whit about Charles Kittridge's money."

"Uh-huh." Sophronia picked up a brush and began drawing it through Abby's tangled curls. "Folks that got plenty o' money is always the ones that say it don't matter."

Footsteps sounded in the hallway, and the door opened. Papa stuck his head into the room. "I heard voices. Are you awake, Abigail?"

"Miss Abigail jus' this minute woke up," Sophronia said. "I was on my way to fetch you."

"Well, I'm here already," Papa said. "You may leave us now, Sophronia."

Sophronia shot Abby an unreadable look and hurried out, the door closing with a click that sounded to Abby like a jail cell slamming shut.

"I'm not properly dressed, Papa." Abby drew the thin cotton coverlet up to her shoulders.

"That didn't seem to be a deterrent to you the day before yesterday."

Even as his harsh words pierced her heart, rage built inside her chest. "You know I despise Charles. It was not at all what it seemed."

"Governor Gist was shocked to find you two locked in an embrace, your dress torn, and you half dressed. I am disappointed in you. More than I can say."

"Papa, I tried to tell you what happened that night after supper, but you were too angry to listen. It was not an embrace. My boat sank in the creek, and I had to wade out. I was muddy and sopping wet and

went to the boathouse to dry off. Charles followed me and took hold
of me and wouldn't let go, even when I told him he was hurting me.
Surely the governor heard every word I said."

"All I know is that he came to me as one concerned father to
another and told me what he had witnessed. He was quite scandal-
ized. Such things have a way of getting out, Abigail, no matter how
delicately they are handled. And the repercussions affect more than
your girlish heart."

"Your political prospects, you mean."

"I won't deny it. I have worked too hard and too long to let my
chance slip away over something like this. Your engagement to Charles
was a foregone conclusion anyway. I simply had to announce it sooner
than I planned. The governor is mollified. I think I've contained the
damage."

"Except the damage to me." Abby swallowed the tears building in
her throat. "Did Dr. Bennett speak to you last night?"

"He mentioned that he wanted to, but—"

"He proposed to me, Papa. Last night, in the parlor. He wanted
to speak to you that very moment, but I asked him to wait an hour
or two. It was such a delicious secret, and nobody knew it but us. But
all the time you were planning this ridiculous announcement of my
betrothal to Charles. And you didn't even—" The last of her resolve
crumbled, and she dissolved into wracking sobs.

Papa drew a chair close to the bed and sat down. He poured
a tumbler of water from the bedside pitcher and handed it to her.
"Drink this. You'll feel better."

She wiped her eyes on her sleeve. "I won't feel better until I have
seen Dr. Bennett and straightened out this whole mess. Because I will
marry him, Papa. If he will still have me."

He waved one hand in dismissal, a gesture that infuriated her even further. "You will marry Charles Kittridge. And furthermore, you will appear promptly at seven this evening with a smile on your face. We're giving a farewell supper for the governor and his lady. They want a chance to congratulate the happy couple. I expect you to—"

"Abby?" Mama knocked once and came in. "Oh, I didn't realize your father was still here."

Papa rose. "I've said what I came to say. I'll see you both at supper tonight." He pointed his finger at Mama. "Don't coddle her, Alicia. She may not want to admit it, but she knows I'm right, about everything."

"How comforting that must be," Abby said bitterly, "to know that you are never, ever wrong."

If he heard her, he didn't let on. The door closed behind him. Mama set aside her cane and perched on the bed. "Oh, my dear girl. I've hardly slept since this whole disturbing business about the boathouse. If only the governor hadn't happened upon you and Charles—"

"If even half the things Cousin Ophelia says about the governor are true, he hardly has room to criticize anyone." Abby threw back the covers. "I must go."

She washed her face and hands, then chose a simple ivory frock and began to dress.

"Where are you going?" Mama's face was pale and drawn.

"To find Dr. Bennett, of course. I must explain the—"

"You're betrothed now, darling. You can't go chasing after another man, even if he is an old friend. It isn't seemly."

Abby finished doing up her buttons and reached for her stockings. "I wanted to tell you last night, but not in front of Mrs. Ravensdale." She sat down and drew on a stocking. "Dr. Bennett and I pledged ourselves to each other yesterday evening. But before he could speak to Papa, Papa up and announced my engagement to Charles. It's all a hideous mistake that must be rectified at once."

Abby finished dressing and peered at her reflection in the mirror. "Mercy. I look awful."

"Abigail." Mama retrieved her cane and pushed to her feet. "Think about what you're doing. Defying your father. Putting his fondest ambition into jeopardy."

"I don't want to cause Papa any trouble. But he has put my fondest ambition into jeopardy too. Perhaps that makes us even." Abby pinned up her hair and reached for her powder box. "Besides, if what he says is true and the governor is keeping that ridiculous scene in the boathouse to himself, what possible harm can come to Papa as a result of it?"

Mama's dark eyes glittered with unshed tears. "Cousin Ophelia feels no such constraints. She told Mrs. Avery all about it last night. Theodosia was so infuriated with Ophelia that she insisted upon leaving the island right away."

Abby sank onto her chair at the dressing table, her back to the mirror. So that's what had happened while she slept. "I'm sure the Averys are not the only ones who have heard the story. And what they heard undoubtedly paints Charles in the most favorable light."

"I suppose any mother wants others to think well of her children."

"You're defending her? Fine. But she is—"

Mama's cane clattered to the floor. She burst into tears.

Abby was filled with remorse. She guided her mother to the chair by the window and poured her a glass of water. "Mama, please don't cry."

"Why shouldn't I? Everything has gone so terribly wrong. For all of us."

"What is so wrong with my wanting to marry a kind man who adores me, and with whom I have things in common?"

"Because to break the engagement now in favor of Dr. Bennett certainly would cause scandal, and your father would not be the only one paying the price." Mama drew a handkerchief from her cuff and wiped her eyes. "People can be very unforgiving, Abby. And with your father away so much of the time, I depend upon my friendships. I know you're disappointed now, but you must believe that your father is—"

"So you're on Papa's side? You would rather see me in a miserable marriage than to bear the brunt of idle gossip. I thought you cared for me more than that."

"Surely you don't doubt my affections after all I've done for you. But I don't think you're giving your father enough credit. He would not approve the marriage if he didn't think Charles would do right by you."

"I know he truly believes we are a good match, but he makes no allowances for feelings. I care nothing for Charles, and he cares nothing for me."

"Perhaps not now, but when you are married, when children come along—"

The prospect of bearing Charles Kittridge's children made Abby shudder. The memory of his viselike grip on her arms, the hard look in his pale eyes, reminded her that he was not the kind and gentle man her parents believed him to be. He was accustomed to getting his way. Her wishes would not matter at all. But anything she might say now about the way Charles had caught her alone on the piazza last summer and pressed his lips to hers, the way he had practically accosted her in the boathouse, would be seen as merely an excuse for breaking the engagement. "We have nothing in common, Mama. He'd rather have an arm amputated than read a book. What will we talk about at supper for the next forty years? The weather? His horses?

The price of rice? And you know what hurts as much as anything? That Papa has no sympathy for my point of view. In some ways he's just like Charles. Utterly lacking in compassion."

Mama looked truly stunned. "I will grant that your father can be stubborn. Opinionated. But he is not lacking in compassion. Hasn't he spoken often enough of the reasons he wants to become governor? So that he can champion more schools and give the poor more opportunity?"

"I'm not denying that Papa has some good ideas and worthy goals. But he—"

"And just look at me." Mama indicated her walking cane. "He chose to marry me despite my crippled leg. He saw beyond my twisted limbs to the woman I am down deep."

Before Abby could reply, Mama went on. "It's true that my father settled a considerable dowry on me when your father and I married. But there were several girls whose families could have offered much more. Beautiful girls with two good limbs. When they ridiculed me because I could not dance, when they mocked me for my cane, it was your father who defended me." Mama's voice broke. "Say your worst about him, but he is a man of great compassion. And I can't bear the defeated look that has overtaken him since yesterday. His fondest dream swept away in a matter of minutes." She dabbed at her tear-swollen eyes. "If only you had stayed away from the boathouse."

Mama looked up at Abby with such brokenness that Abby's own heart shattered. All her life she had been the delight of her mother's life and the object of all her endeavors. Mama had made sure Abby had the riding lessons she wanted, the summer trips to Saratoga with her friends. The expensive French piano in the parlor at Mulberry Hall was there because Abby had wanted it. When Abby went through her awkward stage, gawky and frizzy haired, it had been Mama who assured Abby of her coming beauty and made sure Abby was the best dressed of all her friends. Her mother had tutored her through the difficulties of second-year Latin and had comforted her when the first boy she ever loved jilted her. Everything Abby was, and everything she might become, she owed to the woman who now sat beside her, wracked with sobs.

She drew her mother into her arms and rested her chin on Mama's hair. How could she condemn Papa for his lack of compassion and ignore the cries of her own devoted mother's heart? She released a shuddering breath and felt her heart filling up with sadness and regret. For a moment she had glimpsed the tantalizing possibility of an authentic life, but now both her parents expected her to live out a false one. She could have borne her father's anger and contempt, but she was no match for her mother's heartrending tears.

She kissed Mama's cheek, tasted the salt on her skin, and summoned her resolve. "Don't cry. I can stand anything except your tears. If it will make you happy, I'll marry Charles Kittridge."

"I can't be truly happy knowing that you are not content." Mama released a long breath. "But it is the practical choice."

"However, I must speak to Dr. Bennett regardless of appearances. He deserves an explanation." Abby found her hat and tied the ribbons beneath her chin.

She left her mother sitting by the window, crossed the hall to the back door, and took the back steps down to the beach. It was nearly noon, the spring sun high in the sky, the light breaking and multiplying on the vast expanse of sea. Normally such a sight would have calmed her. But now, thinking of Wade and of what she must say to him, she was wound tight as piano wire. And near to breaking.

She crossed the dunes and hurried past Miss Augusta's cottage, where the Kittridges were staying, praying not to be seen. Marveling at how quickly all her bright hopes had shattered. Remembering a time when she had looked forward to her future instead of dreading it.

CHAPTER SIX

ALL OF THE WINDOWS OF THE BENNETTS' COTTAGE WERE open to a freshening breeze that caused the empty hammock to sway, throwing patterns of light and dark on the piazza's plank floor. Abby mounted the steps and peered inside. "Hello?"

"My son is not at home."

Abby turned to see Wade's mother rise from a rocking chair half hidden behind an enormous potted palm. Mrs. Bennett crossed the piazza, brows raised in question. "After the events of last evening, you are the least likely person I expected to see."

Abby's mouth went dry. "It's all a misunderstanding, and I feel terrible about it. I've come to explain to Wade, to tell him that I—"

"Your father's announcement last night made things plain enough." Mrs. Bennett crossed her arms across her chest. "Wade is in shock. And deeply hurt."

"I know. That's why I want to speak to him."

"If you care for him at all, you'll leave him alone. He has no desire to hear anything from you."

Tears brimmed in Abby's eyes. "Did he say that, Mrs. Bennett? That he won't see me? That he won't even listen?"

The older woman sighed and stared out at the sea. "It won't

change anything, will it? What good is talk, except to ease your conscience?"

"I—"

"I don't wish to be rude, Miss Clayton. But there is nothing you can say that will make any difference, and I have things to do. I'll thank you kindly to leave us in peace."

"I'll go, but please tell me where to find Wade."

Mrs. Bennett whirled and stalked toward the door, shutting it firmly behind her.

Too distraught to return home, Abby continued up the beach, crowded now with swimmers and waders, groups of children launching kites, and ladies in wide-brimmed hats enjoying tea in the shadow of the dunes.

An older man in a fishing hat approached, carrying a string of sea bass. He nodded as he passed her, then stopped and turned around. "Miss Clayton?"

"Judge Bennett." She clapped one hand to her hat to anchor it against the sea breeze and looked up at him.

"Are you all right?" Frowning, the judge peered into her face. "You gave us all a scare, fainting away like that. Do you know you barely missed hitting your head on the corner of the stairs?"

"I spoiled the evening for everyone."

"Well, for my son at least. I expect your Mr. Kittridge is happy enough this morning."

"I haven't seen him. I'm told that Dr. French gave me something to make me sleep. I'm grateful for that since it saved me from having to listen to idle gossip all night."

The judge's face flushed, and Abby saw that he had heard the unsavory story of her encounter with Charles in the boathouse. No doubt Wade had heard it too. But she still wanted desperately to talk to him.

"Judge Bennett, I know what my cousin Ophelia has told everyone. It isn't true, but it seems no one believes me, even Mrs. Bennett. She refused to tell me where Wade has gone."

Two boys rushed past, jostling her, and the judge held out a hand to steady her. "I've been a judge a long time, Miss Clayton. Long enough to learn that things are often not quite as they first appear." He motioned to her, and they continued walking along the beach. "Long enough to feel that everyone deserves a chance to tell his own side of things."

Abby kept her eyes down as they neared the Bennetts' cottage. Did this mean he would help her?

"Do you know how to drive a horse and rig?" he asked.

"Of course. I have my own rig at Mulberry Hill. Papa declined to bring it over this summer. He said walking to the ferry landing would be good for me."

"I expect it is at that. But in this case a rig will get you there faster."

"Sir?"

"Wade is taking the noon ferry to Georgetown. If you go now, you can catch him."

"But I was hoping we could talk someplace quiet. Maybe I should just wait here. When will he be back?"

"Not for a good long while. He intends to overnight aboard the *Nina* and return to Charleston tomorrow."

They had reached the Bennetts' cottage. The judge summoned a servant and handed him the string of fish. "Scipio, please take these to the kitchen. And hitch the rig for Miss Clayton."

Abby placed a hand on the judge's sleeve. "Thank you."

"I hope I'm not making things worse for either of you." He started up the stairs.

Minutes later Scipio returned with the horse and rig. He nodded toward the chestnut dancing sideways in the traces. "He's liable to be a bit feisty this mornin', miss. He ain't had his run yet."

Abby climbed into the smart little rig and picked up the reins. The horse soon settled and trotted down the road, his hooves churning up clouds of sand. At the ferry landing she rolled to a stop, jumped out, and looped the reins over a hitching post next to a couple of other waiting rigs.

The landing was crowded. Many of the passengers were guests from last night. Abby recognized two of Papa's lawyers and his rice factor, Mr. James. Several ladies sat atop their traveling trunks, their parasols raised against the late-morning sun.

Abby scanned the crowd, looking for Wade, but it was Theodosia Avery she spotted. Abby looked away quickly, hoping Theo hadn't seen her, but her friend pushed through the crowd, caught Abby's arm, and turned her around. "Oh, Abby, are you all right? What are you doing here?"

"I'm not injured. Unless you count a broken heart."

"Oh, I know! I nearly fainted myself when your father said you're to marry Charles. I'm sorry that Mother and I left so abruptly. But honestly, Charles looked so smug—and that mother of his too—that I could not bear to spend another minute in their company. Mother agreed with me. The Ravensdales' cottage is finally open for the season, so we spent the night there, and Mr. Ravensdale drove us here this morning. We planned to take the earlier ferry, but by the time we got here it was already too full." Theo paused for breath. "You haven't said why you're here."

"I'm hoping to see Dr. Bennett before he leaves."

"He's here. I saw him just a few moments ago, talking with Mr. James." Theo stood on tiptoe to scan the crowd. "There he is—with Mr. Drayton. I haven't seen Jane this morning. I'm sure she is just as astonished and miserable as you are."

Abby nodded, her throat too full of tears to speak. Her first glimpse of Wade, his dark head bent to the older man, broke her heart all over again.

"Shall I tell him you're looking for him?"

"Please."

As Theo made her way through the crowd, Abby blotted her face and hands with her handkerchief and pinched some color into her cheeks. It wouldn't do for Wade to see her looking so wan.

In a moment he was beside her, his expression unreadable. "You shouldn't have come, Abigail."

"Your father thought I deserved a chance to speak to you. Though your mother does not share his opinion."

"Well, here I am. What do you want to say?"

She drew him aside. "That I am utterly miserable. That my heart has not changed toward you in the least. That I will always regret asking you to wait just for a moment before speaking to Papa."

"It wouldn't have mattered. After what happened in the boathouse—"

"Surely you don't believe idle gossip. You know there is nothing between Charles and me. You can't think that I encouraged him in any way."

"I know you didn't, but not everyone—"

"Isn't it breathtaking how a life can be turned upside down in a heartbeat? Everything you ever wanted gone for good."

He swallowed hard, his eyes fixed on some point in the distance. "Come with me to town. Just for today."

"Then you don't hate me."

"How could I hate you?" His expression was as somber and defeated as her own. "Your father wouldn't let me into the house when he carried you inside. I was awake all night, worrying about you and hoping there might be some honorable way through this situation. But I don't suppose there is one."

Abby slowly shook her head. "This morning I told Papa I intended to marry you regardless. But my mother is entirely broken at the prospect of being ostracized, and I cannot condemn her to such a fate. I owe her everything." She reached for his hand and held on tight. "You will always have my heart. But I have agreed to a life I don't want. Because of her. Can you understand?"

"I can. You've been made to choose between love and duty."

"Yes. And I expect to regret it forever."

The ferry rounded the bend. People picked up their baggage and began lining up.

"We are denied a lifetime together," he said softly. "But we can have this one day. If you will come with me."

"There is nothing I want more. But tonight Papa is hosting another dinner, and—"

"Yes. I know. For the governor and his wife. I heard your father talking about it last night."

"I'm to make an appearance. With Charles. And pretend to be happy." Her voice broke. "From this day until my dying breath, I must pretend."

Wade heaved a sigh. "The last ferry leaves town at four o'clock. You'll be back here in plenty of time for supper." He indicated the hitching post. "Plenty of time to return my father's horse and rig."

"It was generous of him to let me use it. I'm glad he gave me a chance to explain."

"He believes in fairness above all." Wade drew back to look into her eyes. "Will you come with me?"

Abby imagined an even bigger scandal if anyone should report to Papa that she had spent a day with a man not her relative and not her intended. But she had given up her entire future for her family. Surely she deserved one day for herself. One day that she could store away like a precious treasure, to be taken out in years to come and remembered when reality was too difficult to bear.

She followed Wade onto the ferry. He chose a spot near the back, where they were partially hidden by stacks of suitcases, hatboxes, a horse and rig. They spoke little on the crossing. For Abby it was enough simply to stand next to him. To imprint upon her memory the play of sunlight on his dark hair, the sad and tender look in his eyes, the exact timbre of his voice when he spoke her name.

When the ferry arrived in Georgetown, Wade took her hand as she stepped from the landing onto the busy street. The clock tower announced the hour, and Abby realized she had not eaten since the three o'clock barbecue the previous day.

"Mother insisted on packing food for me." Wade held up a small basket as they strolled past shuttered shops and the slave market, quiet now on this Sunday afternoon. "There's plenty to share."

"Last night I thought I might never want to eat again, but I admit I am hungry."

He smiled then. "Even a condemned prisoner gets a last meal."

They made their way along the waterfront, past rows of wooden sheds and brick storage buildings, past cargo ships riding at anchor in the Sampit River. Wade found a grassy patch at the end of the pier and spread his jacket on the ground. He opened the basket and took out sandwiches, boiled eggs, and a glass jar of berries and cream.

"I've told my mother I don't like boiled eggs," he said. "But she makes them anyway." He offered Abby one, and she bit into it. He unwrapped a sandwich and lifted the top slice of bread. "Ham and cheese?"

"Beggars can't be choosers."

They ate in a silence broken only by the faint sound of music coming from a group of sailor-musicians gathered at the stern of a cargo ship.

"Listen," he said. "Remember that song?"

"Of course. The St. Cecilia Ball. Six years ago."

"The first night we danced together." He rose and reached for her hand. "How about it, Abby? One last dance?"

It was a bad idea, being so close to him, feeling his arms around her and knowing that this moment was all they would ever have. What could come of it but more painful memories? But she placed her hand in his. He drew her to her feet and hummed softly in her ear as the song drifted on the breeze. She closed her eyes and rested her head on his shoulder, listening to the shuffle of their footsteps on the wooden wharf. It was more than her battered heart could take.

"That's enough." Abby pulled away before the song ended and fumbled for her handkerchief.

"It will never be enough." He took his time packing away the remains of their meal, giving her time to regain her composure, to return the conversation to a more even keel. "I finished editing my article for the Medical Society journal."

"I'm glad." She managed a smile. "When will you know whether it's accepted?"

"Perhaps not for some time. When I get to Charleston, I'll have clean copies made and sent to Dr. Percy. He'll send them on to the editor, and then we must wait for a decision." He opened a leather pouch and withdrew a sheaf of papers. "Would you like to read it?"

She resumed her seat on the grass and began reading, tucking each page under the edge of his lunch basket to prevent its blowing away. Wade leaned back on his arms, his long legs stretched in front of him. Abby was aware of his eyes on her face as she read, and now and then she glanced up at him. When she set aside the final page, he caught her hand. "What do you think? Be honest."

"I can offer no suggestions for improvement. It's complete, succinct, and factual without being boring."

He laughed. "I'm relieved it isn't boring."

"I don't see how anyone who reads it can fail to be excited by what you and Dr. Percy are trying to accomplish. It seems to me that the goldenseal in particular may hold great promise as a preventative for disease."

"That's what we're hoping." His eyes lit up the way they always did when he talked about his work. Abby felt another stab of disappointment that she would not be working alongside him as his experiments progressed.

"I have great hopes for the coneflower extract too," he continued. "I'd like to be able to offer my patients more than dried huckleberry tea and molasses. The trick of course is to figure out how to ensure that each dose of the extract is of uniform strength and purity."

Abby placed a hand on his. "You'll figure it out. I know you will. I only wish I could be a part of it."

"So do I." He took out his watch and snapped it open. "The *Nina* will begin boarding soon. Shall we walk a while first?"

He took her hand to help her to her feet. Then he donned his coat and picked up his belongings. They strolled to the end of the busy wharves, skirting stacks of lumber, barrels of molasses, kegs of spirits. The calls of gulls hovering above a fishing boat mixed with the music still coming from the stern of the cargo ship. Farther on, eager passengers carrying travel satchels, hatboxes, and portmanteaus milled about the *Nina*. Smoke drifted from her stacks into the clear spring sky.

Crossing the street, they passed a group of girls whispering together, the pastel flirtation ribbons on their Sunday hats lifting in the wind. Her hand resting lightly on Wade's arm, Abby stopped to admire a silver tea service and a pair of jade lions in the window of a secondhand shop. In the next block they paused to listen to a black-clad street preacher reading from the book of Isaiah.

They strolled past a bakery, a leather-goods shop, a tobacconist's.

The clock tower rang again. Wade turned to her, his eyes darkened with pain and regret. "I suppose I ought to walk you to the ferry landing. You don't want to miss that supper tonight."

"I want to come with you to the *Nina*."

He shook his head. "It's better this way."

"I don't want to leave you."

"I'll be in Charleston until the autumn, looking after my patients." He brushed a loose strand of hair from her cheek. "Sixty miles is not the ends of the earth."

"No, but it might as well be."

Wade removed a ring from his pocket and pressed it into her palm. "This is not the ring I hoped to give you, but it means a great deal to me. My father had it made from an old coin as a present for Mother on their honeymoon in Greece. Mother gave it to me when I went to medical college. She said it would bring me luck. I pray it will bring you good fortune."

Her fingers closed around it. Tears leaked from her eyes.

"The image on the coin is that of Thalassa, a spirit of the sea." He smiled down at her. "Mother loves the sea more than anyone I know. Except you."

She swallowed her tears and tucked the ring into her pocket. "Sophronia was right."

"About what?"

"One summer, when I was fifteen or sixteen, I came home heart-broken from a picnic at White Point Gardens because Hugh Sumner had invited me and then turned his attentions to another girl."

"What a fool."

She managed a tremulous smile. "Sophronia told me to stay away from the ones I cared about most deeply, because loving them was sure to break my heart in two."

A gentle breeze billowed her skirt and loosened a lock of hair. She brushed it away and rested her head on his shoulder.

Wade's arms went around her. "I don't suppose any of us gets to choose what our hearts want."

"It's a mystery, isn't it?"

"And a great misfortune of the human condition." He offered her his arm. "I hate to say it, but we ought to go."

They headed for the ferry landing, where passengers were gathering for the return trip to the island.

Wade released her. Their eyes met for a long moment.

"Wade, I—" She leaned against him, trembling, and felt the beat of his heart beneath her palm. "God keep you."

"And you." He cupped her face in his hands. "Good-bye, my dear. Try to be happy."

He turned and left her there. She watched him disappear into the crowd of passengers heading for the *Nina*, fighting a furious pain so deep she doubted she would survive it.

"If you goin' to Pawleys, miss, you better come on." The ferryman motioned her on board.

Her fingers closed over the ring in her pocket. *This is not the ring I hoped to give you.*

The ferry dipped as it slid into the river current. Standing near the back, next to the chattering schoolgirls, Abby watched Georgetown recede into the distance. She imagined Wade settling into his cabin aboard the *Nina*, heading off for a life that would not include her.

If only she could turn back the clock to last summer, when Charles had caught her alone and bruised her lips with his rough and furtive kiss. If she had told Papa then, perhaps he would have changed his mind. But she had kept silent. How terrible it was to look back and realize where she'd made her mistake. And to know that now it was too late to correct it.

CHAPTER SEVEN

Abby waited at the open parlor window, watching the play of light cast by the flickering candles in the adjacent dining room. The setting sun drenched the beach in a rich amber glow and threw long shadows across the sand. The ocean's steady breath was a soft caress against her skin, but tonight even the sea couldn't soothe her.

This afternoon's return from Georgetown had been uneventful. The ferry arrived on time. She disembarked quickly and returned Judge Bennett's horse and rig. If he was surprised that she had been gone all afternoon, he kept such thoughts to himself, merely nodding when she handed over the reins and thanked him for his generosity.

The parlor door opened. Holding firmly to Mama's arm, Papa ushered her and Governor Gist and his lady toward the dining room. Behind them came Charles and sharp-faced Cousin Ophelia, one pink-gloved hand resting on her son's arm. Abby knew she should join them. To be late was rude. But she stood rooted to her place in the shadows, studying the man who all too soon would become her husband.

He was handsome enough, with his dark-gold hair and clear blue eyes. Tonight, dressed in a gray suit of fine wool with a dark-blue cravat at his throat, the candlelight glinting off his hair, he looked quite dashing. Most girls would be pleased by a betrothal to such a handsome and wealthy suitor. But his lack of curiosity about the world, his lack of passion for anything that mattered, left Abby cold. As his wife she would be expected to be at his side as he engaged in endless, frivolous amusements, observing life but not living it as she wanted. And the disregard he had shown for her last summer—and again in the boathouse—filled her with dread.

Shaking off her sense of doom, she stepped into the light and forced a smile.

"There you are," Papa said. "You look quite lovely, my dear."

She acknowledged her father's compliment with a nod and forced a smile that included everyone. "Good evening, Governor. Mrs. Gist. Did you enjoy your outing this morning?"

Mary Gist smiled. "We did indeed. I think this is the nicest time of year on Pawleys, don't you?"

"Oh, Abigail loves Pawleys in any season." Charles spoke before Abby could form a reply. Did he not think she was capable of answering a simple question on her own?

"Actually, I agree with you, Mrs. Gist," Abby said. "August can be quite uncomfortable here, even in the shade. I do prefer May's more temperate weather."

Molly and two kitchen girls appeared in the doorway carrying platters and serving spoons. Mama took her place at the foot of the table. The governor sat to her right. At the head of the table sat Papa with Mrs. Gist seated to his right and Charles next to her. Abby took her place on the opposite side, settling into her chair between Cousin Ophelia and the governor.

Mama picked up her spoon, the signal that the meal could begin.

"Well, Governor," Papa said as they began the soup course, "I'm delighted you and Mrs. Gist were able to join us this year. I hope you enjoyed the barbecue."

Mrs. Gist dabbed her mouth with her napkin. "Everything was lovely. I don't know how you do it, Mrs. Clayton. Even with your staff to help, organizing so many guests for a three-day affair seems more daunting than any entertaining I do at Rose Hill."

"Will you be returning directly to the governor's residence tomorrow?" Cousin Ophelia asked. "I imagine you're eager to get home. I've always thought your plantation is the loveliest place in all of Union County."

"Actually, we're going to New York first." Mrs. Gist smiled at her husband. "William has acquired tickets to Adelina Patti's concert. I was lucky enough to hear her debut performance last fall, and I've been wild to hear that lovely voice again. William wants to meet with a senator from Massachusetts while he's in the city, so we'll kill two birds with one stone, as they say."

Papa's brows rose. He took a sip of Madeira. "What's the meeting about, William?"

The governor finished his soup and set down his spoon. "We're discussing ways to prevent another strike like the one the shoemakers staged in February. I'm sure I don't have to tell you it caused quite a lot of concern among all of the manufacturers in New England."

"They were right to stand their ground," Papa said. "Nobody likes to issue threats to their workers. Heaven knows I don't. But in this case, the possibility of losing their voting rights was enough to quell the rabble-rousers and keep the businesses open."

"From what I read in the papers last winter, not everyone agrees with you, Papa." Abby paused while the soup bowls were cleared and the next course was served. "Most of the churches sided with the workers."

"That's because the women in the congregations got involved in the situation." Charles motioned for Molly to refill his glass. "I find it shocking that they inserted themselves into a debate where they clearly didn't belong."

Abby frowned. "Why is that, Charles? What makes them unfit for comment on an issue that clearly threatened the women and children as deeply as it threatened the workers themselves? Surely the wearing of petticoats instead of breeches hasn't addled their brains."

Mrs. Gist laughed and turned in her chair to smile at Charles. "My word, Mr. Kittridge. I do believe you're betrothed to quite a little firebrand."

His face reddened, but he smiled. "I believe you're right, Mrs. Gist."

"Mary," Mama interjected smoothly. "Mrs. Ravensdale told me that you and she visited Niagara Falls last summer. I've always wanted to see the falls. Is it as spectacular as they say?"

"Every bit of it." Mrs. Gist finished her pork pie and waved away more wine. "We happened to be there on the day that Frenchman—what was his name, William?"

"Blondin." He glanced up briefly as Molly served the fish and rice. "Charles Blondin."

"That's right," Mrs. Gist said. "Mr. Blondin walked clear across the falls on a tightrope. I thought I might faint dead away from sheer fright. One little slip and he would have plunged to his death. But he made it, and the crowd applauded for ever so long."

"I can imagine they would," Mama said. "Though I cannot fathom why anyone would take such a foolish risk for no good reason."

"I quite agree." Cousin Ophelia sent Abby a hard, accusing look. "Sometimes I am sure I don't understand human beings at all."

"Perhaps we should ask Abigail," Charles said. "I'm certain she can enlighten us."

Abby saw the challenging gleam in his eyes and knew he was

still smarting from her earlier comments about the shoemakers. She took a long time setting down her coffee cup, refusing to let his barely concealed sarcasm silence her. "I suppose some people take enormous risks in order to feel truly alive. When one risks everything, whether in pursuit of some ideal or for personal pleasure, the reward must seem that much sweeter."

She smiled demurely and lowered her gaze. "But that's only my opinion. I could be completely wrong."

"No, I think you're quite correct, Miss Clayton," the governor said. "Though of course one must be judicious when it comes to taking a risk for an ideal." He set down his fork and sat back in his chair, apparently sated. "John Brown learned that lesson last winter after he raided Harpers Ferry."

Mrs. Gist caught her husband's eye across the candlelit table. "Now, William. I don't think—"

The governor held up both hands, palms out. "You're right, my dear. Murder, conspiracy, and hangings are hardly appropriate topics for dinner conversation. We must confront the problem of the abolitionists sooner or later though." He caught Papa's eye across the candlelit table. "But my term is up in December. Whatever happens, it won't happen on my watch. You might want to reconsider whether you truly want the governorship, John. If Lincoln is elected this fall, the next man to occupy my chair will get much more trouble than he bargained for."

Molly reappeared to serve cake and coffee, then quietly withdrew as talk of John Clayton's potential campaign continued.

"My cousin is up for the challenge, sir," Charles said, spearing his last bite of cake. "I can't think of a steadier man to lead South Carolina through whatever turbulence is coming."

Papa smiled. "Thank you for that vote of confidence, Charles."

"You've my vote of confidence as well." The governor drained his coffee cup. "And on that note, I suppose Mary and I ought to retire. I hate to conclude such a pleasant evening so early, but we'll be away at first light tomorrow, and we've still some packing to attend to."

Mama inclined her head toward Mrs. Gist. "Shall I send Sophronia up to help you?"

"Thank you." Mrs. Gist smiled. "I do wish it weren't necessary to travel with so many dresses. Sometimes I feel as if I need a special dray just to transport my hats and gowns. It's ridiculous, really."

Mama rose, and the rest of the table rose with her. The governor kissed Mama's cheek and thanked her for her hospitality. "No need to get up with us in the morning. Your Hector said he will call for us in time to make the first ferry."

"You'll need breakfast by the time you get to town," Mama said. "I'll have Molly pack a basket for you."

"That would be most kind." The governor shook hands with Papa. "I'll see you in the city in the fall."

He turned to Charles. "Congratulations again, my boy, on your engagement."

"Thank you, sir." Charles snaked an arm around Abby's waist and squeezed so hard she winced. "We intend to be very happy. Don't we, dear?"

Abby swallowed. "Yes."

Cousin Ophelia kissed Mama's cheek and retrieved her reticule from beneath her chair. "We ought to go too, son. I'm sure Hector is waiting to drive us over to Miss Augusta's."

"You go on ahead, Mother," Charles said. "I'll be along in a while."

"But it's getting dark."

"I'm not afraid of the dark. And it's a beautiful night. I think I want to walk home, enjoy the moonlight."

"What a lovely idea." Mrs. Gist linked her arm through her husband's. "Let's take a walk before we turn in."

The governor suppressed a yawn. "A walk? We've a long day tomorrow, Mary."

"We won't stay out long. And a walk in the night air will make us both sleep better."

Mama motioned to her guests. "Go ahead if you like. I'll find Sophronia and send her up whenever you're ready."

Once the Gists and Cousin Ophelia had left, Papa retired to his study. Mama kissed Abby's cheek and went in search of the housemaid, her cane tapping along the wooden floor.

"Well, good night, Charles." Abby turned and started for the stairs.

"What's your hurry?" He reached for her hand and pulled her toward the door. "Let's take a walk as well."

"I'd rather not. I've had a long day. I'm tired."

"Tired? From doing what?"

"Have you forgotten I was under Dr. French's care last evening?"

"Hardly. And while we are on the subject, I want to say I didn't appreciate your theatrics."

"Theatrics?"

"Your swoon when your father announced our betrothal. I know of your objections, but it wasn't necessary to call attention to them in such a dramatic fashion. It was embarrassing."

"Papa told me I could take time to think about it, and the next thing I knew it was a fait accompli. I was shocked." Abby rounded on him. "Though not as shocked as all my friends were by the vicious gossip your mother seems to have encouraged. It drove the Averys from our home. Did you know that?"

"That accusation does not deserve a reply. Where were you all day anyway? I looked for you after breakfast, but Sophronia said you'd gone off somewhere."

"Yes, I had some things to do." Eager to end the conversation, Abby crossed the hallway, but he blocked her way.

"What sort of things?"

"Nothing of interest to you."

"Try me."

She fought a rising sense of panic. Pawleys was nothing more than a narrow spit of land, only half a mile wide. There was hardly a place one could go without being seen. And people talked. It would be all too easy to be caught in a lie. "If you must know, I paid a call on Mrs. Bennett."

"And that took all day?"

"No. I walked on the beach after I saw her. I had a lot on my mind." She pressed a hand to her midsection. "I really would like to go up to my room now. I'm afraid I'm not feeling well."

"You felt well enough to make a fool of me at supper tonight."

"I'm sorry. I didn't mean to make you angry. I was merely stating my opinion."

He propelled her across the wide hallway to the parlor and closed the door behind them. He yanked her to him, so close she could see spittle forming on his lips. "Don't you ever do that again," he said, his voice hard-edged and insistent.

"Are you telling me that in the future I am to remain silent at meals like a monk in a monastery?"

"If all you can contribute to the conversation is a joke at my expense."

"I've already apologized. Now please let me go."

She spun away with such force that the ring hidden in her pocket came out and rolled across the floor. Terrified, she bent to retrieve it, but Charles got to it first and halted it with the toe of his black boot. He picked it up and held it to the light. "What's this?"

"It's mine. Please give it to me."

He turned it over in his palm. "I've never seen it before."

"I've hardly given you an inventory of my jewelry. I have plenty of things you've never seen."

"Where did you get it?"

"It's a keepsake from an old friend. It means a great deal to me."

"And yet you carry it your pocket rather than wearing it. Why is that, Abigail? Were you afraid to wear it in my presence?"

"It's too large for my finger. I was afraid of losing it."

"Ah." He walked to the window and stared into the darkness. "Hector said he saw you returning from the ferry landing this afternoon."

Abby's heart pounded. Was it true, or was he playing a game of cat and mouse, trying to trick her into confessing her whereabouts? She certainly had not seen Hector on her way to return Judge Bennett's rig, but that didn't mean he hadn't seen her. "After I saw Mrs. Bennett, the judge lent me his rig. I took the ferry to Georgetown."

"The landing is not that far. You could have walked it easily." He turned, his eyes darkened with anger. "Why the hurry? What was so important in Georgetown?"

She shook him off. "Very well. After Papa's surprise announcement I felt I owed Wade Bennett an explanation. The judge offered the use of his horse and buggy so I could get to the landing before the ferry left."

"And you went with Bennett to town."

"I told you when you first got here that my heart belongs to him. It still does. But for my family's sake I am prepared to forgo my own happiness and marry you. Though I expect I will soon live to regret it."

He slapped her so hard her ears rang. Pain exploded in her cheek, and she tasted blood. Charles loomed over her. "Don't you ever mention him again in my presence. Do you hear me? And don't you dare lie to me. About anything. Because I will find you out, and you will regret it more than you can possibly imagine."

His words sent a raw fury coursing through her. She wanted to rail against him and everything he had done, but she was afraid of making him even angrier. Her cheek throbbed, and she felt a trickle of blood beneath her eye. She headed for the door. "I'm going to bed."

"Do not walk away from me, Abigail."

"I'm through with this conversation."

"But I'm not through with you." He crossed the room, his arm raised, his face a mask of anger. She grabbed a heavy jade-colored vase from the table by the fireplace and threw it at his head. It grazed his cheek and shattered as it hit the floor.

The parlor door crashed open, and Papa rushed inside. "What in the name of heaven is going on here?"

Abby sank to the floor, sobbing, her wounded cheek dripping blood onto the rich silk of her skirt.

"Charles? What is this all about?"

Charles tossed Wade's ring onto the floor and stalked to the door. "Ask your daughter."

———

"Abigail?" Papa drew her to her feet. "What happened?"

Before she could explain, Mama appeared, a wide-eyed Sophronia trailing in her wake.

Mama opened her arms. Abby, overcome by fresh sobs, collapsed against her mother.

"Sophronia," Mama said. "Please fetch a basin of water and some towels. Then bring the broom and sweep up this mess before the Gists return. And not a word of this to the others."

"Yes, ma'am."

"Not even to Molly and Hector."

"No, ma'am. I won't." Sophronia hurried away.

Mama led Abby to the sofa and sat down beside her. "Is Charles Kittridge responsible for this?"

Abby nodded.

Papa knelt in front of her and examined the open wound on her cheek. "I'm certain it was an accident. I've known him his entire life, and I've never seen any tendency to violence in him."

Abby fished her handkerchief from the cuff of her dress. "It wasn't an accident. He's angry with me for the remark I made at dinner. And for going to town without his knowledge. Apparently I'm to behave as another of his slaves. Silent and obedient."

Papa opened his palm to reveal Wade's gold ring. "What does this have to do with it?"

"It's a keepsake. From Dr. Bennett."

"Oh, Abigail," Papa said, his expression pained. "Surely you know how inappropriate it is to accept a gift from a man who is not your—"

"Miss Alicia, here's the water." Sophronia came in carrying a blue-enameled basin, a white towel draped across her arm. "I brought the broom, and some elder-bush ointment too."

"Thank you," Mama said.

Sophronia set down the basin. "I'll take care o' this mess in no time."

Mama dipped the towel into the water, pressed it to Abby's cheek, and leaned over Abby for a closer inspection. "I don't think it's a very deep wound. It looks terrible just now, but I don't think it will leave a scar."

"In the meantime, we must think of a logical explanation for your injury," Papa said. "We can't have people thinking poorly of Charles."

Abby gaped at him. "Why not think poorly of him? He deserves it. He hit me, Papa."

"I know that. And I'm not excusing him. Striking a woman is dishonorable, to say the least. But sometimes even the most careful man can succumb to momentary madness. And he will apologize in the morning. I will make certain of that."

"And what happens the next time he gives in to his dishonorable impulses?" Abby looked up at her father through a blur of angry tears. Did he really care so little for her own safety and happiness?

"I'll have a talk with him. But we don't want to make any rash decisions. This will blow over. I'm sure of it."

Mama blotted Abby's wound and smoothed on the ointment. She wiped her hands, pushed to her feet, and stood toe-to-toe with Papa. "John Clayton, I'm shocked. And what is more, for the first time in the thirty years of our marriage, I am ashamed of you. Say to Charles Kittridge whatever you will, and make whatever excuses for him that you like. But I will not stand by and watch this child wed a man who would do such a thing."

Papa frowned. He opened his mouth to speak, then turned and walked out of the room, the shards of glass crunching beneath his feet.

CHAPTER EIGHT

July 10, 1860

THE *NINA* ARRIVED IN CHARLESTON AN HOUR LATE. ABBY helped her mother with her hat and reticule and handed her cane to her. The gangway was lowered, and they stepped off the steamer into the stifling city heat.

Mama blotted her face and emitted a long sigh. "I must say, as delighted as I am for Theodosia, I don't see why she could not have waited until the fall to hold her engagement party. This disagreeable weather is enough to make a preacher swear."

Abby laughed. The incident with Charles had freed something inside her mother. When it came to expressing an opinion, Mama was no longer the circumspect lady she used to be. Now she was fearless, and her insistence that Abby not marry Charles had drawn the two of them closer than ever.

A handsome carriage drew up at the pier, and a liveried driver jumped down. "Mrs. Clayton?"

"Yes." Mama opened her reticule and took out her fan.

"Mrs. Avery sent me to fetch you to Meeting Street." He craned his neck and looked past them to the pier, where trunks, travel satchels, hatboxes, birdcages, and wooden crates were being off-loaded. "You say which are yours, ma'am, and I'll fetch 'em for you."

Mama pointed out their trunks and hatboxes. He retrieved their belongings, helped them into the carriage, and began the short drive to the Averys' graceful three-story home on Meeting Street. Situated behind a tall wrought-iron fence, the redbrick home boasted a tall mansard roof and twin white pillars. Rows of wide windows with deep-green shutters flanked an elaborately carved mahogany front door. On the front lawn a small fountain was encircled with rose-bushes, the white blooms now browning in the summer heat.

As the carriage drew up in the porte cochere, the front door opened and Theo Avery rushed out, her green satin skirts swirling around her ankles. Before the driver could get down to open the carriage door, Theo wrenched it open. "Abby, you're here! I kept watching for the *Nina*, but it was so late I feared you'd been lost at sea. Oh, Abby, I can't wait for you to meet Nathaniel. He's—"

"My word, Theodosia." Mrs. Avery had appeared on the front steps. "Give these poor ladies a chance to breathe." She smiled at Mama as the driver helped her alight. "Alicia, I'm delighted you could come. Please come inside. Peter will see to your things."

Abby and her mother followed the Averys to the parlor, where tea had been laid and the windows flung open in hopes of capturing a breeze. While their mothers caught up on the latest news, Theo drew Abby aside and peered at her intently. "Your face has healed perfectly."

Abby nodded.

"And Mother says your father has released you from your promise to marry Charles."

"Yes, thanks to my mother. I agreed to the engagement only because I felt I owed it to her. It came as such a relief when she told Papa she would not stand for the marriage."

"So you said in your letter. And now you are free to marry Dr. Bennett." Theo paused. "You have written to him? He knows you are no longer expected to marry Charles?"

"I wanted to write to him. I began half a dozen letters, but—" Abby drained her teacup and set it down. "I thought he might write to me, but I've heard nothing." She clasped her friend's hand. "Have you seen him, Theo? Is he all right? Is he happy?"

"We arrived here from New York only last week, and we've been so busy arranging my party that I've scarcely had time to breathe. But yesterday Mrs. Middleton's niece Emmaline came calling." Theo refilled their cups. "Emmaline knows everything that goes on in Charleston. I'm sure if there were news of Dr. Bennett, Emmaline would have told us. But in any case, now that you're here, you can find out for yourself. You can't expect that he would write to you, thinking you are still promised to Charles."

"Theodosia?" Mrs. Avery stood. "Why don't you take our guests up to their rooms? I'm sure they'd like to freshen up and change."

Ten minutes later Abby was installed in a spacious room overlooking the back garden, unfolding her dresses and placing them in the clothespress that stood next to a tester bed covered in a pale-blue coverlet. Mama was unpacking in the room down the hall.

Theo plopped down on the bed. "Did I tell you that Nathaniel is taking me to Paris for our wedding trip?"

Abby set her hairbrush on a dressing table scattered with silver powder boxes, hairpins, and tiny crystal perfume bottles. "You've hardly had time to tell me anything. When you left Pawleys after the barbecue, bound for New York, I had no inkling you were about to become engaged."

Theo released a merry laugh. "Nor did I. Nathaniel and I hadn't spoken since the Middletons' ball last winter. I had no idea of his romantic feelings until he appeared one day in Saratoga. But after that everything happened quickly."

Abby grinned. "To say the least. Mother and I were quite surprised to receive an engagement-party invitation in the middle of the summer."

Theo waved one delicate hand. "Oh, I know the proper thing is to wait until the start of the social season this fall. But Nathaniel doesn't want to wait to get married, and neither do I." She looked up, her expression suddenly grave. "He thinks war might be declared by Christmas."

Abby perched on the slipper chair by the open window and lifted her hair off her neck. "Papa thinks so, too, but the governor says Britain and France will come to our aid and any war will be hardly more than a skirmish. He says that by this time next year, the South will be stronger and more prosperous than ever."

"I hope he's right. If your father is elected governor this fall, perhaps he can persuade the Yankees to leave us in peace and secession won't become necessary."

Theo's mention of Papa brought a hot prick of tears and swelled Abby's throat. "Papa doesn't think he will be elected now."

"What? Because of your broken engagement to that odious Charles Kittridge?"

"Not entirely. Last week some men from the General Assembly came up to Pawleys to go fishing with Papa, and they told him several members are supporting Mr. Pickens. Apparently Mr. Pickens holds the same political views as Papa but has the advantage of being a cousin of the late Mr. Calhoun. Even Governor Gist has switched his allegiance." Abby shrugged. "I suppose it's difficult for anyone to compete with the memory of someone so powerful as John C. Calhoun."

"Yes. My father invokes Mr. Calhoun quite often, even though the poor man has been dead these past ten years." Theo fanned her face. "What does your mother say about all this?"

"She's sad for Papa, of course, but I think she's secretly relieved. A governor's wife is expected to host countless parties and balls and teas, and all of that would be taxing for her. It's all she can do to organize our yearly barbecue on the island. By the time everyone leaves, she's completely done in."

"You'd never know it—she runs things so smoothly. Which reminds me." Theo got to her feet. "I have some things to attend to before my party tomorrow night, so I must leave you for now. But I'll see you at dinner. It's a small group tonight. The Ravensdales will be here, and Penny's cousin Henry Plowden is in town. He and Nathaniel were at school together."

Theo picked up her reticule and tucked a fresh handkerchief inside. "I'm so relieved you're all right. And glad you're here to share in the happiest time of my life."

"Then it's truly a love match—you and Nathaniel."

"Very much so." Theo inclined her head until her brow briefly touched Abby's. "I'm so deliriously happy, and I want you to be happy too. Go to Dr. Bennett. Tell him what's happened."

"Oh, Theo, you know how people would talk if they knew I'd sought him out. Especially now that all of Charleston knows I've broken my engagement to Charles."

"What could they say? Dr. Bennett has been your friend for years. Judge Bennett and your father were in the army together. Both your families have cottages on Pawleys. Nobody can say a word against your wanting to say hello while you're in town."

Abby felt for the gold ring suspended on a delicate chain that she wore concealed beneath her collar. "I do want to see him. On the journey here I could think of nothing else. But now I'm afraid. What if—"

"Oh goodness. Look at the time." Theo hurried to the door. "I won't be long. We'll figure this out. I promise."

———

Though many in the Averys' circle of friends were still away for the summer, Theo's stately home rang with music and the voices of guests assembled to celebrate her engagement. Half an hour ago, Theo had knocked on Abby's door to announce that she was going down to greet her guests. Now, dressed in an ivory gown trimmed in pale-lilac lace, her hair held in place with her diamond clips, Abby hurried along the carpeted gallery hung with Thomas Sully portraits of Avery ancestors and with gloomy Dutch paintings of pale, round-faced women swathed in black.

"Abby, there you are!" Penny Ravensdale, dressed head to toe in canary-yellow silk, clasped Abby's hand and drew her to the top of the staircase. "I'm so sorry we missed the dinner last night. Mother wasn't feeling well. It's this heat, I think." Penny fanned her face with her hand. "Of course it's hot as the hinges of hell on Pawleys, too, but at least there is some semblance of a breeze."

Abby grinned, happy to see her friend. "You'd better not let your mother hear you talking like that."

"Well, it's true. I haven't been dressed for half an hour yet, and already I am perspiring all the way through to my drawers. Honestly, I think Theo decided to get engaged now just to make me suffer."

They went downstairs to a buffet table laden with an array of meats, fruits, and sweets. Candlelight from a magnificent glass chandelier glinted on fine bone china and delicate crystal glasses rimmed in gold.

"I'm starving." Penny reached for a plate. But Theo appeared and drew them to the double doors that opened onto the broad second-floor piazza. "Come and meet Nathaniel."

"But I'm hungry," Penny said. "What kind of a hostess are you anyway?"

"You can eat later."

Penny grabbed a thin cookie and munched on it as they threaded through the crowd of well-wishers. Nathaniel stood with his back to the room, talking to an older man. But he turned to face them when Theo spoke his name, his entire face lighting up at the sight of her.

Theo made the introductions. Nathaniel, a tall, angular man with prominent cheekbones and a merry gleam in his eyes, bowed to Abby and Penny. "I do apologize, ladies, for holding our celebration during such uncomfortable weather, but Theo and I want to marry as soon as—"

A flash of lightning and a rumble of thunder shook the house, momentarily halting all conversation. "Perhaps we'll get some cooling rain," Abby said, scanning the crowd. Mama and Mrs. Ravensdale were seated near the doors opening onto the piazza, talking with Mrs. Avery. Most of the menfolk had gone outside to smoke.

Abby was sorry now that Papa had not made the trip from Pawleys. Somehow the evening felt incomplete without his imposing presence. But Hector had returned from Mulberry Hall last week with news that one of the storage barns had been damaged by a fire, and Papa had gone home to assess the damages and see to repairs.

Perhaps it was for the best. Though he had agreed with Mama that her marriage to Charles could not proceed, Abby couldn't help feeling that Papa still blamed her for Charles's behavior.

Mr. Avery drew Theodosia and Nathaniel to his side and tapped on his glass to get the guests' attention. "Thank you all for coming. Mrs. Avery and I have the honor of announcing that the marriage of our daughter, Theodosia, to Nathaniel Butler will take place here at home in three weeks' time."

Everyone applauded.

"You're all invited to the nuptials." Mr. Avery signaled the musicians assembled beside the black marble fireplace. "Now, please enjoy yourselves."

Everyone paired off for the first dance. After Nathaniel danced with Mrs. Avery and his mother, he danced with Abby, guiding her around the room with practiced ease, making small talk that Abby found pleasant but instantly forgettable.

"Abby." Theo appeared at her side as another song began and Nathaniel whirled away with Penny in his arms. "I need you for a moment. It's of utmost importance."

"What's the matter?"

Wordlessly Theo led Abby out of the ballroom and through the open doors leading to the piazza. "Stand right there. Don't move."

"What's— Why?"

Theo heaved an exasperated sigh. "Will you for once in your life just do as you're told? I'll be right back."

Abby stood at the railing looking out over the darkened city. A few raindrops plopped onto the porch, and she turned her face to the slight breeze coming off the river. The lilting strains of a waltz floated on the evening air.

"Abigail." Wade's quiet incantation of her name was a whisper falling into the darkness.

She turned, tears already starting behind her eyes.

He crossed the piazza and stood beside her, so close that she could smell the clean warmth of his sun-browned skin mixing with the earthy scent of summer rain. "Miss Avery sent for me. Why didn't you tell me you were coming to town?"

"I wanted to. But I wasn't sure how you would receive the news."

"She says your engagement is broken."

"Yes. Charles isn't my intended anymore." One look at Wade's dear face and the entire story came pouring out. Her innocent remark at the dinner table and Charles's angry reaction. His rage when he discovered the gold ring Wade had given her. The unexpected blow that had left her stunned and bleeding.

"I ought to kill him for that." Wade caressed her cheek. "It was wrong of me to give you the ring. I had no right. But I wanted you to have some reason to remember me."

"As if I could ever forget." She drew the ring from beneath the collar of her dress. "I wear it every day."

He nodded. "How is your father taking this turn of events?"

"He is resigned to it, I think. But I suspect that deep down he still thinks it's due to my imperfect understanding of Charles's true worth."

"Still, I believe your father had your best interests at heart. Everyone is worried about secession and what will come after it. I can't blame him for wanting to be certain you will be as safe and protected as circumstances allow."

"But none of us will be safe if war is declared."

"That's true."

They grew quiet as the rain intensified. He drew her away from the railing and into the protected corner of the piazza. Abby wanted to lose herself in his arms, to rest her head on his chest and hear the steady beat of his heart. Instead she said, "Is there any news from Philadelphia? Will your article be published in the medical journal?"

"Yes. In the winter issue. We're very pleased about it."

"When will you leave Charleston again?"

"I'm not certain yet. Perhaps in September. At present I have one or two older patients who need constant looking after. And—" He broke off and took her in his arms. "Ah, Abby. Why do we speak of such things when there is only one thing that matters?"

She lifted her face to look at him, and in the pale spill of light coming through the tall windows, she saw the gleam of tears in his eyes.

"Do you love me, Miss Clayton?"

"I most certainly do, Dr. Bennett."

"You'll marry me then." It was not a question.

A river of joy coursed through her, flooding her heart. She smiled into the darkness. She could afford to tease him now. "I will give it serious consideration."

"Hmm. Serious consideration, you say? When may I expect your answer?"

Oblivious to the rain leaking through the roof of the old piazza, Abby stood on tiptoe and lifted her face for his kiss. "How about now?"

TO MEND A DREAM

Tamera Alexander

To everyone who ever made a perfect plan, then had God change it—for the better.

We can make our plans, but the
*L*ORD *determines our steps.*

PROVERBS 16:9 (NLT)

CHAPTER ONE

Nashville, Tennessee
June 13, 1870

WHAT SHE WOULDN'T GIVE FOR THE CHANCE TO BE BACK IN that house again. If only for a day . . .

Savannah Darby carefully refolded the stationery and tucked it back inside the drawer of her bedside table alongside the family Bible—and her impossible wish.

"This is my side of the dresser!"

"No! It's *my* side!" The metallic scrape of her brother's leg braces punctuated his frustration.

"I know it's mine because—"

"Andrew! Carolyne!" Savannah pierced her younger siblings with a look, then lowered her voice by a degree, not wishing for the mothers and children on both sides of their room and across the hall to hear them. Again. They'd waited for months for an opening to move in here. She couldn't afford for this not to work, in more ways than one. "I've already received two warnings about your arguing, and we've not been here three weeks yet. Please," she added firmly, seeing Carolyne's mouth fly open, "keep your voices down."

Carolyne pouted. "At least in the boarding house we had our own dressers."

"No, you didn't." Savannah gathered her sewing satchel. "In the boarding house you each had your own overturned crate."

Guilt bowed ten-year-old Carolyne's head. But Andrew, two years older and impatient to become a man, merely scowled.

"We all must share. And no more arguing." Savannah kissed them both on the forehead, despite Andrew's halfhearted attempt to dodge her affection. "I'll see you back here this afternoon. Andrew, be careful with the deliveries. And remember, only one crate at a time."

His frown deepened.

"Carolyne, when you finish your chores in the kitchen, read your lessons I outlined and study your French. Work the arithmetic equations I wrote out for you last night too. Andrew, see to your studies, including the reading in *Macbeth*. There's a volume in the library downstairs. And remember you have a—"

"I know, Savannah." He turned his back to her. "I've already said I'll go."

Hand on the doorknob, Savannah schooled a smile. "Next time, I'll do my best to be excused from work to go with you, but—"

"I'm not a child. I can go by myself."

"I know you can. I want to go for me, to hear what he has to say. Not because I think you're incapable of going alone."

His expression softened a fraction, and Savannah seized the momentary truce and took her leave, already late for work as it was. And dreading the price she would pay with Miss Hildegard.

She hurried down the two flights of stairs.

While she used to dream of getting married and having children, she'd never expected to become *mother* to a six- and eight-year-old at the age of eighteen. Now, four years later, her father and mother gone, along with her older brothers, there were moments when she thought she was handling the responsibility fairly well. The rest of the time she desperately prayed she wasn't botching the job.

At a quarter past eight, the common room of the Nashville Widows' and Children's Home buzzed with life. Moving here represented a new start for them and was a great deal safer than where they'd been several blocks east. And not a rat in sight. Mice she could handle. But rats . . .

She shuddered, remembering what it had been like awakening at night in the boarding house to hear the rodents scurrying about in the dark. Or worse, when she felt one scuttle across the foot of her bed.

The succulent aroma of freshly baked cinnamon bread drifted from the kitchen and helped to banish the bad memories even as the homey scent encouraged her hunger, as did the promise of coffee. But the queue for breakfast was already twenty deep, and the clock on the wall insisted she keep moving.

Outside, the skies boasted a crystalline-blue color, and the sun already felt warm on her face. Summer had staked its claim.

Monday mornings always seemed busier somehow, both in foot traffic and on the streets. Scores of farm wagons and carriages vied for passage, with freight wagons only slowing their progress, the drivers pausing as cargo was loaded and unloaded. At every corner she was delayed. And the minutes rushed past.

She spotted the mercantile ahead and, once closer, saw Mr. Mulholland, the proprietor, standing just inside the doorway. Aware to the penny of how much she owed on her account, she thought of the bill she'd received last week reminding her of the outstanding balance, and a stab of guilt pierced her when she averted her gaze as she passed.

The man had been so kind to extend her credit. And though she had no idea how she would manage it, she intended to repay every penny. Someday.

Out of breath, she raced down an alleyway, her mind turning again to Andrew's visit with the doctor. Determined not to borrow trouble until trouble left her no choice, she hurried inside the back entrance of Miss Hattie's Dress and Drapery Shop, then down the hallway, hoping to get to her sewing station before anyone realized she was—

She ran headlong into a red-faced Miss Hildegard.

Savannah reached out to steady the older woman, then quickly realized it wasn't Miss Hildegard who was about to go sprawling. Hand against the wall, Savannah managed to steady herself, only too aware of the veins bulging in her employer's neck.

"Pardon me, Miss Hildegard! I didn't—"

"*Finally*, Miss Darby, you see fit to grace us with your presence!"

Savannah's face went hot. "My apologies for being tardy, Miss Hildegard." She knew better than to try to offer an excuse. Nothing short of sudden death would satisfy this woman. And even then, Miss Bertha Hildegard would demand forenotice.

The woman huffed. "We are *all* in a state, Miss Darby! Betsy Anderson has taken ill and only now sent word, the slothful girl! So *you* must take her appointment this morning."

Not yet trusting she'd escaped with so minor a scolding, Savannah nodded quickly. "Of course, ma'am. I'll leave straightaway, right after I finish hemming the draperies for Mrs. Garrison's—"

"Mrs. Garrison can wait! This appointment is for redecorating an entire house, Miss Darby. Draperies, bedcovers, duvets, pillows, window shades . . . everything. The patron also mentioned furniture, for which we'll work with Franklin's." An odd look crossed the older woman's face. "The newly arrived owner, a Mr. Aidan Bedford, and his fiancée, Miss Sinclair, are expecting you. Or rather, are expecting Miss Anderson. But you'll have to do."

Accustomed to the woman's disparaging comments, Savannah found them easier to endure when remembering that the former owner, Miss Hattie, had held her work in the highest regard. Miss Hattie's was the finest dress and drapery shop in town, and Savannah needed this job.

Miss Hildegard started down the hallway and gestured for her to follow. "The soon-to-be Mrs. Bedford visited the shop day before last and perused fabric samples. Our most *expensive* samples." If it were possible for a woman to salivate over the sale of fabric, Miss Hildegard was doing just that. "The couple has moved from Boston, and Miss Sinclair—such a cultured, lovely young woman—made it quite clear they're eager to make this house their home."

Savannah was already making a mental list of what to include in her sewing satchel. At the same time she found herself assessing the earnings a job like this could bring. Andrew not only needed new leg braces, but she'd also read recently about a physician up north who had developed boots made especially for people born with clubfeet. The boots were expensive, as were the leg braces. But what a difference they'd make for her brother. Plus, both of her siblings had grown several inches since last summer, and though she could sew anything, fabric didn't come cheaply.

She hated that Betsy's illness—and therefore her coworker's loss of this extra commission—meant personal gain for herself. But if Betsy couldn't do the job, somebody else would. And it might as well be her.

"I'll gather what's needed, Miss Hildegard, and leave straight-away. What's the address?"

Miss Hildegard's dark eyebrows drew together. "Let me make

myself clear, Miss Darby. I will *not* have you ruining this opportunity *or* making Mr. Bedford and his fiancée uncomfortable. The couple has every right to make that house their home."

Savannah frowned. "Why would I ruin such an opportunity, ma'am? And as for the couple, I've not met either of them, so—"

"The house you'll be redecorating . . . where they're living? It's Darby Farm."

CHAPTER TWO

Savannah froze, the frenzied pace of her world suddenly slamming to a halt. She felt certain she'd heard the woman correctly, and Miss Hildegard's cautionary expression confirmed it. Yet somehow, she still worked to grasp the request.

Over a year had passed since her family home had been auctioned and sold. How many nights had she lain awake wishing she could get back into that house? Just that morning she'd reread the letter her father had written to her mother, even though she knew it by heart. She had hoped for this very thing.

But who was the new owner? A *Yankee*.

She knew better than to be surprised. Still, she'd prayed the family farm might remain in the Southern lineage instead of falling prey to one of those money-grubbing carpetbaggers who'd descended from the North like vultures, intent on making money and taking advantage of someone else's misfortune.

"Will this be a problem for you, Miss Darby?"

Grateful the woman couldn't hear the tone of her thoughts, Savannah shook her head. "No, ma'am. No problem at all, Miss Hildegard. I assure you."

The woman eyed her as though unconvinced.

Savannah began gathering the needed supplies from the shelves.

"If you'll show me which fabrics piqued Miss Sinclair's interest, I'll pack my satchel and be on my way."

And she was. In ten minutes flat. She hurried back across town, dodging wagons and carriages, oblivious to the blur of faces and storefronts she passed.

A legitimate reason to be inside her family home again. A chance to search for what her father had hidden in the house before he died in the war—something she would never have known about if not for the letter she'd found a few months ago following her mother's passing.

Yet as determined as she was to make the most of the opportunity, she had an inkling that once she stepped inside the house, her deeply rooted sense of propriety would do its best to thwart her determination. Which meant only one thing . . .

She would have to keep propriety in its place—outside on the porch.

And considering the unfortunate fact that a Yankee now owned Darby Farm only emboldened that resolve. In fact, this newly acquired truth made her intended action seem almost noble. Like just retribution! She would succeed. She had to.

Because a chance like this wouldn't come a second time.

She hastened her stride down the familiar dirt road, consumed by one thought: she would find what her father had hidden inside that house, or she would tear it apart trying.

———

Everything about living at Darby Farm was exactly as Aidan Bedford imagined it would be. Or at least it had been—until four days ago.

"Do you agree with me or not, Aidan? It's important to me that you do. Surely you know that."

The insistence in Priscilla's voice all but drowned out the call of the lush green meadows and hills lying just beyond the open windows of the study. The meadows and hills he'd ridden every morning since arriving here a month ago, save the last four days since she'd arrived.

"What I know, Priscilla, is that whether I agree with the changes you'd like to make to the house is ultimately of little importance to you. Of that I'm certain." Smiling, he turned, fully expecting the arched curve of her dark eyebrow. "And while I never had a sister, nor did my late mother gain pleasure from decorating a home, I realize the activity is generally one of immense pleasure for the female gender. So . . . alter a few things to your liking. Make the house your home."

One . . . two . . . three . . . He silently counted, waiting. And there it was.

Her lower lip pudged. "But I want you involved in the changes too, dearest. This is our home. Yours and mine. Or it soon will be. And I want it to be a reflection of our combined tastes."

He laughed, knowing better. "If that were truly the case, then half of everything in this home would stay precisely as it is."

Her expression went from one of gentility to that of someone smelling something putrid. "But the furnishings are all so . . . quaint. And . . . Southern."

"I find them full of character and warmth. And they're called antiques, Priscilla. Surely you've heard of them."

She scoffed. "Antiques are works of art, Aidan. Think of timeless pieces from the Elizabethan era, or William and Mary. Or Louis the Sixteenth." Her sigh hinted at infatuation. "Admittedly, there are a few good pieces in the house. But the rest of the furniture"—she grimaced at the massive oak desk separating them, then at the matching breakfront bookcases across the room that shouldered a small but impressive library, including the leather-bound works of Shakespeare— "I'd categorize more eighteenth-century pioneer than heirloom."

Accustomed to the woman's expensive taste, Aidan overlooked her pretension and impatience and reminded himself of her finer qualities. Priscilla Sinclair was cultured, intelligent, beautiful, from one of the finest families in Boston, and their pending marriage— while not one planned since infancy—had most definitely been the object of both sets of their late parents' wishes for as long as they could remember. And with good reason. He and Priscilla were well suited to each other. The perfect Bostonian couple. Only . . .

They weren't in Boston anymore. And things about her that had only niggled at him over the past three years now gnawed.

Likely the last fleeting thoughts of a man too long a bachelor. Or at least that's what he hoped.

He ran a hand over the top of the desk, the object of her momentary disdain, and found the workmanship exemplary, just as he had the first time he'd stepped foot into this house. When business had brought him to Nashville a year ago, he'd seen this land, this house, and he'd known he would purchase it. Same as he'd known, somewhere deep inside, that he would live in Nashville. Someday. He simply hadn't thought it would be so soon.

How a conversation with a complete stranger six years ago had so altered the course of his life, he couldn't explain. A most unlikely exchange on a field in North Carolina during the lull of war. With a Johnny Reb, no less. It was a conversation—and battle—he would never forget.

He'd never told Priscilla about what happened that day. He'd never told anyone. But for sure Priscilla Sinclair, daughter to one of the finest families in Massachusetts, wouldn't understand.

Since finally closing the door to the most prestigious law firm in Boston nearly two months ago, he'd not once looked back.

But she did.

Even now, as she studied the draperies framing the windows, the table and chair to the side, he sensed her longing for home, her thoughts undoubtedly returning to the handsome redbrick brownstone he still owned in Beacon Hill. He'd thought about selling the home in recent months but had held back, wanting to make certain he enjoyed living here as much as he thought he would.

And he did.

Darby Farm was exactly what he wanted, what he'd been searching for. The house was older, yes, but it was well built and full of character and had cost a fraction of what he would glean from selling his brownstone.

But even without the capital gained from the sale, he had the funds to get the farm up and running again. Which was a good thing, because despite his investment thus far, there was much yet to be done.

"Aidan," Priscilla purred, moving around to his side of the desk. She pressed a hand against his suit jacket, her pale-blue eyes hinting at conspiracy and her coy smile saying she didn't mind him knowing. "Now that I think of it, why don't you leave the redecorating to me? It's one of my fortes, after all. Your job is to transform this"—she hesitated, her brow quirking the way it did whenever she sought a word other than the one that described her true feelings—"*humble* little property into the grand estate we both know it can be."

"'Humble little property'? It's nearly four hundred acres, Priscilla. And as I've told you, this will be a working farm. Not an elaborate estate. Remember that as you're putting your touches on things."

Her lips firmed, then just as quickly formed a smile. "It's such a beautiful morning, Aidan. You should go for a ride."

He eyed her, knowing something was amiss. "You began this conversation by telling me a seamstress—"

"A Miss Anderson," she supplied.

"*Miss Anderson*," he repeated, "was coming to discuss proposed changes to the house and you wanted my input. Now you want me to go riding? And this after the last four mornings you've said that leaving you to go riding would be considered rude since you're only here for a matter of days."

She met his gaze, then gave a seductive little laugh. "No wonder you'll soon be Nashville's leading attorney. Nothing escapes your scrutiny. Or memory."

She stood on tiptoe to kiss his cheek, then lingered, making her mouth available to him. When he didn't respond, she moved closer, yet not even the brush of her body against his stirred his desire as it once had.

And she knew it.

Early on, he'd found these games she played mildly intriguing. Not so anymore. Aidan planted an obligatory kiss on her forehead, unable to reconcile this distance between them and the growing unease he felt when they were together. She sensed it, too, he knew.

Hence why she was trying so hard.

But he was trying as well. He knew how painful it was to lose both parents. Her father, a good man he'd greatly respected, had passed last fall. Her mother a month later. The adjustment had been difficult for her. Especially as an only child.

"Give it time," a trusted colleague had told him. And he was. He only hoped things smoothed between them soon.

"I believe I will go for that ride," he said gently, sensing subtle triumph in her eyes. "It'll give me a chance to check with the foreman before leaving for town. The office is expecting me midmorning."

She smoothed a hand over his lapel. "That sounds splendid, Aidan. And when you return, I'll give you a full accounting of everything Miss Anderson and I have discussed."

"Which will contain far more detail than required, I'm sure."

All smiles, she preceded him into the hallway where Mrs. Pruitt, his housekeeper from Boston, was busily dusting the marbleized pier table. When he'd told the older woman he was moving to Tennessee, her request to move with him had caught him off guard, something which didn't happen often. But widowed and childless, Mrs. Pruitt seemed almost as happy to be here as he was.

Besides her skills, there was another reason he was grateful for her presence. Though he was no prude, and Darby Farm was likely too far from town to draw gossip, he was grateful to Mrs. Pruitt for playing the role of chaperone during Priscilla's visit. The housekeeper's quarters were on the main floor, while the rest of the bedrooms were aloft on the second story, but having her in the house fulfilled the letter of the law. And for the time being, at least, his present feelings toward Priscilla more than fulfilled its spirit.

"Good morning, Mrs. Pruitt," he offered, noticing Priscilla didn't even look her way.

"Good morning, Mr. Bedford." The housekeeper offered her customary smile, curtsying to them both. "Will you be taking lunch here today, sir?"

"No, Mrs. Pruitt. It will be only Miss Sinclair today. But I'll be back for dinner."

"Very good, sir." She moved on to the small study.

"Aidan, before you go . . ." Priscilla paused in the entryway to the central parlor. "Have you given further thought to the date?"

Knowing to which date she referred, he resisted the urge to look away. "Not since we discussed it last night after dinner."

Her pouty smile said she'd caught his meaning. "I know I'm being a trifle impatient, dear. But it's only because I want to be with you. As your wife."

The response he knew she wanted to hear, the words he would've said to her only a few weeks earlier, wouldn't come. "You're not being impatient. I said we'd set a date for the wedding before you return to Boston, and . . . we will."

With effort, he pushed past the doubt inside him, trusting it would fade and trusting in the wishes of so many they'd known in Boston who'd said how *splendid* they would be together. He hoped they were right. Because in asking her to marry him, he'd given her his word, something he didn't do lightly. He'd never gone back on a promise yet, and he didn't intend to start now.

Priscilla's expression brightened. "So within a month I'll know when I'm going to become Mrs. Aidan Gunning Bedford."

He smiled, but the gesture felt traitorous.

Remembering his portfolio in the study, he retrieved it and was on his way to the front door when he caught sight of Priscilla in the parlor. She ran an index finger over the draperies, the settee, the chairs, even the mantel over the hearth, then cast a frown about the entire room, including the Persian runner beneath her feet, as though she wished she could make it all disappear in a blink.

He'd told her she could redecorate, and he'd meant it. After all, what harm was there in allowing her to make a few changes? But sensing the woman's fervor . . .

"One request, Priscilla, as you meet with this Miss Anderson this morning."

She looked up, her expression first conveying surprise, then guardedness.

"Not a single change to my study."

———

Savannah stared up at the house, her heart heavy as the gap between the present and the past swiftly evaporated. Seconds slowed to a crawl.

The last she'd seen her family home it had looked so neglected and lonely, with the grass gone to seed and the weeds leggy and wild, the occasional shutter hanging at odds with its window. But now the grounds were neat and tidy, grass clipped, weeds tamed, all shutters behaving nicely. She'd even seen workers in the fields.

Her gaze moved beyond the house to the apple grove, then, in her mind, to her favorite part of the farm—the land that had belonged to her maternal grandparents. "Meant more for beauty than for farming" is what her grandfather had said, so neither he nor her father had ever planted it.

Her legs like lead, she managed the climb to the front porch that wrapped the house like a hug. Colorful pots of coleus and fragrant mint adorned the steps, similar to the flowers and herbs she'd glimpsed growing on the second-story porch above.

The house had sat untended for so long she knew she should be pleased to see it being loved and cared for again. But the discovery only brought a lump to her throat.

Her gaze went to the porch railing, and her throat tightened as memory conjured an image so clearly in her mind's eye. She could see Jake, her eldest brother, balancing on the top rail, her father laughing as her mother commented with feigned worry that the balusters might not support his weight. But they did. And Jake had sung one of his silly made-up songs as he strode back and forth before ending the performance with a faultless backward flip off the porch, landing flat on his feet as he always did.

Oh, how she missed him. Adam too. She didn't know the details of her brothers' deaths in the war, or her father's. Only that they'd been killed in battle. She hoped, as she'd done many times before, that they'd somehow been at peace in those final moments, even in the midst of such unfathomable carnage.

A breeze rustled the leaves of the oak and poplar trees overhead like a whisper from a ghost and sent a hushed murmur through the magnolias. The sound resembled susurrations from the past, and she reached for confidence beyond herself and prayed that, by some stroke of mercy, God would see fit to saying yes this time to her heart's desire—to helping her find what her father had hidden—instead of responding with His customary silence.

Even a definitive no would be better than that. Because at least then she'd be assured He was listening.

A squeak drew her attention, and she looked to her right.

The swing her father had crafted from poplar wood—the same swing in which she'd read, studied, and dreamed as a girl, in which she had curled up tightly, swallowed by grief, following her father's and older brothers' passings, then her mother's—swayed gently, carefree in the breeze.

Savannah stepped up to the front door, hearing the echo of Miss Hildegard's parting instructions. *"Don't you dare let that couple know you once lived there."*

She had no intention of telling Mr. Bedford or his fiancée she'd lived here. But how hard would it be for them to put two and two together? Her last name was Darby, and this was Darby Farm.

Taking a deep breath, she knocked on the door and heard the muffled sound of voices coming from within. Her stomach knotted, and memories dearly cherished but firmly packed away suddenly tugged at frayed emotions, threatening to undermine her confidence.

Leave propriety on the porch. Leave propriety on the porch.

She'd scarcely drawn her hand away before the door opened.

CHAPTER THREE

The gentleman filled the doorway.

Savannah lifted her gaze to meet his and read frustration in his face. His very . . . handsome face. Able to guess the source of his annoyance, she hastened to offer apology. "Please forgive my tardiness, sir. My coworker has taken ill and—"

"Miss Anderson." He moved to one side. "Miss Sinclair is expecting you. Please, come in."

His tone, while polite, possessed a quality that brooked no argument. But his accent—she bristled—was like a burr in her stocking, despite the cultured gentility in his voice. Because no matter how well spoken, or darkly attractive, the man was still a Yankee.

Yet understanding he was also likely the one controlling the purse strings, she quickly masked her annoyance beneath a polite facade, accepted his invitation, and stepped across the threshold.

And in the time it took to draw breath, she realized she'd underestimated what effect being back in this house again would have on her. Memories pressed in from all sides, siphoning the air from her lungs. But oddly, it wasn't familiar surroundings that threw her off kilter. Nor was it seeing precious family treasures—among them the side table crafted by her paternal grandfather and the grandfather clock crafted by her mother's father. It was something more furtive that threatened her undoing.

Something the past year of living in the boarding house had all but erased from her memory.

The *presence* of this house, the warmth it exuded. As if every bit of love and laughter that had been shared within these walls, along with every tear, had somehow been absorbed and translated into a wordless language only the heart could comprehend.

And hers did. A swell of emotion rose inside her to—

"Miss Anderson? Are you well?"

Savannah blinked. The gentleman's expression was keen, and she swallowed, her throat parched. "Yes, sir. I'm fine. But actually, I'm—"

"Late!" a female voice interrupted. "That's what you are, Miss Anderson. *Late.*" A striking brunette in a beautifully tailored teal ensemble strode toward them from the central parlor. Her smile was lovely, but her clouded features told the truer story. "I believe the agreed-upon hour was nine o'clock, was it not?"

Sensing Mr. Bedford tense beside her, Savannah nodded, the momentary web of nostalgia swept clean. "Yes, ma'am. Please accept my apologies. However, as I was about to explain, I'm not—"

"No excuses, please." The woman glanced at Savannah's satchel, then cast the gentleman a parting smile. "You're here now, and we have *much* to do, you and I. Let's not waste any more time, shall we?"

The woman turned on her heel and retraced her path to the parlor, leaving Savannah feeling firmly put in her place.

Feeling pressure to follow the woman, she still hesitated, knowing decorum demanded that someone in her position of employ be dismissed before leaving the presence of such a man.

"Allow me to introduce myself, Miss Anderson."

Hearing a hint of apology in his voice, she turned.

He gave a tilt of his head. "I'm Aidan Bedford, the owner of Darby Farm, and that . . . is my fiancée, Miss Priscilla Sinclair."

His mouth curved, but the tightness in his expression led Savannah to believe this particular smile wasn't one nature had given him.

"Nice to meet you, Mr. Bedford," she said, telling herself the statement was partly true—the part that connected her meeting him with the opportunity to be in this house again.

He glanced toward the closed front door. "I don't believe I saw a carriage just now."

"No, sir. I walked."

"All the way from town?"

Seeing such a man perplexed helped her to relax a little. "I enjoy walking."

His gaze held appraisal, and the intensity in his gray eyes gave her the impression that divining truth from fiction was one of this man's talents. She was grateful her actions warranted no fear of it.

Yet, anyway.

"May I offer your guest some refreshment, sir?"

A petite older woman, features soft with age, hair white as snow, stood at the base of the stairs.

Mr. Bedford nodded. "That would be appreciated, Mrs. Pruitt. We'll take it in the parlor."

We? Savannah turned. In her experience, husbands usually made themselves scarce as soon as she arrived. But Aidan Bedford—not quite a husband yet—seemed unaware of the freedom afforded his gender.

He gestured for her to precede him, and she soaked up the nuances of the house and what it felt like to be *home* again.

Miss Sinclair sat poised on the edge of the settee, posture erect, countenance attentive, if not a tad impatient—until seeing her fiancée. "You're joining us?"

"Only for a moment." He placed his portfolio on the side table.

Feeling something pass between the couple, Savannah deposited the satchel by her father's favorite chair, grateful to be relieved of the burden. Without the additional weight, her arm felt as though it might just float up and out of its socket.

"I trust Miss Hildegard sent samples of all the fabrics I chose the other day while in the store?"

"Yes, Miss Sinclair. She did." Savannah unlatched the satchel, aware of Mr. Bedford standing off to the side, watching. She reached for the fabrics, wondering what she sensed between the couple. Tension, most certainly. But something else. She hoped, for Miss Sinclair's sake, that Aidan Bedford wasn't the controlling type. Although, from what little she'd seen, Miss Sinclair didn't seem the type of woman to be easily controlled.

Savannah quelled a smile. *Good.* They deserved each other.

She withdrew the swatches, dozens of them in every imaginable fabric and color. "As you requested, Miss Sinclair, I brought silks, satins, taffetas, *failles*, *moirés*, silk poplins from Ireland, and velvets. In mixtures of florals and patterns including everything from the richer earthy tones of umber, green, and crimson to the more vibrant hues of purple, saffron, and blue."

Taking into account the stylishness of Miss Sinclair's fitted skirt with bustle and matching jacket—the latest in fashion—Savannah chose the most recent fabrics from Paris and draped them across the settee for her perusal.

Miss Sinclair gave a satisfied sigh, her hand moving to the most expensive first, and lingering. *"C'est belle."*

"Oui, il est très belle," Savannah answered, fully expecting the surprise in the woman's face.

"Parlez vous français?" Miss Sinclair asked, glancing at Mr. Bedford.

Savannah nodded. *"Oui, mademoiselle. Je l'ai étudié le français pendant des années."* It was a little prideful on her part, she knew, but she had indeed studied French for years, and she wanted women like Priscilla Sinclair to know she could do something other than merely sew.

And she didn't mind Mr. Aidan Bedford knowing either.

As Miss Sinclair studied the swatches, Savannah let her gaze roam the parlor. Strange how you could be gone from a place, and have changed so much while away, only to return and find the place that had so influenced you remarkably unchanged itself.

But even with her surroundings familiar, she found herself viewing the room in a different way, wondering where someone would hide something they didn't want discovered. Say, for instance, a box. She had no idea what size it would be, but certainly something small enough to be well hidden.

Her father wouldn't have put it in a drawer or tucked it on a shelf behind something. She knew from his letter he'd chosen more wisely: *"I left additional monies in the box as well. Save it if you can. Spend it if necessary. Even if the house is commandeered, it will be safe."*

No, the hiding place had to be somewhere more . . . permanent. Somewhere that even a Yankee soldier scavenging a home wouldn't find it. And having witnessed neighbors' homes searched during the war, she'd seen firsthand how thorough—and brutal—a Yankee soldier could be.

Her gaze slid across the room to Mr. Bedford who, much to her surprise, was watching her. It wasn't difficult to imagine him dressed as a bluecoat. But imagining him in blue made her think of her own father and older brothers clad in gray, and she found she couldn't contrive even the faintest smile before looking away.

The housekeeper entered and set a tray containing a silver service and a plate of biscuits on a side table, then served each of them. The silver service was similar to what Savannah's family had owned, but it wasn't theirs. She and her mother had sold all of those niceties during the war and in the months following, to keep food on the table.

"Thank you," Savannah said softly when the housekeeper came to her. Famished, she helped herself to two biscuits. She had heard of the dry, tasteless fare served by their Northern neighbors, yet after taking a bite of a biscuit, she wished she could sit down to the entire plate. She ate the second and finished her tea.

"Is this your first assignment, Miss Anderson?"

Noting skepticism in Mr. Bedford's voice, Savannah saw it in his face as well and gradually realized why he'd stayed. He'd mistaken her behavior upon first arriving for nervousness.

The man thought her a novice.

"No, sir." She lifted her chin, taking more pleasure than she should have in setting him straight. "I've been employed at Miss Hattie's for several years. I'm actually a master seamstress. I'm pleased to say that my draperies hang in some of the finest homes in Nashville, and I've also served as dressmaker to many of the mistresses of those homes. Should you require references, I'll happily provide them."

He said nothing, only nodded. But his eyes hinted at a smile.

"How long have you been in the home, Mr. Bedford?" Savannah asked, surprising herself. And him, too, judging by the furrow of his brow.

"About a month now. Though I purchased the property last year."

She remembered hearing the painful news of that sale as though it were yesterday. "Why the delay in moving, sir?"

He sipped his tea, eyeing her over the rim of the cup. "I had business to conclude in Boston. And upon first seeing the property and the house, I knew if I waited it would be gone."

"But what he apparently didn't know"—Miss Sinclair rose from her place on the settee and walked to the front window—"was how dreadfully dated his *new* home was and how much it needed a sophisticated woman's touch. Just look at these draperies."

Savannah did, and remembered sewing them with her mother before the war, nearly a decade ago now. They'd had such fun choosing the fabric together—a heavy rust brocade with flecks of silver that caught the light. Savannah had added the black piping and customized the elegant tie sash herself. Her first attempt on her own. Her mother had praised her for weeks.

"Honestly." Miss Sinclair scoffed, grasping the leading edge of the curtain between her thumb and forefinger as though it were the tail of a rat. She quickly let go and gave a shudder. "Who among us with a shred of taste would choose such a drab color?"

"I like them."

Savannah's gaze swung to Mr. Bedford. Guarded challenge lined his expression, and though she told herself not to allow it, she felt her opinion of the man softening the slightest bit.

"You *like* them?" Miss Sinclair laughed. "Oh, my dear. You really must reserve your opinions for your clients and the courtroom and leave the redecorating to me."

"Which I will agree to do." He returned his cup and saucer to the tray and reached for the portfolio on the table beside him. "With one repeated exception. Not the slightest alteration to my study."

CHAPTER FOUR

AIDAN CRESTED THE HILL AND REINED IN THE STALLION, HIS breath coming hard. The thoroughbred pawed at the dirt, still wanting to run, but a firm hand persuaded him otherwise.

Morning mist still ghosted the trees in breathy white, the delicate haze draped from the branches like Spanish moss. Aidan looked out over the countryside at the endless rise and fall of meadows and hills, so green and lush, then to the city of Nashville laying a handful of miles east. A world away from Boston.

And a world he'd swiftly grown to love.

He'd asked Priscilla last night to rise early and go riding with him, but she'd declined. She wasn't overly fond of horses. Or of nature, come to think of it. He hadn't asked twice. So . . .

He stroked the thoroughbred's neck. It was just him and Rondy.

Aidan spotted his foreman in the field below. Just about that time Colter raised an arm in greeting, and Aidan returned the gesture. He felt fortunate to have found such an experienced man to run things. Because as knowledgeable as he was personally about the law, that's how *in*experienced he was with farming. His education at Harvard had prepared him for many things. But farming wasn't one of them.

It wasn't Harvard's fault; he'd chosen to concentrate on the law. But he was determined to learn now.

Most of the attorneys he'd practiced with in Boston—and the attorneys here too—had their eyes on someday becoming a judge. He'd shared that aspiration at one time. But this was what he wanted now. Darby Farm, and to continue to practice law.

No judgeship for him. Not anymore.

He clucked his tongue, and the stallion set off at a trot. Aidan guided him down the hill and up another embankment. Their destination: his favorite spot on Darby Farm, just beyond the apple grove, and the reason he was all but certain this was the farm he'd been meant to find. He went to the meadow every chance he could to think and—

Movement through the woods caught his eye, and he reined in. He leaned down to peer through the trees. Miss Anderson, hurrying along the road to the house. She was starting bright and early this morning, and only her third day on the job. She managed a pretty fair pace too.

"She'd give you a run for your money, Rondy." The stallion tossed his head.

Upon first meeting the young woman, Aidan had gotten the distinct impression she didn't care for him, which was fine. He wouldn't have expected her to. After learning where he was from, most Southerners viewed him as death incarnate—only with greater dread and animosity.

Smiling, he urged the blood horse on, hoping Priscilla wasn't still abed. Then again, Mrs. Pruitt's day was well underway. She would see Miss Anderson inside.

He dismounted before reaching the meadow and looped Rondy's reins around a branch. He stood for a moment, drinking in the hushed tranquility of the place, the beauty of the magnolias and the stalwart majesty of the oak and cedar standing guard. To his knowledge, this field had never been tilled, and he planned to keep it that way.

An old cabin sat tucked among the trees a short distance away, and he set a path for it, the timeworn shanty already feeling like a trusted friend. As well it should, considering how he'd come to know about it.

He'd learned a little about the Darby family since moving here. One of the founding families of Nashville, the Darbys were well respected—or had been. The latest Mr. Darby, the former owner, had been killed in the war. As had happened to so many of these properties following emancipation, the farm went bankrupt and was auctioned.

That's when he'd come along.

He'd struggled at first with buying someone else's land and home at auction, imagining what heartache had preceded that event. And yet, someone would buy the place. And he'd paid a fair price as foreclosure and auction prices went.

He might well be pulling the wool over his own eyes, thinking his situation was any different, but he really did want to restore the place—the farm, the house—to what it had been. Only better this time.

Because they were on *this* side of the war.

The cabin lay just ahead, leaning slightly to one side as though resting on its elbow, and the trickling melody of the stream, just a stone's throw beyond, worked to soothe the restlessness that was his near constant companion these days.

He peered through the window opening and caught sight of a squirrel scurrying across the remnants of the old stone hearth. What must it have been like to be in this very place when Nashville was founded nearly a hundred years ago? And what would this spot be like a hundred years hence? He'd be long gone by then. And what would he have left behind? What would he and *Priscilla* have left behind?

There were times, like now, when he wondered why he'd asked her to marry him. And—though this did little for his ego—why she'd said yes.

These questions, and others, stirred inside him. He leaned forward, resting his arms on the split-log sill of the window, and found his thoughts drawn back to that field in North Carolina so many years ago. The soldier's voice was as clear in his memory as was the warble of the mockingbird in the tree above.

"If you've never seen the sun rise over the Tennessee hills, the city set off to the east, with the fog still clinging to the trees and the air so fresh from heaven . . . then you've never seen a sunrise. And my mama's peach cobbler? Oh, sweet Jesus, let me live to taste that again. That's the best stuff around, Boston. Better than anything you bluecoats got up there where you live."

He'd known the Confederate soldier only as "Nashville." That was one of the rules. No names exchanged. They went by their hometowns instead and talked about everything but the war. They traded newspapers and childhoods, shared pictures of sweethearts, and the rebels always wanted to barter for tobacco. Either that or shoes.

If someone had told him when he'd first put on his uniform that, come one summer afternoon, as opposing generals met on opposite hills to decide how best to kill Johnny Rebs and bluecoats, he'd lay down his rifle, kick back in a field, and "jaw" with the enemy, as Nashville had called it, he wouldn't have believed it. But that afternoon, as well as what happened a handful of hours later, had changed his life in ways the Confederate soldier couldn't have known. And that he himself had never dreamed.

Nashville had painted a picture of this setting that still resonated within him.

"There's a meadow a ways from the house, where my grandparents

first lived. It's everything that's best about this world, Boston. The trees, the stream, the way the sun falls across the land. Such a peacefulness to it. Not like the upside-downness of the world we're in right now." Nashville had smiled, a gesture that seemed to come as easily to him as breathing. "Sometimes I go there in my mind . . . and I feel finer than a frog's hair split four ways."

The snap of a twig brought Aidan's head up, and—the memory settling back inside him—he saw her again through the window on the other side of the cabin. Miss Anderson was picking her way through the trees, headed straight for him. But he didn't think she'd spotted him yet.

Curious as to how she'd found this place, he was surprised to discover he was glad she had. He waited until she got closer.

"Miss Anderson," he said softly. But despite his best intentions, she sucked in a breath.

"Mr. Bedford." She looked around. "W-what are you doing here?"

He laughed, finding her question a bit odd, considering the place was *his*. And by the blush that crept into her cheeks, he could tell she swiftly came to a similar conclusion.

"I come here quite often, Miss Anderson." His gaze traveled to the meadow, then the stream, then wove a path through the pines back to her. "It's a sort of . . . haven, I guess you could say."

Her eyes narrowed, and she frowned. "A haven. From what?"

The thinnest sliver of incredulity slipped past her polite tone, and from her perspective he couldn't say he blamed her. He didn't know her personal circumstances, but what he did know was that, compared to the majority of people in this city who were still putting their lives back together even five years after the war had ended, he had so much more than most. So through this woman's eyes, what did he have to complain about? Much less seek a haven from?

Yet he'd learned long ago that a man could have everything he needed to be considered successful while still feeling as though he lacked what was most important and precious.

Because . . . that described him.

How much he'd like to honestly answer her question, to talk to someone about all that was on his mind, including the frustrations roiling inside him. But he took present company into account and knew that was impossible. Not only did he not know this woman, but she was, in effect, working for him. At least temporarily. In addition, he was betrothed.

He should be sharing all these things with Priscilla. Only, hard as it was to admit, *she* was perhaps his greatest frustration. And even with all the other concerns he *could* discuss with Priscilla, he didn't completely trust her to understand them, much less be interested enough to listen.

Which was a rather disturbing realization, considering he'd be spending the rest of his life with her.

Aware of Miss Anderson awaiting his response, he took in the beauty and peacefulness of their surroundings and settled upon one he could safely give her. "A haven from everything in the world that is not this."

She held his gaze, and he could see her mind working, weighing, trying to decide whether he be friend or foe. Then the tiniest smile tipped one side of her mouth, shy, though not coy in the least. Nothing about this woman seemed false.

On the contrary, even on first impression, she seemed authentic and kindhearted—and so much like a young woman Nashville had described as his sweetheart.

"But if everything in the world were such as this," she said softly, "where would the longing for heaven be?"

The words left her lips like a feather on the breeze, and Aidan found it impossible not to stare at her. The woman was a mystery. Master seamstress, fluent in French, patient beyond what any creature without wings should be, and now this. Wisdom and humility wrapped up in all that beauty.

The moment he'd opened the door and seen her standing there that first day, he'd thought her lovely. It hadn't been a consciously formed opinion, rather something he'd simply known upon looking at her. Which he was doing now, likely in a manner he oughtn't.

For though he'd thought her attractive before, he'd not seen her lips as so kissable. Or the slender column of her throat so inviting. She had a quiet strength about her, a strength wrapped in softness, that—

She blinked and looked away, and the moment shuddered and skipped like a pendulum jarred mid-swing.

"If you'll excuse me, sir, I need to be—"

"Miss Anderson," Aidan said quickly, not wanting her to go, yet knowing it was best if she did. He also knew he was responsible for this, even as he told himself *this* had been nothing. He'd only been appreciating her beauty. But seeing how she was looking at him now—gaze wide, watchful—and feeling the pounding of his pulse, even he couldn't believe his own lie. "Thank you . . . for sharing what you did."

He grappled with what to say next that might somehow make the moment less awkward, or—

"Thank *you*, Mr. Bedford." Uncertainty faded from her gaze and warmth took its place. "For reminding me of why, at least in part, this world is the way it is."

Aidan watched her go, the gentle sway of her hips drawing his eye. Finally, with a sigh—both regretting and enjoying her retreat—he purposefully dragged his gaze back to the meadow.

He'd been so certain, when first seeing this place, that he'd found Nashville's farm, that he'd bought it. But since moving to this city he'd seen at least a dozen other arthritic, old cabins situated just beyond the setting of a farmhouse similar to this one, each staring back at him as though mocking his unaccustomed sentimentality. Though none of the settings was quite so beautiful as this one.

He ran a hand over a hewn log of the cabin and felt the roughness of time beneath his palm, almost as if the passage of lives lived out day by day within these walls had left a physical mark on the place. One he could feel both with his hand and his heart.

He'd likely never be certain where Nashville had lived, but he was determined to live with more of the gratitude and zest for life that Nashville had shown him. Even in so brief a time.

CHAPTER FIVE

Nothing had happened. Nothing had happened.

The phrase echoing in her head, Savannah gathered the swatches along with her notebook and hurried from the central parlor to the sitting room where Miss Sinclair waited. But no matter how many times she tried to convince herself, it didn't change the intimate turn her thoughts had taken yesterday as she'd stood there staring at Aidan Bedford.

This woman's future husband.

She didn't know what had come over her. *Embarrassing* didn't begin to describe it. Yes, the man was attractive, but she'd seen attractive men before. No, there was something else about him. Something unexpected, deeper than she'd first thought was there. And kinder. And it had drawn her in.

The way he'd gazed upon the land reflected her own love for its beauty and—

"Miss Anderson."

Savannah's head came up. "Yes, ma'am?"

Miss Sinclair frowned. "Are you well? You seem . . . preoccupied today."

"No, Miss Sinclair. I mean, yes. I'm feeling quite well." Or had been until she remembered how Mr. Bedford had done his best to try to set her at ease after she'd stood there practically ogling the man. Reliving the moment sent heat coursing through her. Though not warmth of a pleasurable nature—like yesterday.

Thankfully, she hadn't seen him since.

Now if she could only manage to sew every new set of draperies in the house and install them before he got home today, she could leave here, never come back, and everything would be fine.

But everything wouldn't be fine. Because she was no closer to fulfilling her main reason for being here: finding the box her father had hidden. So she'd simply make it a point to see him as little as possible, which could prove to be a challenge since this was his—

"Miss *Anderson*."

Savannah refocused and swiftly gathered from Miss Sinclair's irritated expression that the woman had asked her a question. "I'm sorry, ma'am. Would you mind saying that again, please?"

Miss Sinclair sighed, then repeated the question slowly, as though addressing a halfwit. "What do you think about my newest purchase?"

Only then did Savannah see the very *interesting* portrait by which the woman stood. The hopeful anticipation in Miss Sinclair's features clearly conveyed what she wanted Savannah to say. Although Savannah was at a loss as to how to exile thoughts of kissing the woman's fiancée, she did know how to handle this particular question. And with complete honesty. Years of experience decorating for eccentric personalities had prepared her well.

She tilted her head to one side. "That is one of the most thought-provoking portraits I've ever seen." She only hoped Miss Sinclair didn't ask her what she thought it was. If she did, Savannah's nearest guess would have to be . . .

No, she couldn't even hazard a guess. She wondered if Mr. Bedford had seen it yet, doubting it would be to the man's taste. Which, thinking of him again, only resurrected her former mantra.

"Can you hang the portrait for me, Miss Anderson?"

Hang a portrait? Was the woman serious? But Savannah swiftly realized she was. And since keeping this job was paramount . . . "Yes, ma'am, of course. I'll get the tools." Savannah turned to leave the sitting room.

"Miss *Anderson.*"

Hearing a trace of condescension in the woman's tone, Savannah paused in the doorway.

Miss Sinclair shook her head and gave an airy laugh. "Do you even have the slightest idea of where the tools are kept?"

Realizing what a mistake she'd been about to make, Savannah let out a breath. Of course she knew where they were. She'd left the remainder of her father's hand tools on the lower shelf of the cupboard off the kitchen. But from this woman's perspective . . .

Savannah covered the near mistake with a smile. "I thought surely Mrs. Pruitt would know."

Miss Sinclair stared, her eyes narrowing the tiniest bit. "Very well. See to it, then."

Savannah skirted down the hall, wondering if the woman suspected anything and vowing to be more careful. Enlisting the housekeeper's assistance, she *found* the needed tools and supplies and set to work. After measuring twice, she gripped the hammer and nail and struck her mark true and firm, just as Papa had taught her.

Before she and Carolyne and Andrew had vacated the house over a year ago, she'd managed to pack a few of her father's hand tools for her younger brother. Right now he only used them on occasion to repair his leg braces. But someday he would appreciate having them for the heritage of skill and craftsmanship they represented.

Her parents had left such a precious legacy for their children. One she'd been reminded of yesterday. *"Don't allow the world to teach you theology, Savannah. It'll not teach you right."* She could hear her father's voice and see his smile even now, his large hand resting atop the family Bible. *"Take it directly from the Source instead."*

"Are you certain you can manage it?"

Seeing Miss Sinclair struggle with the cumbersome gilded frame, Savannah smiled. "Yes, I'm certain." Lugging around her heavy sewing satchel had its advantages.

Mindful of how much the portrait likely cost, Savannah made certain the wire had caught on the nail before letting go. She stood alongside Miss Sinclair and eyed it. Then smiled.

"It's slantindicular," she said, aware of how Miss Sinclair was looking at her.

"I beg your pardon?"

"I said it's slantindicular." Savannah crossed the room and nudged the portrait up a little on the right side, then walked back, thinking of her brother Jake and about how he used to make up nonsensical words and phrases. "It means it's slanted."

Miss Sinclair looked from the portrait to her, then back to the portrait again. "You Southerners are a *strange* breed, Miss Anderson."

Savannah didn't know whether it was the wary tone Miss Sinclair used when saying it, or if it was the woman's proper Northern accent, but she laughed out loud.

And was still smiling when she walked home briskly that afternoon, keeping watch for a black stallion and the master of Darby Farm.

Later that night, as she helped Carolyne with her French and answered Andrew's questions as he struggled with *Macbeth*, Savannah thought again of what Mr. Bedford had said about a haven. She was grateful the plot of land meant something to him and hoped he would decide as her father and her mother's father had in regard to tilling it: that there was plenty of cultivated land on Darby Farm. Best leave that foretaste of heaven alone.

Thinking about her maternal grandfather made her think of her mother, which brought a sense of melancholy. She wished again that the two could have made peace with each other before her grandfather passed.

"Savannah?"

Seated by Carolyne on the girl's bed, Savannah looked across the room at her brother. The careful way he'd said her name told her he desired her full attention.

"I was at the mercantile today, and Mr. Mulholland asked about you." Brows knit together, he hesitated, then glanced at their younger sister, whose head was still buried in the textbook. "He asked if you were going to stop by the store anytime soon. He said you hadn't been by in a while to . . . visit with everyone."

Clearly hearing what he wasn't saying, Savannah hated the worry edging his voice. She'd been able to hide the dire state of their finances from Carolyne, but Andrew was far too perceptive. And him working at the mercantile didn't help. She knew Mr. Mulholland needed his money. The proprietor had been more than patient with her. But to inquire about it to Andrew? The boy already had enough burdens to deal with.

"Not to worry." Savannah pasted on a smile. "As soon as I finish the job I'm working on now, I'll drop by and say hello to Mr. Mulholland and his family."

Andrew held her stare then discreetly reached down and touched the braces on his legs. "These are fine," he said softly. "I really don't need any new—"

Savannah silenced her younger brother with a look, her throat straining with emotion. "We're going to be fine," she mouthed, then swallowed hard.

As though sensing something, Carolyne peered up at her. Savannah smoothed a hand over her sister's golden-blond hair and checked the girl's writing on the slate. *"Très bon,"* Savannah whispered. "You're almost finished. Continue, please."

With Carolyne's attention refocused, Savannah looked back at Andrew. "I'll visit the mercantile again very soon. I *promise*. And yes"—she looked pointedly at the braces on his legs, loving her brother with a fierceness that sometimes surprised her—"you do."

Reading uncertainty in his eyes, she smiled to let him know everything would be fine, and remembered her mother doing the very same thing with her, even when Savannah knew otherwise.

Later, once both siblings were in bed asleep, her gaze went to the drawer of the bedside table, and her heart to the letter within. She retrieved the missive, wanting to hold the stationery in her hand again and see her father's handwriting. Her gaze moved down the page to the paragraph she'd thought of earlier in the evening.

You will remember what we spoke of when last we were together, after the children were abed. I ask you again to forgive me for keeping what I did from you. It was most lovingly done. However, I understand how hurtful a revelation it was for you. It was never my intention to add to that past wound, my dearest.

She turned the page. A heavy watermark marred the ink on the time-crinkled stationery, but the words were still legible. Besides, she knew them already.

Your father was a most persuasive man, and even now I can see the determination in his eyes. Though I know the relationship between the two of you was never the same, I do believe your father entered eternity with overwhelming love for you and with a desire that you forgive him for the decision he made all those years ago. And I hope, my love, that you will. The longer I fight this war, and the more men I see taken so swiftly from this world to the next, the more I am convinced that harboring unforgiveness is a costly debt. One that is paid over and over not so much by the one needing forgiveness as by the one withholding it.

The ink blotched the page as though her father had hesitated overlong in lifting the pen, and she wondered what her mother had felt when first reading his next words.

What your father gave me—gave you—he did in a spirit of reconciliation, and I hope that in time you will receive his gift as such. Before I left, I placed it with the rest of our valuables for safekeeping.

Andrew stirred, and she looked up to see if he'd awakened. Sometimes the pain in his legs kept sleep at a distance. But his eyes remained closed, so she continued reading.

I'll adhere to your wishes and will wait to share the story with our entire family once the boys and I return home. But know that this was far more than a simple gesture on your father's part. It was an olive branch intended to heal, and I pray its roots spread deep and wide through our family. I left additional monies in the box as well. Save it if you can. Spend it if necessary. Even if the house is commandeered, it will be safe.

Oh, Papa. Where did you put it? And what is in it? Money still, perhaps?

Her mother had never said anything about it and had died so quickly herself. She'd been fine one moment, then complaining of a severe headache the next. Then she'd collapsed. When she finally came to, she'd been unable to move or speak, and within hours, even to breathe.

She'd been gone by the next morning.

Her throat tightening, Savannah didn't reread the last paragraph of the letter, her father's parting thoughts especially painful tonight for some reason. She slipped the folded stationery back into the envelope, then reached for the Bible. She laid her hand atop the worn black leather, much as her father had done, and wished she felt as confident about God's providence as he and her mother had.

She opened the Bible and took care turning the pages yellowed with time and dog-eared with a thirst for understanding and comfort. Contrary to the front and back of the book that contained the scribbled history of the Darby family, the pages themselves were clean and unmarked.

Every night she read to her siblings and silently to herself. But that habit had slipped in recent years as work grew busier and time shrank by half. Some days the words spoke to her more than others. Though she realized this had more to do with *her* heart than anything to do with the Lord.

The lamp oil burning low and the hour growing late, she returned the Bible to the drawer, then snuggled into the bed, weary from the long day. But apparently her body hadn't informed her thoughts because they turned with startling clarity to Aidan Bedford. She could see his face. And how he'd looked at her yesterday. For a moment, her imagination almost convinced her she hadn't been the only one doing the looking.

Then her saner side resumed function. Why would a man like him look at a woman like her? On the other hand, how could a woman like her take a second look at a man like him? From two different worlds, they were.

But she had to admit, even though the sensations she'd experienced had been one-sided, it gave her hope that maybe someday she'd find someone. A solid Southern man who would not only love her, but who would love Carolyne and Andrew too.

As she willed sleep to come, the last paragraph of her father's letter returned, insistent. But instead of seeing the words on the page, she heard the memory of her father's resonant voice across time.

When last you wrote, Melna, you told me you believed without fail that it was God's design for me to see home again. I cling to that hope and your faith in it, for my own grows less day by day. I pray to God that I am wrong. But if I am not, and heaven is soon within my sight, know that with my last breath I will be thinking of you and thanking God for the gift of your love and for all of our children. Jake and Adam are doing well, fighting bravely, as you would imagine. Though I know they are frightened. As are all brave men, from time to time. I am attempting to keep them safe and am so proud of them both. They send their love.

We all look forward to being home soon.

With deepest affection,

Merle

She hugged her pillow close, her tears dampening the smooth cotton beneath her cheek. "I love you all," she whispered aloud, hoping the hushed stillness might somehow cause her words to be heard in eternity, even as she prayed Eternity would answer.

CHAPTER SIX

Four days later, the fabrics for all windows receiving new treatments had been chosen, and Savannah had measured each of the windows numerous times, both for new shades and draperies. Then she'd measured them again to confirm her calculations. Save for one room she'd particularly avoided.

As she stood outside of her old bedroom, Miss Sinclair's current quarters, she felt much like the girl depicted in a novel by Lewis Carroll she'd recently read to Carolyne. Only there was no White Rabbit racing by with his pocket watch, and she knew with certainty she wasn't about to tumble down into a curious hall full of locked doors of all sizes as young Alice had. Still . . . she felt a hesitance she couldn't account for. Except that for all the dreams she'd dreamed in this bedroom, for all the paths she'd thought her life might someday take, very few had come to fruition.

Hearing footsteps on the staircase, she guessed Miss Sinclair had returned early from her shopping trip, and she hastened to her task, smiling to herself as she playfully checked the bedside table for a tiny key like in the story.

As she measured the windows and recorded the dimensions in

her notebook, she waited for Miss Sinclair or Mrs. Pruitt to pop into the bedroom at any moment. No matter where she went in the house in recent days, one of the two women always seemed to be either in the room with her or in another close by. At this rate, she could come here every day for the rest of her life and never find what her father had hidden.

She glanced about the room, noting the subtle changes from when she'd last lived here. The entire house had been given a thorough cleaning. Yet it was comforting to still see familiar scuff marks on walls and slight dents in the wooden floor that she'd personally authored.

But the lacy undergarments peeking from the wardrobe and the black silk nightgown draped over the chair in the corner were most definitely new additions. She didn't even want to think about whether Mr. Bedford had seen them.

And yet, she did wonder.

Purposefully refocusing, she moved to the next window.

Draperies for the dining room were already being sewn in the shop in town. She'd stopped by before coming this morning to make certain her coworkers understood the instructions on the ruching and trim. For a Monday morning, and so early an hour, the shop had been in a flurry. But a happy one.

To say Miss Hildegard was ecstatic with how the project was progressing was like saying a fish tended to prefer water. And why not? Miss Sinclair was asking for nothing but the best. The cost of the rich blue silk for the dining-room draperies was more than Savannah earned in a year, never mind the beading and tassels. For that reason alone, she hoped Aidan Bedford was a wealthy man. Because his fiancée was spending money almost faster than she could keep tally.

But his generosity to his future wife would also pay for Andrew's new leg braces. *"They'll be much better and less cumbersome than your old ones,"* Andrew had quoted the doctor.

So thank you, Mr. Bedford.

Though, much to her relief, she hadn't been alone with him since that day by her grandparents' old cabin. She'd seen him in the house along with Miss Sinclair or Mrs. Pruitt, and he'd acted completely normal. Whether it was just an act or he truly hadn't noticed how taken with him she'd been that day, she was grateful. Either way.

She stood back and eyed the double windows, still loving the curtains she'd sewn years earlier, although the blue-and-yellow floral was a tad girlish now. But they'd soon be gone. Because next on the list were the draperies for this room—soon to become the guest quarters—once Miss Sinclair approved the design. Miss Sinclair had requested that every room in the house be measured for floor coverings as well. Carpet was to be installed wall to wall in some of the rooms, and new Persian rugs had been ordered for others.

Savannah had identified the woman's taste early on, a skill honed from years of learning to set aside her own preferences and see the project through her clients' eyes. Miss Sinclair loved everything French and expensive and "unlike anything Nashville has ever seen." Savannah found it quietly amusing that so many of Miss Sinclair's "unique conceptions" were nearly identical to drawings in the latest editions of *Godey's, Harper's,* or *La Mode Illustrée.*

Personally, she appreciated fashion as much as anyone. But why was it that so many women, instead of listening to their own vision and creating a style unique to them, that fit their personal taste, let their style be dictated by someone in another part of the world? Say, Paris, New York, or . . . Boston.

After all, a home belonged to the people who lived in it. Not to the world.

But she'd also learned in recent years that a house didn't necessarily make a home. People did, and the love they shared. Wherever Carolyne and Andrew were, that was where her home was now, and she was determined to be grateful, however challenging that was at present.

Certain she'd heard someone on the stairs moments earlier, she crossed to the door and peered up and down the hallway. But the corridor was empty. Apparently she'd been mistaken. Seizing the opportunity, she combed the room for loose floorboards or ill-fitting bricks in the hearth, just as she'd done in most of the other rooms in the house. She even reached beneath the larger pieces of furniture to see if her father had somehow secured the box to the underside of—

"Miss Anderson?"

Hearing Aidan Bedford's voice, Savannah froze on all fours in front of the wardrobe. Then she did the only thing she could think of: quickly tossed her measuring tape underneath. The round cylinder rolled clear to the back.

CHAPTER SEVEN

SAVANNAH LOOKED UP, HAVING NO NEED TO WONDER IF HER face was flushed. "Good afternoon, Mr. Bedford! How are you, sir?" And why on earth was the man home from work so early?

Still in his suit, and looking quite the successful young attorney, he tilted his head as though to better match the angle of hers. "I'm well, Miss Anderson. Question is . . . how are you?"

"Fine. Other than my measuring tape having gone for a little stroll."

"Oh, please, allow me." He crossed the room and knelt, facing her, then reached beneath the wardrobe. Just as swiftly, he grimaced and pulled his hand back out.

Savannah winced. "A spider?"

He shook his head, then grinned. "A joke." He reached beneath the wardrobe again and a second later dropped the measuring tape safely into her palm.

Savannah laughed, finding his humor a little off center. And liking it.

He offered his assistance as she stood. His hand was warm and strong. And spoken for. Startled by the thought, she tucked the measuring tape into the pocket of her skirt and her hand along with it. Then she realized . . .

She'd never had a man visit her room before. At least not one who wasn't a family member. It felt a little . . . impolitic. Especially when all she could think about at the moment was how striking Aidan Bedford was. With his dark hair cropped close, just above the collar, and his jaw closely shaven yet showing signs of tomorrow's beard, he had an air of sophistication about him. Some might even say arrogance. Which fit with what she knew of Northerners.

Yet he seemed polite enough and had a perceptiveness about him that must certainly aid his profession. An attorney-at-law, the man was no doubt good at what he did.

Which, thinking of what she'd just been doing, only intensified her unease.

His gaze moved about the room, briefly catching on the nightgown before he looked back at her. His expression sobered. "May I ask, Miss Anderson, what you're doing in this room?"

She eyed him. "I'm measuring for draperies and carpeting, sir."

His eyes narrowed. "I was under the impression that *my* bedroom was the only room receiving alterations on this floor."

She opened her mouth, then quickly closed it. It wouldn't be the first time a wife—or almost wife—had been caught redecorating a bit more than she'd admitted to her husband. Which made her wonder if Miss Sinclair had told him yet about the stonemason or the marble fountain to be situated in the front courtyard. Once the courtyard was designed and built.

Mr. Bedford smiled. "I'm sorry, Miss Anderson. Please forgive the statement. It's clear you're only doing as you were instructed."

"Thank you, sir." Seeing the tension behind his eyes, she heard it in his voice, too, which prodded her uncertainty. She might have been tempted to let it pass if not for the order she'd told Mrs. Hildegard to place for fabric last Friday. An order worth several hundred dollars. Savannah felt sick inside.

Miss Sinclair had guaranteed the order with Mr. Bedford's name, and Savannah had accepted. But if for any reason the woman changed her mind, Savannah knew it would cost her her job. And Andrew's leg braces. And her ability to pay the outstanding debt at the mercantile.

"Mr. Bedford . . ." She tried to soften her query with a smile. "All the fabric for the draperies Miss Sinclair commissioned has been ordered. Which means the shop will be responsible for the bill if—"

"Don't worry, Miss Anderson. I'll guarantee whatever obligation Miss Sinclair has made."

Savannah breathed a little easier. "Thank you, sir."

"But in the future, I would prefer all orders be paid for in cash."

Understanding his meaning, Savannah nodded. "Yes, sir."

He turned to go, then paused. "And just where is Miss Sinclair at present?"

Savannah hesitated. "She left awhile earlier, sir. She said she was going into town."

He stared, waiting, as though certain there was more.

"To do some shopping," she added quietly.

He nodded, and she noticed then the tiny lines at the corners of his eyes, as though something were weighing on him. Or had been for some time. But Aidan Bedford's business being none of hers, unless it involved fabric or carpet of some sort, she offered a quick curtsy, gathered her notebook and pen, and took her leave.

She barely reached the stairs, however, when she heard her name— or Miss Anderson's name. She paused, again feeling the nudge to tell him the truth about who she was. But the anonymity *was* alleviating some potentially awkward moments. And she couldn't risk anything taking her off of this assignment.

"Thank you," he said, his voice gentle, "for the work you're doing here. Miss Sinclair is quite pleased thus far."

Which is no small feat, Savannah heard faintly in the subsequent silence. "Thank you, Mr. Bedford. And on behalf of Miss Hattie's shop, I'm most grateful to you for engaging our services."

He smiled then, the ease of the gesture and warmth in his gray eyes telling her *this* smile was natural. The effect it had on her was heady. But when his gaze lowered from her eyes to her mouth, Savannah was certain the house shifted beneath her.

To say she knew a lot about men was like saying she knew next to nothing about sewing. She'd had a beau. Once. Before the war. But she'd scarcely been thirteen years old. And he'd died in battle along with all the other boys she'd known.

But Aidan Bedford was no boy. And she got the distinct feeling he wasn't looking at her as an employee anymore. Which sent a simultaneous shiver—and shudder—through her.

He broke their gaze a heartbeat before she did, and the seconds lengthened as they purposefully looked anywhere but at each other.

Finally, he cleared his throat. "So . . . the fabric for the draperies has been ordered."

"Yes." She nodded as though telling him something he didn't already know.

"And I believe you said the project should take six weeks?"

"Perhaps a little less, based on the number of seamstresses we have assigned to your order. And, of course, contingent upon any changes that might yet be made."

"Of course." His eyes briefly grazed hers. "And here I thought I was buying a house that was already homey and ready to move into." He sighed, then smiled, or tried to. But the expression didn't hold. "Things without all remedy," he said quietly, finally looking at her again, "should be without regard."

Savannah tried to follow his meaning, thinking she should be able to, yet fell shy. "I . . . beg your pardon, sir?"

He blinked then ducked his head, his manner suddenly elusive. "I beg *your* pardon, Miss Anderson. I'll leave you to your work. Thank you again for your service."

CHAPTER EIGHT

THE KITCHEN AND STUDY. TWO ROOMS SAVANNAH HAD YET TO search.

She'd been here over two weeks, yet every time she visited the kitchen, Mrs. Pruitt was there. The housekeeper, kind though she was, might as well just drag her bed down the hallway and set it up by the stove.

Savannah peered down the corridor to her right and, even now, heard the clang of pots and pans as the older woman sang softly to herself. Then she looked back toward the left to her father's study.

No, *Mr. Bedford's* study.

How was she supposed to legitimately search in there when he'd expressly requested that nothing be changed? But he wasn't home right now, and Miss Sinclair was in the central parlor with a fresh pot of tea perusing the latest issue of *La Mode Illustrée*, with several past issues of *Godey's* beside her on the settee.

Savannah checked the time on the grandfather clock and knew Mrs. Pruitt's schedule well enough to hope the woman would be occupied with dinner preparations for at least a little while. With the rush of a thrill up her spine, she sneaked inside the study, then turned and pushed the door just shy of closed. She stood in the silence and breathed in the scent of old books and cigar smoke, the aroma of her father's favorite tobacco thicker in her memory than in the room. Still, amazing how the aroma lingered in the carpet and draperies after all these years, as though clinging to his memory just as she did. *Comforting* didn't come close to describing being in here again—the sun slanting through the windows, falling across the desk and the bookshelves, bathing the familiar room in a golden hue.

She gave herself a moment to drink it in, then hurriedly set about checking every nook and cranny, starting with the floor, then the bookshelves. But . . . nothing. Knowing anyone moving in to the house would've checked the drawers of her father's old desk, she didn't even bother looking.

She spotted a pipe on the desk and lifted it to her nose. The aroma bore a faint scent of vanilla and something else woodsy and sweet, and she wondered why the scent seemed so familiar to her, then realized she'd caught the scent on Mr. Bedford's clothes before. Something else familiar to her returned: *"Things without all remedy should be without regard."*

What he'd said days ago had stayed with her, and on a whim she crossed to the bookshelves and the familiar leather-bound copies, hoping her hunch was correct.

But now to find the right one.

Three volumes, four comedies, and two tragedies later, she happened upon the passage as she skimmed the pages. She wanted to throttle herself when she realized to which Shakespearean tragedy the phrase belonged.

She read the passage aloud softly, trying to give Lady Macbeth the Scottish accent the woman, however guilty, deserved. "'How now, my lord, why do you keep alone, of sorriest fancies your companions making.'" Impatient, she skimmed. "'Things without all remedy should be without regard: what's done is done.'"

She lifted her gaze. *What's done is done.*

She stared at the words again. She was familiar with Lady Macbeth's tenuous circumstances, but what had Aidan Bedford meant by quoting the literary character? Unless, of course, he'd murdered someone and was having trouble sleeping. She laughed to herself.

Then her smile faded. Not because she thought the man a murderer. Rather because she knew the meaning of the passage. It reflected a heart of regret. One of frustration. And she wondered what he'd been regretting in that moment when he'd quoted it. Was it giving Miss Sinclair permission to redecorate, perhaps? Understanding all the money the woman had spent? Or . . . was it another kind of regret entirely? What if he'd been referring to something far more personal?

That possibility caused her to go still inside. What if he'd been referring to—

"Mrs. Pruitt!" Miss Sinclair called out, the sharp staccato of fashionable boots approaching.

Savannah hastily returned the leather tome to the shelf and raced to stand behind the door in case Miss Sinclair looked inside the room. But the footsteps continued on toward the kitchen, and Savannah leaned her head back against the wall and allowed herself to breathe again.

The last three or four days, Miss Sinclair had seemed bent on accomplishing everything she'd planned and more, and with good reason. She was set to return to Boston later that week.

At the woman's insistence, Savannah had brought her sewing machine last week and had set it up in the boys' old bedroom upstairs in order to sew decorative pillows to the woman's *precise* specifications. And Savannah had sewn a dozen so far, with another dozen cut out and ready to be sewn. Where visitors were going to sit when they came calling, she didn't know.

But there was a new desperation to Miss Sinclair's efforts to make this house her home, and Savannah didn't have to wonder long as to why. Even she sensed the distancing between the couple. She wasn't privy to details about the pending nuptials, which was just as well. She got a sinking feeling in her gut every time she thought about it. Which she tried not to do.

Listening for footsteps and hearing none, Savannah opened the door as Mrs. Pruitt's voice carried toward her from the kitchen.

"Yes, Miss Sinclair. Last I saw Miss Anderson, she was upstairs sewing the pillows you requested, ma'am."

Peering down the hallway and seeing the back of Miss Sinclair's dress, Savannah made a dash for the stairs and raced up, avoiding the risers with the worst creaks and half deciding that whatever box her father had hidden was gone. Or perhaps . . . Heart pounding, she slipped into the boys' bedroom and took her seat at the sewing machine. Perhaps it had already been found.

Miss Sinclair's steps sounded on the stairs, and Savannah picked up one of the partially sewn patterns, trying not to appear as guilty as she felt. It had been hard enough to be in Priscilla Sinclair's company before. But with what had happened with Mr. Bedford—

But what *had* really happened? After all was said and done? Nothing. He'd looked at her. That was all. And as she and Maggie and Mary—her closest friends—had said in younger years, "It doesn't take much to get a boy to look. It is getting him to look at the right things that matters."

The same was true for men, she guessed. Even though she wanted to believe Aidan Bedford was different. But in the end, how much did she really know about the man? Other than that he'd purchased her family's farm, he was searching for a haven, and he held an apprecia-tion for Shakespeare.

As well as a tiny part of her heart.

"Miss Anderson?" Miss Sinclair peered through the doorway, breathless. "Quickly! I need to discuss something with you in the cen-tral parlor. Posthaste! It's about the furniture!"

CHAPTER NINE

"—AND EVERY PIECE OF FURNITURE IN THIS ROOM MUST GO. Surely you're in agreement, Miss Anderson."

Aidan overheard Priscilla's voice as he opened the front door. His interest more than piqued, especially after the day he'd had, he paused in the foyer. The door to the central parlor on his right wasn't quite closed, and he spotted Miss Anderson, her back to him. But he couldn't see Priscilla.

"Do you know of an establishment in town that will take such pieces, Miss Anderson? *Passé* though they may be?"

Miss Anderson glanced about the room as though taking inventory of its contents, and Aidan sensed her hesitance.

"Yes, Miss Sinclair. There's a . . . Widows' and Children's Home in Nashville that might be able to make use of the furniture. I could speak with the home's director, if you wish. But are you certain Mr. Bedford doesn't wish to retain any of it?"

Aidan's appreciation for the young woman increased tenfold.

"There's no need to mention any of this to Mr. Bedford, Miss Anderson. I'm still choosing the last of the pieces, but I'd prefer the new furniture be a surprise for him. Do you understand?"

Aidan rubbed the back of his neck, the muscles taut. Oh, it would be a surprise all right. Or would've been. If she'd managed the purchase. Which she certainly wouldn't now.

Work in recent days had been unrelenting. Regardless of the personal grudge people in this town held against Northerners—to date, he'd been called arrogant, aggressive, and brutish—it appeared they desired those traits in an attorney. His desk was piled high with files, and his satchel bulged.

He'd finally left the office a little early in hopes of getting some work done in his study this afternoon. He sighed. Returning home was supposed to be a man's respite. But since Priscilla's arrival, it had been anything but. Between his attempts to avoid Miss Anderson while also trying to spend time with Priscilla, he felt a little like a prisoner in his own home. When Miss Anderson was in a particular room, he tried to avoid going in, while doing his best not to make it look intentional.

The young woman had done nothing wrong. It was *his* mistake. He was the one who had overstepped his bounds. Yet, if her behavior when he *did* see her was any indication, she seemed to have forgiven him completely, for which he was grateful.

And also not.

Because even as fleeting as those moments had been with her, and as silly as it sounded to him even now, he'd felt more of a connection with her in that brief space of time than he'd felt with Priscilla in months. Perhaps ever.

Which left him feeling like an entirely different kind of prisoner.

He glimpsed Priscilla briefly through the open doorway, her back to him. He'd told her she could redecorate, and it had seemed fitting since the house was going to be hers as well. But she was going far beyond anything he'd imagined. Replacing entire rooms of furniture? Furniture he liked?

"I found a borne settee this morning," Priscilla continued, her voice overly dramatic as though she might swoon. "Rococo Revival period with rich damask fabric. I bought it immediately, of course, and believe it will work best right over . . . *there*. What do you think, Miss Anderson?"

The grandfather clock beside him ticked off the seconds.

"A borne settee?" Miss Anderson finally answered, her tone polite but clearly questioning. "That's a rather large and formal piece for a central parlor, Miss Sinclair."

"Which is precisely why I bought it. This house is starved for elegance. My future husband is an attorney for now. But someday he'll be a judge, and I want this house to—"

Having heard enough—for his wallet, his respectability, and his patience—Aidan stepped back to the front door and opened and closed it again, louder this time.

Shushed whispers came from the parlor. Seconds later Priscilla waltzed through the doorway, arms outstretched as though they'd been separated for seven years instead of seven hours. She clasped his hand and offered her cheek for a kiss. He obliged, aware of Miss Anderson watching from the other room before she quickly looked away.

"Dearest." Priscilla linked arms with him. "You're home early."

Along with surprise in her voice, he also detected another quality, one that had a definite note of falseness to it. Aided by what he'd just overheard, he found himself viewing the woman in a somewhat different light, and he realized he'd heard that tone from her before. Many times. "I wasn't getting any work done at the firm, so I decided to come home and work here."

"Wonderful! I'll ask Mrs. Pruitt to fix us some tea. We can sit on the front porch and visit for a while before you—"

He gently squeezed her hand. "I'm sorry, Priscilla, but I have two very important cases coming up next week, and I must read through some briefs."

Her smile faltered. She removed her hand from the crook of his arm. "Of course. You're busy. More so, it seems, than you were in Boston."

"That's not true. I've—"

Knowing Miss Anderson could hear their conversation, even without trying, Aidan urged Priscilla into the sitting room to their left, then eased the door closed.

CHAPTER TEN

Aidan kept his voice quiet, not wishing for Miss Anderson to hear them. "Since you've been visiting, Priscilla, I've gone in late most every morning so we can spend time together. But I'm getting further behind, so—"

"I didn't realize spending time with me was such a burden, Aidan."

He looked at her. "I didn't say that. What I'm saying is that my schedule here is every bit as demanding as it was in Boston."

"But there's nothing for me to do here."

His laugh held no humor. "Quite the contrary, from what I'm seeing. You're changing nearly every room in the house."

"And can you blame me?"

Tempted to answer more honestly than was fair in the moment, he took a deep breath. "I don't blame you for being lonely. You haven't had the opportunity to make friends here yet."

"These people are so . . . different from us. The land is handsome enough, I guess, as you said it would be. But all the rest . . ." She bowed her head, and the silence completed her thought with unmistakable clarity.

Still dwelling on the "different from us," Aidan looked at the woman beside him and heard the echo of another conversation from years earlier.

"My sweetheart, she's a pretty little thing. Hair all buttery and golden, like wheat in the summer sun. And kind too. She's a lady through and through, but she can hold her own, let me tell you that. Shoots as well as I do, baits her own hook. But can still cook up a mess of ham and biscuits the likes of which you ain't never tasted up north. Let me tell you, Boston, you're on the wrong side in more ways than one."

Had Nashville known what a gift he'd possessed? In his family? In his sweetheart? How fortunate he'd been? Most people went through life without a fraction of that depth of love and commitment.

"But if everything in the world were such as this, where would the longing for heaven be?"

Like guarding a priceless nugget, he'd carried what Miss Anderson had said with him, taking it out now and again, examining it, then tucking it away again for safekeeping. As he did now.

It occurred to him then: he didn't even know the woman's first name.

"Come back to Boston with me for a few days, Aidan. It'll do you good." Priscilla took hold of his hand, and her touch already felt foreign. "I know you miss it. I see it in your eyes."

Knowing what she was seeing wasn't him missing Boston, but him missing Darby Farm—the way it had been before she arrived—he took his time in answering. "I can't," he finally said. "My job is here now."

"But you kept a home in Boston too." Fragile hope lit her eyes. "And I know your former partners would welcome you back."

He looked at her, then slowly shook his head.

"I leave in two days, Aidan. And I won't be back for a month. Perhaps even longer."

He was fairly certain he heard an ultimatum, or at least a threat.

What bothered him most about that was how *un*bothered he was by it. "I understand. So we'll spend as much time together as my schedule allows before you leave."

Her jaw went rigid, and she turned to go. He debated whether to say anything further, then decided it was best to get it out now rather than for her to try and lay the blame with Miss Anderson for having revealed a confidence.

"Priscilla."

She looked back.

"Draperies and rugs are one thing. But not a stick of furniture leaves this house without my approval. Is that clear?"

Her blue eyes went cold. "Perfectly," she whispered, then left the room and wordlessly ascended the stairs.

Feeling wearier than he had in ages, Aidan crossed the foyer and found Miss Anderson straightening the room, of all things. Taking books off the shelves and lining them up again, then smoothing her hand over the surface of the wood, presumably checking for dust. Although she seemed particularly intent on her job.

"I do have a housekeeper, Miss Anderson."

The woman jumped nearly a foot into the air.

"I'm sorry," he offered, the look on her face so comical it tempted him to grin. "I didn't mean to startle you. But . . . it seems I keep succeeding."

"Yes." Hand on her chest, she laughed. "You do."

Her breathlessness told him he'd truly given her a fright. And as much as part of him wished he could ask her to stay and sit with him in this room and converse, or to walk outside with him to the old cabin, he knew better.

He gestured. "Miss Sinclair has gone upstairs for a while. So it might be best if you—"

"I was planning on leaving a little early today anyway, Mr. Bedford."

She quickly gathered her things and had opened the front door when the question he'd fought to sequester finally won out.

"Miss Anderson . . ."

She looked back.

"You've worked here for several weeks, and I just realized—I don't even know your first name."

She smiled, and he was certain the sunlight framing her from behind dimmed by a degree.

"Savannah," she said softly, then closed the door as she left.

Several minutes passed before Aidan realized he was still standing at the front window, long after she'd turned the corner and disappeared from sight.

Later that night, unable to sleep and feeling a pressure building inside him, Aidan rose and went outside to the second-story porch to get some air. He filled his lungs with the tantalizing scent of fresh pine, the summer sweetness of honeysuckle, and . . . the stench of skunk.

He smiled, figuring that pretty well represented his life right now. And life in general. Some good along with the bad. But the bad surely made one more grateful for the good. And likewise, the bad surely had a way of ruining what was more pleasant.

He looked up into the star-studded night, heaven's canopy stretching forever all around him, covering him, making him feel both infinitesimally small and yet not without purpose. Because he was here among it all. And surely the One who had gone to such fantastic lengths to create this world wouldn't have plopped mankind down in the midst of it only to leave him to flounder without meaning, without guidance.

No, he'd been long convinced that the Creator had a master plan. Regardless of him not quite knowing what it was at certain times. Like at the present moment.

Aidan walked to the porch railing and looked out into the darkness, wondering about the man who'd lived here before him. The last Mr. Darby. Had he ever awakened at night, unable to sleep, unable to wrestle the anxiety inside him into submission? Had that man ever stared across the fields as he did now, asking for the Divine to whisper wisdom and discernment?

Nashville had spoken of having a girl back home. Someone much like Miss Anderson—*Savannah*—he'd bet. The way the soldier spoke about the girl, about his home and family, about the very land itself, had reached deep inside of Aidan that day and hadn't let go. Not even hours later when, on the battlefield, he looked over to see Nashville take a bullet to the chest. The young man lurched forward and fell facedown into the field of wildflowers. Aidan fought his way through the fray, trying to get to him. And when he finally did, he turned Nashville over, only to find him gasping, a hole ripped open in his chest.

Nashville tried to speak, but blood gurgled out in the place of words. Still, Aidan had read the look in his eyes. And there, in the midst of battle, he'd gripped Nashville's hand, feeling the life slip from him, watching it pour from his heart. "I'll see that sunrise, Nashville," he'd whispered. "I'll taste that peach cobbler again for you too."

Body shaking, gasping for breath and finding none, Nashville had smiled a smile that Aidan already found familiar. Then he'd breathed his last. And the light that had burned so brightly within his friend awhile before had snuffed out.

His friend.

They'd known each other for all of perhaps three hours. Yet in that short time Nashville had shown more love for his family and dedication to his country than Aidan had ever encountered, regardless of their differing views on the issues that had brought them there.

Aidan wanted to know what that felt like. To love and be loved that way. Had he made a mistake leaving Boston to come here? He didn't think so. Had he made a mistake asking Priscilla to marry him? Most definitely. But how to fix it?

He didn't quite know. But he was determined to find a way. He owed that much to Nashville's memory.

CHAPTER ELEVEN

THE BLAST OF THE TRAIN WHISTLE SENT STEAM BILLOWING up against the pale blue of early morning. The air wasn't cold, but Aidan thought he saw Priscilla shiver. And he felt a bit of one himself, though not because of fear or of any doubt of what he needed to do.

On the contrary, after the night he'd spent on the porch, searching his own heart and seeking God's, there wasn't a shred of doubt left within him. And he was all but certain that down deep Priscilla felt the same as he did. If only he could get her to realize it.

"You've changed, Aidan," she whispered, her demeanor lacking its usual confidence.

"*We've* changed, Priscilla."

She frowned and looked away. Her lower lip trembled. "My father . . ." She drew in a breath. "He was always so fond of you."

"As I was of him. He was a good man."

She nodded.

"But, Priscilla, your father would have wanted you to love the man you're going to marry. Not just be with him because your father liked him. Or because"—Aidan hurried to finish, recognizing by the narrowing of her eyes that she was gearing up for battle—"marrying him will offer you security. You have security, Priscilla. Your father's estate will allow you to live comfortably for the rest of your life."

"But I want to be with you."

"No, you don't," he said gently. "You want to feel safe again. Something you haven't felt since your parents passed. I know. I've felt what that's like. It's lonely, and can be frightening. Loss makes you reexamine your life, who you are, and what you really want. But that's a good thing, however painful the personal revelation can be at times."

She looked up at him, and for reasons he understood, he didn't see disagreement. Only fear.

"What if"—her voice faltered—"when you look at yourself more closely, you don't necessarily like who you see?"

He smiled. "Then know you're not alone. But also know that it's recognizing your faults and being honest about them that's the first step to overcoming them. To changing who you are, becoming who you want to be."

She returned a feeble smile.

"I'm selling the brownstone, Priscilla. I'm wiring my broker as soon as I leave here."

She nodded. A tear slipped down her cheek. "I never did want to live in this city, Aidan."

"I know."

"But I also don't want to be alone."

"And knowing you"—he pressed a parting kiss to her forehead—"and all the single men in Boston, I don't believe there's the slightest chance of that happening."

Now if only he could muster the same hope for himself.

Leaving the telegraph office, Aidan headed to the mercantile only to find his way blocked by a freight wagon. He was maneuvering around it when someone across the street caught his eye. He slowed his pace, then finally paused.

A young boy was unloading crates of potatoes, one at a time, from the back of the freight wagon, his progress slowed by the braces on his legs. But Aidan read unwavering determination in the boy's halting stride.

Another boy about the same age and with a shock of red hair worked alongside him, carrying two crates at once but more slowly, even stopping occasionally to jaw with some buddies who stood off to the side. But not the crippled boy. Back and forth he went, in and out of the store, unloading goods, steady and right as rain.

One of Red's friends said something to him on his way out, and Red and his buddies laughed. The tallest one in the crowd held a forefinger to his mouth, then followed him to the wagon, and—

Realizing what the bigger boy was about to do, Aidan tried to get there in time. But couldn't. A shove from behind sent the lame boy sprawling, and the crate of potatoes went everywhere.

As Aidan reached the scene, another man strode from the store and the instigators took off. All except for Red. The man grabbed the coworker by the arm, apparently having seen it all unfold.

"You're done, Walters! Now get yourself out of here. And don't be askin' me for another job!"

The lad wisely obeyed, and the man, his Irish accent thick, reached down to help the boy to his feet.

"I'm all right." The boy waved off his help, but the clank of metal against metal as he tried to straighten his braced legs suggested otherwise. His face and neck were a deep crimson. "I'll pick them all up and wash them, Mr. McGrath."

The man hesitated, then nodded. "Good man, Andrew. We get knocked down, but we get right back up." The man tousled the boy's hair, which drew the ghost of a smile.

Andrew righted the crate, and a few passersby helped toss some potatoes in. And despite sensing the boy's desire to make his own way, Aidan couldn't resist helping too.

"Catch," Aidan said, tossing a potato his way, already guessing at the lad's dexterity.

With quick reflexes, Andrew caught the spud in his grip. And smiled. "Thank you, sir."

"These for sale?" Aidan eyed the potatoes, impressed. Scarcely a bad mark on them.

"Yes, sir." The boy pointed. "You can get them by the crate here. Or out at Linden Downs by the wagonload."

Aidan nodded, recognizing the name of the farm from dealings in town. "I'll remember that."

"You're not from around here, are you, sir?"

Aidan smiled, appreciating the respect in the boy's voice, while clearly hearing an opinion. "No, I'm not. I'm from Boston."

"Where Paul Revere's from." Andrew's face lit. "And the two lanterns, telling the British were coming by sea."

"That's right." Impressed, Aidan studied the boy. About eleven or twelve, he guessed. The lad's chambray shirt, though slightly worn at the elbows, was of fine stitching, and his britches, a little short, boasted the same quality tailoring. But it was the maturity in the boy's manner that impressed him most.

"Having lived in Boston, I've actually ridden the path Revere took that night. All the way up to Concord."

Fascination swept Andrew's face. "What's it like up there? In Massachusetts."

"It's nice." Aidan looked toward the hills of green. "But I think it's prettier here." That earned him a grin. He offered his hand. "Mr. Aidan Bedford."

The boy rubbed his palm on his pants before accepting. "Andrew Darby, sir."

Aidan's grip tightened subconsciously. "Darby," he repeated.

The boy nodded.

"Well . . . Andrew, I've enjoyed our discussion." His thoughts racing, he released the boy's hand. "You certainly have studied your history."

Andrew shrugged. "My sister Savannah makes me. Sometimes it's not so boring though. But I wouldn't want her to know that." Grinning, he gestured back to the wagon. "I'd best get back to work, Mr. Bedford. Thank you again, sir, for your help."

His thoughts having moved beyond racing to fully broken rein, Aidan finally managed to respond. "My pleasure, Andrew. *My* pleasure."

CHAPTER TWELVE

SAVANNAH STOOD IN THE MIDDLE OF THE CENTRAL PARLOR and studied the draperies, knowing Miss Sinclair was going to be more than pleased. The most complicated and ornate of all the window coverings in the house, these had turned out even finer and more elegant than Savannah hoped, though pressing the endless folds had taken hours, and her back was still paying for it.

She gestured. "Let's bring the rod up about an eighth of an inch on the right, Freddie."

"Yes, Miss Darby."

Savannah winced at the name and glanced toward the front hall. Mrs. Pruitt was the only other one in the house, and she was busy in the kitchen. Still . . .

"Like I told you, Freddie, you don't have to call me Miss Darby here. It's just us. And I've known you since before you were born."

The boy, a little older than Andrew, grinned as though he'd just been handed a bag of penny candy. "Okay, Savannah."

"Better." She smiled, then looked up. "Secure them there and we'll be done for the day." And none too soon. Since Miss Sinclair had returned to Boston, Mr. Bedford kept longer office hours in town and was rarely home before half past five. She always made it a point to be gone by then.

Although some days he surprised her by meeting her in his carriage as she walked back to town. Each time he insisted on taking her the rest of the way and acted the perfect gentleman. She enjoyed talking to him, and his slightly tilted humor always found its mark with her. She only hoped Miss Sinclair was deserving of such a man.

And that perhaps God had a man just like him for *her* someday.

The last two weeks had been so very pleasant working here, just her and Mrs. Pruitt. She felt as though God had given her a gift. Time to say good-bye to her childhood home and time to touch, one last time, all the tangible reminders of her family lineage.

In a way, she wished she could have shared this experience with Andrew and Carolyne. But besides being impossible under the circumstances, she knew it wouldn't have been wise. While she was grateful for this opportunity, it hadn't been easy.

Yet one thing she'd learned: with so many of the possessions she'd once considered essential, in seeing them again, she'd realized how *un*essential they were. Treasured, to be sure. But luxuries. Most of which she'd learned to live without. And some she'd honestly forgotten they'd ever owned.

But the one thing she'd wanted to find most still remained hidden. She'd looked everywhere she could possibly think of for the box. It simply wasn't here. She would've found it if it was.

"Is it strange, Savannah?" Freddie asked, packing up his tools, folding up his ladder. "Being back here?"

"Yes," she answered readily. "A little. But . . . it's also been very nice."

He nodded.

"Freddie."

The boy turned at the door.

"Thank you for keeping this—my working here—between us for now. I'll tell Andrew and Carolyne after the job is finished."

He looked around the room, his features sobering. "It's been kind of sad for me. Being back in the house, ma'am. Makes me think of your brothers. And your papa."

"I know."

He sighed, then smiled in parting.

Savannah saw him to the door, then closed it behind him and turned and stared at the house. The house that would soon belong to Miss Priscilla Sinclair . . . Bedford. She sighed, feeling in the act a loosening inside herself. She'd surrendered this house to the Lord so many times. How many would it take before her heart finally let go?

She didn't know. She just prayed the Lord would give her a peace about it. Someday.

The grandfather clock chimed on the hour, four long-lasting strokes, each echoing throughout the home as the comforting timbre had for years past and likely would for many years to come. Unexpected tears rose at the sound and the thought. The clock had passed from her maternal grandfather to her mother, and even though he and her mother had never reconciled that Savannah knew of, she thought it said something that her mother had kept the clock in the main foyer all those years, faithfully wound, its large brass pendulum swinging back and forth over the wide base, its movement sustained by weights as it marked the passage of time.

She followed the pendulum's sway. Slowly, her gaze moved downward to the ornately carved base where her grandfather, a gifted craftsman in his day, had sculpted magnolias, her grandmother's favorite flower, in the wood along the bottom.

And as the last note of the chimes faded, Savannah's eyes narrowed. *But know that this was far more than a simple gesture on your father's part. It was an olive branch intended to heal, and I pray its roots spread deep and wide through our family."*

The beat of her heart bumping up a notch, she recalled the words her father had written, and she crossed the foyer, knelt, and ran a hand along the base of the clock.

The piece was so heavy. There was no moving it.

She reached underneath but felt only cobwebs. She quickly withdrew her hand, thinking of Aidan and how he'd made her laugh that day he'd caught her snooping in her old bedroom.

She peered inside through the glass front, then stood and reached for the key on top where they'd always kept it. Her fingertips first to deliver the good news, she grasped the key and, hands trembling, unlocked the door. She knelt again and felt along the inside bottom of the clock. Then she rapped on the wood.

The hollow echo caused her pulse to race.

Quickly she retrieved her sewing scissors from the central parlor and slid a narrow point down along the inside edge . . . and felt the wood along the bottom give way. Her breath coming in short, shallow gasps, she pried open the false bottom and there—her throat ached at the sight of it—was a cigar box, her father's favorite brand.

She took out the wooden box and reverently opened the lid, thinking of how one of her parents had been the last one to close it. The first thing she saw was her maternal grandfather's pocketknife, its handle inlaid with ivory. Then her grandmother's wedding ring, a simple gold band, one side nearly worn clean through. But the band with the companion diamond was gone, no doubt having been sold to help pay the taxes as they'd slipped further into debt.

She fingered an old money clip she remembered from her paternal grandfather. A poor excuse for one—she smiled—as the clip had obviously failed to do a very good job.

No money was left in the box. But sundry other treasures were. Among them lay a thimble she recognized as her mother's, a hair clip she thought had belonged to her maternal grandmother but couldn't be sure, and a tiny pearl button, all on its lonesome, perfectly lovely, but whose story was likely forever lost. There was also a sketched likeness of her mother's mother and father, very much like them too. Or at least as Savannah remembered them.

She turned the drawing over, hoping there might be a date. And there was: *April sixth, eighteen hundred and sixty-three*, and a scripture reference below it: *Deuteronomy 29:29*.

Savannah frowned. The date made no sense since it was nearly seven years after her grandparents' deaths. And the scripture reference . . . She hated to admit, if only to the Lord and herself, that Deuteronomy was not a book of the Bible to which she often went for comfort or daily reading. So she had no idea what the scripture said. She'd have to look it up.

Beneath that picture was a photograph that took her breath away. She hadn't seen it in years. It was one of the family taken just before the war. She remembered her mother insisting they have it done. A photographer had set up a studio in town, so they'd all dressed in their Sunday best and sat for the photograph. How hard it had been for Andrew, a toddler at the time, to stay motionless for so long. And how tiny Carolyne had been, just a baby. Savannah smiled, remembering how Jake had bribed Andrew with the promise of candy and one of his stories.

Her gaze moved over the faces of her precious family. Jake and Adam looked so young. So handsome. She took a deep breath. Nearly a decade ago now. And what change the decade had brought.

She continued looking through the box. And there, at the bottom, was a slip of paper.

She carefully withdrew it, noting its heavier feel—like fine stationery, only without the deckled edge. The set type bleeding through from the other side of the page lent resemblance to a legal document, but even as she unfolded it, she knew whatever it said was too little, too late. Everything had already been legally sold at auction. The land, the house, the belongings.

And yet . . . Her gaze scanned the page, and she felt a frown forming. A deed. From her maternal grandfather.

The sunlight faded, and she moved the page toward the light. But just as quickly, the sun shifted again. And she realized . . .

It wasn't the sun. It was Aidan's shadow, and he was staring down at her, a most quizzical look on his handsome face.

"And what have we here . . . *Miss Darby?*"

CHAPTER THIRTEEN

MISS DARBY?

Savannah scrambled to her feet, nearly dropping the cigar box and sending its contents racing for cover. Heart pounding, she took a cautious step backward. "H-how long have you known?"

His smile came slowly, deliberately. "I first suspected two weeks ago when I met your younger brother."

She nearly choked. "You . . . met Andrew?"

"I did. Nice young man. Hard worker too. A few discreet inquiries later . . ." He gave a one-shouldered shrug that was definitely *male*. "And my suspicions were confirmed."

Andrew hadn't said a word to her about meeting Mr. Bedford. But then, why would he? Andrew didn't know she was working for the man.

Mr. Bedford looked at the box in her hands, then at the clock and back at her again.

"I can explain," she said quickly, hoping she could do so to his satisfaction. "But first . . . I didn't tell you who I was because I feared it would make the situation uncomfortable and then I might lose the assignment. And I need this job, Mr. Bedford." Reading questions in his features, she rushed to continue. "On that first morning, I did *try* to tell you and your fiancée, Miss Sinclair, that my coworker had taken ill and that—"

"I believe you mean my *former* fiancée, Miss Darby."

Caught midsentence and completely off guard, Savannah moved her mouth, but no words came. And then, "I-I don't understand."

The smile in his gray eyes deepened. "Miss Sinclair and I are no longer engaged, Miss Darby. It was a . . . mutual parting of the ways. When she left for Boston."

The gleam that moved in behind his eyes did anything but set her at ease. On the contrary, it set her pulse racing, as did the meaning of what he was telling her. She shook her head. "So . . . you're not—"

"No. I most certainly am not."

She took a quick breath and felt the tug of a smile, then just as quickly banished it, realizing how inappropriate the reaction was. "I'm sorry to hear that, Mr. Bedford."

"Are you?"

His gaze dropped from her eyes to her mouth, and her heart vaulted from her chest to her throat. She smiled again. She couldn't help it. And the telling flicker of his response, similar to hers, only encouraged it. The subtlety of the exchange was potent. Even intoxicating.

"Now . . ." He glanced at the box. "Might you explain what you have here?"

Having all but forgotten about it, she nodded. "Of course. And please know that I realize everything in this box belongs to you now. You are, after all, the rightful owner of Darby Farm."

"Your home," he said softly.

"My *former* home," she whispered, then looked at the box and the pieces of her life it held. "Before my father died, he wrote my mother a letter and referenced something he'd hidden here in the house."

She explained it all to him, sharing parts of the letter from memory, even sharing how she and her friend, Maggie, had tried to find a way to sneak into the house last summer. "But there were no open doors or windows. No way to get inside without breaking something. Which . . . I knew was wrong."

As she spoke, she watched the curiosity in his expression give way to disbelief and surprise, then—as she told him about the items in the box—to an emotion that moved her so deeply she could barely finish her story. "I realized, again, that this isn't my home anymore. And that I needed to accept it."

"So . . ." He looked at her with a knowing gaze. "Those times I walked in and found you cleaning . . ."

She blushed and glanced away. "I was searching for this." She relinquished the box, their hands touching briefly in the exchange. The warmth of his felt so familiar somehow. "And there *are* treasures inside. Though none of great monetary value, I'm afraid."

He said nothing for a moment, then lifted the piece of paper. "And this?"

"It's a deed. From my grandfather. But it's obsolete now. Everything that belonged to the farm—my family's land, the house, what belongings remained—was included in the auction to cover the taxes."

As he read the document, his eyes narrowed. "And you found this just now?"

She nodded. "In the bottom of the clock." She laughed softly. "No telling how many times I've passed right by it. Both before we lost the house and again since I've been here. I was standing here in the hallway awhile ago and the clock chimed and . . . I don't know. It drew me somehow. Almost as if the box wanted to be found."

He looked at her again, but this time his expression was absent the gleam from before, yet held an intensity all the same. "Are you the oldest living child of Merle and Melna Darby?"

Authority edged his voice, and she could well imagine him in a court of law. "Yes," she whispered, "I am."

He smiled as though recalling a joke, though not an altogether funny one. "Then you, Miss Darby, are the legal owner of a portion of land on this farm. *If* this deed proves valid, which I have every reason to believe it will."

She searched his expression, then the deed when he handed it back to her, not following. Her gaze went to the description of the property. "The original land purchased by Wesley Tripp . . ." She looked up.

"The meadow," he said softly. "And the cabin. That's the plot of land that belonged to your grandparents. Isn't it?"

She briefly closed her eyes. "Yes, but . . . This can't be right. Everything was sold in the—"

"Property can only be sold by the legal owner. Which appears to be you, Miss Darby. This deed, dated September nineteenth, eighteen hundred fifty-four, supersedes the one I have. So it seems you own a portion of my land. Or what *was* my land."

Contrary to what she would have thought, his voice held a warmth that hinted at pleasure. And the smile she'd felt before returned, but not to her face. She felt it solely on the inside this time, as though the veil between this world and the next lifted ever so slightly, and Eternity whispered to her that she wasn't alone. God heard her. He saw her. He was leading her, every step of the way.

Still, she couldn't fathom that a part of Darby Farm was *hers*. Then it occurred to her. "The oldest living child," she said, voice weak. *Jake.* Her grandfather had intended for that land to go to him.

Aidan Bedford lifted a hand to her face and wiped away a tear she hadn't realized she'd shed, and his fingers lingered there, cradling her cheek. Her breath quickened, and she didn't know whether she moved closer or he did, but suddenly there was very little space between them. And she liked it that way.

"That land is what led me to Darby Farm." He fingered a strand of her hair. "It's what led me to you."

"Led you to me?" she whispered, again trying to follow and yet not. She didn't know how it was possible, but staring at his mouth, she could almost feel his lips on hers. "That land has always been my . . . favorite place." Her voice caught. "That's why you saw me there that day. Being there helps me to feel my family's love and . . . to remember I'm not alone."

"Savannah Darby," he whispered, tipping her chin upward. "It's nice to finally, *formally*, make your acquaintance."

"Likewise, Aidan Bed—"

He kissed her full on the mouth, a touch of mint on his breath. His lips were gentle at the start, then gained insistence. His hand moved to cradle the nape of her neck, and he deepened the kiss. She felt the delicious sensation all the way to the tips of her toes and back. But too soon, he broke the kiss and drew back slightly.

"Since I'm assuming you won't be open to selling your land, Miss Darby, I'm wondering if we might work out another arrangement."

All the warm places inside her warmed even more. Remembering how Jake had held a straight face longer than anyone she knew, she did her best to keep her humor in check. "And just what kind of arrangement are you referring to, Counselor?"

He smiled, then set aside the box and deed and took her in his arms. He kissed her again and cradled her face in his hands. "Do you have any idea how much I've thought about you? How much I've wanted to be with you? Ever since that day I saw you in the meadow. Ever since you said that to me." He briefly closed his eyes. "'But if everything in the world were such as this, where would the longing for heaven be?'" He kissed her again, slower this time, as though savoring her as she was him. "I'll do my best to make this house your home again, Savannah. The same for Andrew and Carolyne."

She peered up, eyeing him. "You know about Carolyne too?"

"I've been doing my homework." He broke into a grin. "We're already well on our way to filling this house with children, Savannah."

Her cheeks flamed, but she smiled. "I'm afraid we Southerners don't speak so openly of such matters . . . Aidan." She spoke his given name softly, and his eyes warmed.

"I'll do my best to remember that." He reached for her hand and entwined his fingers through hers. "And I'll do my best to make you happy."

"No need to worry on that count. I'm finer than a frog's hair split four ways." Seeing the surprise on his face, then how his smile faltered, she laughed. "That's something Jake, my oldest brother, used to say. He was always making us laugh." She briefly bowed her head. "He was killed in the war."

"Your brother," he whispered.

An urgency in his voice brought her head up. His eyes had gained a sheen—and a seriousness that leveled the emotion in the room.

"What's wrong?" she whispered.

"Only one other person I've known has ever used that phrase." He swallowed hard, his jaw tightening. "Where did your brother die, Savannah?"

She searched his eyes. "Near Charlotte, North Carolina. Why?"

He exhaled.

When he didn't answer, she retrieved the family photograph from the box and pointed to Jake. "You would have liked him, Aidan. And he, you."

He took the picture from her, his hand shaking, and stared at it for the longest time, then looked at her. "I knew him, Savannah," he whispered, voice hoarse with emotion. "I knew your brother. We—" He took a breath. "We met in a field one day. Between battles." He stared at the picture. "He spoke with such love of his home and family. It made me want what he had. *He's* why I'm here. We were on opposite sides of a bitter war, but . . . we were friends. However briefly."

Her chest aching, Savannah gripped his hand, unable to speak.

"I saw him get shot. I ran to him, but"—he shook his head—"there was nothing I could do. He died right there . . . in my arms. I closed his eyes, but . . . I swear I saw heaven in those eyes before he passed. Along with a peace I knew I wanted in my own life. And found . . . soon after."

As Aidan stared at the image of her brother's face in the photograph, all she could picture was Jake's sparkling smile, his laughter. And him lying there on the battlefield in those final moments. "He didn't die alone," she whispered, searching Aidan's eyes, remembering how many times she'd prayed for that very thing. For both her brothers and her father. "You were with him." She smiled through tears. "At the very last . . . he wasn't alone."

A faint smile tipped Aidan's mouth. "'Finer than a frog's hair split four ways.' Your brother had a unique way of phrasing things. And his love for his family and this land . . . it's what brought me here."

"It's what led you to me," she whispered, touching his face, silently marveling at God's quiet orchestration of lives and realizing she'd likely never know how often the Almighty did this. How often He interlaced such painful parts of this earthly journey with such joyous ones, weaving them together with such skill and grace. And beauty.

And she'd be forever grateful He did.

EPILOGUE

Almost three months later

"Toss me the ball this time, Aidan!" Andrew yelled.

"No!" Carolyne called. "Toss it to me."

Aidan grinned. "I'm going to toss it to the one person who isn't yelling at me right now!" He lofted the baseball in the air to Savannah, who caught it one-handed, then threw it back—right between her brother and sister down the road leading to the house. Carolyne took off running for it, but Andrew in his newly fashioned boots and leg braces gave quite a respectable chase.

Savannah laughed, watching them.

Aidan came up from behind and slipped his arms around his wife. She leaned back into him, and he felt as though he had the world in his embrace. A breeze stirred the trees overhead, and leaves of burnished gold and crimson fell like snowfall in autumn.

Savannah sighed against him. "Mrs. Eleanor Geoffrey at the Widows' and Children's Home said to thank you again for the draperies. She told me she never dreamed they'd ever have draperies so lovely."

"She's welcome to them. I'm just grateful you'd saved the ones from our house."

"*Our house.* I love the sound of that. Though I still can't believe you had me continue to sew the curtains even after you knew you didn't want them."

"I had to have *some* reason to keep you coming back out here. Until I was ready"—he kissed her left hand, looking at the gold wedding band and band with companion diamond—"to give you this."

She turned in his arms and kissed him, which earned a wince from her younger brother and a smooching sound from her little sister. Which didn't bother him or Savannah in the least.

Mrs. Pruitt rang the bell beside the front step, signaling lunch was ready, and they ate at the table on the porch, Mrs. Pruitt included. The older woman adored Andrew and Carolyne and was happier than he'd ever seen her. He looked around the table at the faces and knew that no amount of human orchestration could have brought together what had happened here—and on a faraway battlefield in North Carolina.

Jake Darby . . . Nashville.

His throat tightened, thinking about that young soldier, and he pledged again—as he did every day—that he would not only live this life to its fullest, but that he would live it for the One who had given him life.

He and Savannah had looked up the scripture reference scribbled on the back of the sketched likeness of her grandparents. Deuteronomy 29:29: *"The secret things belong unto the Lord our God: but those things which are revealed belong unto us and to our children for ever, that we may do all the words of this law."*

The verse had become even more touching when they'd discovered the note Merle Darby had written beside it in the margin, almost hidden in the binding of the Darby family Bible. Along with the verse,

Aidan had committed it to memory. *"May what is hidden within the covers of this book bring life to the souls of my children and also serve as an inheritance, both in this life and in the one to come."*

And the date written beside the note, *April sixth, eighteen hundred and sixty-three*, was the same as on the back of the drawn likeness of her grandparents. As best they could piece together that was the date Mr. Darby had finally told his wife about the land Savannah's maternal grandfather had left to their oldest child years earlier.

Aiden realized they'd likely never be certain, but they guessed that Melna Darby had refused the land due to the rift between her and her father. But Merle, in wisdom and love for his wife and children, had accepted it, then had held it in trust all those years.

Thinking again of the scripture and note, Aidan intended to do all he could to make good on Merle Darby's petition for the Darby family. *His* family now.

Savannah disappeared and returned minutes later. "Be careful. It's hot!"

"*Ooh!*" Carolyne swooned. "Peach cobbler! That's my favorite. It's heavenly."

The golden-brown juice from the cobbler had bubbled over and baked onto the sides and looked every bit as good as Aidan knew it was. Savannah spooned the flaky crust and savory fruit into dishes, serving him first, then Mrs. Pruitt, then her siblings.

And with every bite, he thought of Nashville. And of home. Both this one and the better one to come.

A NOTE FROM THE AUTHOR

Dear Reader,

Thanks for taking yet another journey with me. Your time is precious, and I appreciate you investing it with me.

The idea for *To Mend a Dream* came while I was writing *To Win Her Favor* (a Belle Meade Plantation novel) and when I first *met* Savannah Darby on the page. Savannah is a secondary character in that novel, but her story and all that she'd been through and endured in her young life spoke to me—and demanded its own story.

I love stories about hidden things. A hidden letter, message, or treasure. A trinket with a special meaning that's discovered only once the mystery is solved. But I'm so grateful that in Christ nothing is hidden.

He sees everything. Both the good and the bad in all of us. There's no use pretending with Him. In fact, pretending with Him is really only pretending with yourself. I firmly believe in God's master plan in our lives and in how He weaves our lives in and out of one another's, like He did with Jake, Aidan, and Savannah.

If you're hurting right now and are wondering if Jesus sees you, rest assured that He does. And He not only sees you, He's working for your eternal good this very moment, working in details of your life

He has yet to reveal to you, and that you may never know about until we reach Home. But trust Him. He's working.

As Proverbs 16:9 says, "We can make our plans, but the Lord determines our steps" (NLT). And aren't we grateful He does?

For you baking enthusiasts, I'm including the recipe for Savannah's Truly Southern Peach Cobbler featured in the story. This really is like the "good ol' days" cobbler my granny Agnes Preston Gattis used to make. Hope you enjoy!

I'd love to hear from you! Let's connect through one of the venues listed on my About the Author page.

Until next time . . .

Tamera Alexander

LOVE BEYOND LIMITS

Elizabeth Musser

With much love
for my precious daughter-in-law,
Lacy Elizabeth Musser,
and for my nieces,
Sadie Rosebud Wren
Lynnette Musser Haizlett
Rachelle Ashley Granski
Leighanne Michaelee Nichole Granski
Emily Joy Musser
Hannah Kaye Musser
Rachael Katherine "Katie" Goldsmith

All of you are beautiful young women who are finding your place
in this world. Hold tight to Jesus as you move forward
with all the strength and exuberance that I admire in each of you.

CHAPTER ONE

Wilkes County, Georgia
April 1868

THE ROCK SAILED THROUGH THE OPEN DOORWAY OF THE one-room schoolhouse, landing near Emily's feet. Startled, she bent down and saw that a piece of parchment had been tied around the stone. She removed it and read the words, printed in childlike block letters: KLAN IS ON THE WAY.

Emily stepped out into the encroaching darkness, gathered up her dress in one hand, and took off running toward the cabins of the freedmen, calling out, "Sam! Sam!"

An elderly Negro met her in the middle of the road, and she thrust the note into his hands. Sam had only learned how to read last year, but he deciphered the words quickly, then looked up at Emily and said, "Get outta here now, Miss Emily. Go on!"

"I'm not afraid of the Klaners, Sam. I'm staying with you."

Sam looked at Emily with wide eyes and shook his head. "You ain't never been afraid a nothin', Miss Emily. I knowed that. But you ain't goin' a stay here. Git yourself on upta the Big House now."

"The Klan's never killed a white woman." Emily lifted her head and squared her shoulders. "I'm staying."

185

The look on Sam's face changed from surprise to something dark, so dark it jolted Emily. "I done seen you come into this world, Miss Emily, and I don't aim ta see ya taken from it jus' now."

"They won't kill me!"

"They'll do worse. They'll make you wish you was dead. They'll make you watch while they kill us! Go on now!"

"But I care. There must be something I can do."

"You is young and brave, Miss Emily. But the only way you can help is ta git yourself back up to the house and fall on your knees and beg our Creator for mercy."

She saw both fear and anger smoldering in Sam's eyes. And then she heard the thunder of hoofbeats pounding the ground far in the distance. It sounded like death approaching.

With a sweep of his hand, old Sam grabbed her and pushed her toward the little white clapboard church. "You cain't git back to the Big House now. Get into the church and don't make a sound, Miss Emily. I beg you."

His hands were trembling so hard that Emily grabbed them in hers. "I'll stay here, I promise," she said. "You go on home."

She watched Sam leave and felt her heart breaking. He was the oldest of the Derracotts' former slaves, now a freedman. All of their slaves had stayed, trying to eke out a living on the thousand acres of farmland. *Sharecropping* was the word Father used. The slave quarters were gone, and now two dozen or more independent cabins formed a small community. With Father's reluctant permission, the Negroes had built a church and a school on the property.

Even the adults were going to school, educating themselves right along with their children. Every day Emily stood before them in the little schoolhouse they had erected two years ago and taught them to read and write.

And now horrible men, driven by hate, were terrorizing plantations, seizing the freedmen, beating some, hanging others, committing sheer butchery for no reason at all except the one that had plagued their little part of the world for so long: the need for white people to believe they were superior in every way to Negroes.

The hoofbeats grew louder, closer, and Emily fell to the floor, her heart hammering in her chest. *Lord God, dear Lord, please protect them. Protect us.*

The freed Negroes were not the only ones who lived in fear of these night riders. Many white Republicans were now picked out by this demented group, the Ku Klux Klan, for punishment—beating and even murder. But Emily did not fear for her father. He was a sworn Democrat through and through. Still, he was a fine man who had treated his slaves kindly on the plantation.

Before the war.

Emily collapsed on the floor, brushed her black ringlets of hair from her eyes, and wept. "Before the war!" she said out loud. Her whole life had made sense before the war. Now the plantation was practically in ruins, her two brothers were dead, and Mother looked frail and old. Father was a fine, good man, but he was weak. And afraid.

In 1867 Congress had divided the South into military districts and registered only voters who could take a loyalty oath to the United States and swear that they had not aided the Confederacy. These conditions had resulted in many white Southerners—including her father—being disenfranchised.

Emily brushed her fists across her face to swipe away the tears. For all those antebellum years, she'd been naïve and young. But at twenty, with three years of caring for dying soldiers behind her and two years as a teacher at the schoolhouse for the former slaves, she was no longer naïve and she no longer felt young. She wanted the freedmen to have all that was due them by the Constitution. Their rights. With the new Reconstruction Act passed in 1867, black men were granted the right to vote. They could learn and own property and even hold political office.

And die simply for being free.

She'd read the stories in the papers, heard the whisperings of raids in nearby Greene County and the horrible beating that Mr. James Corley had undergone, in front of his wife and daughter. Sixty-five assailants, hooded men, some of whom were the aristocrats of the town, had brutally beaten him to within an inch of his life. He would be forever scarred physically and in ways that went much deeper. The Klan had chosen James Corley because he was a black legislator from Georgia.

She felt the bile rise in her throat. And now the Klan was here in Wilkes County, on her father's plantation. As she knelt on the wooden floor of the church, she wondered who had delivered the warning.

Why had she stayed so late at the schoolhouse? She knew it wasn't wise to be out alone after dusk. But she loved the stillness after the adults and children headed to their cabins. Alone in that room, she could prepare lessons for the next day . . . and, if she was lucky, get another glimpse of Leroy.

There. She admitted it even as she heard a horse whinny, then the tramping of dozens of hooves. Light from burning torches glowed and blurred in the window as the angry mob rushed past the church toward the freedmen's cabins. Emily knew the Klaners were enraged at the thought of the black men on the plantation exercising their new rights to vote or hold a legislative office. These changes were making the South into something that was anathema to the hard-line Democrats, who were intent on taking the South back to antebellum days. Perhaps the black man was free, but he would live in terror of the white man's power.

How true it was.

The first shrill cry made her jump. Then the night exploded with terrifying, gut-piercing screams and the sound of the horses dancing in their places. Emily huddled in terror for perhaps ten minutes, though it felt like an hour. Then came boisterous shouts of victory from the men on the horses, and the hoofbeats again sounded past the church, going in the opposite direction. As Emily cowered in the corner, a lit torch crashed through the church window, landing only a few feet away by a stack of weathered hymnals. Before she could fling the torch out of the church, the hymnals had caught fire and her dress was singed.

She threw open the church door as the flames spread to the makeshift wooden pews, igniting them like kindling. Emily ran outside, watching through her tears as the white-hooded riders galloped into the night. In the distance she saw three cabins lit up on fire, and the families scrambling out into the open. Crying, choking on the smoke, she started toward them.

Then she stopped. Emily screamed, and her whole body began to shake. Washington Eager was swaying from a rope tied around a tree not ten feet away.

"Cut him down! Cut him down!" She heard Leroy's voice over the hysterical crying. He was beside her, then climbing on another man's shoulders, and with a wretched grunt, Leroy sliced the rope in two. The body fell in a heap to the ground. Washington, Leroy's older brother, was dead.

Emily stood riveted in her place. Leroy's face was covered in sweat and blood. He bent down, picked up Washington's lifeless body, and held it in his arms, sobbing and screaming to heaven.

Dizzy and nauseated, Emily forced herself to run to the Eager cabin. She was halfway there when she met Sam and his wife, Tammy, coming toward her.

"Where did they take our boy? What they done to Washington?"

Emily grabbed Tammy in her arms and held her tightly. Tammy had been her nursemaid, confidante, and personal slave for many years. It was Tammy whose strong black arms had held Emily when the soldier had appeared on the doorstep of the Big House with news of her brother Luke's death in some valley in the North. Tammy had held Emily again when, only four weeks later, another soldier had come to announce her brother Teddy's death.

And now Emily held her friend, her *friend*, and wept with her as Leroy walked the long path back to the cabins, his dead brother in his arms.

CHAPTER TWO

August 1868,
four months later

EMILY LEFT THE SCHOOLHOUSE FEELING ONLY SLIGHTLY reassured. No warning note had been thrown into the room. Still she felt wary, even full of dread, because of the news she had received that morning.

Before she turned to go to the house, she walked far out into the fields, fields that were fast turning white, as if it were snowing in the middle of August. King Cotton! That was what they called it throughout the South. Harvest time would soon be upon them. She loved the feel of the downy cotton in her hands; from an early age she had taken pleasure in sitting with the slaves and passing the cotton through the cotton gin.

Emily did not think much of Eli Whitney. Maybe he was famous for inventing the cotton gin way back in 1793, but to Emily he was *infamous*. It was his invention that had caused more slaves to be brought to Wilkes County, more slaves to be needed all throughout the South. The soil here was good for the special short-staple cotton foreign to the Sea Islands. Better soil, better cotton, bigger plantations—and that equaled more slaves.

More slaves. And now, here on her father's plantation, they were freedmen. Freedmen who still picked cotton. Tammy and Sam and Leroy and seventy-five other freedmen, women, and children would soon head out to the fields to pick King Cotton and share the revenue with her father. If there was any revenue.

Oh please, Lord. Don't let the crops fail again. For all of us. And please, Lord, keep the Klan away.

"Emily Joy!" Her father's voice startled her as she entered the parlor. "Where have you been? Your mother's been beside herself looking for you."

She moved quickly to her father and hugged him tightly. He looked old, his black hair tinged with gray, his shoulders slumped, his suit ill-fitting. She had always considered him strong and determined. Before . . .

"I was down at the schoolhouse preparing lessons."

Her father's face went pale. "At this hour? After what happened in the spring?"

"The time got away from me. And then I went out to the fields. It will be a good harvest this year, Father."

"We pray that it is so, Emily."

She hesitated before speaking her other thoughts. "I heard about the lynching yesterday in Oglethorpe County. What if the Klan comes back here tonight?"

She felt her father's body stiffen, and he moved one hand to cradle her head against his shoulder. "Shh, Emily. They won't come tonight."

"How do you know?" She sounded almost accusatory.

Her father let out a long sigh. "I don't know," he admitted. "I am just praying they don't come back. I pray they overlook Leroy's decision to join the Georgia legislature. He is foolish to be so outspoken."

"He is speaking out for the honor of his slain brother," Emily retorted.

Father stared at her sadly. "Yes, I know. And what good will that do? Does he want his parents to witness his hanging too? We are powerless against the Klan."

Emily let go of her father and walked into the library, where she pretended to peruse a book. Father was wrong! She had read in the papers of several states that had dared to stand up to the horrible Ku Klux Klan. Martial law had worked in Tennessee, Arkansas, and Texas.

But not here in Georgia.

In Georgia, the Democrats were taking back political power, moving backward toward white supremacy—through terror. Father had always disapproved of her strong Republican leanings, but she could not, would not, change. She had known, had *known*, since she was a girl of six, that slavery was wrong. From her earliest memories Emily lived with two juxtaposing beliefs: life on the plantation was heaven on earth, and slavery was one of the worst evils ever known to man. She had not known what to do about this evil at that age, but gradually she had learned.

And now the slaves were freedmen. Now she stood before them in their little one-room schoolhouse and taught children and adults together to read and write. She closed her eyes and saw the deep pride and wide smile on Leroy's face the first day he'd written his name.

Leroy! Emily slammed the book shut and shook her ringlets. *Get Leroy out of your mind*, she reprimanded herself. But if anything happened to him, to Sam and Tammy . . .

"Dinner's ready!" It was her mother's feeble voice. Once a stunning beauty, now Mother looked haggard, her auburn hair dull, her cheeks sunken. All sparkle had long since left her eyes, buried with Teddy and Luke.

Emily entered the dining room, smoothing her dark-blue dress that had gotten dusty as she had walked outside to the fields. She glanced at the long cherrywood table that could easily seat ten. Tonight it was set for five. That meant a visitor was expected.

Father and Mother came into the room, and Mother gave a quick glance around, inspecting the table setting. At least she still cared that her table was well set, with the fine china, crystal glasses, and silver inherited from Emily's grandmother.

Gladys, a former slave and now the kitchen maid, bustled by with a dish as Emily and her younger sister, Anna, took their places at the table.

"Lieutenant McGinnis is dining with us tonight," Mother said, and her gray eyes met Emily's. Solemn eyes communicating something important. Emily knew what she was supposed to read in those eyes.

Moments later, Thomas McGinnis entered the room. He wore civilian clothes and he was smooth-shaven, his blond hair combed back from his face, his blue eyes soft and, Emily thought, sad.

"My thanks, Mrs. Derracott, for this kind invitation." He bowed his head slightly and then said, "So good to see you, Anna. And Emily. You are as lovely as ever."

"How kind of you, *Lieutenant* McGinnis." Emily's eyes twinkled mischief briefly. For heaven's sake—why the formality? "If you give me another compliment, I'll arm wrestle you and win."

Lieutenant McGinnis laughed. "I have no doubt of that."

She gave him a peck on the cheek and noted her mother's approval. "It's good to see you again, Thomas."

They all sat.

Childhood friends, Emily and Thomas had played together, ridden horses together, even gotten into a fistfight once. She loved him like a brother, like the brothers she had lost. But only like a brother. And Mother, she knew, wanted it to be more.

"When did you get back to Wilkes County?" Emily asked once grace had been said.

"Only a few days ago."

"And for the work in Atlanta, any news?"

"Plenty of work on the railroads. Not much for a former farmer and soldier." His light-blue eyes rested on Emily. "Besides, Father needs me back at the plantation if we hope to make any profit this year. The cotton's almost ready for harvest, and the slaves won't work normal hours now."

"They're not slaves anymore, Thomas," Emily said.

"No, of course not," he conceded. She watched a muscle in his jaw harden. "They're high-and-mighty equals who refuse labor. Leave the black man alone and he does not know how to work. Without the means to discipline him, he becomes lazy."

"Oh, Thomas. Please don't tell me you're spouting the party line of the other crazy Democrats," Emily remonstrated.

"Thomas is right, Emily," her father said. "Our Negroes may have stayed on, but it's not the same as before."

Before the war.

"They won't work correctly," Father added.

"By 'correctly' you mean twelve-hour days for men, women, and children?" Emily replied.

"Well, yes."

"But Father, you wouldn't want to work out in the fields for that amount of time, would you? You wouldn't want me to, I'm sure!"

Father stared at Emily with a familiar twitch of annoyance. "I don't know how it has happened that I have raised a daughter as insubordinate as the slaves! Perhaps you are the one who has taught them these crazy ideas. They are not, nor will they ever be, our equals."

Emily felt the heat rising to her cheeks as the familiar conversation resurfaced. She preferred not to argue in front of Thomas.

"Your father is right, Emily. Blacks are ignorant; they are unable to learn. They are lazy and foolish. It's their race." Thomas said this quietly, steadily, but with a firm conviction.

"It's *our* race that has caused it," Emily blurted. "We have kept them ignorant, and I tell you, Thomas, Father, you're wrong! They are not lazy. They can learn, and they *do* learn. Every day they are learning! Quickly. With pride."

"Why you ever had the foolish idea to help at that schoolhouse with those uppity Northern women, I'll never understand," Father said, wiping a white starched napkin across his mouth.

How dare he humiliate me in front of Thomas, Emily fumed. Father was the one who was ignorant. "I beg your pardon, Father, but Miss Lillian and the other Northern women are many things, but certainly not uppity!" *And all men* are *equal.*

"That's enough, Emily," her mother broke in. "Gladys, we're ready for the next course."

Later Emily stood outside on the wraparound porch, leaning against one of the six fluted white columns and staring out at the magnolia trees that lined the drive to the plantation house. One of the prettiest homes in the whole state of Georgia, her father had often bragged. Now she wondered how much longer he could keep the house. And she could not watch the trees without seeing poor Washington's body swaying from that other tree down by the little church.

Thomas came out on the porch and stood beside her. "You were certainly contentious at dinner tonight."

She turned and looked up at him, her handsome friend. He was only a year older than she, but at twenty-one his face held the marks of war. He had a fatigue about him that perhaps nothing could erase.

Thomas, too, had lost two brothers in the war. He had been standing right next to Joseph when a bullet brought his brother down.

"I've always been contentious, haven't I, Thomas?"

He gave that tired smile and shrugged.

"I haven't changed, you know. I've always held these beliefs."

"Yes, but now you are too outspoken, Emily. You know what my soldier buddies say when we're together?"

"I have no idea." She turned her nose up and looked away.

"They say I've got myself a scalawag bride."

"How dare they!"

"I agree it's quite rude, but your Republican ideas are not a secret."

She didn't dare to correct his misunderstanding. She supposed she *was* a scalawag of sorts, if by that it meant she had opposed slavery and supported the Northern war effort. But it wasn't the discussion of her politics she was protesting—she was furious to be considered his *bride*.

Thomas reached for her hand. "My dear scalawag bride."

She pulled it away. "Aren't you being a bit presumptuous?"

"Yes, I suppose I am. But sometime soon, I'll make it formal. I promise you that, Emily."

She looked at him sadly. "Dear Thomas . . . you don't want a scalawag bride. I hope we will always be friends. I hope I will always respect you. But I know I can't change your beliefs, and no one will ever change mine. I won't make you miserable."

"You could never make me miserable, Emily."

She almost lost resolve when he looked at her like that, with love in his eyes. But she did not love him as a woman ought to love someone who would become her husband. Marrying a man with such differing basic beliefs would spell disaster. She could not do it.

Besides, she loved someone else. But the prospect of becoming *his* wife was not improbable. It was completely impossible.

CHAPTER THREE

On some afternoons after school, Emily sat in a pew in the little church on Father's property that the freedmen and women had built with their own hands, and had *rebuilt* after that dreadful night last April when it had burned to the ground, along with three of the freedmen's cabins. She sat and prayed. Often Miss Lillian, the other schoolteacher, joined her.

"You look deep in thought today, Emily."

"Yes, Miss Lillian. I suppose you'd say my heart is heavy. If people within the same family cannot even agree on the Negroes' position in society, how do we ever expect the issue of emancipation to be settled?"

"I don't believe it will be settled, at least no time soon," Miss Lillian replied. "Shortly after the war's end, I read something in the *Enquirer*—'Slavery is dead; the Negro is not; there is the misfortune.' Discussion about the meaning of free labor led to a nearly impossible conundrum between planters and former slaves. The past has to be unlearned by both parties, Emily." She gave a deep sigh. "I'm not telling you anything you don't already know. Between the planters' need for a disciplined labor force and the freedmen's quest for autonomy, conflict is inevitable. Change is difficult and comes oh so slowly."

Emily brushed her ringlets over her shoulder. "Whites and blacks will never trust each other, will they?" She didn't wait for Miss Lillian to answer. "It's just as Father and Thomas say—the whites are sure that blacks aren't industrious enough to work hard. But we know differently, Miss Lillian. Look at all they've accomplished in just three short years since the war. They've got their own churches and schools, the freedmen have the vote, they can even hold political office. They are becoming an important community. They are learning well how to exercise their rights."

Miss Lillian furrowed her brow and gave a slight shrug. "Emily, I believe the biggest problem in the South is that most of the white public still cannot conceive of the fact that blacks have any rights at all."

Emily nodded. *"Change is difficult and comes oh so slowly."* Miss Lillian was right. How in the world did anyone expect the South to suddenly adopt a whole new set of values, to amicably agree to the end of slavery, the enterprise upon which the South's economy had been based for almost two hundred years?

"I don't want to tear my family apart, Miss Lillian. You know that. I love my parents, and they have suffered so greatly. I cannot bear to have them suffer more. But they want me to marry a man who is good and true and a Democrat to the core. I cannot do that." She stood quickly, hands on her hips. "And it's so much deeper than my family! I cannot abide the hypocrisy of my nation! Look at the way the United States fought for its freedom from England. And then we went right back to living in the same way, with a worse forced-class structure on the slaves."

She walked to the window and stared out at the thick oak tree, the one that had held the swaying body of Washington Eager. She could not look at Miss Lillian when at last she whispered, "And I think that in my heart of hearts, I'm afraid. Afraid for myself. Afraid that my concern for our freedmen and women will hurt people I love. But I don't want to change. What should I do?"

She glanced at her friend, this lovely woman in her early forties with her reddish-brown hair swept back in a chignon. Miss Lillian was poised and gracious, and her bright-green eyes seemed to carry a sort of holy wisdom in them. There was nothing "uppity" about her.

"The Lord is not surprised by these circumstances, Emily." Those green eyes met Emily's and did not waver. "Throughout all of time, families have been divided over the issue of human rights. Ask God for guidance. He will surely give it to you." Miss Lillian's face was peaceful, radiant. "And I believe you, my dear child, are attuned to his voice." She winked. "In spite of that fiery exterior." Miss Lillian stood up also. "And now I'll be getting home."

Emily watched Miss Lillian leave the schoolhouse. She was one of many Northern women from the Missionary Aid Society who had come to the South to help educate the newly freed slaves. Emily remembered their first conversation two years before. "Wasn't it hard to leave your family?" Emily had asked. "Why did you come?"

"I figured it was best to obey God rather than man," Miss Lillian had replied, "and my Lord has given me the orders to be his servant to these needy people."

Emily hadn't forgotten the woman's words. She had called herself a *servant*, here to serve those who had been slaves. It was ironic and perplexing. And right. Absolutely the right way to think.

Emily figured that the South was one of the most confused places on earth. She agreed with Miss Lillian, that her place before God was to serve the freedmen and women. For three years she'd watched her father's former slaves work tirelessly to build a school and a church, to educate themselves and learn how to defend their rights. They had come so far. But it all felt very fragile. And dangerous.

CHAPTER FOUR

THE FOLLOWING DAY SHE ASKED LEROY TO WAIT FOR HER after the others had left. She needed to warn him again. At least that was the excuse she used to convince herself that she needed to see him. Alone.

"Yes, Miss Emily? Is there something I can do for you?" Leroy stood at the door of the one-room schoolhouse, proud and reserved, his eyes turned down. Her face flushed, just seeing him there. He was tall and broad-shouldered, like his father, but thicker, stronger. His profile was like a statue sculpted by one of the artists she had studied in school. A fine, chiseled ebony face, with a wide forehead and a straight nose and deep-brown eyes, intense and beautiful. He had loose, soft black curls that fell past his ears.

Standing in the doorway with him for anyone to see made her nervous. Yet she knew that was safer than being hidden from view. Much safer. Still, her voice caught when she tried to speak. "I . . . I wanted to . . ." She cleared her throat. "I need to talk to you about the delegation going to Atlanta. I'm afraid for all of you."

Leroy narrowed his eyes. "What exactly is you afraid of, Miss Emily?"

Not Miss Emily! Just Emily! Call me Emily! We're equals.

How much could she, should she, say? "Leroy, you know what happened to Mr. Ashburn. The Klan murdered him in his own house, that white man who had done so much for the cause of the Negro."

"The whole country knows what happened to Mr. Ashburn, Miss Emily. That was only the beginning of the Klan's business in Georgia. We seen worse since then."

"Yes, of course we have." Again the image of Washington's swaying body filled her mind. "Yes, I know, but I fear the danger for you is greater now that you have been appointed as a Georgia delegate. Father is afraid the Klan may seek you out. So am I. Please, can't you simply remain a preacher? Must you mix politics in?"

Leroy had walked outside and was leaning on the railing of the schoolhouse porch. "Cain't help it, Miss Emily. I aim to learn as much as I can about the law and run for office, just as Washington was planning to do. Being a delegate is the next step." He took a deep breath and turned his gaze to the cotton fields. "We'se in a critical time, Miss Emily. We Negroes. We have ta move forward while we got the vote, while the ex-Confederates is still banned from voting. Ain't no Negro goin' ta ignore politics before his Lawd. They goes together, Miss Emily, preaching the Word of God and helping my people keep their rights and move up in the world."

"But look what they did to Washington! Surely you can't help from the grave. Please consider that."

When Leroy looked at her, his eyes were hard. Usually they held a tender look, but today she saw determination and great sadness. She wished she could brush the sadness away.

"The way of the white man is to intimidate through fear. If'n he can keep us afraid, don't matter none about any laws being passed. No Negro will dare to vote if he thinks the Klan will pay a visit."

He turned, now facing Emily. "But I'm not afraid. I'll hold office. We can't give in ta fear and terrorizing. Our freedom is a very fragile thing, Miss Emily."

She nodded, biting her lip to keep back her tears. "I need to get home. Mother will be worried." She longed to reach out and touch his hand. Just one touch to communicate that she cared.

Oh yes, she cared. Much more than that.

She loved him.

Every night she twisted in bed, trying to figure out a future with Leroy. And every night she knew the dream was more than impossible. If nothing else, it was against the law for a white woman to marry a black man. So why did she love him so?

Emily said good-bye and turned to walk to the Big House. Mother had asked her to come home promptly from school today because Thomas was coming to dinner again. Mother was hoping for a proposal. Emily was not.

Anna stood in front of the oval mirror, admiring her new violet dress with its lace ruffles that brushed the floor. "Emily, it's perfect! My first new dress in so long. Thank you."

Emily accepted her little sister's quick hug with gratitude. At sixteen, Anna was stunning and smart. She deserved to look beautiful. Emily was not interested in catching the eye of any young man. Besides Leroy. Perhaps Thomas would take notice of Anna tonight.

She heard her mother ascending the staircase and hurried to survey her wardrobe, hoping to find something Mother considered suitable.

"Don't you look lovely, Anna! Where did you get this dress?"

"Oh, Mother, Emily bought it for me from the teaching salary she gets from the Missionary Aid Society. Isn't it the loveliest thing you have ever seen?"

Mother gave a glance at Emily. "Did you buy yourself a dress too?"

"Oh no," Emily said dismissively. "I still have several fine dresses to choose from."

"Indeed?" Mother said, but she couldn't conceal the irritation in her voice.

Throughout dinner, Emily noticed approvingly, Thomas gave Anna admiring glances from across the table. Anna was strong of spirit and character, but not like Emily. She would never go against her parents' beliefs and wishes. She could be the wife that Thomas deserved.

The wife that Thomas deserved.

Who was she to decide such a thing for him? Emily castigated herself for once again trying to control something else that was out of her control, for running ahead of reason. Ahead of reason and ahead of faith. Yes. Hadn't she seen enough damage done through love triangles? The Bible served up many stories, as did history. Jacob with Rachel and Leah. Anne and Mary Boleyn vying for Henry VIII. Did she dare entangle her sister in sentiments with Thomas? She scolded herself. No matter that Thomas admired Anna. She knew, they all knew, it was Emily he loved.

And what shall I do about that, Lord? I suppose you have in mind something a bit more noble than buying a dress for my sister.

She had no intention of breaking Thomas's heart. The Lord would have to give her a better idea. And soon.

After dinner, Emily walked with Anna and Thomas and her parents out to the gardens, where late-summer roses were in bloom. Off to the left, the view of the cotton crops was a mirror of white. Father put an arm around each daughter. "If the good Lord desires, we'll have a fine crop this year. I see it there spread across the fields, by God's mercies."

Emily wondered herself. Before the war her father's plantation had been one of many to contribute to the seven hundred thousand bales of cotton produced in the South. But the last two years, the total production was only a quarter of that, and the plantations were close to ruin.

Tomorrow Leroy and Sam and Tammy would head with the other freedmen to the fields, as sharecroppers instead of slaves, and work long, hard hours to harvest the cotton.

She felt a hand on her elbow and turned to see Thomas standing beside her.

"My dear friend, my dear Emily."

She felt her body stiffen at his gentle words, then relax as his hand took her by the elbow and guided her along a path in the rose garden.

"Do you know the memory that kept me going at times during the war?"

"I can't imagine."

"It was of you and me galloping through these fields as mere children."

Emily laughed. "Yes, those were lovely times, weren't they? We were invincible back then. Those rides seem to belong to a completely different life."

"It would give me great pleasure if we could take a ride together again. Would you consider reserving next Saturday afternoon? For a ride and a picnic?"

"That would be lovely," she answered before she'd thought better of it.

"Yes, it will be just like old times." But he looked at her so intently that she was afraid to think what that meant.

CHAPTER FIVE

OF COURSE EMILY COULD NOT TURN DOWN THOMAS'S REQUEST for a ride together. How many afternoons had she spent riding with him across dusty fields picked clean of cotton—laughing, carefree?

Before the war.

She closed her eyes and was only fourteen, galloping at full speed on her bay mare, Brandy, while Thomas pulled ahead, laughing, on Trooper, his steel-gray gelding, perhaps the most beautiful horse Emily had ever seen.

And here he was again, riding beside her on Trooper. The dappled gray gelding had a flaxen mane and tail. She had never seen another horse with the same distinct coloring. Trooper arched his neck under Thomas's tight rein. Then, as Thomas loosed his hold, the gelding shook his head so forcefully that his whole neck vibrated, and his mane, that magnificent flaxen mane, danced in all directions.

"He weathered the war well," Emily commented. "He is still as beautiful as the first day I saw him."

"He's the smartest horse on the planet. And the bravest, Emily. He saved my life a dozen times." Thomas patted the horse's neck, and Trooper threw his head in response, almost as if he understood what Thomas had said. Emily caught Thomas's eyes and saw they were not laughing, not happy. They held a deep sorrow in them, something almost akin to dread.

"He's faithful. That's why I am the only one to ride him. He knows I trust him."

She could not bear to let Thomas live with whatever memories were haunting him. "Come on, friend!" she called, nudging Brandy into a trot and then a canter. "Catch me if you can!"

Within a moment Thomas had taken the lead, bent over the gelding's neck, the flaxen mane whipping in his face and Emily following behind. She stopped worrying about his hinted proposal and thought only of the kindness and mischief that had once been in her friend's eyes when they rode together. She wondered if she would ever see that again.

———

Later they sat together on the blanket, the picnic Gladys had so carefully packed half eaten. Thomas's posture seemed more relaxed, and yet she knew he was not at ease. She was pestering him with her incessant questions. She should stop this conversation, but she could not. Why must she always bring up the subjects that divided them? Why, when she longed to see her friend rediscover some tiny bit of joy in life? But the words were already out.

"And you believe in the Klan? You cannot possibly support terrorism, Thomas. Barbarism. Butchery."

She felt her face flush, her temper flare. She closed her eyes momentarily, tried to pray for the ability to hold her tongue. She hated her rash, insensitive words, especially as she saw what they did to him.

"Emily, I have lived through a war that was only that. Barbarism. Butchery. I will spare you the details, but you saw it yourself as a nursemaid to the wounded and dying. You saw what we soldiers did to one another."

He glanced at her, and she thought she saw tears in his soft blue eyes. He turned and stared out into the field. "I stood on a hill in Virginia and watched a Union boy, a boy younger than myself, Emily, fire point-blank at my brother. I watched the bullet rip Joseph apart, and then I watched myself take careful aim and fire and kill that Union boy. I killed five men that day. Five boys, really. I shot them down, galloping on Trooper." Thomas met her eyes. "I wanted some sort of holy vengeance, I suppose. But it did me no good. I could not bring back my brother. He died in a puddle of blood with a swarm of gnats around his head. I could only cradle him there when the battle was over, and cry. And know that I was a murderer as sure as anyone else."

Tears sprang to her eyes so quickly that she could not stop them, and soon they were streaming down her face. Without thinking she reached over and took Thomas's hand. "I'm so sorry. Please forgive me for making you recall such painful memories."

He didn't respond to her touch; he sat stiff and almost cold, almost as if he were in a trance, or worse, as if he were reliving the scenes from that day over and over again in his mind.

At last he withdrew his hand from her grasp and whispered, "No, Emily, I don't approve of the Klan. And yet sometimes I wonder, am I any different from them? Sometimes I wonder if my hate is as strong as theirs. Sometimes I am afraid of what I became during the war." Now at last he looked straight into her eyes. "And I wonder if that man still lives inside me in some deep and godforsaken part of my soul."

Emily stared at the ceiling in her room, the hour long past midnight. She could not stop thinking of Thomas's eyes, of his voice, broken, almost afraid. "Forgive me, Lord," she whispered into the night. "I injured him. I did not mean to. I cannot seem to learn temperance. I cannot stop this mouth of mine from spouting all that runs through my head."

She thought of Miss Lillian—her quiet wisdom, her firm convictions, her peacefulness. Yes, Emily trusted God, sought to obey Christ. She *was* obeying him, she told herself. She was caring for the freedmen, speaking up for their rights. And yet, her zeal was fueled by a righteous anger. She did not feel peaceful.

She got out of bed and fell to her knees. "I want your peace, dear Lord. I want to do what is right out of love, not hate. I confess I do hate the Klan. I hate them all, and I hate the terror they have brought on this region. I don't know what to do with this hate, Lord. I simply have no idea."

She got up from her knees and returned to bed. She saw Thomas's sorrowful eyes, and then she thought of Leroy's eyes and the pride and determination that shone in them. She did not know which made her more afraid.

"Do you mind if I ask you a question that is rather personal, Miss Lillian?"

The older woman looked around from where she was stacking books and smiled. "Of course not, Emily. Ask away."

"How did you learn temperance? And peace? And wisdom? How did you gain these qualities? Or perhaps you possessed them all along?"

Emily wasn't prepared for Miss Lillian's hearty laughter. "Forgive me, Emily. I suppose you are the first person to assume I have those qualities. Thank you. I can assure you that my husband never said such a thing about me."

"You're married?" She had always thought of Miss Lillian as a spinster and couldn't imagine that she would have left her husband in the North to come and serve the Negroes.

"I am widowed. Years ago." She was silent for a few moments. "My dear husband put up with many things, one of which was my being so very opinionated about slavery. Not that he didn't oppose that evil. He, too, was against slavery and fought for the Union as a colonel. He was killed in battle in 1863." She looked off, lost in thought.

"I'm so sorry to hear it."

Miss Lillian turned to face Emily. "Yes, it was dreadful. But I shan't go down that path today. You asked how I learned temperance and peace and wisdom, and I will tell you that the good Lord put me with a man who modeled these things to me. Somehow, after living together for so many years, they rubbed off on me, I suppose."

"Ah. So I will have to wait to find that kind of husband."

Miss Lillian laughed again. "Not at all. God will teach you in his own way and in his own time. He chose my husband to show me how sharp was my tongue, how quickly I could injure the one I loved the most. I believe the Holy Ghost began his work on me in this realm after I had hurt my husband so deeply."

Emily didn't dare ask how Miss Lillian had hurt her husband. She could see that she'd spoken truth by the stricken look in the woman's eyes. After a long silence, Emily asked, "What was his name?"

"His name was Benjamin."

"Do you have children?"

"No, we were never able to have children. And so I have adopted all of these into my heart."

Emily had a hundred other questions she longed to ask Miss Lillian, but the older woman simply said, "You keep asking the Lord to teach you wisdom and temperance and to give you his peace." She cocked her head. "You know, his peace doesn't feel like the peace we naturally get when it's a lovely day and all seems well in the world. His peace comes in the midst of the hardest days. It's something a bit mysterious and supernatural. Ask him for that peace, Emily."

After she left Emily thought for a long time about Miss Lillian's comments. She had hurt Thomas. She had to make it right. She would figure out a way to have gentle, kind words, even if in the end they would perhaps break his heart. And she would ask for that special kind of peace. Miss Lillian said it was supernatural. Emily didn't know if she had ever in her life experienced something like that.

CHAPTER SIX

OF ALL THE PROGRESS THE NEGROES HAD MADE SINCE Emancipation, the church was their shining star. Once, many slaves throughout the South had cowered in the fields before dawn on Sundays, afraid of their masters' wrath if they were caught in worship. Others had sat silent on the back rows of the "white churches." Now they exercised the freedom to worship in their own churches in their own way, with buoyancy and joy. It seemed to Emily that they worshiped with their whole bodies and souls. She wished that a little of their enthusiasm and fervor could spill over to the white Methodist church her family attended.

She should not have gone to their church that morning, but she could not stop herself. Maybe prayers, even fervent ones, could not change a heart that was lovesick. She told herself that she simply wanted to listen to the Negroes sing. In reality, she wanted to hear Leroy preach; more than that she simply wanted to see Leroy, fresh back from his time in Atlanta.

So intent was she on her thoughts that she didn't notice Sam standing at the door watching her approach until she was nearly at the church herself.

"You ain't got no need to be here, Miss Emily. Go on home and git ta yur church now."

"But I want to hear Leroy's sermon."

Sam came to her, his brow a mass of wrinkles, his long, thin fingers pointing down toward the Big House. "Miss Emily, ain't nothing good a comin' of you staying with us. We be jus' fine worshipin' the Lawd here in our little church. You go on now."

She nodded and left the front porch of the reconstructed church building. But as soon as Sam went back inside, she stopped and retraced her steps, hiding on the side of the clapboard building, listening until she heard Leroy's voice floating out of the opened window.

". . . And so we is like those Israelites following that mighty warrior Moses to the Red Sea, yes, we is! And we is heading to our Promised Land, ain't we ever! Amen!"

A chorus of amens rang throughout the packed church, where over eighty Negroes crowded to worship.

She listened to Leroy's strong, solid voice, closed her eyes, and pictured herself out in the fields as a young teen, picking cotton beside him. The war had forced her into the fields, and she had happily complied to be near her friend.

"You be the toughest white woman I ever did know," Leroy had said back then.

When Emily had frowned, he put back his head and laughed. "Ain't nothin' but a compliment, Miss Emily. You knowed that. You out here workin' in the hot sun like us slaves. Ain't right."

"We're the same, Leroy. Before God we're just the same. And when this war is done, you'll see. You'll be free, and you will be able to choose whatever work you want. You'll be as free as I am!"

He had laughed at her and shaken his head and simply said, "My, my, Miss Emily, you shore does have a big imagination."

Not only was he free, Leroy had become a preacher among the freedmen as well as a delegate. That meant he also could be considered as one of the next political candidates. Emily heard Leroy again saying that it was impossible for him to separate religion and politics. A preacher had a duty to protect the political interests of his people. Emily thought of Washington and shivered.

Leroy's voice rose stronger, and anger spilled into it. "I was in Atlanta, and I'll tell you what happened. They's taken away our rights. Forced us out of the politics. The General Assembly conservative Democrats—and even some of the white Republicans—have taken away the offices of our three black senators and twenty-five black representatives. Expelled every one of them, even those who were only one-eighth black!"

Emily heard murmurs and protests of "It cain't be true!"

"It is true, my brothers and sisters. And I was there to hear the speech that Henry McNeal Turner gave in Atlanta on September 3, 'On the Eligibility of the Colored Members to Seats in the Georgia Legislature.'

"Mr. Turner is a finely educated Negro, one of the three black freedmen elected as a representative to the Georgia State Legislature. I wish you coulda seen him, standing up so tall and proud and confronting those otha representatives with his eloquent words."

There was a pause, and Emily strained to hear through the silence. Papers rustled, and then she heard Leroy's voice again.

"I will read you a part of Mr. Turner's speech. This is what he said: 'The scene presented in this House, today, is one unparalleled in the history of the world. From this day, back to the day when God breathed the breath of life into Adam, no analogy for it can be found. Never, in the history of the world, has a man been arraigned before a body clothed with legislative, judicial or executive functions, charged with the offence of being of a darker hue than his fellow men.'"

"Amen! Amen!" Emily heard the fellow freedmen and women saying over and over.

Leroy continued to read, "'Never in all the history of the great nations of this world—never before—has a man been arraigned, charged with an offence committed by the God of Heaven himself.'"

There was a roar of approval. Emily felt sick to her stomach. Leroy's voice resounded with eloquence and conviction. She could well imagine him making a speech like Mr. Turner's. And she heard the fury in his voice, the holy righteousness.

She left the window and hurried up to the Big House, where she would join Father, Mother, and Anna for a carriage ride to the Methodist church in town.

CHAPTER SEVEN

THE MOOD ON THE PLANTATION WAS GRIM AS NEWS OF A massacre in South Georgia flashed over telegraph wires and was printed in newspapers across the nation. Even Father and Thomas had expressed complete outrage. Now every eye in the schoolroom was riveted on Emily as she read the article from the front page of the Wilkes County newspaper.

She whispered the headline, "A Dozen Negroes Massacred in Camilla, Georgia," and heard the ripple of fear throughout the schoolroom.

Then she began to read. "'Although our state of Georgia at last fulfilled the requirements of Congress's Radical Reconstruction and was readmitted to the Union in July of this year, there was no peace. Earlier this month the Georgia state legislature expelled twenty-eight newly elected members because they were at least one-eighth black. Among those removed was southwest Georgia representative Philip Joiner. Yesterday, September 19, Joiner, along with northerners Francis F. Putney and William P. Pierce, led a twenty-five-mile march of several hundred blacks and a few whites from Albany to Camilla, the Mitchell County seat, to attend a Republican political rally.

"'Mitchell County whites, determined that no Republican rally would occur, stationed themselves in various storefronts and opened fire on the marchers as they entered the courthouse square in Camilla. A dozen marchers were killed and at least thirty others wounded. As the terrified survivors returned to Albany, hostile whites assaulted them for several miles. This is the worst case of racial violence reported in Reconstruction Georgia.'"

Some of the students began weeping, others simply moaned and shook their heads. At last Leroy stood and raised his fist high. "They aim to scare us into not voting! We will not give in to fear!"

Though his voice sounded strong and adamant, the amens in the schoolhouse were much less enthusiastic. Emily felt the fear in her stomach, set down the newspaper, buried her head in her hands, and cried.

A few days later, as the children filed out to go to their homes at the end of their lessons, the freedmen gathered in the schoolroom again. They had requested a special teaching session that had nothing to do with reading and writing, and everything to do with self-defense. A special guest was their "instructor"—Colonel Willingham, a carpet-bagger who had arrived in Georgia in 1866 and was a fervent supporter of the Negroes' rights.

Emily knew that Father would have forbidden her to stay for this "class," had he known, but if Miss Lillian was staying, she would listen too. The two women sat quietly in the back.

Colonel Willingham stood before the freedmen and asked, "How many of you served during the war?"

Twenty-three of the forty men in the room raised their hands.

"And how many of you know the proper way to use a gun?" The same hands rose again, plus a few more.

"You know that there are only a very few cases of the Negroes standing up to the Klan? You realize the risk could be complete annihilation?"

Emily felt weak at the word.

"Beggin' yur pardon, sir," Leroy said, "but do you have a better idea than us defendin' ourselves?"

The colonel did not answer at first. Finally he met Leroy's eyes and said, "What you're doing is right, men. Lord, have mercy on us all."

Sam stood, clutching an old rifle. "Word bin leakin' through the grapevine that the Negroes on the Philips' plantation has stood up to the Klan."

Several men nodded their agreement.

"Somebody done warned them of trouble," Leroy informed the men. "If we're ready with our weapons, and if the Good Lord sees fit to warn us ahead of time, I am sure we can hold off the Klan."

"Who warned them?" another freedman asked.

"Word is that two of the freedmen heard about it from someone who sneaked into the Klan meeting."

Emily thought of the note that had come crashing through the schoolhouse window last April right before the KKK's attack. *Klan on the way.* She remembered the childish block print. Yes, someone had known back then. Doubtless a freedman. But the warning had come too late.

She shuddered to think of the risk taken by a freedman spying on the KKK. What if Leroy decided to do that too?

CHAPTER EIGHT

Emily tried to concentrate on teaching the children as the perspiration trickled down her back. The men were out in the fields harvesting the cotton while the women and children fanned themselves in the schoolroom. But all Emily could think of were her father's words: "Impending storm."

Her heart had sunk when he pronounced those words early that morning. If there was a downpour, the rest of the cotton crop could be ruined, as had happened in 1865.

"The rain weakens the cotton fiber. Too much rain, and there is nothing you can do but watch all the hard work be lost." Her father's explanation from years ago wiggled its way into her thoughts.

The sky outside was still sunny, but off to the left gray clouds hovered.

With only the men working the fields, they would never harvest all the cotton in time. Emily couldn't stand there a moment longer.

"Children, today we're going to do a different kind of learning," she announced. "Today we're going to learn how 'many hands make light work,' as a wise man named John Heywood said a long time ago. You see the storm clouds gathering? We need to get the cotton harvested before the storm. How many of you have harvested cotton before?"

Every child over ten waved a hand in the air.

"How many of you would be willing to help harvest cotton today?"

The children broke into smiles and spoke almost in unison. "Yes, ma'am, Miss Emily. We's good at it. We be helping you. Yes, ma'am, we is."

The sky was almost black with clouds, and the children's hands were bleeding from picking cotton. Still they refused to leave the fields. Emily swiped her hand across her face and continued to pick. She could barely straighten her back, it was so sore from being perpetually bent over.

"Come on now, Miss Emily. Time for you to get yurself back up to the Big House," Sam said, his tall, skinny frame covered in dust and sweat. "You and Miss Lillian done a good thing for all of us today by letting the children and women help. But the storm's coming in strong now."

"But, Sam, there's so much left. We can't leave it now. I'll pick through the night if I have to." She stood up and put her hand to her brow, squinting as she gazed at the field. "A little rain never hurt any-one, Sam," she continued. "We have to keep going. Send the children home to eat. Anyone who wants to leave can do so. I'm staying. I'm picking this cotton for my father. I promise you I am."

"Yes, Miss Emily. I believe you."

She knew he didn't. Sam knew as well as anyone that Emily was picking the cotton so the sharecroppers would have enough to survive another year of freedom.

She couldn't help but notice Sam's smile.

The sky was black when Emily saw the first bolt of lightning zigzag its way toward the field. The ensuing thunder made her jump. The white flashes lit up the field enough for her to see the other workers, men and women, still picking.

"Get yurselves into the cabins!" The deep voice of Sam reverberated across the fields as the rain began to fall in little droplets. All day long they had picked and then hauled the bags of cotton to the storage shed. Now they hurried to get in the last bags before the rain soaked it.

Emily had just picked up her bag and was headed to the shed when a bolt of lightning split open the sky and flashed down in a knifelike stab at her feet. She screamed with the scorching pain and fell to the ground.

When she awoke, she was aware of Tammy leaning over her and a horrible stabbing pain in her head.

"Praise Jesus, she done opened her eyes." Tammy's voice sounded far away.

Now Sam spoke. "Miss Lillian's gone on up to the Big House to git the mistress. She be here afore long."

Emily tried to speak, but she had no strength. She couldn't even muster the energy to open her mouth. And the pain in her head!

She heard another voice now—Leroy's. "I thought she was dead for sure. Saw that bolt a lightning come fer her like it was thrown down by the devil hisself. Found her lying right there by her bag and paler than the cotton."

"Lord, have mercy. What wud we ah tol' her mamma ifn the lightning had kilt her?"

But Emily wanted to know the rest. Leroy had seen it; Leroy had found her.

"Picked her up right there, and dagburned lightning chased us all the way to the storage shed. Miracle we's okay."

He had picked her up! Leroy had bent down and touched her white skin and lifted her into his arms. And she had not one memory of it. All she had was a searing headache and the sound of hail popping off the roof of the cabin.

CHAPTER NINE

"I DON'T KNOW HOW YOU'RE NOT DEAD, EMILY!" ANNA WAS saying, leaning over her sister's bed in the bedroom of the Big House. "Tammy kept telling me how you simply refused to leave the fields."

Emily tried to smile. Two days after the incident her head still ached fiercely. "I'm thankful to the Lord for sparing my life. It all happened so suddenly. Sam called out the warning, and then the sky lit up as if it were a fireworks celebration and then we were all running for the storage shed and lightning was chasing me." She shut her eyes and shivered. "It was terrifying. Like trying to win over nature and realizing I have no power at all. None at all."

Anna fluffed her pillow and then passed another wet rag over Emily's forehead. "I don't suppose you feel like a visitor?"

Emily closed her eyes and sighed. "He's back?"

"He never left."

"Poor dear Thomas. If you could bring me some hot tea, I think the pain will subside. Yes, of course I'll see him."

"Don't frown so, Thomas. I'm alive. And I will be well."

Thomas was seated by her bed, and now he grasped her hand. "I have been so worried, Emily. If anything happened to you . . ."

Emily tried to focus on her friend, tried to push the pain away. "You see, nothing has happened at all. I'm quite fine. Better than that, Father says that almost none of the crop was lost. The hail only ruined a tiny percent. All the sharecroppers will have their due." She tried to smile, tried not to wince, as the pain pierced her forehead. She didn't want Thomas to continue in his line of thought. All she could think was that she had been in Leroy's arms. Leroy had saved her.

"I have had a discussion of sorts with your father, my Emily."

She frowned, irritated with the way he addressed her.

"We have agreed on a dowry and a date for the wedding." Now he let his hand tighten on her own. "We are thinking of—"

Emily turned to face him. All strength to answer seemed to vanish. She mumbled, "Thomas! Thomas, how dare you make plans without even consulting me . . ."

"I am consulting you now, my dear." He fell to one knee. "I am asking you to make me the happiest man in the world by agreeing to become my wife."

Emily's hand went to her brow, and she choked back a cry. He thought she loved him. He had never truly heard her protests, her insistence that she could not marry someone with such differing views on what she considered so important. And now she would have to wound him, perhaps more deeply than the memory of holding his dying brother in his arms in a battle somewhere in the North.

Unexpectedly, her eyes filled with tears. "Thomas, I . . . I can't answer you tonight . . ."

"Shh. I have taken you by surprise. Forgive me, dear. You are weak and tired. We will talk of this at another time, when you are stronger. Then we will have all the time in the world to talk and plan, alone . . ."

Emily lay back in her bed in tears. Why did Thomas love her? Why did he think that a marriage between them could work? How could she explain it in a way he would understand? Perhaps a letter would be the best way to communicate.

She would destroy her family if she refused to marry him. She knew it in her soul. Her mother could not stand another disappointment. The horror of death, the tragedy of Luke and Teddy, had stolen all the fight out of her. Now Emily saw bitterness and anger in her eyes, if they ever communicated anything other than deep, deep sorrow.

"Emily, Mama thought you were dead," Anna had confided. "When she first saw you at the cabin, so still and pale, she thought you were dead, like Teddy and Luke. She died a little bit more that day, I swear she did."

Now if she dared turn down Thomas's offer, could her mother bear the strain? But she must explain it to Thomas clearly.

"Anna," she said. "Could you bring me a pen and paper?"

"Are you sure you feel like writing?"

Emily was sure she did not, but she felt she had no other choice.

But when Anna returned with the fountain pen and paper, the throbbing in Emily's head was so fierce that all she could manage was a moan of "Thank you" before she closed her eyes and fell into a restless sleep.

The letter arrived the next afternoon as Anna spoon-fed Emily the thick potato soup that was Gladys's specialty.

"Delicious," Emily whispered, but even opening her mouth to receive a spoonful of her favorite soup drained her feeble energy.

"Do you want me to read it to you?" Anna offered.

"No, no. I will read it later." Emily's eyes were closed, but she had opened them long enough to know that the envelope bore her name in Thomas's handwriting.

She finished the soup, and Anna left the room with a loving glance back at her sister. "Soon you'll be back to your mischief-making ways," Anna teased, but Emily read the worry in her eyes.

"Thank you, dear little sister. I'm sure you're right."

Would the pounding in her head never end?

She reached for the letter, then hesitated. She leaned back on her pillow, closed her eyes, and thought of Miss Lillian. *Give me your wisdom, Lord, as I read Thomas's words.*

Seeing his fine cursive brought tears to her eyes. She did care for him. Then she slowly tore open the envelope, took a deep breath, and removed the single sheet of parchment.

> *My darling Emily,*
>
> *What can I do to convince you that our marriage will work? I am not your enemy in this time of confusion in the South. I do not share the strong convictions you have, and yet I will not oppose your voicing your opinion. I am proud to know you as an intelligent, caring, and faithful woman.*
>
> *But I cannot force you to love me as I love you. I have tried to woo you, to show you my love and concern and respect. But I can read your eyes. I will not talk of marriage again. I will wait for you to address the subject with me. And if your decision is no, I will respect you for this even as I grieve it.*
>
> *You are right, Emily. I do not want a wife who does not love me.*
>
> *Yours,*
> *Thomas*

Emily set down the letter. How was it that she felt such relief and yet such grief at the same time?

After she had spent two weeks in bed, Emily's headaches finally subsided. Thomas kept his word. He visited her often but did not speak of marriage. Instead, he read her the latest news in the paper, news of the successful cotton crop, news of the upcoming presidential election between Republican General Ulysses S. Grant and Democrat Horatio Seymour, news of their families and friends.

And then he would spend the remainder of his time trying to make her smile.

"Today, Emily, I will introduce you to a fascinating new board game. It has been all the rage in the North for several years now."

Emily smiled. A board game! Her mother considered dice from the devil and looked down upon games in general.

"I assure you this one is a 'morality game,' created by a fine young man by the name of Milton Bradley." Thomas placed a board on the table and opened it up. "It's called, most appropriately, 'The Checkered Game of Life.'"

Emily laughed at the pun, for indeed the board was checkered red and white. In the red squares were words such as *Fame*, *Ambition*, and *Wealth*, as well as *Gambling*, *Intemperance*, and *Prison*.

"The goal is to accumulate a hundred points by the time you reach the top right-cornered square marked *Happy Old Age*."

For over an hour Emily lost herself in the game, as she moved from a square marked *Poverty* to *School* to *Industry* and *Bravery*. Thomas laughed and laughed with each spin of the "teetotum"—a simple cardboard hexagon with sides numbered one through six. It had a wooden peg through the center, creating a spinning top. When Emily landed on *Politics*, she felt the heat rise in her cheeks, but Thomas said nothing at all. Instead he spun the teetotum again and moved forward three squares, landing on a square marked *Matrimony.* Their eyes met then, and Thomas's were filled with love.

That night, as she lay in bed, Emily realized that for a brief time she had forgotten about Leroy. In her dreams Thomas was riding Trooper while she followed happily behind on Brandy.

CHAPTER TEN

FATHER WOULD NEVER UNDERSTAND HER NEED TO BE AT THE festivities, but she would face his anger tomorrow. Tonight was a time of celebration at the Eagers' cabin. A miracle. It was simply a miracle. Timothy, their eldest son, sold into slavery as a boy of ten and separated from the family for twenty years, had returned.

Emily had always known of the deep heartache that Tammy bore. As a young girl, Emily had listened to the story.

"Our Timothy done be sold on the auction block before we's come to work for yur father. Praise God yur father done bought the rest of us when the old master got rid of us. But before he come along, the old master done sold Timothy, our oldest boy. Done it just to break my heart when I got too sick to pick cotton one fall. But I knowed our good Lawd be lookin' afta my boy. I pray for him every night and day. Sometime, sometime, our boy goin' ta come back to us. I knowed it. I do."

Indeed she had been right.

The week before, a telegram had come, and yesterday Timothy Eager had walked purposefully down the path to his parents' cabin and embraced them. Tammy's squeal of delight had blotted out her cries of terror over Washington's hanging, at least for the time being.

"Tomorrow we's killing the fatted calf and we's havin a feast. Yessir, we is," Sam had proclaimed.

Now every freedman, woman, and child on the plantation, along with Miss Lillian and Emily, gathered in the little church to celebrate. Timothy, a grown man of thirty, every bit as tall and sturdy as Leroy, stood beside his father, telling his story of being a slave on a plantation in Mississippi. A pig roasted on a spit outside, and vegetables and breads crowded the tables. Gladys had prepared five different pies, and now she stood, laughing and smiling, with Sam and Tammy.

Surrounded by the freedmen and women, Emily felt at home.

Sometime in the evening she made her way over to Leroy. "I'm so thrilled about Timothy's homecoming."

"Yes, Miss Emily. I ain't seen Mama so lighthearted and joyous in a long, long time. Mebbe never!"

Emily could not imagine the emotions of being reunited with a loved one after twenty years. But she imagined very well sharing other celebrations with the Eagers in the future. And then she chided herself for such thoughts, even as she let her gaze linger on Leroy for a few extra seconds.

The meal had ended and dessert was being eaten when Father and Mother came into the small church. Emily braced herself for the reproach. But then she saw her mother walk over to the dessert-laden table and set something down. Her famous coconut cake! Mother, who had not baked a cake since the war began eight years before.

Emily watched in amazement as her father hurried to Sam and Tammy and embraced them both warmly.

"We are mighty thankful for this day," Father said, first holding Sam by the shoulders and then repeatedly shaking his hand.

Mother held onto Tammy as tears streamed down her face. "Oh,

Tammy! How we have prayed for this day. Our Lord has heard our prayers. Praise be his name."

When Emily came up beside her father, he put his arms around her and kissed her softly on the head. In a voice cracking with emotion he said, "The good Lord has given us something to celebrate amidst all of the years of sorrow."

CHAPTER ELEVEN

THE DAY DAWNED WITH THE BRIGHT-BLUE COBALT SKY OF autumn and the sweet scent of fallen leaves, the perfect weather for a ride with Thomas. Now that he no longer spoke of marriage, Emily enjoyed her outings with her dear friend. Galloping behind Trooper, her face nestled in Brandy's black mane, Emily momentarily forgot her fear of the Klan's attacks, forgot the thrill of being close to Leroy. She was a young girl again, and the horrors of war and present difficulties did not exist.

It was almost like life before the war.

At last they slowed the horses and walked side by side. "What is the news from the freedmen, Emily?" Thomas asked.

Emily happily related the joyous reunion of Timothy with his family and the party that had ensued the night before. "Mother and Father participated. It was as if, as if they *did* see Sam and Tammy and the other freedmen as their equals. I was . . ." She searched for a word. "I was overcome."

Thomas reached down and patted Trooper's sweaty neck. "Give them time, Emily. Their world has changed dramatically. Your parents are fine people."

"Yes," she agreed. "As usual, I have been impetuous in my

judgment." After a few minutes of silence, she dared to broach the subject of politics. "I'm nervous about the presidential elections."

"Understandably so." Thomas met her eyes. His were impenetrable. "Do you believe your freedmen will vote in the elections?"

"I don't know. The Klan's continued violence has certainly intimidated some of them." Then she thought of Colonel Willingham's visits and his discussions of self-defense with Leroy and the others.

"I'm afraid that the Klan will be successful with their intimidation," Thomas said.

"Wilkes County had over a thousand Republican votes cast in April for Governor Bullock. Many of those were black votes, Thomas."

"Yes. But even though the ex-Confederates are still disenfranchised, I believe the results will be far different this time."

"You think that the Negroes and white Republicans will stay home?"

"Yes. I fear the Democrats will carry the vote."

"You *fear* that, Thomas? But you *are* a Democrat."

The way he looked at her made her stomach turn. "Yes, my dear Emily, but I want you to be prepared for such a disappointment. Perhaps you will be able to convince your freedmen to be very careful."

"What do you mean, Thomas?"

"I mean that I believe the Klan will do anything it takes to gain back its Democratic rule."

She thought of his statement over and over that night. Was Thomas trying to warn her? Did he want her to warn the freedmen on the plantation? And if so, of what?

Emily could not grasp the news that Reverend Hill related to his members sitting in the pews of the First Methodist Church the next morning.

"I am distressed to tell you that the Jacksons' plantation was visited by the Klan last night. Three Negroes were hanged, and Mr. Jackson was shot to death in front of his own family."

Emily felt the blood leave her face. Mr. Jackson, a member of the church, was one of the few white plantation owners who was now a Republican, supporting black suffrage and equal representation.

Whispered words of shock and anger filtered through the congregation.

"Let us take a moment for silent prayer in memory of those who lost their lives. Let us pray for their families. Let us pray for peace during the elections on Tuesday."

But though his voice communicated sorrow, in his gestures Reverend Hill did not seem sorrowful. Emily knew he was as much in favor of the Democratic return to power as anyone. While every head bowed, Emily wondered which of the members of the congregation were secretly thinking that if white supremacy had to be gained through terrorism, then so be it.

Thomas was waiting for Emily when she and her parents returned to the plantation after church. As she stepped out of the carriage, he approached, and she let him draw her into his arms. "How can it be true?" she said. "Please tell me it is just a rumor."

Thomas led her to the rose garden where she sank onto a bench. "I thought nothing worse could happen than what they did to poor Washington. Can you imagine Mr. Jackson, as fine a man as there ever was, being shot in front of his family?"

She began to sob, so hard she could not stop herself. And although Thomas held her, he said nothing comforting. Rather, she felt him stiffen, felt his grip so tight on her arm that she cried out in pain. "Thomas, you're hurting me."

When she met his eyes, they were hard and angry and tired all at the same time. "I'm sorry, dear. Forgive me. Yes, what a shock. What an absolute shock for you. For all of us."

But Thomas did not look shocked. He looked as if he knew exactly what had happened, and Emily could not tell if he was repulsed or secretly in favor of this atrocious act.

After sitting in silence for a few minutes, he said, "Even with this news, Mother still would like for you all to come to dinner on Wednesday evening."

"We are planning to come. But some of us will be rejoicing in the election results and others lamenting them."

"My hope is that we will be able to put politics behind us for one evening and simply enjoy one another's company."

Emily nodded, but she doubted that was possible.

He sighed heavily. "Do you think your freedmen will still vote?"

"I believe some of them will."

Now Thomas looked desperate. "Then you must convince them to stay away from the polls. Try. Please, Emily."

"What do you know, Thomas? What are you saying?"

"I'm saying that strong convictions can cause otherwise good, fine men to do horrible things."

Emily sucked in her breath. "You're frightening me, Thomas. Even more than I already was."

"I'm sorry, Emily. I am frightened too." He looked away, toward the freedmen's cabins, and ran his hands over his face.

"You look so tired, Thomas." Indeed, he once again resembled the tormented young soldier who'd returned from the war.

He made no comment but gave her hand a kiss. "I must be getting home."

Emily fled to the freedmen's quarters and banged on the Eagers' door. Tears streaming down her face, she cried to Tammy, "It is so awful about the Jackson plantation. Oh, Tammy." She closed her arms around her friend's thick waist, rested her head on the black woman's shoulder, and cried.

"Good Lawd done see them men. Good Lawd the one to get retribution, Miss Emily. We cain't fight them. They's too many, too strong."

"Please tell Leroy not to vote on Tuesday! Lieutenant McGinnis fears the worst from the Klan. And tonight, please tell everyone to be ready, in case there is violence. Tammy, I know the Klan is numerous, but the men have been preparing. Tell them to watch and pray!"

But Tammy was shaking her head, her face now covered with tears. "I kin tell them to be ready, yes I kin. But I cain't make my Leroy listen to me, no sirree. Cain't stop him from living out his convictions, Miss Emily."

Tammy had lived with suffering all of her life. She had worked in the fields from the time she could walk and had buried three children as babies. *And one as a young man*, Emily thought. Tammy wasn't afraid of suffering. She would not stop her son. If freedom meant death, the Eagers, and so many others, would choose death.

Tammy would not try to convince her son, and Leroy would not listen to his mother. Perhaps that was true. But he might listen to someone else. With Thomas's dire words ringing in her ears, Emily determined she would find a time to make Leroy listen to her. Very soon.

CHAPTER TWELVE

THE NEXT MORNING MISS LILLIAN JOINED EMILY IN THE schoolhouse before the students arrived. Emily had never seen the Northern woman look so completely shaken. Her face was drawn and alarmed. Even in the worst times, Miss Lillian had modeled peacefulness. But not today.

"Emily, you heard that the Jacksons' plantation was visited by the Klan Saturday night."

Emily nodded. "Yes, I know of the horror."

"I'm sorry to tell you the rest," Miss Lillian said, her voice quivering. "My dear friend and teacher, Isabella Jenkins, was there when the Klan came. She recognized some of the men." Miss Lillian reached out and held Emily to steady her. "She said she is sure that one was Lieutenant McGinnis."

Thomas! Emily braced herself on one of the students' desks. "That's impossible. Simply impossible, Miss Lillian. Were not the men hooded? She could not know them for certain."

"Yes, they were hooded. And on horses. She knows the lieutenant's horse well. She has seen him before at the Jackson plantation."

Emily felt her legs give out. Trooper. There was no mistaking Trooper.

"Perhaps someone else took the horse. Surely . . ."

"He's faithful. That's why I am the only one to ride him. He knows I trust him."

"I know how you care for him. I'm sorry to tell you, but I felt I must warn you. You could be in danger too. If Lieutenant McGinnis knows of the goings-on with our Negroes here . . ."

"Thank you for telling me," Emily whispered through the catch in her throat. It was all that she could get out.

It simply could not be true.

Somehow Emily got through the school day, numb. As soon as the children left the building, she walked in a daze in the empty cotton fields, trying to imagine it. Thomas a member of the Klan. Thomas riding Trooper to the Jackson plantation, along with a mob of other white-clad phantoms. Did his hand place the noose around the Negroes' necks? Had his hand fired the gun that killed Mr. Jackson?

"I believe the Klan will do anything it takes to gain back their Democratic rule."

Had he pronounced those words on their ride Saturday, knowing that he was planning on fulfilling them that very night?

Emily fell to her knees and vomited.

She tried to picture his face again as he sat with her in the rose garden the day before. Hard, angry, and definitely not surprised.

Oh, Thomas! Please, no.

And what had he said? He had looked at her with eyes worn from exhaustion. *"Strong convictions can cause otherwise good, fine men to do horrible things."*

She sank onto the ground with feelings of love and rage battling in her heart. What should she do? Betray Thomas? Warn the freedmen? Say nothing?

Emily trudged up toward the Big House, tears streaming down her face. As she passed the schoolhouse, she saw a crowd of sober-faced freedmen entering the small building along with Colonel Willingham. She waited for them all to go inside, then stood outside the opened window, straining to hear.

"We must be on our guard tonight," Colonel Willingham was saying. "With the election tomorrow and the murders at the Jackson plantation, I fear the worst."

Just as Thomas had said.

"We will be ready tonight." Leroy's voice resounded, loud and confidant. "We cannot give in to terror. We must band together and encourage one another to vote. Tomorrow is the day."

For a moment Emily heard nothing. Then a voice sounded in the stillness.

"Our families is afraid, you know it well, Leroy. Our women is beggin' us not to go down to the polls tomorrow. They's afraid it's goin' ta be jus' like in Camilla. The Klan'll be there to shoot and kill us. The women is terrified. We don't want ta leave them to raise our chillen alone."

Leroy's voice didn't waver as he replied. "I understand your fear. I still see Washington's body swinging from the tree in my worst nightmares. But I will be going to the polls to vote. I promise you that. I will go."

The sun was setting behind the bare fields as the men left the schoolhouse, each carrying a rifle. She supposed they would post an all-night vigil, awaiting the Klan's visit.

Thomas, please. It cannot be true.

She needed to talk with Leroy, but her father would start to worry if she didn't arrive at the plantation house soon. Anxiously, Emily waited for Leroy to exit with the others. When he did not, she entered the schoolroom where Leroy stood, alone, his back to her, his head bowed as if in prayer.

"Leroy?" she whispered, and he turned around.

"Miss Emily! What are you doing down here? It's almost dark."

"Yes, yes, I know. I must get up to the Big House. But . . ." She took a deep breath. "But I wanted to beg you not to vote. It's too dangerous. I'm afraid for you, Leroy."

"Klan wants us to be afraid. I've got to abide by my conscience, Miss Emily." He gave a sad smile. "Don't you be worrying for me. I'll be careful."

"But I love you, Leroy! I don't want anything to happen to you!" Emily threw her arms around the broad black shoulders of her former slave.

Leroy quietly and quickly removed her arms, moved away from her, and turned his back. "Don't you ever say those words again, Miss Emily. Them's dangerous words. Go on!"

"But I know you love me! I've seen the way you look at me . . ."

At that Leroy turned around, terror on his face. He shook his head, and his tangled hair touched his shoulders. "I never looked at you no way, Miss Emily. You say that to anyone, they'll hang me from the nearest tree and won't need no Klan to do it." Now his eyes were staring straight at the ground.

Emily stepped back, her face on fire. *Foolish, foolish girl!*

"I'm sorry, Leroy!" Her words came out in a gut-wrenching sob. "I didn't mean it. No. Of course you've never looked at me."

Her heart hammered in her chest, the only sound in the silent schoolroom.

He moved to the other side of the room, eyes turned away from her. "Miss Emily, these are hard times, good times, too, with some possibilities for us freedmen still out there. And I aim to fight for our rights. But ain't no time for a white girl to declare her love to a colored man. Ain't evah goin' ta be that time—least not in this future."

Emily felt the slow crawl of humiliation cover her face, and she stared at the ground. Tears stung her eyes, and she again reprimanded herself for her foolishness. Now Leroy would hate her!

"You've been our friend for all these years, Miss Emily. You've worked with us, cared for us, fought for our rights, and taught us." Now he turned back around, and his face was warmed by a smile. "You taught me to read my first word."

She met his eyes, and they murmured in unison, "Free."

Free.

It had seemed like such an appropriate word for him to learn back then.

"I'm mighty thankful for you, Miss Emily, for your teachin'. For your kindness. But all the good things you've done will be for naught if anyone ever suspects you have feelings for me. They'll crucify me, Miss Emily. I swear they will."

Now she could no longer keep the tears from spilling down her cheeks. She felt ripped in two and turned upside down.

"I'm so sorry, Leroy," she whispered. It was all she could get out.

Leroy walked onto the porch, and Emily followed, the two standing on opposite ends.

Then he spoke again. "If times was different, Emily"—he pronounced her name in the softest of voices—"if they was different, I'd talk to you 'bout otha things. But they ain't, and it's dangerous to dream. Besides, you got a fine young man who loves you. I seen you two togetha."

A fine young man! A member of the Klan!

She shook her head. She would tell Leroy about Thomas! And yet she hesitated as Leroy continued to speak. "And I am seeing a young woman in Atlanta. She was a former slave right here in Wilkes County on the Turner plantation."

Emily felt faint with his words.

"Please, please let go of your dream and know how thankful I am for you, Emily." Their eyes met, and she saw it there—the love, the sorrow, the understanding. For one brief second he touched her hand, and then he walked down the steps and back toward the freedmen's cabins.

Emily thought she had cried every tear in her body, but they came again, flowing freely, as she prepared for dinner with her parents and Anna. She could not face them with the truth of Thomas's betrayal and Leroy's confession. Despair tugged at her heart. No hope for Leroy. Of course not. Foolish, foolish girl. He loved someone else. She had to do what he said. She had to let her dream go.

And what of Thomas? If she told her parents that he was part of the Klan, surely they would agree that she should not marry him. Perhaps she wouldn't hurt them, split the family now, if they realized his loyalties were with terrorism. Surely they wouldn't wish her to marry a violent man.

But how could she tell them? She did not trust herself even to be able to sit at the table and bring a fork to her mouth. Everything inside her had plummeted with Miss Lillian's announcement about Thomas, and even further with Leroy's confession. She regarded her splotchy face in the mirror; no amount of powder could cover her humiliation and fear. She sank to the floor, her dress fanning out around her.

Anna knocked lightly on the door. "Ems? Are you all right? We're waiting on you for dinner."

"I . . . I cannot come," she said.

Anna opened the door and, finding her sister in tears, knelt down beside her. "Poor dear. I know the murders on the Jackson plantation have upset you." Her little sister took her shoulders and looked her in the eyes. "And you are worried for the freedmen and the elections tomorrow."

"Yes, Anna. I am too distraught to come to the table. Please apologize to Mother and Father."

Anna gave her a long embrace. "Rest, my dear sister." Before she left, she turned and said, "You cannot change history by yourself, Emily. Please don't try."

Never had Emily felt so confused, so heartbroken and alone. The flood of emotions crippled her. She sat on the floor unable to move, having no idea what to do.

And then, at last, she did.

She rose to her knees and cried out, "O Lord! Show me. Should I betray Thomas to our freedmen, to my family?"

Miss Lillian's words came to her. *"The Lord is not surprised by these circumstances, my dear Emily. Throughout all of time, families have been divided over the issue of human rights. Ask him for guidance. He will surely give it to you."*

On her knees she prayed out loud. "Lord, I do ask you for guidance. I feel so alone and terrified. I don't know what to do with this information. Nor with my heart."

She sat for an hour or more, her head bowed, her hands clasped, praying, crying, and listening for the Klan. At times she nodded off, only to reawaken with fear and heartbreak lodged deep inside.

Long after the tears had dried on her face, leaving it rough and salty, she sat and listened to the silence. She had poured out her heart to the Lord. Miss Lillian always said it was easy enough to cry out to God, but much harder to wait to hear his answer.

She waited.

Two scripture verses drifted into her memory, the first from somewhere in the Book of Isaiah: *Fear thou not; for I am with thee: be not dismayed; for I am thy God: I will strengthen thee; yea, I will help thee; yea, I will uphold thee with the right hand of my righteousness.*

She could not quote the second scripture reference, but she knew it occurred right when Moses led the Israelites out of Egypt and they were stuck—the Red Sea in front of them and the Egyptian army behind them. In that predicament, Moses had spoken these words: *The Lord shall fight for you, and ye shall hold your peace.*

Hold your peace. Be silent. Wait.

Peace.

And then she remembered something else that Miss Lillian had told her: *"His peace doesn't feel like the peace we naturally get when it's a lovely day and all seems well in the world. His peace comes in the midst of the hardest days. It's something a bit mysterious and supernatural. Ask him for that peace, Emily."*

"Give me that peace, Lord," she whispered many hours later, as she climbed into bed and fell asleep.

CHAPTER THIRTEEN

Wednesday, November 4, 1868

ALTHOUGH THE NEWSPAPER CLAIMED A HUGE REPUBLICAN victory with the election of General Ulysses S. Grant as the new president of the United States, Emily could only read the headlines with a sickening feeling of defeat as she remembered the scene from yesterday. Her father had forbidden her to go to the polls, but when Miss Lillian offered to accompany her and they promised to stay at a distance, he had acquiesced.

And she *had* seen: only one black voter had shown up.

Leroy.

Emily had trembled as she watched him walk forward to cast his ballot while the Klan members paraded by the polls on foot, silent and menacing. Emily's stomach cramped as she imagined Thomas hidden behind one of those flowing white sheets.

Oh, Leroy.

Oh, Thomas.

She had held her breath as Leroy left the square unharmed and then wept with relief.

And the truth came out this morning: Leroy's was the sole vote cast for General Grant in Wilkes County. The only one! The Klan's tactics had succeeded in terrifying the freedmen and even the white Republicans, with the result that only Georgia and one other state had not voted the majority for Ulysses S. Grant.

She tried to acknowledge the positive side of the election. This was, after all, the first time the black man was allowed to vote in a presidential election, thanks to the First Reconstruction Act. In all, over seven hundred thousand black men *had* voted. Surely that was great progress, no matter the defeat in Georgia. And Grant *had* carried every state but two. A Republican who believed in equal rights for the freedmen was the new president.

And the other news, the most important of all to Emily, was that the Klan had not visited their plantation on Monday night. Now that the election was over, surely there would be peace.

Peace.

Later that day, as Emily prepared to leave the schoolhouse, she found Leroy waiting on the porch. "May I speak with you, Miss Emily?"

"Of course." She felt her face on fire.

"Thank you for coming to support me at the polls yesterday."

"Of course," she whispered.

Leroy stood, bracing his arms on the railing and looking out toward the barren fields. He spoke as if to the wind. "I am heading to Atlanta this weekend, and I aim to ask the young woman I told you about to marry me."

Emily let out a breath and leaned against the railing on the other side of the porch. She could think of nothing to say.

"I wanted you to know."

"Thank you," she whispered. Then, "What's her name?"

"Her name is Clara."

Clara.

"And she has a little son, Jesse."

Emily's cheeks warmed. She didn't want to hear any more.

Leroy turned slowly and looked Emily straight in the eyes. "I had ta tell you, 'cause you two will surely meet one day. And you will wonder . . . for she looks white as you. Her mother became pregnant by her slave owner and birthed Clara. And Clara became pregnant by the same slave owner and birthed Jesse. She looks white, but she ain't. She's a former slave like me."

Emily tried to process this information, but her mind felt foggy. At last she said, "I pray you will be very happy with Clara."

"Yes, I believe we will be."

Then she dared to speak the rest. "You can marry a Negro woman who looks white because her father is a horrid slave owner, and that is fine. But when a girl who happens to be completely white loves a black man, it is forbidden. It seems so unfair."

Leroy nodded slowly. "I agree. But our Lord ain't never been tricked by that ol' devil. He sneaks around and makes life unfair, but you'll see, Emily. Our Lord will make good from it. I promise he will."

When her emotions had calmed enough, Emily took a deep breath. "Thank you, Leroy. May our Lord bless you."

As she walked back to the Big House, the sun slowly making its way west, Emily thought to herself, *Leroy is marrying a white Negro, and Thomas is a member of the Klan. There were two men that I loved, and I have lost them both. I am alone.*

The words throbbed in her head until only one remained. *Alone, alone, alone.*

Fear thou not, for I am with thee.

The thought whispered above the throbbing accusation, floating like a sweet memory in the evening chill. *I will strengthen thee; yea, I will help thee.*

"Help me, Lord," Emily whispered out loud, and then, as suddenly as the lightning had split the sky that fateful night in October, a feeling sizzled through her—the Holy Ghost's presence. Then it enveloped her softly, so the dread and the sorrow and the fear fell away, and what remained was something deep and unfathomable.

God's peace.

CHAPTER FOURTEEN

She had waited and prayed. She had kept silent. But now she knew, she knew as surely as she was to keep silent two days earlier that today she had to talk with Thomas. This conviction came amid the strange, strange peace that had captured her on the way back to the Big House. Now Emily's heart beat with a holy excitement. She had to confront him with the truth and beg him to stop. Tonight the whole family was invited to the McGinnis mansion for dinner. Before the meal, she would talk to Thomas. She must.

As the sun set across the naked cotton fields, she turned back to the house, walked inside, and began to ready herself for the dinner date. In a fog she pulled on her petticoat. Her fingers trembled as she buttoned the gold buttons on her deep-violet gown.

When she came downstairs, she found Father sitting in the library. She tried to keep her voice calm, tried to sound nonchalant.

"Father, would you mind terribly if I rode Brandy to the McGinnises' and met the rest of you there?"

He looked up from his paper. "My dear, you look stunning."

"Father, please answer my question."

"It will be dark soon."

"Not for another thirty minutes. Plenty of time for me to get to the plantation, and I'll have their stable boy bed down Brandy for the night. I can ride back in the buggy with you and Mother and Anna."

He looked skeptical.

"Please, Father. I've been so pent up over the election. I could use the fresh air."

"Go on, my child." Then he mumbled, "I can't imagine women-folk taking to horseback in their dinner finery! Only you, dear rebellious Emily." But he gave her a halfhearted smile.

Emily hurried to the barn and tacked up Brandy while Willum, the stable boy, stared after her, offering, "Please let me help you, Miss Emily."

She was in too big a hurry. Hurry! Was it the Holy Ghost or simply holy fear that propelled her to the McGinnis plantation, covering the five miles that separated the two plantations in lightning speed? She arrived completely out of breath, her dress crumpled, her ringlets clinging limply to her face. She dismounted and led Brandy into the McGinnises' stable and through the hallway, looking for Freddy, their stable boy.

That's when she saw it—Trooper's empty stall.

Emily stifled a cry. Where had Thomas gone? She *had* to talk to him.

Leaving Brandy with Freddy, she hurried to the McGinnis mansion and knocked on the door.

Lissy, the McGinnises' kitchen maid, answered. "Why, Miss Emily! Are you all right? You done look like you's seen a ghost!"

"Is Lieutenant Thomas at home? I must see him at once."

Lissy's eyebrows arched even higher, and a look of fear passed across her face. "I be thinking Lieutenant Thomas done left the plantation awhile ago."

"Are Mr. and Mrs. McGinnis here?"

"Yes, ma'am. I'll tell 'em you's here."

Emily tried to calm the rapid beating of her heart, tried to slow her breath.

When Mrs. McGinnis appeared, she said, "Emily, my dear! We weren't expecting you for another half hour."

"Yes, forgive me, Mrs. McGinnis, for arriving early, but I needed some fresh air, and Father said I could ride my mare over as long as I did so before dark. I had hoped to speak with Thomas before dinner."

The setting sun wove its beams between the columns on the porch of the McGinnis mansion, casting shadows that resembled ghosts on the wide expanse of lawn in front of the mansion.

Mrs. McGinnis looked exasperated. "That boy! I'd like to have him tarred and feathered! He rode off about an hour ago. He said he had important business to attend to in town." She frowned. "When I reminded him of our dinner date, he just smiled at me and said, 'Don't worry, Mother, I'll be back for dinner—my business in town has precisely to do with tonight.'"

Now Mrs. McGinnis's eyes held a sparkle of mischief. "I believe he was checking with Mr. Dubois, the jeweler." She raised her eyebrows and then winked at Emily.

"The jeweler?" Emily felt the blood drain out of her face. From the conspiratorial look Mrs. McGinnis was giving her, there was no mistaking her meaning. Thomas was planning to ask her to marry him that night, in spite of his promise not to bring it up again.

Surely not.

Mrs. McGinnis seemed not to notice Emily's discomfort. "But he warned us he might be late. He asked his father and me to keep the company 'occupied and in good spirits' until he got home." Then Emily's ashen face must have registered, for she said, "I'm sorry, Emily, are you well? You look quite distressed."

"No, I'm, I'm . . ." Emily struggled to make her lips form a smile. "I'm quite shocked! I don't know what to say." *Think, Emily. Think!*

"Say nothing, dear. Why don't you let Lissy help you freshen up, and I'll have refreshments brought in."

"No!" she said too quickly. Then, "I . . . If what you are implying is true, well . . ." She gave her best giggle. "Well, I want to meet Thomas alone."

Mrs. McGinnis nodded. "Of course you do. We'll give you plenty of time alone tonight."

"Oh, I don't think I can wait. Let me ride out to meet him!" *Slow down, Emily. You have got to make this believable.* "Oh, I'm dizzy with it, Mrs. McGinnis. Please forgive me. I feel I must see him first." She spun around and hugged her arms around herself, trying to sound like a girl in love. "Please assure my family that I have ridden out to join Thomas—so they won't worry."

"But, dear, it's dark. Please wait here. He won't be long now, I'm sure."

"It's not far into town. I'm sure I'll meet him before I've gone even a little way. Please understand. This is important to me."

Mrs. McGinnis was shaking her head. "You two will make a fine pair—both of you lovesick and impetuous." But she was smiling.

Emily clutched her stomach as she fled toward the barn. *If only Mrs. McGinnis knew. If only they all knew.*

She arrived at the stable out of breath. "Miss Emily! What's the matter?" Freddy asked.

"I need to take Brandy. I must go to town to meet Lieutenant McGinnis." When the boy didn't move, she added, "Don't worry, Freddy. Mrs. McGinnis knows I'm going. Please help me get Brandy ready."

Freddy nodded, looking confused, retrieved Brandy's tack, and went into the stall. The mare snorted her disapproval at having been taken from her hay as Freddy led her into the hallway. He bridled her and cinched the girth and then brought the stepladder and helped Emily remount.

"Thank you, Freddy."

She glanced back at Trooper's empty stall. Then she saw outside the stable that Father, Mother, and Anna had just arrived and were climbing out of the carriage. Before they could speak, Emily explained. "Thomas is coming back from town. I'm riding out to meet him!"

Father's face registered guarded surprise, and Mother's eyebrows rose. Anna shot her a questioning look.

Again Emily forced a silly giggle. "Don't worry, it's for a good reason. Ask Mrs. McGinnis. I'm sure you'll approve! We'll both be back soon." And she spurred Brandy into a canter.

In the short amount of time she'd been at the McGinnises' home, the sun had slipped away. Dusk grew thick and then darkness swallowed up the road. In a blur Emily rode back in the direction she had come from, toward her home. The way to town veered off on a road a half mile before the Derracott plantation.

Her mind was racing. What could she say to Thomas? How to confront him?

She had just arrived at the *V* in the road and taken the one leading away from her home, expecting at any moment to see Thomas loping toward her on Trooper.

Then she did see him, but he was not alone. Brandy reared and whinnied as a mob of white-sheeted riders came toward them, fiery torches lighting up the dark, and in the lead, a dappled horse whose flaxen mane shone like the moon against the pitch-black backdrop.

The Klan! Racing toward her home.

Fighting to stay on Brandy's back, Emily mouthed an astonished

Thomas as the horses with their ghostlike riders rushed past in a dazzling blur of fire and white.

Once again she had been wrong. *Thomas didn't go into town to meet a jeweler and pick up my wedding ring. He must have invited us to his home to make sure we would be absent when the Klan attacked the plantation.* Emily was shaking so hard she could not gain control of the mare, who danced wildly, throwing her head in the air and rearing again. At last she pulled Brandy to a halt and turned her in the direction of the mob. She sat on the horse, staring as the eerie glow gradually disappeared. She listened to her labored breathing, matching that of Brandy's. At last she recovered enough to spur Brandy forward again.

She had barely crossed the entrance to the plantation when once again she spied lighted torches far ahead. Brandy danced on pins and needles, whinnying loudly in response to the other horses' whinnies far in the distance—down toward the freedmen's cabins.

Emily galloped past the Big House, past the schoolroom and the little church, pulling Brandy to a halt as she watched at least thirty, perhaps forty, hooded men on horses surrounding the freedmen's cabins. And in the lead, a dappled gray horse with a flaxen mane and tail.

She watched, dumbfounded, as the freedmen spilled out of the cabins, dozens of them, all carrying rifles. All at once Trooper reared, and she heard Thomas, *her* Thomas, shouting, "Beware! The freedmen are armed!"

Shouts rang out and horses whinnied as the Klan faced the freedmen. Then Leroy appeared, his face set and determined, glowing in the light of the torches, his rifle aimed at the rearing gray horse.

She heard the weapon fire.

In another instant, the ghostlike figure riding Trooper had fallen to the ground. The gray steed bolted and galloped off in the wake of the other horses, with the Klaners fleeing as gunshots rang out from the armed Negroes.

Emily dismounted and ran to where the man lay, praying that it would not be Thomas, that she had been mistaken all along, that the voice she had heard was not his. But as she lifted the sheet from his face, Thomas's glazed eyes stared up at her.

Emily screamed.

Then Tammy and Sam and Leroy were beside her, kneeling over the bleeding man. "Lieutenant McGinnis!" Tammy was crying. "Is you hurt? Is you hurt bad?"

Leroy cupped Thomas's head in his hands, and Emily watched in disbelief as a faint smile spread across Thomas's face.

"Sure am glad your son is such a good shot," Thomas murmured. "Sure am thankful for that, Miss Tammy."

Then he fainted.

As Sam and Leroy carried Thomas into their cabin, Tammy held Emily and explained. "He bin informin' the freedmen now for almost six months. Eva' since before they done hanged our Washington. Bin attending them Klan meetings, bin ridin' out to the plantations, to the freedmen's cabins to warn them, to beg them to arm themselves, to be ready. Bin bringing rifles and such to us. He bin tryin' to protect us."

Tears streamed down Tammy's face. "Sometimes it's worked. Otha' times, like with Washington, waddna nothin' he could do." Tammy reached out and grabbed Emily's hand, her grip firm. "He's one of us, Miss Emily. He saved my Leroy tonight. They was coming for Leroy, and Lieutenant McGinnis done told him what to do."

Emily sat in stunned silence, trying to process Tammy's words as Tammy and Sam busied themselves with Thomas.

"Someone's gone to fetch Gladys—she done removed many a bullet during the war," Leroy was saying.

Emily knelt beside Thomas. "Oh, my friend. I'm so sorry. So sorry for everything."

"The Klan have to believe it was all real," he whispered to Emily. "Foolish girl! Go back to my house." His breath was heavy, his eyes closed. She reached for his hand and clasped it. "Make up whatever story your wild imagination can find, but don't you ever let anyone know you were here. Do you understand?" He managed to open his eyes, and Emily nodded.

"My friend. My dear, dear friend. I misjudged you so."

"You couldn't know, dear Emily. Go now. Quickly."

"Yes, yes, I will. But I must do one thing first." She bent down and softly kissed Thomas on the lips.

CHAPTER FIFTEEN

A DOZEN ROSES OF DIFFERING COLORS SPREAD THROUGHOUT
the garden, stubbornly displaying their colors in the fading November
sun. Emily looked at a soft yellow one and admired its tenacity.

Thomas caught her gaze and said, "It will be absolutely breathtaking out here for a spring wedding."

"Yes. Mother is beside herself with joy."

"And you, my dear scalawag bride?" As he spoke, his soft blue
eyes came alive with love.

Emily smiled at his term of affection and kissed him softly on
the forehead. His shoulder was bandaged, and a sling held his arm in
place. He swore it was healing, but Emily was unconvinced.

"I, my dear Thomas, am simply overcome. It is all so unexpected.
The veil has been lifted, and I still have not recovered."

"Then I hope you never recover, if it means you becoming my wife."

She snuggled closer to him, drawing a quilt around their shoulders. "I will delightedly be your wife. But you, *you* are the scalawag,
my Thomas."

My Thomas.

They had spoken of it every day since the Klan's raid on the plantation, but she whispered it again. "It was something so strong. I felt

it, Thomas, felt a piercing inside that I must, I *must* find you. Do you believe it was the Holy Ghost?"

"Yes, I believe that God propelled you to the plantation so you would see the truth." Thomas drew his good arm more tightly around her. "I would never have wished it so, but now I thank God for it."

"Yes."

"You know, though, Emily, that someday I would have told you, when I felt it safe." This he had also repeated to her a dozen times in the past days.

"Yes. But that would have been a long time in coming."

"Certainly," Thomas admitted.

"It isn't safe even now."

"No, especially not now. And what we do *now* is what we must determine." He kissed her hand.

"Yes, tell me of your time in Atlanta. What have you learned? Will you formally resign from the Klan?"

"Moving to Atlanta will be a big enough breach. I'll have much more freedom there."

"But you love the plantation." This she had not dared to say before. "How can you leave it?"

"It is better for all of us that I move to Atlanta. On my last trip I met several businessmen who wish to help me find employment."

"And your parents?"

"Father has encouraged me to leave." He met her eyes. "When I explained my situation to my father and yours, they both supported my decision to seek employment in Atlanta and find a suitable home for us."

Emily thought back to that night when she had ridden back to the McGinnis plantation, fumbling with her words, trying to explain the news while Thomas lay in a bed at her house surrounded by Tammy and Gladys and Sam and Leroy. Later she had described to him the reaction of her parents and his. "They were confused, terrified, angry, relieved, dumbfounded. I've never felt so many emotions bumping around in one room all at the same time."

She smiled at Thomas. "You know that Father was completely baffled at first about my change of heart toward you."

"Baffled, perhaps, but delighted too. I have appreciated his trust, his support of my desire to marry you, even though I had not been completely honest with him for all those months."

"Father respects you, Thomas. And Mother, as I've said, is simply beside herself."

Thomas nodded. "Emily, our parents have watched their whole way of life come crashing down. They will come around, but it takes time, perhaps a long time, for people to learn to accept those who are different. Some will never change, but our parents will, I am sure of it."

"I trust it will be so."

"I suppose you've heard that Leroy is marrying and moving to Atlanta too."

"Yes, I have heard this." Now she wanted to tell him the one thing that she had not yet dared to admit. She cleared her throat and whispered, "I thought I was in love with him."

"I know."

She pulled back from his embrace. "You know?"

"Leroy and I spoke often. It was he who in fact told me I should reveal my true loyalties to you before it was too late."

Emily managed a smile. "I misjudged so many things!"

"You could not know."

"And you are very sure you want to spend your life with the likes of me? A woman who is strong-willed, impetuous, lacking wisdom."

"I am absolutely positive that I want to spend my life with a beautiful woman who is learning temperance and grace while still holding firm to her convictions."

Temperance! Would not Miss Lillian laugh to hear Thomas pronounce that word? Then Emily pouted. "And what will I do for all these months with you so far away in Atlanta?"

Now Thomas brought her close again and met her lips with his in a long, luxurious kiss. Emily melted into his arms as Thomas whispered, "You will plan our wedding, and I, my dear, will plan the rest of our life."

EPILOGUE

EMILY'S DAUGHTERS, RACHEL AND NICOLE, HELD ONTO HER legs tightly as Emily stood at the edge of the cotton fields on her parents' plantation. She breathed in the fragrance of late summer on the plantation, so different from the fast pace of their lives in Atlanta.

She sighed, feeling the pinching in her heart as she thought back to her former life.

"It looks like white fluffy clouds growing in the field," three-year-old Rachel exclaimed, exuberant.

"Clouds," chimed in two-year-old Nicole.

Yes, yes it does.

"This is where Mama grew up. And sometimes I went into the fields and picked cotton."

"Can we pick cotton, Mama? Please, please," begged Rachel.

"Yes, perhaps we will tomorrow, girls."

Emily closed her eyes and saw herself bending and picking on that night when the lightning had chased and stabbed her. Then she winced as the memory of Washington's body swinging from the oak tree flashed into her mind. In another memory, Leroy was aiming his rifle at Thomas and pulling the trigger.

So many difficult memories from the year of 1868.

And yet Emily always thought back to those days as short and bittersweet parentheses in time. A time of exponential change and possibility.

She knelt down beside her daughters, drawing them close as she looked out to where the sharecroppers worked in the fields.

The freedmen.

But not truly free.

Earlier in 1872, Georgia had been completely "redeemed," as the Democrats called it, meaning that the state had returned to conservative white Democratic control. She thought of the defunct Ku Klux Klan, defunct only because there was no longer a need. White supremacy reigned again in Georgia, as it had before the war.

Antebellum, Emily thought sadly.

Thomas came up behind her, encircling her waist with his arms. "Here you are! All my beautiful girls!"

"Mama says we can pick cotton tomorrow," Rachel squealed, now grabbing hold of her father's hand.

"Then I suppose we shall," Thomas said, laughing.

How Emily enjoyed hearing her husband laugh, and seeing a spark of hope in his eyes.

He came beside her, and she rested her head on his shoulder. Many things had changed for the better, and yet she wondered how many years would pass before true equality between whites and blacks existed in Georgia.

Leroy still fought for it. Just the week before, she and Thomas had attended his church in Atlanta and listened to his eloquent sermon, punctuated with scripture and politics. After church, the two families dined together at Leroy and Clara's home, Emily and Clara sharing stories of their children's antics.

There in the sanctuary of that home for that afternoon, they tasted true equality. And brotherly love. Love beyond the limits of what society imposed.

As Emily, Thomas, and the girls turned from the fields and made their way up to the Big House where they would share dinner with Father, Mother, and Anna, Emily prayed for the day when that kind of love and equality would be spread throughout the land.

A NOTE FROM THE AUTHOR

ALTHOUGH I AM FROM ATLANTA AND TOOK PLENTY OF HISTORY classes in high school and college, I did not remember the hope and horror of the Reconstruction period in Georgia, and was frankly embarrassed at my lack of knowledge as I began delving into this 'parenthesis of freedom' in the life of black Georgians. The following information (taken from www.georgiaencyclopedia.org) gives a few details about the end of Reconstruction:

Conservatives used terror, intimidation, and the Ku Klux Klan to "redeem" the state of Georgia. One quarter of the black legislators were killed, threatened, beaten, or jailed. In the December 1870 elections, the Democrats won an overwhelming victory. Black Georgian voters, first manipulated, were ultimately disenfranchised, beginning in the 1890s. The last black member of the General Assembly, W. H. Rogers, resigned in 1907 as the final representative of the Reconstruction-era coastal-Georgia political machine. Not until 1963, during the civil rights movement (also called "Second Reconstruction" by some scholars), would another black politician, Leroy Johnson (a Democrat) enter the General Assembly, with black Republican, Willie Talton of Warner Robins, not following until 2005.

In large part, for the masses of Georgians, black and white, the major legacy of Reconstruction would be a sharecropping life. Property taxes, which had previously fallen most heavily on slave owners, now fell on landowners, and during Reconstruction tax rates increased as well. For this and other reasons, a transformation took place. While the majority of Southern whites had owned land during the antebellum period, the majority had become landless sharecroppers by the early 1900s. Though landownership by Georgia's black farmers had grown to 13 percent by 1900, most remained sharecroppers. White and black Georgians awaited another transformation of the economy; it would take World War II (1941–45) to bring it about. Where black political rights were concerned, another Reconstruction would be necessary.

AN OUTLAW'S HEART

Shelley Gray

To Mendy.
Thank you for years of friendship, beautiful
smiles, and, of course, for spending one eventful
evening with me at the Menger Hotel bar.

CHAPTER ONE

July 1878

RUSSELL ANDREW CHAMPION HAD KNOWN BEFORE HE'D SET one dust-covered boot on the parched Texas ground that it had been a mistake to come home. No good ever came from seeing things that had haunted a man's dreams for well on seven years.

The outlaw Scout Proffitt had been correct when he'd muttered under his breath that some things can never be undone.

Instead of returning to Broken Arrow, Russell should have taken another drink, ridden in another direction, agreed to another job.

He should have done something. Heck, anything, in order to avoid the pain he was about to bear. After all, some things were marked too deeply in his memory to ever attempt to erase. He shouldn't have even thought to try.

In his case, it was sorely obvious that some wishes and dreams were never destined to become reality. Not any of the good ones anyway. He would've thought he could have figured that out by now.

But it seemed he hadn't. Long ago, he reckoned he must have some need to refuse to live in peace. He needed to shake things up in his life whenever he felt like he was almost the right sort of person.

But now, as he looked around the Iron Rail Ranch, it wasn't his past fears that painted everything in front of him the color of rust and pain. Instead, a deep feeling of dismay colored his vision.

It turned out that the Iron Rail Ranch was not prettier or nicer than his middle-of-the-night nightmares. In fact, it was all a whole lot worse than he remembered it.

Dismounting from Candy—his sorry-named mare he'd never had the gumption to rename—Russell cursed his weaknesses. A real man would have long ago pushed his past firmly where it needed to go. Somewhere deep in the ground. Preferably six feet under.

Yet here he was.

"Looks like I haven't learned much in twenty-two years of living, Candy," he murmured.

When the mare merely blew out a rush of impatience, Russell figured his fall was now complete. Even his horse couldn't see the benefit of what he was doing.

He couldn't blame her for that however. At first glance his house looked like it had fallen upon hard times a good five years ago and then had determined to stay standing out of sheer stubbornness. It appeared as if no one had gone near it with a paintbrush or a hammer since he'd been gone. Paint was peeling, the two windows were cracked, and one of the front steps had given in to decay and collapsed.

The whole thing made him kind of sad, and he hadn't thought such a thing was possible. After staring at the door shut tight against the stifling heat, he turned away and guided his horse to the barn.

It, too, looked like it not only had seen better days, but it wasn't as if it hadn't been all that good in the first place. Course that was probably because it hadn't been all that much to begin with.

Spurs clicked against dirt as he guided Candy into the dark confines of the barn. The horse fussed a bit and pawed the ground with her hooves. She wasn't happy about her new surroundings.

"I know, girl. Place looks worse than a ghost town in Nebraska. And where in the world is Ma's gray mare?"

Candy, of course, had no answer.

Lost in old memories again, Russell didn't need it. Thinking about his stepfather's horse, he reflected that the gelding had had the best of Emmitt Johnson. Such that it was. Kismet had been everything Candy had never been. A fine specimen of horseflesh who'd been coddled like a favored child all his life.

But now all that remained of the beautiful horse with that exotic-sounding name was one long saddle slung over the rail like a child's leftover toy. The leather was dry and parched. Cracking. Russell couldn't stop staring at it—he would've gotten beaten well and good for even thinking about leaving a saddle in such a state.

Rubbing his backside at the memory, he frowned. Matter of fact, he had gotten beaten more than once for not putting tack up like he should.

But now all that seemed to care were his memories.

Candy nervously sidestepped and whinnied when he opened the stall door.

Wrinkling his nose at the scent of soiled straw, rotten wood, and a multitude of things better left unidentified, Russell sighed. "Can't say I blame you, girl." Dropping her reins—'cause Lord knew she sure wasn't going anywhere—Russell found a rake and began mucking out the stall. Subconsciously, the muscles in his arms and shoulders settled into the forgotten rhythm. And just as automatically, his mind drifted away from where he was, imagining other things. Imagining a sweeter life.

Years ago, those daydreams had been his refuge.

When he'd ridden with the Walton Gang, fanciful daydreams had kept him alive. For a man with so very few good things to think about, dreams were the only things worth saving. In the bitter years after, those thoughts had kept him from giving in to despair. Now, his dreams embarrassed him.

Once he'd removed the old straw and smoothed the dirt, he breathed a sigh of relief. But fresh oats and hay would have to be found soon. Because even though Candy was not real fancy, he didn't have the heart to let her stay in such a dirty place for even a few minutes.

When the stall was as good as he could get it, he took off the saddle, found her some water, and rubbed her down. "Come on in, Can," he said, gently pulling on her bridle. "It's not good, but it's all we've got." When she planted a somewhat skeptical eye on him, he chuckled. "We've had worse. You know that."

After he closed the stall's door, he faced the inevitable. He couldn't put it off anymore . . . it was time to see his mother. Russell turned and walked to the house, finally admitting to himself the awful truth. He hadn't come back to see the land or a ramshackle barn or an old house on the verge of ruin.

No, he'd come back to see his mother.

He had no idea if she was going to let him in. There was a pretty good chance she wouldn't. After all, only a cold woman without a heart would cast out her son when he was fifteen.

There was a real good chance she wasn't going to feel any kinder toward him even after all these years. Especially since he never sent her a single note or card since he'd left.

He could only hope that she'd tell him what happened to Nora before she asked him to leave. It would ease his mind to know that she was happily married and looking over a slew of kids.

Steeling his shoulders, he marched to the door and knocked twice. When no one answered, Russell jiggled the handle, fully prepared to bust open the lock if he needed to.

Instead, the handle turned easily. The door swung open on well-oiled hinges, allowing him entrance to a bare entryway.

"Hello?" he called out as he stepped over the threshold. He felt like a fool, calling out the way he did. No one did that. Not returning sons. Definitely not men who'd ridden with an outlaw gang.

For a moment he considered turning around and retrieving his treasured Colt out of his saddlebag. That was the smart thing. But though every man in the Walton Gang would have cuffed him on the side of the head for walking into a place unarmed, facing his mother with a pistol in his hand didn't seem like the right thing to do.

After all, there had to be somewhere in the world where a man could let his guard down. Somewhere a man could go without looking at it through the narrow confines of a weapon.

But as a telltale itch traveled up his spine, he began to think he had seriously misjudged the situation. His gut told him something was wrong. And though he hadn't been an especially good outlaw, he had learned a thing or two.

Cautiously, he entered the kitchen. To his relief, it lay still and ordinary. Recently used and recently tidied. But what, really, did he know about such things anymore?

"Hello?" he called out again. Now he found himself fighting a lump in his throat. He pretended it was from nerves instead of raw emotion. "Anybody here?"

When only silence continued to meet him, Russell swallowed and tried to think on the right side of things.

Maybe it was good he wasn't calling out for his mother. Maybe she was long gone, and all that remained of her here were his memories.

The suspicion that had curved around his brain started to take hold. That had to be it. She had passed. Made sense, he supposed. A lot could happen in seven years, and times had been hard. Very hard.

A weak call came from the back. The bedroom his mother had shared with his mean-as-a-snake stepfather. "Who's here?"

Even after so long, he knew that voice. Recognized it as easily as if she'd called him to come in for supper.

Relief made him close his eyes. His mother was still here. He was going to see her one more time.

Russell needed to get a grip on himself, as he was currently fighting the urge to both cry and run. But he was no longer a stubborn, dreamy child.

And his mother was no longer a person he feared disappointing.

"Who's here?" she called out again. This time panicked. Suspicious.

Swallowing the lump that threatened to cut off his air supply, he rushed through the short hallway and burst into the room.

Only to come face-to-face with the wrong side of a pistol.

As he heard the trigger click into place, two things came to mind.

One was that his homecoming wasn't going to be the happy occasion he'd hoped it would be.

The other was that Scout Proffitt had been right. Russell really should have brought his gun.

CHAPTER TWO

"Who are you?" his mother asked as the worn-out pistol in her hand looked to be in danger of either bouncing on the mattress ticking or firing. If the latter happened, Russell sure hoped it would end up hitting the wall behind him. It would be a real shame to die at his mother's hand.

As she glared at him through rheumy eyes, she rasped, "What do you want?"

He didn't know what he wanted anymore. So he made do with telling her the obvious. "It's me, Ma. Russell."

She blinked in the dim light. "Russell?" The pistol in her hand wavered.

He held up his hands. Whether it was a gesture of surrender or an attempt to calm her, he wasn't really sure. "How 'bout you set that gun down?" He attempted to smile. "You're scaring me."

After staring at him for far too long, she lowered her right hand and loosened her hold on the weapon.

Russell breathed a sigh of relief.

"I can't believe I'm seeing you again," she said. "I just can't believe it."

She hadn't yet said that she was glad to see him. That was notable.

"I can hardly believe I'm here either." Not daring to walk any closer, he remained where he was. Hands hanging loose by his sides, staring at the woman who'd birthed him. One of the two women he'd loved beyond all else. The one whose betrayal had cut him the most deeply.

Her hair was pinned up. And though she was in bed, she wasn't in a white linen night rail. Instead, it looked to be a faded and worn calico. Her eyes were the same though. Like his, they were dark brown and framed with thick, dark lashes.

She said nothing as she looked her fill. He did the same thing. Then, at last, she spoke. "Russell, you're a grown man now."

"Yes, ma'am."

"I had hoped you would do all right. I had hoped . . ." Her voice drifted off as if what she was thinking was too painful to dwell on. After a brief shake of her head, she said softly, "I'm fair surprised you even recognized me as your ma. I reckon I look a sight different than I used to."

Although her eyes were the same, much was different. Her skin had always been supple and ruddy, the consequence of being a rancher's wife. Now, her skin was pale and papery. As delicate looking as tissue paper. While he remembered her hair a chestnut brown, the same shade as his own, it was now liberally lined with gray.

But her tentative smile? That looked almost exactly as he remembered. After marrying Emmitt, she'd been too afraid to trust herself. Too afraid to do anything to cause her husband's meaty hand to strike.

"Your smile's the same," he said, because he couldn't bear to lie to her. "Your voice is too."

"You think so?" That smile deepened, bringing with it a spark of light in her eyes before she looked at him like he could give her everything she'd ever wanted. "Law, Russell. I can't believe you're standing here at the foot of my bed. It's like I conjured you up in a dream."

There were so many things he should say. So many things he

wanted to. But none felt right. He wasn't in any hurry to bring up his last day at home, though most of the time that last day was all he ever remembered of this place.

Instead, he stuck to the present. "Why are you in bed? Are you ill?"

She shrugged. "The doctor don't know exactly how to classify my illness. About two or three years ago my muscles started getting weak. I seem to be wasting away."

In spite of his best intentions, her words pierced his heart. "Wasting away?" And it had been going on for years?

"It's been a progressive thing. Used to be, I needed to sit down frequently. Then I had to cut back on my chores." Not meeting his eyes, she said, "Then about eight months ago that became too much."

Pity for her circumstances slid into him with the stealth of a viper. She had been hurting for some time. For quite some time.

She, too, had suffered.

Unable to focus on that, he again guided the conversation to an easier path. "The house looks clean. How do you manage that?"

Her brow wrinkled. "The house? Oh, a woman comes in for a couple of hours every day. She helps me bathe. Runs a mop now and then. Keeps things good enough."

"Does she bring you meals?" Russell couldn't tell much about her weight under the voluminous faded dress and pile of quilts and covers. But she seemed to have wasted away, especially given the warmth of the season.

"She brings me food."

"Enough?" Though why he asked he didn't know.

"She brings enough. I, um, don't eat much anymore."

"I'm sorry about that." To his surprise, he actually was. After all the bitterness and all the hurt, he never would have imagined that he would feel anything toward her but disappointment.

Those first words of kindness seemed to do everything his

presence had not. She looked away as her voice turned hard. "Don't you start feeling sorry for me, Russell. We both know my suffering ain't nothing I don't deserve."

He gaped at her. "What are you saying?"

"You heard me. We both know God saw fit to punish me for my behavior toward you."

Her words were so surprising that he did the very last thing he thought he'd ever do. He defended her. "Emmitt beat you."

"He did. He beat my son as well." She looked at the pistol lying next to her hand.

He stepped closer, snatched up the gun, and placed it out of her reach. "He catted around on you."

"Yes, he sure did. That was never a secret, I'm afraid." Her lips tightened. "He was a difficult man with many faults."

He'd actually known his fair share of difficult men plagued by faults. Emmitt Johnson hadn't been like that. He'd been cruel. Heartless. "He was far worse."

"I know that too. Only a man who was far worse would ever try to force himself on his stepson's girl." She winced. "In this very house."

Even now, seven years later, the agony of hearing Nora's cries, of seeing Emmitt with his rough hands tearing at the collar of her dress, practically forced every last bit of air from his lungs.

If he'd been alone, Russell would have closed his eyes tight, done anything he could to push away the image. But he was a grown man in his mother's house.

And, it seemed, she expected him to be able to talk about it.

Therefore, he looked directly in her eyes. "Yes. Yes, he did. He tried to force himself on my girl. On Nora."

The pain in her eyes reflected the stinging in his heart. "It wasn't right, what he did. Nora was special, of course, but no girl deserved that."

"No, it wasn't right," he agreed. But it had been more than that. It had been so very, very wrong.

Remembering that moment, remembering Nora's face, Russell knew that while what he'd done wasn't right, he would have done it again. If Russell hadn't stabbed Emmitt, if he hadn't struck him hard through his ribs with that bowie knife, Nora would never have been the same.

"It wasn't right. And that is why I killed him."

"Yes, you did. You killed my husband, the man who'd given me nothing but shame and pain from the day I said my vows. You stopped him from hurting me further. From hurting that sweet Nora Hudson."

The tension in her voice accentuated the tremors in his muscles. All the anger and frustration and pain returned tenfold. "I had no choice," he said.

"No choice at all," she whispered, staring at him with wide, pain-filled eyes. "You did what you had to do. And for that, I sent you away."

The words were unadorned and plainly spoken. Said quietly without added guilt or hurtful blame or excessive emotion.

Which was why Russell was able to stand stoically at the foot of his mother's bed and hold the tears at bay.

It was why he was able to hold her gaze and at long last come to terms with what he'd always secretly believed to be true but had never been brave enough to admit out loud.

He didn't regret murdering Emmitt Johnson. Fact was, he would have done it again in a heartbeat.

It seemed he, like this poor, broken-down ranch and his ailing mother, was in no great hurry to get fixed.

Perhaps it wasn't even possible.

———

After Russell composed himself, he brought a chair in from the kitchen and sat down next to his mother. He had no idea what was going to become of the two of them. All he knew was that he needed these next couple of minutes with her. He needed it like food and water. Needed it like the comforting hand of God's healing grace.

When she gazed up at him in wonderment, a true mixture of disbelief and joy, he realized he felt very much the same things. Never would he have thought to see his mother smile at him, or to look at him the way she was, as if she was doing everything she possibly could to refrain from clutching his hand to her side.

"I know I keep saying it, but I truly can't believe you're here," his mother said after the silence between them began to pull a bit. "I hoped and dreamed and prayed, but I never thought that the Lord was going to forgive me enough to give me this gift." Wonder filled her tone.

"I never thought it would happen either," he allowed. "However, I needed to return. One last time."

Something in her eyes faded. "Ah." After visibly regaining her composure, she spoke again. "Is that what brought you here at long last? You wanted to see everything before you moved on for good?"

Russell wasn't really sure. He'd wanted to ease his mind. Come to grips with what had happened. Maybe even a part of him yearned to feel justified. Maybe he simply wanted to be able to sleep at night.

But all of that would reveal too much.

"I happened to be nearby," he murmured. "Figured I might as well stop and see the place." What a coward he was! He wasn't even able to speak the truth.

A little more light extinguished in her eyes as it became evident that she believed every word he said. "I see. Well, as I'm sure you noticed, everything here is older and more worn down. Worse for wear." With a grimace she ran a hand along her brow. "Myself included."

Guilt slashed through him, though he had no cause for that. After all, he hadn't left by choice. "Saw you don't have any horses."

"The expense grew too dear. Plus, it wasn't like I was riding. I figured they needed something better."

"I guess so." His collar started feeling tight. Constricting. He needed to get out of this room. Heck, he needed to get off the land. Away from the hope that was teasing them both.

But responsibility clawed at him. Maybe underneath his violent ways and lies there really was some of his father's goodness inside him. "Would you like me to do something for you before I leave?"

Her expression fell. "You . . . you're leaving? Already?"

"Well, within the hour. No reason for me to stay."

She closed her eyes. "No, I guess there isn't. I mean, not anymore." She cleared her throat. "You can go ahead and leave now. Like I said, a girl comes in once a day to help me. I'll be fine."

Feeling like he was being sent away again, though it made no sense because this time he was the one doing the leaving, he jerked his head into a nod and got to his feet.

Then, just as he was picking up the chair and turning away, she spoke.

"Do you ever think about that day, Russell?"

Glad his back was turned, glad she would never see the pain that was now surely shining in his eyes, he replied, "All the time."

"I think of it too. Quite a bit, actually."

He was sure she did. Though he ached to leave it alone, the silence hanging between them practically begged him to respond. Feeling as if each word choked him, he muttered, "It was . . . it was a hard day to forget."

"I know I said things I shouldn't."

He reckoned that was true. But for some reason, he couldn't bear to remind her of what she'd done.

Therefore, instead he said softly, "A lot happened that day that shouldn't have."

"Emmitt was a difficult man. He often let his temper get the best of him."

No, it was more than that. And while Russell might be okay with covering up a lot of things, he wasn't okay with remembering Emmitt any differently than the way he was. "He was mean and selfish. Violent. Cruel." Still afraid to turn back around, he continued. It seemed he was unable to stop saying things she didn't want to hear, but he was too tired of keeping them to himself. "We both know he beat you every chance he got."

"He treated you the same way."

"I know." As violent, painful memories flashed in his head, he forced them away. "He was an evil man."

"You took his life."

He heard it. Even though his back was turned, he heard her condemnation. And even now, after all this time, he found himself being surprised that his mother still didn't understand why he'd done what he'd done.

"I killed him because he was going to taint the only thing good in my life, Ma." Stealth-like, those memories forced him to recall the name. Nora.

Nora Hudson, with her honey-golden hair and bright-blue eyes and pretty, sunny smile. His girl.

Emmitt Johnson had been just seconds from forcing himself on Nora. The collar of her dress had already been torn. So many worse things had been about to take place.

"He was going to hurt Nora," she said in a matter-of-fact way.

As if that reminder wasn't capable of clawing deep marks of regret inside him.

"Yes. Yes, he was." Even now, it was hard to remember. To even speak of what had almost happened to her. Longingly, he stared at his mother's door. He was just two steps away from ending the conversation. From never having to talk about it again.

Behind him, she sighed. "You know, Son . . . back then, I couldn't imagine another life. I couldn't imagine not living each day in Emmitt's shadow. The War of Northern Aggression had been so painful. So many good men died, including your pa."

"I know." It was hard to acknowledge her pain. Harder to realize that he could now almost understand why she'd put up with so much. She continued, lost in her reminisces. "So much had happened. We were barely scraping by even then." Lowering her voice to a mere whisper, she said, "What you did shocked me."

"What I did *upset* you. You didn't care to understand what I did."

"No, I didn't dare to understand what you did. Or what it meant to me." Looking bleak, she added after a moment's pause, "Or what it meant for the rest of my life."

As much as he wished he could make her feel better, he couldn't allow her to brush aside days and months and years of hardship and heartache. "You understood. You stood by when he'd abused me for years."

"I had no choice. He was my husband. I took vows, Russell. Vows before the Lord."

"He did too, Ma." Even now as a grown man, he cringed to think of the life he'd lived here. It had been so bad.

Russell stopped himself from saying more. She didn't need more guilt. And even if it would have made himself feel better, it wouldn't change a thing.

Instead, he focused on his actions. "I didn't have a choice either.

If I had let Emmitt Johnson lay one hand on Nora, what would that have made me? What kind of man would I have been?"

"You were a boy."

"I was more than that. I was fifteen."

"Fifteen sounds so young now."

It sounded like a lifetime ago. "Ma, talking to him wouldn't have worked. And I had nothing to threaten him with." Instead, he'd ended so much pain by grabbing his hunting knife.

Russell had no regrets for what he had done. He couldn't, because the alternative would have been too awful to bear.

"Before you leave, I want you to know that I regret saying the things I did to you. As time went by, I realized that I had been under his influence for so long, I had let myself slowly die inside. I should never have sent you away. I am truly sorry, Son."

At one time, her words would have felt soothing. He would have clung to them, grasping for hope. But now? All he felt was empty. "It don't matter anymore."

"I suppose not." After a pause, she spoke again. "Are you going to leave now?" She sounded resigned. Disappointed.

Suddenly he realized that she didn't want him to leave. And because he had nowhere else to go, he took the coward's way out and let her think that he still had ties to this pile of wood and stone and dirt.

That he still had ties to her.

"Not yet. I'll let you know when I do." Then, because he was no longer able to relive the past for another second, he walked out of the room, stormed down the hall, crossed the shabby kitchen, and threw open the door.

The blast of hot air on his face felt clean and fresh. He breathed deeply, forcing air into his lungs as he attempted to regain his composure. Doing his best, he inhaled again. Exhaled. Attempted to shove the past back where it belonged.

"Russell? Is that really you?"

His eyesight focused. Then he blinked, sure his vision was betraying him all over again.

Because standing there on the red dirt, wearing a faded gold calico that had seen too many washings and a pair of boots that should have been handed over to the less fortunate several years previously, was Nora.

His one true love. The reason he'd killed a man.

And the reason he'd felt empty ever since.

"Yeah," he finally replied. "Yeah, Nora, it really is me."

CHAPTER THREE

Nora Hudson had stopped believing in miracles seven years ago. But the sight in front of her made her wonder if the Lord had seen fit to grant her one beautiful dream at long last. "Russell Champion, as I live and breathe. Look at you."

The muscles in his cheek twitched, almost as if it was taking everything he had to reply. "Nora. I could say the same thing about you," he replied, his voice sounding hoarse and unsteady. Deeper.

Had he always sounded like that? Or was he feeling just as befuddled as she was? The idea that he might be feeling the same way was as exhilarating as it was curious.

"What are you doing here?"

He looked embarrassed. "Reliving old hurts, I guess."

She flinched, though she imagined it was no less than she deserved. "I never thought I'd see you again."

After meeting her gaze, he averted his eyes. "Sorry to disappoint you."

"I'm not disappointed. I didn't think you would return here. Plus, last I heard, you were part of the Walton Gang. I lost track of you after that."

Of course, the moment Nora said that, she wished she could

take the words back. He didn't need to know how many times she'd thought about him over the years. Or, perhaps, that she only thought of him as part of the most notorious gang of thieves west of the Mississippi.

"I was with Walton for a time."

"Are you still?"

Russell shook his head. A melancholy smile curved his lips. "The gang was broken up by the Rangers. Walton swung. Other men faded off into the distance." He looked beyond her for a moment before blinking. "That was years ago."

"Were you sorry about that?"

A line formed between his brows. "About what?"

"The gang disbanding." Inwardly she groaned. She had no idea what she was talking about. She didn't even want to be thinking about a terrible outlaw gang, certainly not the fact that Russell had been in it.

Why was that easier to discuss than their past?

He blinked. "Nora, I joined the Walton Gang because I had no place else to go. I was alone in the world. Don't you remember?"

All she could do was nod. The memory of sending him off would be something she would never forget.

"I stayed with Walton because once you join, you only leave in a pine box." He frowned. "Well, unless you're Scout Proffitt."

A dozen questions filled her head. She wanted to know how Russell had survived. What the infamous gunslinger Scout Proffitt was really like. What Russell had done since.

But all that really mattered, she supposed, was how he came to be standing in front of her. "What brought you back home?"

"This ain't my home."

"All right. Um, what brought you here after all this time?"

Grasping at straws, she said, "Independence Day? We're gonna have a picnic in the square, just like we used to."

"Definitely not that. I didn't come for a picnic, Nora."

Though it shouldn't, his brusque, unapologetic tone made her wince. "Of course not."

Something flashed in his eyes. "What does it matter anyway? It's not like we're ever going to need to know each other again."

Each word crushed a little bit of her heart. "Ah."

"Now, why don't you go ahead and tell me why you're here."

"Your mother didn't tell you? I come every day. Help her out."

"*You* are the girl who comes to help?" Russell looked horrified.

She gave a little bow. "I'm afraid so. Why do you look surprised?"

"I imagined you would be long gone. Or busy with your own husband and family?"

Nora noticed that his statement was carefully posed as a question. A minute sense of satisfaction coursed through her. He had thought about her. And he was curious. "I don't have a family of my own." Her parents were long gone, and she'd certainly never had the chance to have her own family.

"Why not?"

He looked so appalled, she almost laughed. Almost. "A couple of reasons." The main one being that she'd lost the man she always imagined she'd marry the day Russell Champion had left town.

But instead of letting her comment pass, he strode forward, his eyes skimming her body, concern and what surely had to be pain etched in his features. "Was I too late, Nora?"

"What? Too late?"

She braced herself when he ran his hands over her body, actively looking for hurts. It made no sense, given the fact that anything he was looking for would have happened seven years ago.

She jumped back from his rough exploration. "Russell. Stop."

But he didn't stop. He reached for her shoulders, ran a shaky hand along the collar of her dress as if he was searching for bruises or other malformations that had, of course, faded so long ago.

Yet she wasn't afraid. Though it had been a very long time since any man had done more than hold her hand, she wasn't scared of Russell.

"You need to stop," she murmured slowly. "Remember? All that happened years ago." She attempted to smile. "Look at me, Russell. See? I promise, I'm fine."

"Did Emmitt hurt you after all?" His voice was so filled with pain it was almost unbearable to hear. "Nora, did he ruin you? Did everyone find out? Did the dim-witted men in this town forget that no matter what happened, you were still everything?"

Everything? Her body responded, her breath turning shallow. Just like more than two thousand days hadn't passed, every inch of her once again became attuned to him.

And that was why she suddenly found herself leaning toward him, like he was someone who could heal her.

She caught herself just in time.

After she got her bearings, she lifted her chin up to his . . . then shook her head. "You weren't too late."

Relief settled in his eyes. "Sure? Nora, are you sure?"

Unable to help herself, she reached out, curved her fingers around his arm, felt the hard, sinewy muscles of his bicep under the worn cloth. Realizing as she did so that he had grown into himself, just like she had. She was holding a man now. A grown, sinfully handsome, exceptionally strong man.

"You got there in time," she said softly. "Russell, if you believe nothing else I ever say, please believe that." Because he still looked a bit wild-eyed, she repeated herself. "Emmitt never did what you fear. You got there in time."

His hand dropped quickly, almost as if her skin had burned his own. "Good." Then he blinked, met her gaze, and flushed. "I'm sorry. I had no cause to touch you like that."

Yes, she had been startled, but she was honest enough with herself to admit the truth. Even on this hard Texas soil that had held little beauty for a very long time. She hadn't minded. It had been such a long time since anyone had acted like she mattered. "No need to apologize. I'm glad we got the chance to clear that up."

"I would have died if you'd been hurt."

Nora knew he spoke the truth. He was a man who felt deeply, and a man who had learned to cover up his feelings too. He'd learned to cover them up so no one could hurt him further.

Seven years ago she'd been drawn to his contradictions as much as the tenderness and attention he'd constantly treated her to. She'd been under the impression that no other man would ever love her as much.

But of course, no other man had ever set her so on edge. She'd been in a constant state of awareness when he'd been around. Expecting him to either kiss her senseless or make her want more than she should.

"But I wasn't hurt."

"If your honor was intact, why are you alone?" His eyes flashed. "Or did you marry and your husband passed?"

"I never married." She swallowed. "Did you, Russell?"

"Of course not."

"Because you never settled?"

"No. That's not the reason."

Before she could ask what that reason was, the muscles in his neck relaxed as the lines between his brows eased.

"I'm surprised no one ever caught your hand, Nora. You're still lovely."

"Thank you."

"What happened? Did all the men stay blind?"

For a time she'd been tainted by what happened. But that hadn't been the reason she'd stayed alone for so long. For several years she'd been too torn up with guilt about how she'd rejected Russell when he'd come over seeking help just moments after his mother had thrown him out of his house.

But she'd been so afraid of the blood on his hands, by the fierce anger in his eyes, she'd ended up doing the very same thing. She'd asked him to leave. And then she'd asked him to leave her alone forever.

"I don't know if the men were blind or I was," Nora finally answered. She shrugged. "It hardly matters now."

"Why? You're still young. I mean, it's not too late to live those dreams."

She started to nod, becoming mesmerized just like she used to by his warm, deep-chocolate eyes. Eyes everyone used to joke were wasted on a man.

Then she remembered Braedon.

"It hardly matters because I, uh, have a beau now."

He froze. Stared hard at her. "You do?"

She nodded. "His name is Braedon."

"Braedon?" His lips twisted, telling her without words that he wasn't too impressed with the name.

"Yes. Uh, his name is Braedon Hardy. He's a gentleman. God-fearing."

"I don't remember him. Is he new?"

"Yes. Um, well, he lives in town. In the boardinghouse over the diner. He moved here last year."

"What's his story?"

"His story?"

"What does he do? Living there in the boardinghouse, I mean."

"Oh! Well, he's a traveling preacher. He, uh, was the third son of a wealthy man. He's looking for a place to settle."

Russell's eyes narrowed. "How is he wealthy? Is he a Northerner?"

"No." She bit back a smile. "He's from Texas. Near San Antone, I think." Until that moment she had never really wondered how a Southern gentleman had managed to accumulate or hold on to any wealth. Confederate banknotes were worthless, and well, the Yankees had taken what they could and the carpetbaggers everything else.

"He must be quite the catch then."

"He seems to like me," she commented. Of course, the moment she said such a thing she ached to take it back. She sounded so full of herself.

"I'll look forward to meeting him."

"Oh?" Her heart started to pound. "You plan to stay for a while?"

"I reckon I might stay a little while. Just to be sure, you know."

"To be sure about what?" Did she sound as jittery as she felt?

"To be sure it's the right time to leave again," he said cryptically. "I'll be seeing you, Miss Hudson," he said formally before turning into the barn.

His words sounded like a promise. Or maybe a threat.

Both filled her with a restless impatience and the smallest amount of dread. Something had happened between them.

And just like all those years ago?

She wasn't quite sure what it all meant.

With her mind still filled with questions, she walked into the house and prepared herself to see his mother. No doubt Corrine was at the end of her rope.

CHAPTER FOUR

"How was Corrine today, Nora?" Jolene, her great-aunt, asked over her shoulder from her spot at the stove.

If Nora had had her way, she would have slipped inside her house without her great-aunt noticing. That way she could have spent the next couple of hours coming to terms with the fact that Russell Champion was back in her life.

But she'd learned long ago that it wasn't always possible to get what one wanted. Therefore she tried her best to control the shaking in her hands and temper the tremor in her voice. "Mrs. Johnson is about the same," she finally said. "About the same as yesterday."

Healthwise, that had been true. Unfortunately, in every other way Mrs. Johnson had been a bundle of nerves and nearly inconsolable. If Nora hadn't seen the same pain burning so brightly in Russell's eyes, she would have been tempted to march out to the barn and give him a piece of her mind.

But that meeting with Russell had showed that even after all this time, he was holding as much pain in his heart as Nora and his mother. It was obvious he'd learned to hide it. She couldn't help but wonder what it had cost him though. His life hadn't been easy after leaving the Iron Rail Ranch.

Realizing that Jolene was awaiting a better report, Nora added, "I only stayed about an hour with Mrs. Johnson today."

Her aunt turned around. "Nora, your voice sounds off. And you look troubled. Are you sure she was doing all right?" Truly, it was as if her grandmother's younger sister had a sixth sense that allowed her to discern any changes in Nora's mood or appearance within mere seconds of being in the same room.

More softly, she added, "Don't forget, dear, Doc says Corrine isn't going to make a recovery. It's only a matter of time before she goes to heaven. You can't take on her failing health as your burden."

She couldn't talk about Corrine's impending death. It was too much to deal with after seeing Russell again.

After considering the idea of keeping Russell's appearance a secret, Nora elected to go ahead and tell her aunt. No doubt everyone in town was going to learn about it sooner or later anyway. "Actually, there was something new . . ."

Aunt Jolene's eyes lit up. "What?"

"Russell was there."

She blinked, visibly attempting to place the name. "Hey, now. Wasn't he the boy you were seeing years ago?"

"Yes."

As usual, her aunt had a gift for understatement. Everyone knew that Nora had loved Russell, that Russell had killed his stepfather, and that he'd run off and eventually joined an outlaw gang.

Before her parents had perished from scarlet fever, they'd given thanks every single night that he'd hightailed it out of Broken Arrow.

Aunt Jolene, however, was far more circumspect. "Nora dear, you always made it sound like he hadn't been happy here. Why did he come back?"

"I think he wanted to see his mother one last time."

Aunt Jolene stirred her cook pot a moment. "That's a good thing, don't you think?"

"Yes." Though she and her parents hadn't had the easiest relationship after Russell left, Nora would have given every bit of the money they'd left her in order to spend just one more hour with them.

"Did you speak to him much?"

"Not much." Only enough to notice that he was still handsome. And to realize that they both had strong regrets about that afternoon in July.

"People say he's an outlaw. You'd best be careful around him," she warned. "He could be dangerous."

As she took in her aunt's worried expression, Nora realized that Russell's appearance was going to disrupt a lot of things in her life besides her breathing and heartbeat.

Her parents had always mistrusted him. While she and Russell had been dating, they'd never actually come out and said why. It was only after he'd killed his stepfather that her mother and father had admitted their real opinions of Russell Champion.

As for herself, Nora couldn't begin to guess how many times she'd relived that awful afternoon in July.

She'd been so shocked by Emmitt Johnson's pawing her, Russell's explosive temper, and the flash of his hunting knife, that she'd hardly been able to stay on her feet.

Even now, Nora could barely stand the sight of blood. That was what had stuck in her head after Russell had saved her. Emmitt Johnson's knife wound. His blood dripping on the floor. The way it had stained Russell's clothes and his hands. The way it had turned dark and permeated the air with a terrible metallic scent.

That scent had clung to her skin and pores. No matter how many times she'd washed, she'd been certain she would never be free of it.

It was only months later that she'd started doubting her memory and her parents' self-righteous conclusions. She remembered the bruises that had constantly been on Russell and his mother. She recalled how he'd hated to go home and the way he'd been so torn, wanting to get far away from the Iron Rail Ranch but feeling obligated to stay as close to his mother as possible.

She'd begun to realize that Russell had been a product of a violent and broken home. She would also remember how pretty much everyone in town had known about it, but no one had wanted to get involved.

No, Russell Andrew Champion hadn't been a violent man, just a very hurt and injured one.

He'd also loved her.

He'd treated her with such tender care that she'd often teased him that she wasn't fragile. But no matter her protests, he'd simply gaze at her in that patient way he had and say that she was precious. And that he would do anything and everything in order to protect her.

Which, she'd realized when her mind had cleared, he had done. He had done the only thing he could to be certain that his pain would never be hers.

And she'd sent him away for it.

Aunt Jolene dipped a spoon in her pot, tasted the soup, and added a bit more salt. "I certainly hope he goes on his way soon. Do you think he will?"

"I don't know. He said he might stay awhile."

"Hmm. He sounds like a man on a mission. I guess time will tell what he really wants." She glanced Nora's way. "Did you tell him that you are seeing Braedon Hardy?"

Nora couldn't help but notice her aunt's voice sounded as careful as it always did whenever she mentioned Braedon. "I did."

"What did he say about that?"

"Nothing."

She stirred the soup again. "You know, I've always been grateful to have a home here with you. I don't know what I would have done back in Fort Worth if you hadn't asked me to move in after your parents died."

"I've been glad for your company. You've helped me so much. This old house would be lonely without you in it."

"If you'd like me to leave after you and Braedon marry, I will."

"Don't be silly. Of course you'll stay. And we're not engaged, Aunt Jo."

"Sure seems like he's going to ask any moment. You'll have to do what your husband wants, Nora. And I've gotten the feeling a time or two that Mr. Hardy isn't going to be content living in an old house in the middle of a broken-down town."

This was news to her. "What else would we do?"

"Perhaps he would like you to sell your house." Aunt Jolene looked like she was tempted to add more but she pursed her lips.

"Braedon is a good man. A godly man."

"I know that, dear. Forget I said anything." Finally setting down her spoon, she propped her hands on her hips. "Well, you'd best get ready. He'll be here before long."

"Yes, ma'am." Turning from the kitchen, she walked down the hallway to the second door on the left. When she entered her room, its bed still covered in a childish quilt, Nora closed the door behind her and looked in the mirror.

She'd tied her long blond hair back in a simple way before going to Corinne's home. She had forgotten about what it must look like. Russell had only looked at her with admiration.

Now, as she examined her curls, she sighed. Her aunt was right;

she was going to need to spend some time cleaning up and attempting to tame her wild curls.

Ruthlessly, Nora brushed her hair and then tightly braided it into two neat rows. Then she pinned it back, doing everything she could to transform herself into a lady fit to be a minister's wife.

A lady so very different from the girl she used to be.

Next, she opened her wardrobe. She had three dresses that were appropriate for an early-evening caller. None were as comfortable as the faded gold calico she was currently wearing. They were wool and composed of flounces and tucks. In sedate eggplant, navy, and dark gray.

All were flattering and yet modestly cut. Braedon had seen two of the three.

Which left, of course, her navy dress.

After she pulled off her calico, she quickly ran a damp cloth over her skin, then began the laborious chore of fastening the gown at her back.

As she did so, twisting and turning in her efforts, she did her best to concentrate on the gentleman who was so very appropriate for her. Braedon was a gentle soul. He always looked his best and appreciated how she always looked her best too. In some of Nora's worst moments, she reflected on how he seemed to view her as nothing more than a paper doll. A well-dressed, well-mannered woman with little inside.

But that had been part of his appeal to her, she knew. Braedon was always smiling and didn't expect much from her. Didn't actually expect much from himself.

Instead, he seemed perfectly happy to spend his family's money. At least, that's what he said. Nora had never actually met his family.

Last year, when he'd suddenly appeared in Broken Arrow, his tales of being a well-to-do preacher in need of a wife and a home had created quite a stir in their dusty town. When he'd set his sights almost immediately on her, she'd been flattered.

It had felt as if she'd at last moved beyond the shame and heartache that loving Russell had thrust on her.

But now that she'd seen Russell in person, she wondered if she was making a mistake. Braedon Hardy paled in comparison. He seemed false while Russell was everything real. Slippery while Russell was honest.

She looked in the mirror and saw the woman staring back. Her hair tightly braided and pinned into a simple chignon. Her navy dress, with its fine lines and attractive bustle, modestly covered her . . . yet somehow highlighted her pale neck and chest. Nora hardly recognized herself.

This woman looked confident and content. As if she'd never had a moment's worry.

Or a second's regret.

It seemed Braedon wasn't the only person in Broken Arrow who was intent on covering up his true self.

CHAPTER FIVE

Russell spent a good two hours riding through town and exploring all the changes that had taken place in the last seven years.

Much was different, as it should be. The war and the subsequent reconstruction changed everything. While he'd been living on the fringes of society, the town of Broken Arrow slowly rose again. The pair of buildings the Yankees had utilized as their temporary head-quarters had been torn down, as had the old house the women had used as a hospital during the war.

In their place, a hotel, a schoolhouse, and a church had been added. And the new mercantile and the blacksmith and assorted saloons.

But the aura of desolation, mixed in with red dirt and mesquite trees, was still alive and well. He recognized it. Felt it like a second skin. He'd grown up feeling it too. For a time, he assumed that was how all people felt.

It had been a revelation to meet the men in the Walton Gang who were buoyed by feelings of self-worth. Though, of course, many of those feelings were misplaced and misguided, given that half the men in the outfit were known thieves, train robbers, and hired killers.

However, the novel idea that it was possible to feel good about oneself had stuck with him.

From that ragtag band of men, he'd learned that a man didn't have to resolve to be judged by his past. Or even by the company he kept. He'd learned that no one was all good or all bad. Instead, they existed in that broad spectrum of hazy gray.

In fact, the man Russell had admired the most had been working undercover in the gang. And the man he'd feared the most, Scout Proffitt, had later acted so unselfishly that the lines between his reputation and honor had become blurred.

Now, as he rode Candy through the streets of the town he'd once known, old insecurities washed over him all over again. Their return was as unwelcome as they were unsurprising and served to remind him that he was only steps away from going back to that dark place he'd vowed not to ever even think about.

Because, he suddenly realized, he was once again willing to defy all things holy and right in order to protect the honor of the one woman he'd always loved. Even if it seemed she would never hold him in such high regard.

Yes, it was obvious now that he was in a more precarious situation than he'd understood at first.

He entered the mercantile and purchased a few provisions for his mother. He also made arrangements for oats and hay to be delivered the next morning for Candy. Then, still feeling a bit out of sorts, like he was missing something he'd never known he'd had, Russell started toward home.

However, when he passed a rundown building advertising home-cooked fare, he decided to take a break. His mother didn't eat much, and what little she did eat Nora had prepared in such a way as to be gentle on her ailing body.

It was no match for a man like him.

After pulling off his saddlebags, he tethered Candy, then entered the establishment. As the faint aroma of baked chicken and vibrant seasonings filled the air, his stomach growled in appreciation.

"Just you?" a woman perhaps ten years older than he was asked when he set his saddlebags just inside the door.

"Yes, ma'am."

"Table or counter?" She gestured to a trio of mismatched, rickety chairs and tables and a set of six bar stools near the kitchen.

"Counter." Usually, he would have preferred the solitude that a table provided but he was too plagued by old fears and memories to take solace in only his company.

"Pick one of the empty spots, and I'll fetch you something to drink. What'll you have? Tea? Coffee?"

"Tea. Cold, if you have it."

She looked amused. "I've got it. It's too hot to sip near anything else."

Of the six stools, two were occupied by men, one separating them. Russell elected to take the one at the far end. He might need a little company surrounding him, but that didn't mean he was looking for conversation.

The woman came back, a tall glass of tea in her hand, keeping company with a lopsided ice chip still decorated with sawdust. When she saw his gaze flicker to it, she laughed. "Ice wagon's comin' tomorrow. We got sawdust ice or nothing."

He smiled. "Sawdust ice will do. Obliged."

"We keep hoping for a break in the heat, but the Lord hasn't seen fit to answer that prayer yet."

He shrugged. "I'm used to it." There were far worse things than being hot, after all.

After the woman told him about the evening's offerings, he asked for the chicken with potatoes and vegetables, along with a couple of fresh rolls.

"You from these parts, sir?" the waitress asked before giving his order to the cook.

He was tempted to lie, but he figured his presence was going to be known before too long. "At one time I was. I grew up here, then left for a spell. Seven years," Russell added when he saw the waitress was mentally attempting to place him.

"Seven years?" Her expression cleared. "That explains why I don't recognize you. I only got here six years ago."

She left then, and he was glad. It was obvious she was a gifted waitress. She knew how to make a man feel less alone while not pushing into his business. But he had no desire to make friends. He was leaving soon.

After taking a fortifying sip of his tea, he looked to his right. If there was one thing being in the gang had taught him, it was that it was always best to look a stranger in the eye.

Both men were gazing his way. The older of the two nodded. "Heard you tell Trish that you're originally from these parts?"

"Yessir. Name is Russell Champion."

The older man raised a brow. "You're Corrine's boy?"

He nodded. "Not much of a boy any longer," he said by way of warning.

The man lifted a hand. "Don't get on your high horse, now. I didn't mean disrespect."

"None taken," he said just as quickly. He had no desire to pick a fight with a pair of strangers. "Beg pardon. It seems I've gotten a little too used to looking out for myself."

"Makes sense. You look like you've done real well for yourself.

I'm guessing you made yourself into the man Emmitt Johnson never wanted you to be."

Russell had never believed he'd be referred to as someone better than expected, especially in relation to his family. But he couldn't deny that he liked the idea of it. "I'm sorry, do I know you?"

"Jim Bennett. I've got a spread just south of here."

"Ah," Russell said as his pulse started to race. The Bennett Ranch was well known and well respected throughout most of the state. He felt insignificant in comparison. Russell had to remind himself that he'd done nothing to be ashamed about in years.

"This here is Robert Carlisle. He's got an outfit on the edge of Broken Arrow. He's a Yankee; he hails from Ohio. But we try not to give him too much grief about that. War's over, you know."

Russell nodded his greeting. "Sir."

"You planning to stay here long?"

"No. Only a day or two." Long enough for him to get his fill of memories.

"'Spect Corrine is real happy you've returned."

"I don't know if she's real happy or not." His food came then, and he was glad for a reason to end the conversation. Picking up his fork and knife, he dug in.

"You know, I never cottoned to getting into another man's business," Jim said. "But I want you to know that I didn't blame you for what you did. I don't think any man really did."

"The man beat me and my mother for years. He left her with a permanent limp. There's no telling who else he damaged with his fists that I never knew about. No one in Broken Arrow ever stepped in. Therefore I reckon you'll understand when I say that I don't really care if you understand my actions, respect me, or forgive me."

"I don't expect you do."

Ironically, Russell appreciated Bennett's lack of excuses. Little by little the tension along his spine eased. "Emmitt's behavior forced me to do something I shouldn't have had to do. And because of that, I lost everything."

"He had to leave Broken Arrow," Bennett supplied to Carlisle. "'Course, what happened was a long time ago. No reason to revisit it all again."

"I didn't bring it up," Russell retorted. "Like I said, I'm only here for a spell. Then I doubt I'll ever return."

The men left soon. After a mostly silent meal with only Trish asking every now and then if he needed anything else, Russell retrieved his saddlebags, watered Candy, then headed back to his mother's home.

But he was unable to stop himself from riding by Nora's home. Just as he was passing her house, he saw a man about his age alight from a shiny black buggy and stride up her front steps. He knew right then and there that was Nora's caller, the estimable Braedon Hardy.

Abruptly, he pulled on Candy's reins and directed her to Nora's family's drive. Candy whinnied, letting him know she was upset about his rough treatment.

"Sorry, girl. But there's something that needs to be done, the sooner the better."

Candy blew out a burst of annoyance as she *clip-clopped* up Nora's drive, illustrating yet again that she had more gumption than most of the men he'd ever known.

Whimsically, he wished that he had just a portion of the honor his horse possessed. Because he wasn't going to be able to stay away from Nora, no matter how hard he tried.

CHAPTER SIX

BRAEDON HARDY PERCHED PRECARIOUSLY ON THE EDGE OF Nora's settee, almost as if he feared the worn fabric would soil his clothes.

As Nora sat on her chair directly across from him, she found herself wondering for the first time why he always sat that way. Was he really so persnickety in everything he did? Or was it a reaction to her home? She'd always been proud of their three-bedroom house. Each piece of furniture and mark on the walls reminded her of happier times. When she'd spent countless cozy afternoons perched on the same settee, looking out the window for Russell to come calling.

Back before her parents had succumbed to scarlet fever. Back when the rooms had been filled with her father's deep baritone and her mother's careful attention to details.

But now, as she looked around their parlor through this man's eyes, Nora wondered if everything she'd always perceived as warm and comfortable merely appeared shabby to him. Perhaps that was it.

As the silence between them stretched, her beau cleared his throat. "Nora, you don't seem yourself this evening."

She supposed that was true. After all, she didn't feel very much like herself. But then again, how could she when Russell had returned? "Oh? Have I said something wrong?"

"You haven't had a chance to say anything wrong," he said in his exacting way. "By my count, you've hardly said ten words."

"Surely you exaggerate." She smiled to keep the lie a little easier to swallow.

"I never exaggerate." His eyelids drew down to half-mast as he examined her more closely. "Your silence has been most out of the ordinary. Are you ill?"

She was ill at ease. But of course, that had nothing to do with him. "I'm sorry, Braedon. I had thought to shield it from you, but I am feeling a bit under the weather this evening. I'm feeling a little peaked."

"You were over at the Johnsons' homestead today, weren't you?"

"I'm there every day."

"I feel for Mrs. Johnson, but it's becoming apparent that she is not afraid to take advantage of you. It's time to stop going over there."

"I can't do that. She's dying. She needs help."

"Then let someone who has experience in such things tend to her." Piously, Braedon murmured, "Even the most helpful heart understands when things are in the Lord's hands."

"Yes, but—"

"Perhaps you should consider doing something different with your time. It would be better for both of you. Think of it, dear. We both know that she needs more than just a brief visit from a well-meaning young lady." He leaned back at last. Crossing his arms over his chest. "I pity her, but I care more about your well-being. We can't have you putting yourself in harm's way."

"My well-being is not being put at risk."

"Obviously it is. You just told me that you are more tired than usual. Perhaps I can send word to the churches and they can add her to their list of charitable visits. There are no doubt many in our community who would appreciate the benefits of tending to someone in so much need. Especially since that woman is Corrine Champion."

Nora flushed, already imagining the shame Russell's mother would feel, knowing that her weaknesses had become fodder for the public's discussion. "Braedon, I appreciate you caring for me, but the fact of the matter is that she won't be on this earth much longer. Perhaps not even until the picnic."

"Which is more reason you need to let other tender hands see to her needs. You know I'm right, Nora." Before she could respond, he said, "I'll take care of things in the morning. Now, let's talk of the dance that will be held after the picnic." A spark of mischief appeared in his eyes. "You will save me a dance or two, won't you?"

She didn't want to talk about the dance.

Actually, she couldn't seem to think of anything but one particular man. "Russell returned," she blurted. Perhaps if she spoke about his return in her life she would at last get over him.

"Are you speaking of Corrine's vagabond son?"

She lifted her eyebrows in mock concern. "Vagabond, Braedon? To the best of my knowledge, you have never met him. I can promise that he's nothing of the sort." At least, she hoped that was the case.

Umbrage straightened Braedon's spine. "I never would wish to meet him."

"Then you shouldn't speak of him. After all, you're basing your judgment on hearsay."

"I know he killed his stepfather. I know that many people say he was rough and illiterate. And that he joined an outlaw gang. That's all I need to know."

Was it? Did he not care that she'd once been so in love with Russell that she'd thought she'd always live by his side? She'd thought she'd forgive almost anything of him. Of course, she'd soon learned something about herself. She wasn't possessed of much forgiveness.

"There's more to him than that."

"How do you know?" Staring at her intently, he lowered his voice. "Did you see him when you visited Mrs. Champion?"

Nora drew in her breath, preparing to find a way to tell Braedon about their past relationship—and how she regretted her treatment of him—when a knock at the door brought her words to a halt.

She turned her head in time to see Aunt Jolene open the door and then freeze. She heard a murmur, watched her aunt's posture shift. Watched her frown as she stepped backward with obvious reluctance but still made way for the new visitor.

Who just happened to be Russell Champion himself.

His presence seemed to occupy the entire entryway. He towered over Aunt Jolene, with his imposing height, well-muscled body, shoulders that seemed to stretch the limits of his white broadcloth shirt. Almost immediately, he turned her way. "Nora." His voice was deep and his gaze was intense.

Just as it was in her memories.

Suddenly, she felt nervous and giddy. Nora got to her feet. "Good evening, Russell."

"Nora?" Braedon said.

Her aunt glanced from Braedon to Nora to Russell, towering above her. "Russell, I mean, Mr. Champion, perhaps it would be best if you came back another time. Nora is presently occupied with another guest."

Russell continued to stare directly at her. "I'd rather hear that from her, ma'am." After a pause he spoke, his voice as rough as birch bark. "Nora, is that what you want? For me to leave?"

She knew he chose that phrase on purpose.

Nora walked to Russell's side. She was fairly certain that she wasn't ever going to be able to ask him to leave her again. "Of course you are welcome to stay."

Her aunt looked decidedly agitated. "Nora, perhaps now isn't the best time . . ."

"It doesn't matter if it is the best time or not. He's here, and I'd like him to stay."

"Yes . . . with this man suddenly appearing at your doorway, it does seem that the Lord has decided that he should be here. He does work in mysterious ways, of course," Braedon intoned as he joined them. Perhaps with a bit too much bluster?

Resolutely, Nora ignored him. Instead, she continued to face Russell. He was now standing with his arms folded across his chest, one hand holding his Stetson. His skin was tan, his shirt was obviously new, and his dark denims were practically painted on. His boots looked like they'd been worn throughout most of west Texas. But it was the look on his face that answered all her questions and then some.

She'd known that look. It had been absent at his ranch when her appearance took him off guard. But it was back now in force, reminding her of everything she'd once loved and thought she'd lost forever. "I didn't expect you to come by."

"I happened to be in the area," he drawled. "Reckoned it would be rude to not stop by with me being so close and all."

"Most gentlemen wait for an invitation," Braedon said snidely.

But instead of looking embarrassed, Russell laughed. "I reckon you are right. Most men would certainly wait to be invited. With bated breath."

"But not you?" sneered Braedon, obviously determined to make the already awkward conversation even more uneasy.

Russell smirked. "I'm not most men."

While her aunt wrung her hands and Nora racked her brain for some way to defuse the situation, Braedon strode forward with his hand outstretched. "I don't believe we've formally met. I'm Braedon Hardy."

Russell unfolded his arms and shook Braedon's hand. "Russell Champion."

"Your ears must have been burning. We were just talking about you."

Russell looked at Nora. "Is that right?"

"Russell, won't you please come in? We were about to have some chocolate cake and coffee."

"You sure now's the best time?" Aunt Jolene asked.

It surely wasn't the best time. But that said, Nora knew she simply wasn't going to be able to send Russell out the door. "Aunt Jolene, we have plenty. Russell, please do join us," she added, realizing that she now wanted him to sit with her more than she'd wanted anything in a very long time.

Russell darted a look her way. "If you're sure?"

"I'm sure a man like him wants nothing to do with a lady's parlor," Braedon scoffed. "No doubt he's far more used to the comforts of a saloon."

"Not exactly. I don't drink." His voice was cool, bordering on chilly. "Nora, I'd love to have a slice of cake if you can spare one. I can't remember when I've last had cake. Did you bake it, by any chance?"

"I did." She smiled.

"I'll take care of that," Aunt Jolene said as she walked to the back of the house.

Feeling like every nerve in her body was zipping through her, Nora led the way to the parlor. Just as she was about to sit back down on her chair, Russell gripped her elbow and neatly deposited her next to him on the sofa. Leaving Braedon to take the chair. After a small hesitation, he sat down, but Nora knew he wasn't happy about what had just happened.

She felt herself blush. Again, she knew what she should be doing. She should be steering Russell away, not inviting him to join her.

"How long have you been gone from Broken Arrow?" Braedon asked Russell.

"Seven years."

"Long time to ignore one's mother."

"It is."

"Nora here has been looking after her." Braedon smiled. "Of course, that shows what a good Christian she is. Since your mother couldn't count on you, she's lucky to have Nora."

The lines around Russell's lips tightened, but to his credit, he merely leaned against the sofa's back. "She has been lucky. Blessed."

Nora bit her lip. She was afraid Braedon was going to ask exactly why Russell had left and that Russell was being just ornery enough to say it all.

Then her aunt would find out far more than she ever needed to know, Braedon would assume she was damaged goods, and Russell would get that dark look of regret in his eyes again, as he came to terms with the fact that it was his stepfather who'd wreaked so much havoc on her life. If there was anything she wasn't ready to do, it was rehash the past.

"Yes, seven years is a long time. What have you been doing since you left?" Braedon asked, just as Aunt Jolene entered the room carrying a tray laden with plates and coffee cups.

"This and that."

Nora took over the serving duties, uneager for her aunt to become more involved in the evening's events than she already was. After placing a plate and a cup in front of Braedon, she gave Russell his.

"Thank you, darlin'," he murmured, sheer gratitude lighting his expression.

And making her lips twitch. Never had Russell been the type to offer throwaway endearments. She guessed that habit wasn't something he'd picked up while he was gone either. Therefore, he was saying such things to deliberately get a rise out of Braedon, or to make her blush.

Whichever reason it was, it was working. Across from her, Braedon tightened his lips. She felt her neck and cheeks heat.

Braedon's voice turned frosty. "What exactly were you doing? I know you weren't off fighting. Did you venture into the Indian Wars?"

"Where Russell has been is none of our concern," Nora interjected softly.

"Still, I am curious."

"I left home at fifteen years of age. I was a bit too young to join the infantry." He shrugged. "Even if I'd wanted to, the war was over. However, I had no practice with a pistol. No practice with a rifle except for hunting trips."

"Which tells me nothing."

Russell stared at him as he neatly forked over a generous bite of cake. "I drifted for a time, then eventually found work for a number of influential men."

"Is that how you refer to the Walton Gang? As working under influential men?" Sarcasm dripped from every word.

Russell set his fork down as his body stiffened. "I can't say I know anything about you, sir. But if you had ridden with a man like James Walton, you would know better than to ever even consider thinking of him as anything other than what he was."

"Influential?" Braedon asked.

"Powerful. Tough. Deadly."

"Yet you stayed."

"One didn't leave the Walton Gang by choice."

"Yet you joined it."

Nora looked from one man to the other. "Please, let's not talk about this."

"Why?" Braedon asked, his innocent expression looking patently false. "Don't you want to know what a man like him has done?"

"I know enough." When Russell flinched, she immediately regretted her choice of words. "I know enough to know it didn't change you, Russell."

Braedon turned to her. "I'm curious how you know that."

"What about you?" Russell asked. "I hear you're a good Christian man and a preacher. But I don't believe I know of your church."

"Would you even know of such things?"

"Tell me where it is, and I'll tell you where I've heard of it."

"It's no secret that I am without a church at the moment."

"Where was yours?"

"I doubt you've heard of it."

"Try me." Russell's voice was hard. But there was a new calculating gleam in his eyes that told Nora he'd pressed men for information before.

"It was out near San Antonio."

"Where exactly in San Antonio?"

"Why do you need to know?" He bristled. "Champion, you act like I'm telling a falsehood."

"Those are your words, not mine."

Braedon shot to his feet. "Are you calling me a liar, sir?"

Russell shrugged. "I'm not calling you anything. All I'm doing is attempting to figure out who you are and why you're in Broken Arrow."

"I have no need for you to know more about me. Or my business."

Looking as if he was barely holding his temper in check, Russell got to his feet. "See, here's the thing. I think I do need to know more about you. Because Nora says that you've been courting her, because you've been spending a lot of time in her company." He paused, then continued, his voice turning to ice. "And, sir, if you mean to spend even more time in her company, then I am gonna need to feel that you are the type of man who deserves that gift."

Braedon's brows rose. "Gift?"

It looked like Russell was about to spring. "Oh yes, a gift," he bit out. "Therefore you are either going to prove that you're everything you say you are . . . or you're going to need to leave her be."

"Russell!" she exclaimed as embarrassment heated her skin.

"I'm sorry, darlin'. I don't want you to be upset, but I'm willing to do whatever I need to do in order to make sure you're happy and safe before—" Abruptly, he stopped.

"Before?"

"Before it's time for me to leave again."

He hadn't said that he was leaving her. He'd said that he was leaving.

Didn't that mean something?

Didn't that mean he still cared for her?

As they faced each other, her heart beating so fast that she was sure both Russell and Braedon could hear each thump, she gathered her courage. "Russell, what if I asked you not to leave again? What would you say to that?"

As Braedon blustered, her aunt chuckled from just outside the doorway, and every muscle in Russell's body froze, Nora found herself in a place she'd never been before.

It seemed she'd just gotten the upper hand.

CHAPTER SEVEN

STARING AT NORA, A DOZEN REPLIES CAUGHT AT THE TIP OF his tongue. But none of them were what she wanted to hear or what he wanted to say.

As the silence between them stretched even tighter, practically pulling every last bit of oxygen from the room, Russell knew he had to get out of there before he did something stupid like offer her the world.

Therefore, like the coward he was, he turned, walked through Nora's parlor, then opened the front door and strode outside. Immediately, raindrops pelted against his skin.

He'd been so worked up he hadn't even noticed a storm had come.

Thunder sounded in the distance, stirring up the clouds. As the rain fell harder, soaking his skin, he welcomed the discomfort. Welcomed the reminder of what he should be thinking about instead of wishes and dreams and things that could have been but were never meant to happen.

From her hitching post, Candy snorted and pawed the ground in annoyance. Candy had been his mount his last few months with the Waltons. No thunderstorm was going to spook her.

However, her actions reminded him that he wasn't alone. With a reluctant smile, Russell loosened her tether, then gave in to temptation and smoothed the water from her neck. "That's right, girl. It's going to take a lot more than a little bit of rain to wear us down," he murmured as he turned her around. "Once I set things to rights for Nora, it will be back to just me and you."

He should be happy about that, he mused as he swung into his saddle, guided his horse onto the street, then spurred her into a graceful canter.

Oblivious to the water streaming from heaven and the rivulets of mud forming under her hooves, Candy eagerly increased her pace. Now that they were beyond the town's limits, Russell clicked his tongue and gave Candy even further rein. She surged forward. This was as it should be, he decided. A man and his horse, riding as one.

Just as it used to be. Just like it had always been. No ties to a past, no ties to a woman.

He and Candy knew the routine. They'd ridden alone through open plains for days at a time, stopping only when they were too exhausted to go farther. He enjoyed it.

He was good at this life.

It was simply too bad that for most of his life, it had been all he'd ever known.

———

Russell was still thinking about Nora and Braedon Hardy the next morning. After sleeping in the barn on a bedroll next to Candy's stall, he bathed the best he could, dressed, tended to Candy, then headed inside the house to the kitchen. He intended to rustle up something for breakfast for his mother. Things weren't good between them, but something in the rain had cleansed his soul. He'd realized that holding on to his hurt wasn't going to help either of them. He needed to leave their past in the past. It wasn't like they could change it anyway.

To his surprise, he found his mother out of bed, dressed in a loose-fitting calico, and sitting in one of the kitchen chairs.

"Mother, what are you doing up?"

"I noticed you and Candy got home late and that you slept in the barn last night. I didn't want to miss you this morning."

"I'm a little too old to be worrying about."

"I wasn't worried about you getting harmed. I was worried that you might leave before saying good-bye."

Looking at her more closely, he noticed something in the way she was sitting, the way she was holding herself so still and structured that made him realize she meant what she'd said. She'd feared she'd lost him again.

He was stunned.

It had been seven years since anyone had worried about him. Seven years since he'd had to be accountable for his actions—the Walton Gang had proved that his time, body, and even thoughts belonged to them and only them.

Not a single man would have been distressed if he had gotten hurt. He doubted any of them would have even mourned his death. Injuries would be seen as a minor inconvenience. They would have viewed his death in terms of how much trouble it would take to bury his body. Him dying in the winter would have only caused more grumbling because the ground would be hard.

"Sorry you were worried."

"I didn't mean to . . ." Her voice drifted off as she gathered her thoughts. "But I guess it couldn't be helped. Some things can't be helped."

Russell knew if he didn't volunteer any information, she wouldn't press. But he reckoned if he was truly intent on repairing their relationship, he needed to share some of what he was thinking. "I went to the mercantile." He hesitated, then decided to share everything. "Then I paid a call on Nora." He looked down at his boots. "Then, well, Candy and I took a ride in the rain."

She blinked, then seemed to decide to ignore commenting about his ride in the storm. "You saw Nora? Was she home?"

"She was, though she was entertaining her beau."

"Mr. Hardy."

"Yes'm. His name is Braedon Hardy. Claims to be an itinerant preacher. What do you know of him?"

"He stopped by here once. It . . . it was a charity call."

The humiliation in her voice rankled him. It also led him to ask the next question, though he knew he had no right to feel anything on her behalf. "What did you think of him?"

She bit her lip. "I can't rightly say."

"You didn't form an impression?"

"I'm afraid I felt his demeanor and actions left much to be desired," she hedged. "Of course, what really matters is what Nora thinks of him. And her aunt, of course."

"There was something about him I didn't trust."

"How so?"

"He seemed too slick. And awfully full of himself to be a man of the cloth."

She looked long and hard at him, then wearily shifted. "Is it because you haven't been around godly men much?" She swallowed. "Or have you?"

"I haven't been around too many preachers," he confessed. "But I have been around men who I've admired."

"Like who?"

"When I was with the Walton Gang, there was a man by the name of Will McMillan." Russell glanced at his mother, half afraid of seeing a look of derision on her face. If it was there, he wouldn't continue. He'd known far too few men to admire, and he couldn't watch his mother malign the best man he'd ever met.

But instead of dismay or derision, she gazed at him with such yearning that he was struck by it. Making him realize that she was so hungry for his stories that probably anything he told her would be welcome information.

That acceptance buoyed him, encouraging him to be even more honest. "I didn't know it at the time, but Will was a Texas Ranger working undercover."

Her eyes widened. "Gracious."

"When I discovered that, I realized why I'd admired him so much. Because he was an admirable man. But before that, when I simply thought he was Mr. Walton's second in command, I knew there was an honesty and a goodness about him that shined through."

"What did he do?"

Thinking back, Russell said, "Once, when Mr. Walton had targeted a train, a woman had been kept aside as a hostage. Will put his life on the line to not only keep her from getting hurt, but to keep her from being too scared." Remembering how betrayed he'd felt by Will, because he'd chosen a relationship with the woman over his promise to continue to look out for him, Russell added, "Will left the gang in the middle of the night in Kansas. He jumped from the train with her."

She pressed one palm to her chest. "Did they survive?"

"Yeah. He later married her." He swallowed hard. "But that wasn't the only good deed he did, Ma. See, he looked out for me when I first joined."

"How old were you when you joined?"

"I'd just turned seventeen."

Her expression grew more pained. "Too young."

"I was beyond green. So innocent. He helped me become a man."

"You were blessed to know him."

Russell nodded. "I was. He was the best man I ever met, and I have met a couple of those over the years." He thought of Scout Proffitt and how he was later willing to come out of hiding to help his brother. It had been a selfless deed. Honorable, even.

But he refrained from mentioning Scout. He was too famous and the stories about him too distorted to share with anyone who hadn't been in his company. "I knew from the moment I met Will that something was honorable about him. Just like with some men I know within seconds that their characters are as oily as the pomade greasing their hair."

"Which is how you feel about Mr. Hardy."

He nodded. "I don't want Nora to marry him. I can't help but feel that he'll break her heart and then slowly ruin her spirit." He stared down at his clenched hands in silence, trying to organize his thoughts into something of worth. "Ma, I know I have no right to worry about Nora's future."

"You care about her. That's enough of a reason, I think."

Russell took a fortifying breath and made another confession. "I don't know how to make things right."

"I do. You need to get busy and formulate a plan."

"How? I don't know anyone."

"But I do." She smiled, then pointed across the room. "Get me a pen and paper. I need to write a note that you will need to deliver."

He did as she asked. "Who are you writing to?"

"Mr. Talbot."

Russell recalled that someone in the mercantile had mentioned the man in passing. "He's a banker, right?"

"Yes. I haven't had much cause to see him, but I visited with him one evening after church about a year ago. I think he's a good man."

Russell was trying to find a way to tell his mother that one conversation did not make a good man when she continued.

"Russell, I think Mr. Talbot might be able to help you. See, Mr. Hardy told me some things during his visit that struck me as odd. He said that he grew up right in San Antonio. And that he came from money. But if that was the case, why is he traveling? Most wealthy landowners help set up preachers."

"That is curious."

Looking pleased that she could be of help, she added, "He also kept asking me about Nora's parents. He wanted to know how old they were when they succumbed to the fever, how many acres had been left to Nora. I thought his questions were far too intrusive."

"I agree."

"That's why I think you should pay a visit to San Antonio and ask some questions."

"Ma—"

"He's hiding something. If you want to help Nora, you've got to go figure out what that is." Looking like her suggestions were as easy as pie, she said, "Then you can tell Mr. Talbot."

"No banker is going to see me."

"He will, once he realizes who you are."

Russell feared his identity was the exact reason the banker would refuse to see him. "Things aren't that easy. Furthermore, even if he does agree to see me, he's not going to take my word about anything."

"He will. You've simply got to have faith." She bent down and wrote out a short note to the banker. "Go visit San Antonio, then go see Mr. Talbot."

He took the note because he didn't have a better idea about what to do. "I'll follow your advice, but I'm gonna feel like twice the fool when Mr. Talbot has someone escort me out the door."

For the first time since he'd arrived, his ma's eyes glowed. "From what you've told me, I have a feeling that if you do get kicked out it won't be the first time."

"No, ma'am, it won't." And with that, he slapped his Stetson back on his head and marched out to the barn.

Candy whinnied and pawed at the dirt in her stall.

"You're in luck, girl," he said as he buttoned up his duster and pulled out his saddle. "We're going for a ride and it ain't even raining."

With any luck, they'd be in San Antonio by noon.

———

The return to the open fields energized his horse. Candy practically flew across the grassy plains, her hooves navigating the terrain easily.

They rode into San Antonio just before noon. They passed the livery, the jail, and a couple of saloons. Russell had decided to go to the Menger Hotel first. The Menger was well-known, and the men who frequented the hotel's famous bar were reputed to be some of the most famous and influential men of the area. Russell figured if he hung around there long enough he would eventually find someone willing to talk to him.

It turned out he didn't have to wait even an hour. A pair of cattlemen bellied up to the bar on one side of him while the sheriff slid onto his other.

At first Russell felt a familiar wave of panic, sure that they were approaching him about his past. But instead, they proved to be a loquacious bunch. After learning that Russell was from Broken Arrow and was merely in town to ask about Braedon Hardy, the men slowly smiled.

They began to talk. And then they told him everything he needed to know.

CHAPTER EIGHT

Nora was standing in line for the bank teller late in the afternoon when the front door opened and Russell strode in with a rush of sweltering air and red dust.

All twelve people in the building froze, then unabashedly eyed him as if he were the devil himself.

Russell stiffened before starting forward, diligently keeping his gaze focused straight ahead. It was obvious he was uncomfortable with the attention.

Her heart went out to him. And because he looked so terribly alone, she stepped out of line and crossed the lobby to get to his side.

When Russell noticed her approach, his eyes widened, making her think that he hadn't even realized she was there too.

"Hi, Russell."

He swallowed. "Good afternoon, Miss Hudson."

"It is good, isn't it?" she said rather inanely as she watched him move forward, patiently waiting for the person in front of him to finish his business outside Mr. Talbot's office.

His gaze warmed. "My day has recently taken a decided turn for the better."

"Oh? What have you been doing today?"

"I rode out to San Antonio," he murmured before glancing at the secretary.

Nora was still standing at his side when he tipped his hat to Miss Jennifer, Mr. Talbot's spinster secretary. "Ma'am, if you could pass this on to Mr. Talbot, I'd be obliged."

As Miss Jennifer read the note, Russell looked Nora's way. His gaze slid across her features before skittering downward. She shivered as he studied her rather plain dress, worn kid boots, and faded bonnet. Oh, but she wished she looked more fashionable!

"What are you doing here, Miss Hudson?"

Though she knew he was talking about her standing by his side, she played dumb. "Oh, I simply had a little bit of banking to do."

"Just a minute, Mr. Champion," Miss Jennifer said before she stood up, knocked softly, then walked into Mr. Talbot's office with his note.

"You know what I meant, Nora," he said. "Why did you cross the lobby to come to my side?"

"I don't know why." She shrugged. "Maybe I didn't want you to be in here alone."

"I'm used to it."

"Maybe I think that's a crying shame."

Something intense filtered through his eyes before he tamped it down. "You shouldn't worry about me. Don't forget, I'm only staying for a few more days."

For a moment she had imagined that her question the night before had changed his mind. "I understand." Like an old friend, pain slid neatly into her bearing again. "What are you doing after your meeting with the banker?"

"I'm not sure. A lot depends on what Mr. Talbot has to say."

"Oh good. I'll wait then."

Russell lowered his voice. "You can't do that. I know what everyone thinks of me. You've got a reputation to consider."

"I don't care who sees me talking to you."

He sighed. "I'll grant you that I don't think Hardy is good enough for you. But I would also be the first to tell you that you deserve better than me."

"Maybe, maybe not." Knowing if she didn't push, nothing would happen between them, she added, "If I choose to stay until your business is completed, will you see me home?"

"Of course I will. But that doesn't mean us being together is a good idea."

Unable to help herself, Nora threw caution to the wind and grasped his arm. "I'm afraid it's too late to be concerned about something like that."

"My reputation won't do you any favors."

"Maybe mine will do a favor for you." Lowering her voice to almost a whisper, she said, "I was wrong to send you away, Russell. I've regretted it every day for seven years."

Obviously shocked, he opened his mouth to argue.

But Miss Jennifer cleared her throat. "Mr. Talbot will see you now, Mr. Champion."

"Thank you." When Nora simply sat down, he stared at her. "I won't be too long."

"It doesn't matter. I'll wait as long as you need me to."

———

I'll wait. Those words were the stuff of his dreams, and they rang in his head as he walked with measured steps to the banker's office, then knocked.

"Come in, Mr. Champion. I'm anxious to hear what you have to say."

When he stepped inside, Russell couldn't help but show his surprise. Mr. Talbot was missing an arm, and it looked as if a knife had gotten the best of one of his eyebrows too. A thick, raised scar decorated a portion of it.

Immediately, he shook himself and presented his left hand in order to shake the man's remaining arm.

That earned him a smile. "Heard you were back," the banker said. His vowels and consonants sounded odd and clipped. The man was a Northerner. A Northerner smack-dab in the middle of a cow town barely two hours from San Antonio. "Looking forward to seeing why you needed my time."

"Thank you for seeing me."

"Take a seat," Mr. Talbot said. Then, to Russell's surprise, he took one of the two plain wooden chairs facing the desk.

"I have a question about Braedon Hardy," Russell explained.

Talbot stiffened. "Any special reason you're bringing his name up?"

Belatedly, Russell realized he'd let his natural inclination to protect Nora at all costs get the best of his common sense. Feeling the other man's gaze on him as intently as if he had laid a palm on his shoulder, he said, "If you've heard of me, you've probably heard that I left for quite a while."

Talbot nodded, giving away nothing else.

"Well, when I was here before . . . before I was forced to leave, I was close to Nora Hudson."

"Yes?"

"Braedon Hardy has been seeing her. Her aunt seems real eager for a union between the two of them." He took a fortifying breath before diving in. "However, I don't trust the man." He continued on, rushing his words when it became obvious that Mr. Talbot was going to refuse his request. "I've had the opportunity to be around a lot of men in my lifetime. Maybe more than most. I had to learn to judge quickly who was a straight shooter and who couldn't be trusted. I feel in my bones that Hardy is in the latter group."

"Because?"

"Because his appearance seemed fishy. That is why I rode over to the Menger in San Antonio and talked to some folks. They were happy to tell me that Braedon Hardy is a charlatan of the worst sort."

Mr. Talbot sighed. "Even if I trusted everything you have to say, even if I wanted to help you, I cannot. My business depends on my ability to keep personal accounts private."

"I realize that. I'm not asking for the details. I'm merely hoping you can find a way to tell Nora if the man she feels is independently wealthy is, perhaps, lying through his teeth."

Russell knew he was on the right track because the banker's eyebrows rose and continued to rise as Russell added more stories about Braedon's lies back in San Antonio. About how he more than once befriended women, encouraged their trust, then fleeced their money.

"If you are so concerned about Hardy being unscrupulous, the better course of action would be to contact the sheriff."

"With my reputation here, I doubt the sheriff is going to give me much of an ear."

Looking regretful, Talbot nodded. "I hate to say it, but I fear you may be right. Though I doubt Sheriff Canfield is a fan of Mr. Hardy, most everything you told me is based on rumors."

Russell stood up. "I figured this was a long shot, but I appreciate your time, sir."

Mr. Talbot's gray eyes settled on Russell as he stood up as well. "Like I said, I cannot give you any information. Because I find it extremely helpful, I wish I could. I really wish I could." Fixing a hard stare on Russell again, he said, "I hope you understand what I'm saying."

Russell did.

And in that moment he found something deep within himself that he'd been certain he'd lost years before. He found his sense of self-worth. Maybe even something greater too.

Maybe he finally believed in God again. Though he'd always figured the Lord existed, some time ago he'd come to the conclusion that the great man up in heaven had given up on him.

And the majority of Russell had never really blamed Him. After all, he wasn't much.

But now, seeing a glimmer of respect in the banker's eyes, Russell found himself believing again. Believing in something greater than himself.

He figured what had just happened might not make any difference to Nora, but it went a long way toward helping him regain his confidence in himself.

Perhaps he wasn't as lost as he'd imagined he was.

With that in mind, Russell turned away and walked through the office door. He was determined at last to trust his instincts and tell Nora everything he'd learned about Braedon Hardy.

There was a good chance she might not believe him. But there was a chance she might. And if she did, it would make the seven years of suffering well worth it.

But those good intentions fell to the wayside when he scanned the filled lobby.

Because sitting on an iron bench were the two people who'd been occupying his mind for almost every minute of the last twenty-four hours.

Nora Hudson. The woman he knew to be the love of his life even if she never returned the favor.

Sitting next to her was the man he mistrusted with every fiber of his being: Braedon Hardy.

It took everything Russell had not to claim Nora's hand and pull her close to his side.

CHAPTER NINE

Even though Braedon pressed a hand to her arm and commanded her to stay, Nora leaped to her feet the moment she saw Russell.

Just a few minutes after Russell entered Mr. Talbot's office, Braedon had rushed in the bank, looking like his world was about to collapse.

Her first impulse had been to tell him that she'd had a change of heart about him, but he'd sat down on the bench beside her and started talking a mile a minute. Talking about how he'd heard that Russell had ridden to San Antonio in order to collect rumors about him.

Talking about how he was a man of the cloth and Russell had done things no woman should ever think about.

The story he painted about Russell made her start to doubt her feelings for Russell. Made her wonder if she was still thinking of Russell as the boy he used to be instead of the violent man he'd become.

Finally it was time to face the truth. She needed to know the truth about Braedon, about Russell's past, and maybe most important, she needed to come to terms with her own heart.

When Russell stood in front of her, Nora said, "Braedon told me that you weren't here on personal business. You're here telling tales about him. Is that true?"

A muscle in his jaw jumped. "Somewhat."

"Why would you do that?"

With a hard glint in his eyes, Russell looked just beyond her. "Word travels fast around here."

"Why are you surprised that he does anything sneaky or devious?" Braedon asked. "A man like him is probably used to riding roughshod over any person of worth to get what he wants."

A man like him. Braedon's voice held so much venom, Nora regretted that she'd listened to him for even a moment. "Maybe we should not discuss this after all."

"It's all right, Nora," Russell said under his breath. "Mr. Hardy is exactly right, if that is even his name. I haven't been the type of person I wanted to be for quite some time. Years now."

Inwardly she flinched. How many times had she ached to relive that terrible afternoon? If she could, she would have never allowed herself to be in the company of his stepfather. She certainly would have never spent even a single minute alone with him.

And even if she couldn't have prevented the man's hands gripping her shoulders or his lips pressing into her neck, she would have tried harder to remain calm.

Or at least not burst into hysterical tears like she had.

Perhaps if she'd controlled her reaction, Russell wouldn't have risked everything he had in order to avenge her honor.

But even if she hadn't been able to stop that, she knew in her heart that she could have handled his return far better. She could have given him shelter. She could have told him that she understood why he'd done what he did.

She could have forgiven him.

No, she could have said that she loved him.

But she'd done none of those things. And she'd regretted those choices for months and months, until the months melded into years.

Until she'd almost let herself believe that he'd never come back and she'd never get the chance to make things right. Or at least better.

"What did you discover from Mr. Talbot?"

"He didn't tell me a thing."

Nora glanced at Braedon and was dismayed to see a look of triumph in his eyes. She scanned Russell's face. "Then . . . then was everything you heard just what Braedon said it was? Rumors and lies?"

"No." Looking directly at Braedon, Russell explained. "I'm guessin' you see Nora as a lifeline to a better future. And if that is the case, you would be right. There is no better woman on the face of the earth."

His statement was beautiful. But it also sounded like Russell wanted her to accept Braedon's suit. Her heart sank. Was that what Russell wanted to happen? "I don't understand."

"I do. He's come to his senses," Braedon said. After curving his fingers around the soft skin above her elbow, he pulled on her arm. "Come along."

"Not yet," Nora said.

"Our business here is done. From now on I want you to stay far away from Russell Champion. He's nothing more than a dangerous outlaw. A killer. There's no telling what he could do."

Eyeing the way Braedon was clutching her, Russell stepped forward. "You need to release her, Hardy. Now."

Maybe it was Russell's reputation, or maybe it was the cold promise in his eyes. But whatever the reason was, Braedon immediately dropped his hand.

Once she was free, Nora knew she had nothing to lose. She could either go with a man she'd been willing to accept because she'd forgotten how to hope, or at last give Russell her heart.

She turned to the only man she'd ever loved. "Russell, what's going on?"

The corners of his lips curved. "I'm trying to find the nerve to ask you to give me a chance, Nora. Again."

"I suggest you address her in a more respectful way," Braedon interjected. "She is nothing to you."

"She is everything to me." Russell took a deep breath. "I cannot prove anything, but I have reason to believe that this man is merely a charlatan, Nora. He only wants your money. And furthermore, I learned in San Antonio that he isn't a man of God. He's something far from that."

Looking at her carefully, he murmured, "Nora Hudson, I may not ever be good enough for you. I may always be an outlaw in your eyes, but at least I have never hidden anything from you. He has done nothing but lie and evade and hide. He's not worthy of you. Whatever you do, whatever you decide to do with your future, please do not bind yourself to him forever."

As she stared at Braedon, her mouth went dry. "Is this true?"

"You shouldn't believe a thing he says. He's nothing but a murderer."

By now she realized that Braedon had been a master of threats and accusations. Whatever it took to evade the truth. "No, Braedon," she whispered. "What Russell said about you . . . is it true?"

"Of course not."

"There's a group of men in San Antonio who tried to string you up," Russell said. "Seems they don't take real kindly to men preying on women. I'd advise you to stay far away from the Menger Hotel."

Soft laughter floated around them. Startling Nora.

Suddenly she remembered they were standing in the lobby of the bank. She looked around and noticed that everyone—including Mr. Talbot and Jennifer—was listening and watching.

Nora had no idea what to do next. Biting her bottom lip, she met everyone's gaze. Two ladies who'd once been friends of her mother. Mr. Kincaid, the teller. A pair of cowhands. Even Belle Weathers, who many whispered owned a brothel the next town over. All of them were looking directly at them, their expressions rapt.

"Mr. Talbot? Do you think Russell might be right?" She purposefully didn't provide a name to her question.

"I believe he is," he said quietly.

And that kind expression, together with the static expectation in the room, told her everything she needed to know.

Gathering her courage, Nora prepared herself to send away another man.

But unlike seven years ago, when she'd been too young, too scared, and too distraught to completely understand what she was saying, she had no regrets. "I don't want to see you ever again, Braedon."

He flinched. "Nora."

"Don't speak my name."

"I'll call you whatever I want." He reached for her, his expression hard.

Immediately a hand reached out and jerked Braedon away.

But to her surprise, it wasn't Russell who reached for Braedon; it was Mr. Kincaid. "I don't think so," he said smoothly.

"Unhand me."

"Nope. You may be just fine with ignoring a woman's wishes, but I don't cotton to that."

Braedon blustered. "Whom do you think you are talking to? I am a man of the cloth."

"Um, no, I don't think so," murmured Jennifer.

He turned to Jennifer with an angry glare. "You have no call to interfere."

To Nora's disbelief, the person who saved the day was Belle. "Come now, Hardy," she called out, her voice full of sass. "We both know you have better manners than this. Why, you're almost a gentleman when you visit my establishment."

As several of the onlookers gasped, Braedon seemed to shrink before them all. He stood stiff and dejected.

Gently, Russell pressed a hand against the small of her back. "Nora, darlin'. Are you all right?"

"I'm not sure."

Pure concern filled his expression. "How may I help? What may I do?"

"Nothing."

He stilled. "Forgive me." Straightening, he dropped his hand. Looked like he was about to turn and walk out of the bank.

Making Nora realize that he didn't expect anything from her. Or from their future.

But Nora knew she would never again err on the side of protecting herself or her emotions. This time she reached out and clasped his hand. "Russell, wait. I meant nothing right this minute," she said with a smile. "However, if you would care to come see me this evening, I would look forward to your call."

"Is that a promise?"

"Oh yes." She released a shaky sigh.

In his brown eyes appeared a look that she'd almost forgotten. It had been the open way he used to gaze at her, back before either of them had been tested and neither of them was really sure what love was.

He exhaled. Then, right in front of everyone, he lifted her hand and kissed the inside of her palm, finally closing her fist around his kiss.

Just like he used to do.

Braedon's mutter was ungentlemanly and didn't sound very much like something that a man of the cloth would say.

When he raised his head, Russell said, "I'll see you tonight, Nora. Thank you."

After smiling at him softly, she turned and walked down the steps of the bank building, determined to speak to Aunt Jolene, make things right, and think long and hard about what she wanted.

Because nothing, nothing was going to stop her love of Russell now.

CHAPTER TEN

Once Nora walked out the door and disappeared from view, Braedon Hardy gave up the last remnants of his ruse. Pride and disdain evident in every step, he glared at Russell. "What are you going to do now?"

"I have no idea," Russell replied. Oh, he had an idea, but it mainly revolved around walking over to Nora Hudson's house every single day until she agreed to marry him.

"Nothing?" Braedon taunted. Looking around at the men and women still assembled, he waved a hand. "This is the big outlaw everyone talked about? This is the man I'd been warned about? The man to be feared? Why, you're nothing more than an out-of-work out-law, Russell Champion. You're nothing."

"That is probably true."

"You should have let me keep her, you know. I might have wanted her inheritance, but I cared for her too."

"You would have made her miserable."

Behind them, Sheriff Canfield opened the door. He frowned when he looked at Russell, but then his expression turned lethal when he faced Hardy. "Ah, just the man I was looking for." Holding up a pair of silver handcuffs, he said, "You're under arrest, Hardy."

"For what? I've done nothing wrong."

Russell figured he'd done everything wrong. But he refrained from saying a word.

The sheriff, on the other hand, had no such ideas. "I received a telegram from the law out in San Antonio. After Russell here started visiting with folks, they decided to put an end to your foolishness. One of the women you ruined is ready to press charges against you." He seized Braedon's arm in what looked like an iron grip.

Braedon yanked. "Unhand me."

"Not a chance. But if you yank me again, I'm going to be tempted to ask Russell to give you a good right fist to your chin."

"You'd condone such violence?"

"Oh yeah. Because I believe in justice even more."

"You will regret this," Braedon yelled at Russell.

"Never," Russell replied.

After the sheriff roughly escorted Hardy out, Russell breathed a sigh of relief.

But then one pair of hands started clapping, followed by the rest of the room. Stunned, he looked around.

It was Mr. Talbot who provided the answers. "Most times things don't work out, Russell. But today, I think the Lord has let a little bit of His goodness and grace shine through."

"Just in the nick of time too," Jennifer said.

Russell met each person's gaze. "I don't know what to say. I never expected anyone in Broken Arrow would even want to look at me again."

Belle laughed. "This is probably the only time that we'll ever have the occasion to talk, Russell, so listen to me good."

"Ma'am?"

"You'd best go get cleaned up and spit shined. And, well, you heard what Miss Hudson said. She's waiting for you to come calling. Go on now, son, and do us proud."

He tipped his Stetson. "Yes, ma'am."

But then before he reached the door, he cleared his throat. "Just in case I get her to say yes in the near future, anyone know where a real preacher might be?"

"One just happens to be coming this way for the picnic," Jennifer said.

"Thank you." Though Russell ached to tell them all that there would be a wedding, he knew he was going to let Nora decide. He'd wait forever until she was ready.

After all, he already had.

After stopping in the mercantile and purchasing a fresh shirt, a small gift for his mother, and a gold ring just in case Nora would have him, he headed home.

He was pleased to see his ma sitting in one of the kitchen chairs. She was still rail thin and pale, but her dark eyes seemed a little bit brighter.

"Russell? Is everything all right?"

"It's better than all right." After pulling up a chair, he told her everything that had happened in the bank. His conversation with Talbot, the showdown between him and Hardy, the sheriff arresting Braedon, and most especially the fact that Nora was looking forward to him paying a call on her that very evening.

She'd stayed silent the whole time, though the expressions that crossed her features matched his story. Only when he finished did she close her eyes.

Then she rested a hand on his cheek. So sweetly. "You'd best get spruced up, then. I'll light the stove; you go pump the water."

"Ma'am?"

"I didn't want to say anything, but you really do need a proper bath. Rainwater don't do much good, you know."

"I reckon not."

"Get ready now. It's time you went calling."

He was anxious to do that. But he didn't want to leave the house again with so much between them still unresolved. "Ma—"

"Don't worry, Son. I'll be here waiting for you when you come home again."

He turned so she wouldn't see how much her words had affected him. Once again, he had his mother's love and he had a home. It seemed miracles really did happen from time to time.

CHAPTER ELEVEN

IT HADN'T BEEN EASY TO CONVINCE AUNT JOLENE THAT HER change of heart wasn't all that sudden or alarming.

Luckily, though, half the folks in town decided to lend a hand. Mrs. Green and Mrs. Winter, the two friends of her mother who had been at the bank, came by with a plate of cookies and some lovely red satin ribbon.

Mr. Talbot popped in and spoke with Aunt Jolene. Nora wasn't sure if the banker had offered Aunt Jolene a promise of a secure future or merely reaffirmed everything that Nora had said. But when he left, her aunt had looked very thoughtful.

Other ladies came by. Ladies who hadn't witnessed the commotion in the bank but had heard about it mere moments after. One brought along a lovely blue gown. It had been purchased by a woman none of them were supposed to ever acknowledge. Of course it had to be Belle Weathers.

Her aunt had been rather shocked and unsure that Nora should accept such a gift. Nora, however, bathed quickly and slipped it on without reserve. The dress was everything proper and lovely. As far as she was concerned, she was thankful for Belle Weathers. That lady had stood up to Braedon in front of everyone.

For that matter, she knew if she passed Belle on the street, she would look at her in the eye and smile. She'd even stop to say thank you to her. Nora had had enough of doing what was supposedly right for a lifetime.

Even with all the visitors and conversations and the time it took to prepare for Russell's arrival, Nora found herself a bundle of nerves and doubts as the clock passed five o'clock and then six.

When six o'clock turned to six thirty, she began to panic.

Maybe Russell hadn't forgiven her for rejecting him after all. Maybe he hadn't understood that she really had wanted him to pay her a call.

She found herself peeking through the curtains in the front room every two minutes.

"Don't fret, Nora," Aunt Jolene said at last. "He'll come."

"I hope so. But I had thought he'd be here by now."

"It's only a quarter to seven. He probably thinks you're eating supper."

She hugged her stomach. "I couldn't eat."

Aunt Jolene laughed. "I certainly hope that Russell will." Pointing to the array of food that had been brought over by busybodies and well-wishers, she added, "You and I can only eat so much, you know."

She was saved from a retort by a sharp rap on the door. Every muscle in her body froze.

"Breathe, dear," Aunt Jolene murmured before going to the door.

Later, she would reflect that she was fairly sure Russell spoke to Aunt Jolene for at least two whole minutes. That they laughed about something. Or maybe they simply commented on the weather?

All she could remember was the way his eyes had looked when he saw her. And how tall and stalwart he appeared as he strode to her side.

"Nora," he said. "You look beautiful."

She smiled because she didn't trust her voice to not hold a thousand tremors.

But it seemed he didn't need her to say a word. He took her hand, threaded her fingers through his own, and led her to the settee. The one that she used to sit on and wait for him to come calling.

She sat by his side, glad that he still held her hand.

Only then did he seem to notice the wealth of food on the coffee table. "That's a lot of food."

His inane comment made her laugh. "Please say you're hungry."

"I suppose I could eat. Eventually." Reaching for her other hand, he lifted it to his lips and kissed her bare knuckles. "I'm going to be real honest with you. I've probably dreamed and pondered what this moment would be like a thousand times."

"I have too."

"I know I should tell you all the right words, promise you that everything is going to be perfect from now on. But I can't lie to you even about that."

"What are you going to tell me?"

"Probably everything you already know."

"Tell me anyway."

"Nora, I fell in love with you when you were fourteen, skinned your knee, and you trusted me enough to lift up your skirt and tend to it." Flushing, he shrugged. "I guess we should have known right then and there that I was a man of questionable morals."

"I fell in love with you that moment too," she said in a rush. "You treated me as if I was special." He'd treated her like she'd been the most special thing he'd ever seen.

"I waited and waited for you. Waited for us to be older. Waited for my life to get better. We both know it never did."

"I should have told you that I didn't care. I didn't want your family. I only wanted you."

"When Emmitt attacked you, I felt I had no choice but to protect you." He looked down at their linked hands. "People have told me that I should regret what I did. Though I regret you saw it happen, I would never regret keeping you safe."

"I should have told you that I was glad you saved me. I've always been glad about that."

"Nora, I'm staying here. I'm going to take care of my ma and fix up our house and do my best to figure out what I can do to make myself worthy of you."

She smiled. "I'm glad you're staying."

"What I don't want to do is wait another day to ask you something." After a shuddering breath, he slipped off the settee and knelt before her.

A lump formed in her throat, his action was so unexpected. "Russell, you don't need to kneel at my feet."

He gazed up at her, his eyes dark and solemn. "This is nothing compared to things that I've done. Nothing compared to what I'd do to be worthy of you again. Nora, I love you. Please say you'll be my wife. If you will, I promise I'll give you everything I am. One day, I hope that will be enough."

It would be. Because it always had been enough. "Yes."

He looked shocked. "Yes?"

She nodded.

"You don't want me to come back tomorrow and ask again?"

"You can come back if you would like, but I'm afraid the answer is going to be the same. I will still say yes."

His eyes lit up. "A, um, preacher is coming for the picnic. I know it's too soon, but maybe we could talk to him . . ."

"Do you think he'd marry us if we asked?"

"I'll make sure he will, if that's what you want."

She loved that about him. She loved that he was still a little bit rough. Loved that he was willing to share his love for her so unashamedly. So unabashedly.

Getting to her feet, she clasped his hand and tugged. When Russell stood in front of her, she said everything he needed to know. "Yes, Russell. Yes. That is what I want."

He pulled her into his arms and held her close. And after brushing one finger along her cheek, he lowered his head and kissed her. Kissed her with so much passion that she feared her knees would go weak.

But when he lifted his head, looked into her eyes, and smiled, Nora knew they'd made the right decision. She was Russell's, and he was hers.

They'd fallen in love again.

Not that there really had ever been any doubt.

A NOTE FROM
THE AUTHOR

Dear Reader,

Growing up, I spent almost every weekend visiting my father at his ranch just outside of Houston. My dad had a big barn and several horses and lots of cows. He loved that ranch and I loved visiting him. But there was one small problem. I was allergic to horses. And hay. And all the dust and grass and everything else that seems to settle inside a barn's interior. It never failed—within minutes of stepping into the barn I would start sneezing and wheezing. It wasn't good!

Because of that, I spent a lot of time inside, watching my dad ride his horses from the window. Imagining what it would be like to climb into a saddle and ride for hours. Luckily, my dad and I also liked to watch old westerns. At night, we'd watch *Shane* or *Stagecoach* or *Gunflight at the OK Corral*. We'd grin at the old dialogue and how bad those bad guys always were. I loved watching those old movies!

My father and that ranch are long gone now. I also now live in southern Ohio, far from the wide plains of Texas. But I still have a love for westerns. When I write about cowboys and outlaws and beautiful horses, I am back there once again. Remembering and dreaming and pretending.

I am so grateful for the folks at HCCP for giving me the opportunity to write *The Outlaw's Heart*.

Thank you for coming along with me on this ride.

Blessings,

Shelley

RECIPES

MOLLY'S SOUTHERN SPOON BREAD
From A Heart So True

- . 3 cups milk
- . 1 1/4 cups yellow cornmeal
- . 3 eggs, beaten
- . 1 teaspoon salt
- . 1 3/4 teaspoons baking powder
- . 2 tablespoons melted butter
- . maple syrup (optional)

IN A MEDIUM SAUCEPAN, BRING MILK TO A BOIL. ADD CORN-meal and stir until it has absorbed all of the milk. Take pan off the heat and let cool for at least an hour. The mixture will be stiff.

Preheat the oven to 375°F. Lightly grease a 1 1/2-quart casserole dish.

In a large mixing bowl, combine the cornmeal mixture with eggs, salt, baking powder, and butter. Pour into the prepared dish and bake for 30–35 minutes, until the edges are slightly browned.

Serve by the spoonful. Drizzle with maple syrup if desired.

SAVANNAH'S TRULY SOUTHERN PEACH COBBLER

From To Mend a Dream

What you'll need:

- 12–15 fresh peaches, peeled and sliced (about 15–16 cups) (You can use frozen peaches if fresh aren't in season, but you'll likely need to drain off some of the extra syrup. You can gauge that as you're spooning it into the dish.)
- 1/3 cup all-purpose flour
- 3 cups sugar (Yes, diabetics beware! But if you're counting calories and carbs, stevia works wonderfully with this recipe.)
- 1/4 teaspoon ground nutmeg
- 1/4 teaspoon ground cinnamon
- 2/3 cup real butter (Please, no margarine, the southern cook in me begs of you.)
- 1 1/2 teaspoons vanilla extract
- 2 old-fashioned pie crusts (recipe below) OR 2 refrigerated pie crusts may be substituted if you really don't love your family and friends (Just kidding. You love them. Just not enough to make homemade, bless your heart.)
- 1/2 cup finely chopped pecans, toasted (Toasting pecans is easy. Chop finely, spread on a cookie sheet sprayed with oil, then bake for 4–5 minutes at 350°F. Watch so they don't burn.)
- 5 tablespoons sugar, divided
- sweetened whipped cream

Now comes the fun part:

If you're making your dough from scratch (which is best and so easy!), make your pie crust dough first and stick it (flattened according to instructions) in the fridge to chill for 15–20 minutes.

Stir together peaches, flour, 3 cups sugar, nutmeg, and cinnamon in a Dutch oven. Bring to a boil over medium heat, reduce to low heat, and simmer for 8–10 minutes. Remove from heat, gently fold in butter and vanilla (and somehow resist eating the entire pot). Spoon half of the mixture into a lightly greased 13 x 9-inch baking dish. Preheat oven to 475°F.

Take your two homemade pie crusts—or for those of you who don't love your friends and families as much, unroll the two store-bought pie crusts (she says with sweet Southern sass)—and roll to a 14 x 10-inch rectangle. Sprinkle 1/4 cup toasted pecans and 2 table-spoons sugar over the first pie crust. Place pastry over peach mixture in dish, trimming sides to fit the baking dish. Bake at 475°F for 20–25 minutes or until *lightly* browned.

Meanwhile, roll your second crust to a 14 x 10-inch rectangle (or unroll the second pie crust). Sprinkle 2 tablespoons sugar and remaining 1/4 cup toasted pecans over the piecrust as you did the first one. Next, cut into one-inch strips with a knife. If you want to get fancy, use a fluted pastry wheel, but you don't get extra jewels in your crown.

Remove the peach cobbler from the oven. Spoon remaining peach mixture over baked pastry. Arrange pastry strips over peach mixture, latticing if you want to, then sprinkle with remaining 1 tablespoon sugar. Bake 15–18 minutes or until lightly browned. Serve warm or cold with vanilla ice cream or whipped cream.

Let me know if you make this! Better yet, post a picture of you and your cobbler on www.Facebook.com/tameraalexander. I'd love to see it, and you!

OLD-FASHIONED PIE CRUSTS

(MAKES TWO)

Ingredients:

- . 1 1/2 cups Crisco
- . 3 cups all-purpose flour
- . 1 egg, beaten
- . 5 tablespoons cold water
- . 1 tablespoon white vinegar
- . 1 teaspoon salt

Let the fun begin:

In a large bowl, with a pastry cutter (or two knives) cut the Crisco into the flour until it resembles coarse meal. In a small bowl, beat egg with a fork, then add to flour-shortening mixture. Add cold water, white vinegar, and salt. Stir together gently until all ingredients are blended. Separate dough into two parts.

Form two evenly sized balls of dough, and place each into a large Ziploc bag. Using a rolling pin, slightly hand-flatten each ball of dough (about 1/2 inch thick) to make rolling easier later. Seal the bags and place them in the freezer until you need the dough. (If you'll be using it immediately, it's still a great idea to put in the freezer for about 15–20 minutes to chill. Chilled dough is easier to work with.)

When you're ready, remove the dough from the freezer and allow to thaw for 15 minutes (if frozen). On a floured surface roll the dough, starting at the center and working your way out. (Sprinkle some flour over top of the dough if it's a bit too moist.) If the dough sticks to the countertop, use a metal spatula and carefully scrape it up, flour it well, then flip it over and continue rolling until it's about 1/2 inch *larger* in diameter than your pie pan. Or for a cobbler, make sure it's about the size of your dish for latticing.

Using a spatula, carefully lift the dough from the surface of the counter into the pie pan. I fold my pie dough into quarters to move it, but it has to be well floured to do this. Gently press the dough against the corner of the pan (or use as directed for the peach cobbler). Go around the pie pan pinching and tucking the dough to make a clean edge.

I love making pie crusts. It just makes you feel good! Enjoy!

MRS. DERRACOTT'S LEMON-FILLED COCONUT CAKE

From Love Beyond Limits

- . 4 cups sifted cake flour
- . 5 teaspoons baking powder
- . 1 1/2 teaspoons salt
- . 6 large egg whites
- . 1 cup shortening
- . 1/2 cup sugar
- . 2 cups sugar
- . milk as needed*
- . 2 teaspoons vanilla extract
- . lemon filling
- . seven-minute icing or other white icing
- . flaked coconut

Use 1 1/2 cups milk with butter or 2 cups milk with vegetable shortening

MEASURE SIFTED FLOUR, ADD BAKING POWDER AND SALT, AND sift together three times.

Beat egg whites until foamy. Gradually add 1/2 cup of sugar to whites, then beat until meringue stands in stiff peaks.

Cream shortening, add 2 cups sugar gradually, and cream together until white and fluffy.

Add flour mixture alternately with milk, a small amount at a time, beating after each addition until smooth.

Add vanilla.

Add meringue and fold gently into the batter.

Pour batter into three round 9-inch layer pans that have been well greased and lined on bottoms with brown paper. Bake at 375°F for 20–25 minutes.

Cool layers.

Spread two with lemon filling. Cover the top layer and sides of cake generously with fluffy seven-minute icing or any favorite white icing. While frosting is still soft, sprinkle liberally with flaked coconut.

LEMON FILLING

- . 1/2 cup sugar
- . 1/8 teaspoon salt
- . 1/2 cup water
- . 1 tablespoon butter
- . 2 tablespoons cornstarch
- . 1/3 cup lemon juice
- . 1 egg, slightly beaten

Combine sugar, cornstarch, and salt in top of double boiler. Add lemon juice, water, egg, and butter; mix well. Place over rapidly boiling water, then cook, stirring constantly, until mixture thickens. Cool. Refrigerate until cold, and spread between layers.

SEVEN-MINUTE FROSTING

. 3 tablespoons water
. 1 egg white
. 1 tablespoon corn syrup or 1/8 teaspoon cream of tartar
. 1 cup sugar
. 1/8 teaspoon salt
. 1 teaspoon vanilla extract

Heat water to boiling in lower part of a double boiler. Water in lower part should surround upper part.

Place 3 tablespoons water, egg white, syrup or cream of tartar, sugar, and salt in upper part of double boiler.

Beat the mixture with a rotary egg beater or electric beater, rapidly at first, then steadily and continuously for about seven minutes. Keep water boiling in lower part of double boiler during the beating.

Remove from heat, pour out hot water and fill with cold water, and replace upper part of double boiler. Let stand five minutes.

Add flavoring and stir. Frost sides and top of cake and then cover with coconut flakes.

TEXAS SHEET CAKE

From An Outlaw's Heart

MIX TOGETHER IN A LARGE MIXING BOWL:

. 2 cups sugar
. 2 cups flour
. 1 teaspoon baking soda

. 1 teaspoon cinnamon
. 4 tablespoons baker's cocoa

Then bring to boil in a saucepan:
. 1 cup water
. 1 1/2 sticks margarine

Let cool slightly, then add to flour mixture. Use electric mixer or stir until combined. Then add:
. 1/2 cup buttermilk
. 1 teaspoon vanilla (Mexican vanilla if you have it)
. 2 beaten eggs

Mix well. Pour into a greased 13 x 9-inch pan. Bake at 350°F for 35 minutes or until done. Set on rack.

ICING

Mix together:
. 1 stick butter or margarine, melted
. 6 tablespoons milk
. 4 tablespoons baker's cocoa

When combined, add:
. 1 box powdered sugar (2–3 cups)
. 1 tablespoon vanilla (Mexican vanilla if you have it)
. 1 cup chopped pecans (optional)
. 1 cup Angel Flake coconut (optional)

Run knife around the edge of the cake when it is still warm. Pour icing on the cake while the cake is still warm. Let set for an hour or so.

DISCUSSION QUESTIONS

A HEART SO TRUE

1. Abby is forced to choose between duty to her family and her love for Dr. Bennett. Have you ever had to make such a choice? What was the outcome?

2. In the nineteenth century men had very different ideas about the roles of women in society. How does Mr. Clayton see Abigail's role? How does Abby's mother see her daughter's role?

3. How do Abby's friends Penny and Theodosia support their friend? What specific scenes from the story show this?

4. Abby regrets that she kept silent about Charles's behavior last summer. Was she right to keep a secret? How would her father have reacted? Her mother?

5. Do you think Mr. Clayton was thinking first of Abigail's welfare, or of his own? Why?

6. Did the behavior of any of the characters surprise you? If so which ones, and why?

7. What three words do you think best describe Abigail? Wade? Charles?

8. Abigail feels that her parents have forced her into an

inauthentic life rather than letting her choose an authentic one. What did she mean by this?

9. Do you think Abby was wrong to spend the day in Georgetown with Wade, or did the two of them deserve one day of happiness?

10. In *A Heart So True* the author provides glimpses of characters from her other novels. Which characters, if any, did you recognize?

TO MEND A DREAM

1. Savannah Darby lost most of her family, her home, and like many Southerners following the Civil War, was forced to leave everything behind when family land went to auction. What family treasure—a portrait, diary, special possession, perhaps—would you miss most if forced to leave behind your home and belongings?

2. Prejudice was a theme in *To Win Her Favor*, the Belle Meade Plantation novel in which we first meet Savannah Darby. What prejudices are evident in Aidan and Savannah's story? Are those still prevalent today? How so? And do you struggle with them?

3. If given the chance to get back into a home that had been legally taken from you, do you think you would have made the same decision as Savannah? Do you think her search for what her father left was right or wrong? Why?

4. Aidan's motivation in moving to Nashville is guided by what happened when he met the Confederate soldier one afternoon during the lull of battle. Are you aware that this really happened in the Civil War? That Union soldiers and Confederate soldiers would converse between

battles? In what ways do you think these meetings changed these men?

5. Have you ever experienced a "chance meeting" (like Aidan and Nashville) and yet knew deep down that chance had nothing to do with it? Share your experience.

6. Savannah treasures a family letter in the story. Letter writing is all but a lost art these days. Would having a letter from a departed loved one have meant more back then, do you think? Why or why not?

7. In chapter 12, Savannah reflects on the many possessions she and her family owned. With time's passing, her perspective on those has changed. How has it changed? And can you relate to her feelings?

8. God worked to weave Aidan's and Savannah's lives together in ways they couldn't see and certainly didn't plan. Have you ever made a plan that you thought was a good one, only to have God intervene and make it even better? Share your experience, and also your thoughts on Proverbs 16:9.

TAMERA LOVES TO SKYPE/FACETIME WITH BOOK CLUBS WHO are reading her books. Visit Tamera's website (www.TameraAlexander. com) for more information on inviting her to join your group and for recipes from all her novels.

LOVE BEYOND LIMITS

1. Discuss your group's knowledge of the Reconstruction period (1865–1877) in the South and in Georgia in particular. Were any of the details from the novella a surprise for you?

2. What were your impressions of the Ku Klux Klan before reading the novella? After?

3. Could you sympathize with Emily's attraction to Leroy? Discuss the relational "taboos" in twenty-first-century America.

4. Have you ever taken a stand against something that was "politically correct" but "morally wrong"? Why? What was the result?

5. How does Emily change in the course of the novella? What precipitates that change?

6. Consider Emily's thoughts at the end of the novella:

There in the sanctuary of that home for that afternoon, they tasted true equality. And brotherly love. Love beyond the limits of what society imposed.

As Emily, Thomas, and the girls turned from the fields and made their way up to the Big House where they would share dinner with Father, Mother, and Anna, Emily prayed for the day when that kind of love and equality would be spread throughout the land.

7. Has that day arrived in America? Why or why not?

8. Have you ever had someone like Miss Lillian in your life who spoke truth to you? How did you respond?

9. Have you ever experienced the type of peace Miss Lillian describes and Emily ultimately experiences? If so, describe it. If not, is this something you desire to experience? Why or why not?

AN OUTLAW'S HEART

1. What was your first impression of Russell Champion? Is he an outlaw?

2. Both Russell and his mother suffered greatly for the mistakes they made seven years ago. Do you think they could have mended their relationship after just a year had passed? Why do you think they both needed so much time apart?

3. What are some traits that make Nora admirable? What are her flaws? Why do you think Braedon Hardy was able to manipulate Nora?

4. Could you relate to any of the characters? If so, which one and why?

5. Most of the characters in *An Outlaw's Heart* yearn to seek forgiveness for mistakes they have made. Is it more difficult to forgive oneself than other people? Why or why not?

6. What role does each person's faith play in the story?

7. When have you had to ask another person for forgiveness? How did that experience change you?

8. What do you think will happen with Nora and Russell?

ACKNOWLEDGMENTS

Dorothy Love

It's a cliché (which authors are supposed to avoid) to say that it takes a village to produce a book, but it's true. I'm grateful to my publisher, Daisy Hutton, who spent countless hours putting all the pieces of this puzzle together, to my wise and patient editors, Becky Philpott and Anne Christian Buchanan, and to the entire team at HarperCollins Christian Publishing. Thank you to my brilliant agent, Natasha Kern, for wisdom and kindnesses too numerous to list on just one page.

I'm grateful to the staff at the Georgetown Historical Society for their help in locating the resources I have used for all of my books set in the beautiful Lowcountry.

To my colleagues Tamera Alexander, Shelley Gray, and Elizabeth Musser, thank you for sharing this project with me. What a delight it has been to work with you. And as always, to my family and friends inside and outside of publishing who have encouraged me every day for twenty years and more, thank you.

Tamera Alexander

Thanks to my fellow Southern authors—Dorothy, Shelley, and Elizabeth—for partnering with me in this collection. I'm honored to call you ladies colleagues . . . and friends. My thanks also to my HarperCollins publishing team. What a pleasure it is to work with each of you. Continued gratitude to Deborah Raney, my critique partner for over a dozen years now, for sharing her talent and laughter with me, and to the Coeur d'Alene ladies for brainstorming this novella during last summer's five days of "plotting, praying, and praying." I look forward to our time together all year. To Jerry Trescott, bless you for sharing your extensive knowledge of architectural history. To Natasha Kern, my literary agent, you're simply the best! And thank *you*, dear reader, for taking these journeys with me. Your enthusiasm and eagerness to read is such an encouragement to me as I'm writing. I always love hearing from you.

Finally, thanks to Dr. Michael Easley, one of our pastors at Fellowship Bible Church, for his oft-repeated phrase, "Don't let the world teach you theology." Oh, so true. Never judge God's faithfulness by your present circumstances, friend. Instead, trust God who is faithful no matter the circumstance. He's always working for your eternal good. And if you've trusted in His Son, Jesus, then you can trust that—no matter what happens in this life—the best is *always* yet to come.

Elizabeth Musser

So thankful to be a part of this project with Tamera Alexander, Shelley Gray, and Dorothy Love. I've had the pleasure of reading your lovely and entertaining prose—what a privilege to work together on the Southern novella collection.

I'm also thrilled to be working with the great staff at HarperCollins Christian Publishing. *Un grand merci* to Becky "Phil" Philpott, Daisy Hutton, Ami McConnell, and all the others for your enthusiasm and confidence. I love your vision for fiction.

Many thanks to savvy and perseverant Chip MacGregor, the most talented agent out there, for presenting me with this project and for your continual encouragement and expertise. *Passez-moi les pommes de terre!*

To my best-in-the-world editor, L. B. Norton, I am always grateful for your expert eye and the fun we have collaborating.

To my genius brothers, Jere and Glenn Goldsmith, whose knowledge of genealogy and history set me straight as I delved into Reconstruction Georgia, *merci.*

Of course, to my family, all of you, enduring thanks for cheering me on amid the roller-coaster ride that is a writer's life.

And always to you, Paul, the best of my love, beyond the limits of what I thought possible. *Je t'aime.*

SHELLEY GRAY

It was such an honor to be asked to be a part of the *Among the Fair Magnolias* anthology! Thank you to Elizabeth Musser, Tamera Alexander, and Dorothy Love for being so warm and welcoming. I've learned so much from all of you!

Thank you, also, to my editor Becky Philpott for your kindness and enthusiasm. I'll always remember our visit to the Menger Hotel's jewelry store! I am blessed to know you.

Finally, thank you to the readers who enjoyed my westerns enough to continually ask about Russell. This story is for you! I hope you will find *An Outlaw's Heart* to be worth the wait.

ABOUT THE AUTHORS

DOROTHY LOVE

A NATIVE OF WEST TENNESSEE, DOROTHY Love makes her home in the Texas Hill Country with her husband and their golden retriever. An award-winning author of numerous young adult novels, Dorothy made her adult debut with the Hickory Ridge novels.

Visit her at www.dorothylovebooks.com
Facebook: dorothylovebooks
Twitter: @WriterDorothy

TAMERA ALEXANDER

TAMERA ALEXANDER IS A *USA TODAY* BEST-selling author whose richly drawn characters and thought-provoking plots have earned her devoted readers worldwide, as well as multiple industry awards. After living in Colorado for seventeen years, Tamera has returned to her Southern roots.

She and her husband make their home in Nashville, where they enjoy life with their two adult children, who live nearby, and Jack, a precious—and precocious—silky terrier. And all of this just a stone's throw away from the beloved Southern mansions about which she writes.

Visit her at www.tameraalexander.com
Facebook: tamera.alexander
Twitter: @tameraalexander
Pinterest: tameraauthor

ELIZABETH MUSSER

 ELIZABETH MUSSER WRITES "ENTERTAINMENT with a soul" from her writing chalet—toolshed—outside Lyon, France. Elizabeth's highly acclaimed, bestselling novel *The Swan House* was named one of Amazon's Top Christian Books of the Year and one of Georgia's Top Ten Novels of the Past 100 Years (*Georgia BackRoads*, 2009). All of Elizabeth's novels have been translated into multiple languages. *Two Destinies*, the final novel in the Secrets of the Cross trilogy, was a finalist for the 2013 Christy Award.

For over twenty-five years, Elizabeth and her husband, Paul, have been involved in missions work with International Teams.

The Mussers have two sons, a daughter-in-law, and three grand-children.

Visit her at www.elizabethmusser.com
Facebook: Elizabeth-Musser
Twitter: @LizzieSwanHouse

SHELLEY GRAY

SHELLEY GRAY IS THE AUTHOR OF THE Heart of a Hero series. Her Amish novel (written as Shelley Shepard Gray) *The Protector* recently made the *New York Times* bestseller list. A native of Texas, she earned her bachelor's and master's degrees in Colorado and taught school for ten years. She and her husband have two children and live in southern Ohio.

Visit her at www.shelleyshepardgray.com
Facebook: ShelleyShepardGray
Twitter: @ShelleySGray